Dead Perfect

Noelle Holten

One More Chapter
a division of HarperCollins*Publishers*
The News Building
1 London Bridge Street
London SE1 9GF

www.harpercollins.co.uk

This paperback edition 2020

First published in Great Britain in ebook format by
HarperCollins*Publishers* 2020

A catalogue record for this book
is available from the British Library

Ebook ISBN: 978-0-00-838365-7
Paperback ISBN: 978-0-00-838366-4

Set in Birka by Palimpsest Book Production Ltd, Falkirk
Stirlingshire

Printed and bound in Great Britain by
CPI Group (UK) Ltd, Croydon CR0 4YY

For my pops – Thomas Holten (July 1943 – Oct 2019)
Missing you every day.

Prologue

Tap.
   Tap, tap.
Tap.

He watched, eyes glued to the screen.

It was over so quickly. Everything had to be so precise.

He held the small hammer and orbitoclast in his hand. It hadn't been easy to get these. He carefully mirrored the images that appeared on the laptop. Something had gone wrong the first time and he couldn't let that happen again. He restarted the video, tightened the vice and began once more.

Tap.

Tap, tap.

Tap.

Practice makes perfect.

Chapter 1

The Major and Organised Crime Department office at Stafford Police Station had never felt so claustrophobic. DC Maggie Jamieson tried to catch her breath. She prided herself on being able to remain objective but when something personal happened, her judgements were clouded, and she couldn't let that happen now.

During a past case – the Raven case – Maggie's friend and colleague, Dr Kate Moloney, had received sinister gifts and notes. Markston Police Station had taken the items and logged a complaint but with no trace evidence and no direct threats, the matter hadn't been pursued. Maggie thought Kate should take more care in protecting herself, but Kate wouldn't listen. So when her boss, DS Nathan Wright, relayed the message, 'Just had a call come in. Police are already on the scene. Body of a female has been found. Initial description sounds just like your friend, Dr Moloney. I'm so sorry, Maggie ...' his words hit her like a brick to the face.

This can't be real. He could be wrong. But Maggie knew that Nathan wouldn't have said it if he didn't believe the victim could be Kate. Something more must have been said in the conversation. He knew about the stalking and had expressed his own concerns at the time. Nathan also knew that although Dr

Moloney had been with the Domestic Abuse and Homicide team for only a little over a year, Maggie had fond feelings for her that went beyond the realm of friendship. He was the only person she'd shared this with.

Time stood still as Maggie processed the words in her head. She stared at her colleague, willing the words to be something different. But she knew they wouldn't change.

Keep it together, Maggie. She pulled herself into action.

'Well why are we standing around here? Let's go! I'll call Markston on the way.' Maggie's head was spinning as she signalled to Nathan to follow. She grabbed her coat from the back of her chair and checked she had her mobile in her pocket. They ran to the pool car and she didn't bother to argue with him as to who would be driving. Her main concern right now was locating Kate.

As she fumbled with the seatbelt, Maggie took slow, deep breaths. It wouldn't do anyone any good if she was panicking. She reached into her pocket and, with shaking hands, scrolled through her contacts until she found Markston Police Station Domestic Abuse and Homicide Unit – the DAHU. She pressed connect.

It felt like forever before someone answered.

'Domestic Abuse and Homicide Unit. PC Kat Everett speaking. How can I help?'

'Kat, it's Maggie. Is Kate there?'

There was a pause before Kat returned to the line.

'Hey. No. She's not in her office. Do you want me to take a message?'

'Is she due in today?'

'Hang on …'

Maggie heard a muffled voice call out,

'*Does anyone know if Kate is due in today? Maggie's looking for her.*'

Seconds passed but it seemed like hours.

'*Sorry, can't help. No one knows where she is. Has something happened? Your voice sounds strange ...*'

Although she herself had automatically made the connection, Maggie wasn't sure how much Kate had told her colleagues about the stalking situation. She didn't want to upset anyone unnecessarily, so she decided she'd hold back on what had been discovered. It would help her keep her own feelings in check.

'No. I'm just looking for her. Has she mentioned anything out of the ordinary lately? Actually, don't worry about that; if she does happen to come in, can you ask her to call me right away?' Maggie noticed Nathan giving her sideways glances, but he didn't interrupt.

'*She's not said anything to me, but I'll pass on the message. Are you sure there's—*'

Maggie didn't let Kat finish her sentence and pressed the end call button. She knew Kat could tell something was happening, but there was no time to mess about with causal conversation. Kate was her priority now.

'Well?' Nathan remained focused on the road and Maggie was grateful he was so calm as she wasn't sure she could handle her blood pressure rising any further.

'She's not at work and no one there knows where she is. I'm going to try her mobile again.'

Maggie found Kate's number and waited as the phone rang once.

Twice.

Then three more times before voicemail kicked in. *Shit!* 'Hi

Kate. It's Maggie here. Could you do me a favour and call me back as soon as you get this?'

'We're nearly there. Let's not get ahead of ourselves until we see the body, OK? I know how you feel about Kate ... beyond your working relationship. Are you sure you're OK?' Nathan's voice was soft and she appreciated his concern, but he seemed to have forgotten that he was the one who'd contributed to her anxiety.

'I'm fine. You're the one who has me so riled up. Why did you have to say it looks like Kate?' Maggie rubbed her temples, and seeing the strain on Nathan's face she instantly realized he regretted his words.

'I know. I'm sorry. It's just that with the stalking incidents, and then the description of the victim, it was out of my mouth before I could stop myself.'

Nathan may not have intended to upset her, but her heart was racing, and her chest felt like it was being held in a vice.

Why didn't I push the stalking incident with Markston? If something has happened to Kate, I will never forgive myself. Maggie didn't have a lot of friends and she was fiercely loyal to those she did have.

Nathan veered left sharply as they headed down Queensway Lane towards the village of Hartley. They had been told only the bare minimum: the body had been found in a park, face down, by the playground where the local kids played. Two teenagers had stumbled across it when they'd cut through the park to reach the bus stop. As they approached the area, Maggie could see that the forensic pathologist, Dr Fiona Blake, had also just arrived with her assistant, Charlie. She was putting on protective clothing, and Nathan parked behind her vehicle.

He had barely stopped the car before Maggie jumped out and

rushed towards Dr Blake. 'Hey, Fiona. Have you heard any details on the identification of the body?'

'Hi Maggie.' She looked past Maggie and waved to Nathan. 'No. All I know is that it looks to be a young female, long black hair. Black boots and a long black skirt with a black and white striped top. No personal items were found near the body.'

Maggie tensed. The description could easily be Kate. The clothing had a familiar ring to it.

Dr Blake must have sensed her fear. 'What's up, Maggie? Is there something I need to know?' She handed Maggie and Nathan a suit each and nodded. 'Get those on you while we chat.'

Maggie took a deep breath as she put on the required forensic suit and waited for Charlie to leave before speaking. 'Did you know that Dr Moloney is being stalked? The description you've just given sounds exactly like an outfit I remember Kate wearing. No one knows where she is at the moment.'

'Oh. I'm sorry, I know you've worked closely with Dr Moloney but you know my motto: no assumptions. Let's see what we have first. Are you going to be OK?' She squeezed Maggie's arm.

'Yeah, I'll be fine.' Maggie hoped her colleagues believed her. The truth was, she felt anything but fine. Her stomach tensed, and she felt like she could throw up at any moment.

'Shall we get to it then?' Dr Blake gestured towards the crime-scene cordon that had been set up around the perimeter.

With each step she took, Maggie fought to contain her feelings. As they signed in, Maggie looked over her colleagues' shoulders and caught a glimpse of the body.

Black combat boots. Exactly like those Kate wore every day. The victim lay face down. The grass was soggy under their feet and a mist hovered over the grass, shrouding the body like a secret waiting to be uncovered. The crime-scene tent was being erected and Maggie couldn't tear her eyes away.

A scream caught in her throat as she grabbed Nathan's shoulder to stop herself from falling.

Chapter 2

The air felt thick as they headed towards the crime-scene tent, her feet like cement blocks, each step a struggle to take. Maggie looked down and stared at the back of the corpse. The clothes had an air of familiarity. The body shape matched and the hair ...

Maggie could hear voices, but they sounded as if they were muffled. She felt a hand on her arm. 'Maggie. Maggie. Are you sure you're OK?' She pulled herself together and Dr Blake released her arm. She didn't want to risk being taken off the case because she let her emotions get the best of her.

'Yes. Sorry. I just needed a minute. I'm fine. Totally fine.' Maggie took a deep breath.

Dr Blake went over to join Charlie at the body while Nathan and Maggie stood back and watched. The few CSIs on site were busy collecting any evidence in the vicinity. Maggie knew she should be looking around, taking in the scene and talking to the witnesses, but her eyes couldn't leave the body.

A brief look from Dr Blake and Maggie knew that the victim was about to be turned over.

'On three, please.' Dr Blake reached across and grasped the female's shoulder. 'One. Two. Three ...'

A lone tear escaped Maggie's eye as she stared at the porcelain face.

She felt a hand touch her shoulder and give a gentle squeeze. 'It's not Kate, Maggie. It's not her.' Nathan held her for another moment, making sure the reality had sunk in. She had registered the fact that although it was not her friend before them, it was a female who bore a strong resemblance to her.

'Dr Blake. Is there anything you can tell us?' Maggie shook her hands out.

'There are no lacerations or stab wounds. No blood around the body.' Lifting the victim's arm, Dr Blake pulled back the sleeves. 'She was restrained at some point.'

Maggie bent down and looked at the bruising and redness around the wrists.

'Her hair looks unnatural. I think it may have been dyed black. But I won't be able to confirm that until we get back to the lab. There don't appear to be any head wounds either, but look at the bruising around the eyes. I'm curious as to why the eyes and mouth have been sewn shut.' She leaned back and looked at the woman. 'There's a doll-like quality to all this, don't you think? At the moment, I can't tell you anything more. I'll have the cause of death and more details, once the post-mortem is completed.' Dr Blake stood. 'Right then. This isn't a natural death by any means, so I'd best get back to the mortuary and prepare. I'll be in touch soon.' Dr Blake left. Maggie's attention was drawn to Charlie who gently moved the woman's hair away from her face.

'She looks familiar.' Charlie looked up at Maggie.

'She does ...' Maggie's brow creased. 'I'd best let you get on with things.'

Maggie left Charlie to finish up and took in the crime scene.

The body had been placed face down near a tree and only a few feet away from the footpath. Although it didn't appear staged, the positioning was neat, almost careful. Maggie wondered if the killer had hidden her face because he felt remorse or guilt at what he'd done. This wasn't a large park, however; it wasn't fenced off either. Instead, it sat in the middle of the village like a grassy island. Trees and shrubberies were scattered throughout and, intermingled with flower beds, added some privacy. The killer could have entered from any point. This wasn't going to be easy.

'Can you go and talk to the witnesses?' Nathan pointed at the two teenagers sitting on a bench. 'I'm going to speak with the Duty SIO and see if they can tell me anything more.'

Maggie nodded and headed towards the two boys.

'Hi. I'm DC Maggie Jamieson and I wondered if I could have a brief chat with you both.' The boys' eyes were glazed, but they nodded their heads in unison.

'I know this must have been a shock. I promise it won't be long and you can get going. OK?'

More nods.

'Can you talk me through what you were doing before, at the time of, and just after you discovered the body?'

The boy in the striped shirt spoke first. 'We were delivering the morning papers. We always cut through here to get over to the other side of the village. I do one side of the street and he does the other.' He pointed at the other boy, although he continued to stare straight ahead. 'We just saw ... I mean ... we thought she was drunk or something.'

'Take a breath. I know this must be difficult. Why did you call the police if you thought she was drunk?' Maggie bit the top of her pen.

The boys looked at each other. This time, the one in the black shirt answered. He was blushing. 'We shouted out to her ... and when she didn't look up or answer ... we went over and ... and ...'

'Look, you're not going to get in trouble. So why don't you just tell me.' Maggie reached out and touched his shoulder.

'I lifted her arm. When it just dropped to the ground, I touched her hand ... It was cold. I didn't know she was dead – but I thought she was in some sort of trouble ...' The black-shirted boy sank down.

'OK, thanks. Did you see anyone else in the park? Any strange vehicles in the area you didn't recognize?'

'No. Just us and ... her.'

'OK. My colleagues over there are going to want you to go down to the station and make a formal statement. How old are you boys?'

'Sixteen.' They answered simultaneously.

'Well, it will be up to you whether you want to contact your parents, or we can arrange for an appropriate adult if you'd feel more comfortable having someone with you, though given your age it's not necessary. Thanks for your time. Don't go anywhere before speaking to the officer over there, OK?' The boys nodded and Maggie walked over to Nathan.

'What did they have to say?' Nathan was looking around.

'Not a thing. They touched her though. I'll let forensics know. They are shaken up. Pretty sure they never expected to stumble across this on their paper route.'

'There's not much coverage around here, so whoever did this was pretty sure they wouldn't be seen or they're very cocky.' Nathan squinted as he looked at the various points of entry.

Maggie followed his eyeline. 'Do you think the killer wanted her to be found?'

'She doesn't appear to have been posed. Looks more like a dump and run.' Nathan started walking towards the car. 'You coming back with me or sticking around?'

'I'll go with you. I still haven't heard from Kate and I'll feel a lot better when I know where she is. I'd also like to go over the evidence from her stalker; I think it's still at Markston. It may be just a coincidence, but the victim looked a lot like Kate, so there may be something in those letters or gifts that were sent to her.'

'Better safe than sorry, right?'

Before she could answer Nathan, she felt the vibration of her mobile ringing against her leg. Her hands trembled as she pulled the phone out of her pocket and looked at the screen.

It wasn't Kate ...

Chapter 3

He saw her. He wanted her. He'd have her. She didn't even look his way when he brushed past her as she walked briskly towards her flat, swinging a white plastic bag in her hand. Milk, he guessed, for her morning coffee. The street-lamps flickered, they'd soon be off when the sun rose in the sky.

He doubled back.

She was stunning with that long hair. Silky. He could almost feel it dancing between his fingertips. Imagine the shimmer of each strand in the light as he brushed it.

He crossed the road. Over to the alleyway. Watching her.

Soon, sweetheart. Soon we'll be together …

He'd been watching her for a while now. She was perfect. Or she would be.

Looking at his watch his excitement grew. She'd be ready now. He counted the seconds down. Four. Three. Two. One …

The door opened.

Right on time.

Her routines never seemed to falter. He'd have to talk to her about that. It wasn't safe. She should know better.

She stood at the top of the steps straightening her jacket before she bounced down each one, onto the pathway and headed towards the top of the street, where she would turn left at the end of the road.

He stepped out from the alleyway and followed, keeping his distance, while also keeping her in his sights.

He caught a glimpse of her jacket as she headed through the gates and into the park. She always cut through the park on her way to the bus stop. It was a quiet morning. No one about – but he still would have to keep his wits about him. The police would be busy with the last one.

His pace quickened, and his heart raced. It was nearly time. He glanced in the direction of his car – still there. No traffic wardens out and about at this time either.

He reached into his pocket and pulled out the knife. Holding it in his left hand, he came up behind her and placed his right arm around her neck. He held the tip of the knife at her back.

She gasped and before she could scream, he whispered in her ear, 'Do not make a sound. If you scream, I will push this knife straight through you. I don't want to hurt you. I just want you to come with me. You will do as you're told, or you will suffer the consequences. Do you understand?'

He felt her head attempt to move up and down. He took it that she understood.

'Good. Now come with me.' He marched her towards his car. 'Put your hands behind your back.' His arm remained tight across her throat. She did as he asked.

He removed the semi-prepared tie cable from his pocket and pulled it tightly, securing it around her small, fragile wrists. He turned her around so he could look into her eyes.

'Now, without making a sound, we're going to go to the boot of my car.' He grabbed her arms and pulled her towards him.

She was shaking her head now. Eyes wide. Cheeks tear-stained.

'Please. Not the boot. I've done as you asked. I promise, I won't scream.'

He pondered her request for a moment. She seemed genuine, but he had been fooled before and couldn't risk it.

He pressed the button lock on the boot and it popped open. 'Get in.'

'Please. I'll do anything. Don't put me in there.' Her eyes pleaded with him. She looked so innocent ... but no.

'Get. In. NOW.' He shoved her this time. He picked up the gaffer tape and wrapped her legs tightly. Biting off a smaller piece, he covered her mouth.

The look of terror in her eyes surprised him for the briefest of moments.

'It won't be for long, I promise. Soon we'll be just where we need to be. Is that OK? Do you mind if I call you Kate?'

Chapter 4

Nathan had headed straight to DI Rutherford's office when they got back. He would be updating her on the new case. Meanwhile, Maggie filled PC Bethany Lambert in on what they had found and asked her to contact Markston Police Station to see if she could find out more about Kate's stalking complaint. Bethany's small frame was swamped by the large chair she sat in. Often it was only the clacking of her keyboard that alerted Maggie that she was in the office.

'Can you also see if we can get a hold of that evidence to compare it to anything we find from the crime scene today?' Although the cases may not be related, Maggie had a bad feeling and following her instinct, along with over ten years' experience as a detective investigating cases, often proved right.

'Do you think there's some connection?' Bethany turned around.

'I'm not sure. But we're not ruling anything out at this stage. Did Kate happen to call here while we were out?'

'Sorry, no messages at all.'

'OK. Thanks. Let me know what you find out from Markston.'

'Will do. Do you know if we're going to get any help with this case? We're a bit thin on the ground now that Nathan is Acting DS.'

'I haven't heard anything yet. I'll ask him when he's done with DI Rutherford. But given it's one victim, I suspect the higher-ups aren't going to give us any specialist help. We'll probably be linked up with the field team again. Soon they'll be honorary detectives in the MOCD.' Maggie smiled.

She headed to her desk, threw her coat over her chair, and sat. Booting up her computer, she dug her mobile out of her pocket and looked at the screen. No missed calls.

Kate Moloney, where the hell are you?

Although the victim wasn't Kate, Maggie was still worried about her friend. She looked at her watch; only a few more hours before she could head home. She'd stop by Kate's on the way back.

'Right, guys. We don't have a name for our Jane Doe as of yet, but let's not let that stop us from setting up the incident room and start putting together what we do know.'

Nathan really was taking his new role seriously as Acting DS. He had accepted the position during their last case and if Maggie was honest, it suited him. She stood and followed Bethany and Nathan to the room that would be used for the main investigation.

'I know we're short of hands on the ground, so I've asked DI Rutherford, but with the scope of the investigation at the moment, we'll just have to make do for the time being.'

Bethany tutted.

'I tried.' Nathan shrugged. He went to the front and cleared the whiteboard. 'What do we know?'

'Unidentified female. She looked between twenty-five and thirty-five years old. Caucasian. Goth appearance. No ID or valuables located nearby and she was face down when she was found in Granger Park, in the village of Hartley.' Maggie processed the information, making sure she hadn't missed anything. 'Victim was found in the early hours by two teenaged males out delivering the local newspaper. They didn't see or hear anything on their walk to the park. They'll be coming in at some point to complete a formal statement.' Nathan paused.

'Maggie mentioned a possible link to Dr Moloney. Do you think we should be including that? From what she's just said, the victim does sound an awful lot like Kate.' Bethany stared at the board and looked like she was about to add something, before Nathan jumped in.

'Have we had any contact from Kate yet?' Nathan looked at Maggie.

She shook her head.

'For now. I'll make a note of it, but I don't want us to start going down one avenue and get lost in a bunch of what-ifs. Agreed?' Nathan's brows furrowed, and Maggie knew there was no point in arguing. Truth was, without any tangible evidence, they had nothing to go on, other than the victim and Kate sharing a likeness.

Maggie looked around and realized DI Rutherford had not joined them. 'Where's the guv?'

'She had a meeting so asked me to lead the briefing. I'll be updating her later. Anything else to add at this point?'

'I can't think of anything else. We'll need forensics and the details from the door-to-door enquiries in Hartley before we'll be able to add anything else.' Maggie looked through her notes. Nothing else stood out.

'Well, it's a start. Bethany, can you liaise with the Misper Unit and see if anyone matching our vic's description has been reported missing recently? Also, collate the information from the door-to-door enquiries as they come in. Maggie, I'd like you to contact Dr Blake and see if she can tell us anything at this stage. I've got to put something together for the press but can be disturbed if need be.'

The team dispersed, heading back to their desks to start their designated tasks. Something was niggling at Maggie's mind; she just couldn't figure out what it was ... yet.

Chapter 5

Maggie picked up the handset and held it between her ear and shoulder as she dialled the number for Dr Blake. It took nearly ten minutes before she was finally put through to the pathologist.

'Wow. That took ages, Fiona. How are you?'

'Yes. Sorry about that. We have a lot of agency staff here at the moment. Half these people don't know their heads from their arseholes. I'd be better off answering the phone myself! But I'm guessing you didn't call to hear me rant. What can I do for you?'

'I know it's a long shot, but do you have anything for us on the victim?' Maggie held the phone slightly away from her ear in case Dr Blake decided to let off more steam. She didn't think her ear could take anymore.

'I know I'm fast, but not that fast. I don't really have much to tell you as this one isn't as straightforward as a stabbing or strangulation. Other than two black eyes, and bruising where she was bound, I haven't been able to distinguish the cause of death just yet. There are no lacerations or visible wounds. I've ordered some further tests and a scan to see if it was an overdose or something not visible to the human eye. Of course, it may be more obvious once I get a chance to do the full post-mortem, but as she has only recently arrived, I haven't had time to prep for that yet. I can

*tell you that she was bathed before being disposed of – probably
to get rid of any trace evidence. I can't really offer you anything
further at this time.'*

'Thanks. I knew I was grasping at straws, but just thought
we might get something to kickstart the investigation.'

*'I'll be sure to forward all my findings as soon as I have them.
Speak later.'*

Nathan popped his head out of his office and signalled for
Maggie to come over. 'Have you heard anything from forensics
yet?'

'I just got off the phone with Dr Blake. She doesn't have
anything substantial at the moment, but did say that there were
no discernible trauma wounds on the body. She's running further
tests and will be starting the post-mortem soon. Do you think
the victim could have died of a pre-existing condition before
our killer had a chance to do anything?' This had been niggling
Maggie earlier; the injuries at the outset hadn't looked like they
would necessarily kill a person. No visible head wounds. No
knife or gunshot wounds. Just a lot of bruising and some abra-
sions.

'Interesting point. Maybe that's why she ended up in the park
– because our killer hadn't been expecting her to die so soon.'

'Maggie! Nathan! Can you come here for a minute?' Bethany
was holding her hand over the telephone handset.

'I'm just on the phone with Missing Persons and they advised
that a twenty-eight-year-old female—'

Bethany looked down on to her desk where her notepad sat
open, 'name of ... Tracy Holloway was reported missing five
weeks ago by her parents. She was on her way to their house
but never showed up and she would usually call if her plans
had changed.' Bethany returned to her call with the Misper Unit.

'OK so we may have ID'd our vic. Let's wait until Bethany is off the phone and has a picture and address details.'

Maggie's mobile phone rang before Nathan had the opportunity to finish his sentence. She held a hand up to stop him from continuing before answering.

'DC Jamieson speaking.' Maggie's shoulders sagged with relief. 'Kate. Holy shit, where have you been?'

Chapter 6

'What in the world is all the fuss about, Maggie? I've had everyone under the sun ringing me and leaving messages to say that it was urgent I return your call.'

'Where are you now? And why the hell weren't you answering your phone?' Maggie knew she sounded stern, but the sense of relief flooding over her made her feel frustrated at the fact that Kate had taken so long to return her calls. Although Maggie didn't know much about Kate's life previous to working with her in the DAHU, she felt a strong bond with her which at times she couldn't explain and this, along with her attraction towards the criminal psychologist, made her overprotective.

'I forgot my mobile and left it at home by accident. You know what I'm like with this thing. So, are you going to tell me what the panic is about?' Kate sounded exasperated.

'I will. I think it's better I tell you in person though, as there are a few things I'd like to talk to you about. Are you in for the rest of the night?' Maggie hoped Kate would be free.

'I am. What time should I expect you?'

'I'm just going to have a word with Nathan and then I'll shoot over to yours. And Kate ...'

'Yes?'

'Do me a favour and make sure you have your phone with

you at all times from now on. I know you aren't taking the stalking situation seriously, but I think you should still be cautious. You nearly gave me a heart attack.'

Kate laughed. 'OK. I'll do my best. Anyway, there haven't been any more letters or gifts delivered; perhaps I was just being paranoid. Looking forward to hearing what all your drama is about.'

Maggie rolled her eyes, knowing that Kate would probably carry on as normal, so it would be up to her to keep an eye on her friend. They said their goodbyes, and Maggie knocked on Nathan's door.

'I take it that was Kate on the phone then?' Nathan looked up from the computer monitor.

'Yes. I can't even begin to explain how relieved I am. I told her I would stop by hers shortly. Are you OK with me discussing details of the case with her at this stage?' Maggie leaned into the doorway.

'Why wouldn't I be? She may be consulting on the case at some point.'

'I only ask because of the victim's similarity to Kate. If she does turn out to be the target, or if this is somehow related to her, wouldn't it be a conflict of interest?'

'Yes, but for now, other than the physical appearance, there's nothing to suggest there is a link, so Maggie, try and get as much out of Kate as you can in case it does turn out to be connected. The more background we can get now, the better.'

'Sure thing. I'll see you tomorrow.' She closed his door behind her as she left.

Maggie collected her coat and bag and, leaving the office, she headed to Stafford train station. The fresh air felt good in her lungs. Walking through the park, Maggie realized she would have to be careful with what she told Kate, as she didn't want to make her unnecessarily afraid or compromise the current case in any way. If she could collate some features on the various stalker types and look further at common patterns of escalation, she might be able to gather enough information to draw up a list of people they already know who fit the profile. Maggie also thought it would be a good idea to speak to Probation to see if they had anyone on their books they were concerned about. The more details they had, the better.

While she was at Kate's, she would also check Kate's security. If Kate's stalker had now turned killer, they wouldn't give him the opportunity to make a move.

Chapter 7

He hummed quietly to himself as he brushed her long, black hair.

The song in the background was perfect. One of his favourites. 'Living Doll'.

'Just like you, sweetheart.' He smiled.

Glassy blue eyes stared at him – loving eyes. She wants to be here, he's sure of it.

He took her hand in his. Still warm. Turning it over, so it was palm-side up, he placed two fingertips gently in the groove on her forearm, down from the fold of the wrist, and then he felt it.

A faint pulse.

He bent over and kissed her gently on her forehead. Brushing her hair behind her ear, he whispered, 'Can you hear me now, princess?'

No response.

'Don't be shy.' He held back his frustration. 'Squeeze my hand if you can hear me ...'

Was that a twitch he felt?

The excitement mounted, and he hoped he hadn't imagined it.

Her head lolled forward and he had to help her straighten up. He placed the brush on the side table and lifted up a picture.

He held the snapshot beside the woman in front of him and looked over her shoulder into the mirror.

'The likeness is uncanny, don't you think?' He waited for her response.

Then he saw it. Her eyelid. A slight twitch. And he smiled.

She would have to do for now. Practice makes perfect.

His first attempt had been a complete failure. She'd died immediately once the procedure had been performed, and so he'd had to start again. He wished he could have been there when they found her body.

He would have loved to have seen the look on the police's faces when they realized.

He turned his attention back to the woman before him. 'Now, Kate, hair up or down?'

Chapter 8

Dr Kate Moloney felt unnerved when she got off the phone with Maggie.

Something in the way Maggie spoke didn't feel right and she had counted down the hours waiting for her to arrive. She checked her locks and looked out of the window so many times her neighbours probably thought she was up to something. But she couldn't help herself.

Although they seemed to have stopped now, Kate wondered if the creepy notes on black paper and the unwanted gifts of dead flowers, pig-skinned rings and vials of liquid that looked like blood had been a message or just a harmless prank. She had no doubt Maggie would be giving her a good bollocking for leaving her phone at home and, given her situation, she should know better. It reminded her of some unpleasantness she'd had in London. Although nothing had come of the harassing calls, they had really affected her emotional wellbeing. She had worked hard to forget that time in her life and she wasn't going back there again.

The truth was, mobile phones and social media were two things that Kate tried to avoid. She'd never liked the idea that she could be reached or should be available at any time day or night, and she absolutely despised the negative vibe she felt from social media most of the time. Kate only had a small circle of friends and she wasn't interested in knowing about other people's day-to-day goings on, just as much as she was sure they weren't interested in hers.

She felt restless. Looking at the clock again, she knew she still had to wait a little longer before Maggie arrived. She plonked down on her couch, picked up the remote, and flicked through the channels until she reached the news.

More politics. Something else Kate couldn't be bothered with. Just as she was about to turn off the television a reporter mentioned the next village over, Hartley. Kate turned up the volume.

'Early this morning two teenagers discovered the body of an unidentified female. Police have not released many details at this time, but the woman is young, described as goth-like in appearance and was found face down in Granger Park, Hartley. Police have confirmed that they suspect foul play and have launched a murder inquiry. We'll bring you news on this story as soon as more details come to light …'

Kate switched off the television and threw the remote as if it was on fire. A shiver ran down her spine.

Was this why Maggie was coming over? Is that what the panic was about? Had Maggie thought the victim had been her? It sounded ridiculous, even with what had been happening with the strange gifts she had been receiving and she dismissed it immediately.

But Kate's fear soon turned to fury. She was angry that Maggie hadn't given her more details over the phone. Although Maggie was a work colleague, Kate had felt a friendship was growing. Wasn't that what friends did? Keep each other in the loop? Tell them if they should be worried? Kate could feel her insecurities return as she went around and checked the locks again.

She quietly opened the door to her bedroom. She double checked that Salem, her cat, was in, as he'd have to use his litter box tonight. Kate wasn't going to risk leaving the window open for him.

What am I doing? This probably has nothing to do with me. She clenched her hands as she realized she was letting her paranoia take over. The last contact she'd had from her stalker had been an email to her work account. He knew she had been to the police about the items and wasn't happy. Was he punishing others until he could get to her? No, that couldn't be it. There was nothing to say the murder was even connected to her and now she was drawing ridiculous conclusions. She needed a distraction and headed to the kitchen to make sure Salem's litter box was clean.

So focused was she on her task that she jumped when she heard the thumps on her door. She walked down the hall and peered through the peephole. Maggie. Kate unbolted the door, removed the chains and before her friend could say anything, Kate spoke what was on her mind.

'Why didn't you tell me that a female was murdered today – who just so happens to look a lot like me? What are you playing at, Maggie?' She stood firm in the doorway.

Maggie didn't respond. Instead she pulled Kate into a tight hug, and Kate immediately started to laugh before gently pushing Maggie away.

'Christ, we're a dramatic pair, aren't we? Come in, sit down, and tell me what the hell's been going on.'

Chapter 9

Maggie couldn't help herself. The minute she saw Kate a wave of relief washed over her. Generally not one for displaying her emotions, she gave in and pulled her friend close for a hug.

'I'll make us a coffee then, shall I?' Kate stepped aside and let Maggie into her flat.

Maggie nodded and then felt a little foolish for being so emotional. Her affection for Kate was growing but she couldn't let her personal feelings overshadow a case.

After Kate had unleashed her anger, Maggie could finally breathe knowing that at least she was safe. Maggie wanted to keep a clear head so had refused the first beverage offer of a glass of wine – though if she was honest, that was what she really wanted. Something to take the edge off. Maybe later.

Kate returned from the kitchen and handed Maggie a large mug. 'Right then. I want you to tell me everything and please,' Kate gave her a stern look, 'don't leave anything out to spare my feelings.'

'What do you know so far?' Maggie didn't want to frighten Kate into believing that she was a target – even if that was what Maggie was beginning to believe.

'I only saw what was on the news. What freaked me out was

the description of the victim and then your panic calls to me today. I was beginning to believe something more sinister was happening. Am I wrong, Maggie?'

'I don't know. And that's my honest answer. We think we have ID'd the victim through the Misper database, but we're waiting to speak to the family first. When I heard the initial description of the victim, I did think it was you -- Nathan did too. The outfit the woman was dressed in could have been straight out of your wardrobe. When I couldn't get a hold of you and no one seemed to know where you were, my fear was ramped up tenfold. Although the team are not treating your stalking complaint as directly linked to this murder, they haven't dismissed it either.'

The colour from Kate's usually pale face drained even further. 'That's a lot to take in. Do you know anything else about the victim?'

'Not as yet. Between us, Dr Blake has asked for further tests to establish the cause of death as there were no wounds on the body other than two black eyes, which were sewn shut ... as was the mouth. She hadn't started the post-mortem so something may come out of that. I'm hoping we'll know more in the morning.'

'In your honest opinion, forget all the police talk ... I'm asking as a friend. Should I be worried?' Kate rubbed her arms.

'Well, first of all, I think you should keep your bloody mobile phone with you at all times. Tape it to your hand if you have to but don't go anywhere without it. Can you promise me that?'

Kate nodded. 'It's not intentional. I just never really got into the idea that I could be contacted at all times. I guess I'm a bit old-fashioned that way.' She pointed to the landline. 'That's my idea of a phone.'

'I totally understand but given we know someone has been

sending you letters and strange gifts – threats even – for your own safety you should have your phone on you. What if you need to call the police? You can't just run to a phone box these days, Kate.'

'OK. Point taken. Can we move on now?' Kate's brow furrowed. Maggie hoped she hadn't overstepped the mark, but Kate had wanted an honest answer; she couldn't be angry when that was what she got.

'Sorry. I know we haven't known each other for long, but I still consider you my friend. I just panicked when I couldn't reach you. I've said my piece. Have you had anymore letters or contact from whomever is targeting you?'

'The last contact that was made was the email to my work account. Whoever sent it was clever as no trace on the IP address could be found. Markston police aren't really taking it seriously and, as things have calmed down, perhaps they were right. I still can't figure out how they got those details though. Do you think it's someone I know?'

'That's always a possibility. But it could be that someone gave out your details accidentally without realizing the implications of doing this. Or this person has their own ways and means of getting the information they need. Individuals of this predisposition can be very resourceful, in my experience.'

'I guess that's true.' Kate shuddered.

'What kind of security do you have on this place?' Maggie stood and walked to the large windows. She tugged then smiled to herself when the window wouldn't budge. *At least she's keeping herself safe when she's home.*

'Window locks. I have the strong lock on the door and I recently put a chain lock on it. That's basically it. I've been thinking I should get some sort of camera installed as the security in this building is shit. I mean, people let strangers in all the time.' Kate rolled her eyes. 'One of the main reasons I chose this building was because I thought it appeared pretty secure ...'

'I think cameras are a good idea. Do you need some contacts for that? I'm sure I could find a reliable place to get that sorted for you.'

'Thanks, Maggie. I have some details as I began looking into it when everything started happening, but if those don't pan out I'll come back to you.'

'Fair enough. Just make sure you do it sooner rather than later.'

'Yes, ma'am.' One side of Kate's lips curled.

'Do you have anyone who can stay with you or who you can stay with? I know I may be overthinking things, but at the moment I don't want to rule out the possibility that this murder case and your stalker are associated in some way.'

'I'll be fine, Maggie. I appreciate your concern, but like you said, it may have nothing to do with me at all and I don't want to make a mountain out of a mole hill. And neither should you. First thing tomorrow I'll make some arrangements for extra security and we can take it from there.'

'Well, if you change your mind and are at a loose end, you can always stay at mine. I have the spare bedroom. Just think about it, OK?'

'Thanks. I will do.' Kate smiled.

'Oh, and I am sure I can get a panic alarm installed here and have your address flagged. I'm a bit pissed off that Markston police never offered you that option when you made your original complaint, if I'm honest.'

'Just because I work there, I wouldn't expect special treatment.' She paused. 'I'm feeling a bit overwhelmed with all this now.

Any chance we can move on to something different?' Kate ran her fingers through her hair. 'Let me just deal with it in my way.'

Maggie held her hands up. 'Sorry. I didn't mean to panic you. Look, I've put everything on the table. You do what you need to, but please talk to me if there's anything I can do to help.'

'Hmm. OK.' She yawned. 'I'm feeling a bit tired now. I think I'm just going to go to bed. Sorry if I sound ungrateful. Hopefully, some sleep and a clear head will put everything in perspective.'

Maggie stood and gave Kate a hug. 'Get some rest and I'll call you if we hear anything more from forensics tomorrow. Are you working?'

'Yes. I'll be at Markston all day. Thanks again, Maggie. Night.'

Maggie said her goodbyes and stood outside Kate's door as she listened to the locks being put on. Even that didn't put her mind at rest. She had a bad feeling about this whole situation and doubted that Kate would get any sleep. She sure as hell knew she wouldn't.

Chapter 10

Kate leaned against the front door as the details of the situation sank in. Her heart was racing but she didn't want to let Maggie know how she really felt. Maggie would only start to stress out and she needed her focused. She needed her to catch this killer.

There would not be much sleep for Kate tonight. She went into her room, gave Salem a quick tummy rub as he stretched out across her bed, and picked up her laptop. If she could put some of her thoughts down on paper, she'd share the information with Maggie and help formulate a profile. Until she had some details from the current investigation, she decided to focus on what she could ascertain from the notes and gifts she had been sent. Kate had meticulously logged all the information, including her own photos, taken carefully so as not to disturb any evidence that might have been on the items. Her gut instinct that the individual was good at covering their tracks was proven correct when forensics had found no identifying evidence on the items.

The letters had arrived in black envelopes with gold writing. No stamps, so they had been delivered personally. Each had a common theme: possession. They said, for instance, 'I will have you', and although in and of themselves they were not threatening per se, it was the gifts that ramped up the obsessive qualities: dead roses, a wreath with 'together soon' on it, rings made of skin, and vials filled with liquid that looked like blood – sinister and threatening, as if this individual were trying to make a point.

Who are you? Have we met before?

Kate looked at the photos of the items she had received. The hairs on the back of her neck stood on end.

She looked around the room. *Are you watching me now?*

Kate knew that there were various 'types' of stalkers and wracked her brain trying to think of anyone with whom she had recently had an unpleasant encounter. No one in particular jumped out at her. She had been attending a lot of training events these last few months. Could the stalker be someone she had met, or possibly even someone she worked with? Her lips trembled and she wiped the sweat from her palms on her trousers.

Why have I been chosen?

A loud bang at the door made her jump out of her skin.

What the hell was that?

Kate stood up slowly. Her curiosity urged her to see what had happened, but her fear screamed at her to stay where she was. If she didn't check, she definitely would not get any sleep. She tiptoed to the door and put her eye up to the peephole. Inching closer and holding her breath, a loud BANG caused her to scream.

Then she heard the whispers and giggles. Two voices. She peered through the peephole again. A young man and woman were stumbling about in the hallway, trying to hold each other up. She shook her head and laughed.

Maybe Maggie was right. I think I do need to stay somewhere until I can get the security sorted.

Kate packed up her laptop and double checked that all the windows and the door were locked. She turned off the light in the hallway, headed to her bedroom and gently moved Salem over as she settled herself in bed.

It was the first time since her childhood that she slept with the light on.

Chapter 11

Maggie could smell the coffee even before she opened her eyes. Having her brother Andy living with her had some perks.

It was only 6am. Her sleep had been restless, as her brain had refused to shut down after seeing Kate last night. She hoped her friend would reconsider the offer of staying with her, but she wouldn't push the idea.

Unless she had to.

Scrappy, her fluffy ginger cat, was curled up at the end of her bed, resting his big paw across her foot. 'Sorry, boy. I'm getting up now.' He stretched out and meowed in protest.

Maggie picked up the tracksuit bottoms she had thrown on the floor a few days ago. She had only worn them indoors so wasn't too bothered that they were not fresh out of the wash. She pulled them on. Her T-shirt said SMILE but that was the last thing she felt like doing this morning.

'Coffee time, Scrappy. You coming down for some brekkie?' She walked out of her room knowing that she would hear a small thump as Scrappy jumped off the bed and followed her downstairs. He rarely missed an early breakfast call. She'd never found out where he had been when he'd gone missing some time ago. Maggie was still convinced that the serial killer, Bill Raven, had had something to do with her cat's disappearance but couldn't prove it. When Scrappy had reappeared, the vet had confirmed that he had some drug in him which had made him groggy but other than that, her cat was in good form. She was grateful for that as she was fond of the moggy, even though he could be a pain in the arse.

Maggie walked into the kitchen and yawned. 'Morning. You're up early, aren't you?'

'Sorry, did I wake you?' Andy's lips tensed.

'Nah. I didn't get much sleep last night if I'm honest. You look shattered. Everything OK?' Maggie's head tilted. Andy had dark circles under his eyes and was looking a bit pale.

'Yeah. Just working some extra shifts is all. Taking its toll on me, I guess.' Andy had been working overtime to put towards his savings. Maggie knew he was hoping to get enough money together to start his own business and move out. She hadn't pressured him to leave, but understood that he needed his own space. He probably never thought he'd be living with his older sister at this stage in his life.

'Well, don't burn yourself out. You won't do anyone any good if you get sick.'

'Yes, Mum.' He laughed. 'Do you want a coffee?'

'Yes, please. I'll need as much caffeine as I can get. We have another case and I've a feeling I won't be getting much sleep for a while.'

'Oh shit! Already?'

'Yeah. Sadly, these killers don't think it's fair to give us a break in between cases.' She tried to smile, but she could tell from her brother's frown that he wasn't buying it.

'Is this about that girl who was found in the park? I saw

something on the news about it this morning. Do you think she was targeted because she was a Goth?'

'Yes, that's the case. We've no idea why she was targeted just yet. It's still early days. But you're right, it could be because of how she looked. There have been cases like that before, haven't there?' Maggie said this more to herself than to her brother as her mind ran over the few cases she was aware of in which Goths, or others whose appearances were different from the so-called norm, had been the focus of random, and sometimes brutal, attacks. She would discuss this with the team when she got into work.

'Right, I'm off to have a shower. If I don't see you before I go, have a good one and I'll catch you later.' Maggie headed upstairs feeling a bit better about things. The shower would clear the cobwebs. She'd call Kate when she arrived at the office to check that she had arranged extra security for her flat.

Chapter 12

Things weren't working out as he had planned. She just wasn't responding, and he didn't know what he'd done wrong this time. He read the books again. Watched the YouTube videos. He'd followed each step meticulously.

With the first girl, he now realized he had hammered the orbital too hard. She'd haemorrhaged and there had been nothing he could do to save her. The poor thing had seized. But this one, he looked down, she was like a zombie, and that just wouldn't do.

He kissed her forehead as he tucked the blankets in tightly around her and wiped the drool that stuck to the side of her face. 'I'm sorry, sweetheart. I think we're going to have to part ways soon. I really hoped you would snap out of this' – he waved his hand – 'state you're in.'

Maybe if she sleeps? Yes, that might help. When he came home from work this evening, she'd be downstairs waiting for him. He had to remain positive. But he still couldn't shake the feeling that she wasn't the one. In his heart, he always knew. It was always Kate Moloney. The moment he saw her, a connection had been made. He needed his Kate.

I have to see her.

He looked at his watch. If he left now, there would still be time to go round to her flat. She wouldn't have left for work yet.

He grabbed his coat, jogged down the flights of stairs, and out of the door.

The roads were fairly clear and it only took him half an hour to reach Kate's home. He parked at the end of the road and waited. He figured he had at least another half an hour before she left, but she surprised him this morning.

His breath caught as he watched her bounce down the steps. *So beautiful. That's my girl.* Pride swelled within his heart.

He put on the glasses, fixed the hair beneath the cap and checked himself in the mirror. He cleared his throat and tested out his deep voice. *Perfect.* He had been practising.

He started the engine and pulled away from the kerb slowly, so as not to attract any unwanted attention. As he came up beside her, he grabbed the map from the passenger seat and rolled down the window.

'Excuse me, miss. I wondered if you could help me?'

Kate continued to walk. She was staring straight ahead and when a gust of wind blew her hair, he noticed the earbuds in her ears.

He tapped his horn and chastised himself when he noticed her jump. He didn't want her to be afraid of him. She removed an earphone and looked in the car window.

'Sorry. I didn't mean to frighten you. I'm a little lost. I wondered if you could help me?' Kate cocked her head, as if she was deciding whether or not to help the stranger before her.

'Where are you going?' Oh, her accent. *Like music to my ears.*

'I'm looking for Anchor House. Do you know if it's around here?'

'Ah no. Sorry. I'm not familiar with that place. There's a shop on the corner; maybe they'd be able to help you?' She pointed to the end of the road.

'Pardon? Can you come a little closer, I didn't hear that?'

Instead, she spoke louder. Something was making her wary. Surely it couldn't be him.

'Try the shop down the road.' She looked at her watch. 'I wish I could be of more help, but I have to go.' Her pace quickened and she looked back at him before she crossed the road, no doubt heading to the bus stop.

She stole another look in his direction. He had to stop himself from waving. *She wanted to see me again.* He folded the map up and shoved it in the glove box before pulling out and heading into work.

'Living Doll' came on the radio and he cranked it up louder. *It's fate.*

They were playing their song. The feeling of euphoria would last throughout the day.

Yes. It's time. We'll be reunited once again, my darling Kate.

He nearly passed the building because he was so caught up in thoughts of Kate. He took out his pass and held it against the flat surface, waiting for the beep to let him know the bar would rise. The parking lot was busy; he hadn't been to this station in a while. Maybe he would see a friendly face or two, but first he would need to change.

Chapter 13

Kate pulled her coat around her as she looked back before crossing the road. The man in the car was still looking at her.

I'm just being paranoid.

He had been friendly enough and only asked for directions. Kate really hadn't known the location he had asked her about, but there was no way she was going to lean in towards his car either. She'd watched various programmes on serial killers and that was definitely one of the tricks they used. With everything that had been happening, she wasn't going to make it easy for anyone to grab her.

She'd reached the bus stop and looked around again. Kate thought she saw his car pass, but that wouldn't make sense as the shop she'd directed him to was around the opposite side. *Perhaps he'd changed his mind.* She shrugged to herself. The bus arrived and after paying her fare and finding a seat, she put her earphones back in and relaxed as Muse took hold. She ignored the rest of the passengers.

Kate felt her mobile vibrate in her pocket. She smiled when she saw the message from Maggie.

I hope you have your mobile on you. Just wanted to double check that you're sorting out the security we spoke about. Text me when you can. X Maggie

Kate texted back letting Maggie know that she was heading into work early and would update her on the security situation. She reminded her that they had already discussed this and there was no need to keep checking. To soften the conversation, she ended by thanking her for caring. She knew Maggie was only looking out for her, but she didn't want to feel so vulnerable.

When she arrived in Markston she walked the long way around so she could go through the centre of the town. It was quiet at this time in the morning, so she popped into the café and picked up an Americano. She wouldn't let her guard down though and continued to look around as she walked through the public parking lot towards the police station. Kate couldn't help but feel someone was watching her, even though there wasn't a soul in sight.

Once she punched in her password, she waited as the gate opened and then entered via the back door, taking the lift up to her office floor. She jumped when she heard someone call out, 'Kate!'

Looking into the open-plan office, she smiled when she saw Lucy Sherwood. Lucy was an agency Probation Officer now after leaving her full-time post at Markston Probation. She was in the process of finalizing and opening a refuge for men and women who were in, or escaping from, abusive relationships.

'Hi Lucy! How wonderful to see you. Had I known you'd be here, I would have brought you one.' She raised her coffee. She walked towards Lucy, having to shimmy past Luke – the maintenance man from headquarters who was finally changing the flickering ceiling bulbs.

'Well, I hadn't planned on coming, but the accreditation from the Ministry of Justice has come through earlier than expected, so I'm here to talk over some things with Mark and the team regarding referrals. Are you OK? You're looking a little pale.'

'I'm grand.' Kate wasn't up for explaining recent events. 'Great news about the refuge! If there's anything I can help you with, just ask, OK?'

'Thanks so much, Kate. I'm sure I'll be picking your brains, as I'm working on an assessment to include in the referral and would love your input.'

'No problem. We can catch up when you're done here or book some time. I'd actually love to come by and see how you have set things up. I'm particularly keen to see how you have the male and female residential arrangements onsite.' Kate looked at her watch. 'I'm really sorry to cut things short but I need to do something. Make sure to catch me before you go, OK?'

'I will. Nice to see you again, Kate.'

Kate smiled as she walked into her office, put her coffee down and slumped into her chair. It was exhausting putting on an act, but she couldn't let anyone know just how shaken up she actually felt.

She turned on her computer and, while it booted up, she took out her notebook where she had recorded all the information about her stalker. Logging on to her computer, she opened the Google browser and searched for security firms within the area. She had already decided to have her locks changed even though there was no evidence to suggest that whoever this individual was had been in her home. She would much rather be sure that this wouldn't be an option. She would also have the locks on the windows changed and alarms installed. A new alarm for the flat and a camera above the door would also ease her mind. She recalled Maggie's offer to have a panic alarm installed, but decided that with all the additional security she was looking at, this wouldn't be necessary.

After reading some of the reviews of the various companies, Kate settled on one and made the arrangements for them to come round on the weekend and do the work. She hadn't meant to lie to Maggie when she told her she already had details for a company, but the situation had overwhelmed her and she just blurted it out. At least it was all sorted now.

What a relief.

She felt better about things. This was going to cost her a fair chunk of her savings, but in the long run her safety was more important.

There was a light knock on her door. 'Morning, Kate. Are you coming to the meeting this morning?' PC Mark Fielding raised his eyebrow.

'Morning. Um, yeah. Is this about Lucy's refuge?' Mark nodded. 'Right, gimme five and I'll be in.' She pointed to the ceiling. 'Any chance you can ask Luke to pop in here and fix that bulb before he leaves? It takes ages to get maintenance here.' She held her hands together in a kind of begging prayer.

'Ha! Yes. I'll have a word and then let DI Calleja know you'll be through momentarily. I think there's some more news to be shared with the team, but DS Hooper is not saying a word.'

'Intriguing!' Kate waited until Mark walked away before she dug out her mobile and called Maggie.

'Hi, Kate. Everything OK?'

'Yes. I just wanted to let you know that I've a security company coming around this weekend, hopefully, to install a few things and talk about other measures. It's all sorted and you can relax.'

'Well that does ease my mind a bit. But I'm still not happy that you have to wait. The offer of staying with me is still open.'

'I appreciate that and I'll have a think and see how I feel. Is there any news on the woman?'

'There's a briefing later today. Hopefully, Dr Blake has finished the post-mortem and once we have official confirmation of her identity, we can move things forward. I'll keep you posted.'

'Sounds good. I've got to go now – Lucy's here to talk to us about her refuge.'

'Is that up and running now? Amazing! Say hello and we'll catch up later today or I'll give you a bell this evening.'

'You don't have to keep checking up on me, you know?' Kate sighed.

'I know. But it's more for my sake than yours, OK? Talk soon.'

Kate smiled as she ended the call. She'd never admit it, but she was secretly glad to have Maggie watching her back. The more she thought about the stalker, the more anxious she became. She didn't want this to impact her work in the DAHU and she didn't want to have to discuss the possibility of being forced to take time off. Work was her escape. If she didn't have that, she'd be in worse shape.

I won't go to that place again – once the darkness consumes me, it's harder and harder to crawl out of that hole.

Kate's previous bouts with anxiety and depression hung around her neck like a noose and she had fought hard to bury that part of her life. Kate stood and shook her head, plastered a smile on her face, pulled her shoulders back, and headed to the meeting room.

Chapter 14

The overcast sky and spittle of rain hitting her face on the way into work that morning almost seemed to perfectly reflect Maggie's mood that day. She stared out of the window. Kate was still on her mind after their phone call.

Maggie's shoulders were tight, and she hadn't realized how worried she was until this moment. She rubbed the back of her neck, and as she looked up she saw Nathan coming down the corridor.

'Everything OK?' Nathan came over to her.

'Yeah. Just got off the phone with Kate and she's organised some additional security as a precaution while all this is going on.'

'Did you tell her more about the case than we agreed?' Nathan frowned.

'She'd already seen the news, and once she put my panicky calls and the news story together, she pretty much figured things out for herself.'

Nathan turned on his heels. 'In my office now, please.'

Maggie raised a brow. Nathan clearly wasn't happy with her. She stood and followed him back into his office.

'Have a seat.' He pointed to a chair.

'OK. You look pissed off. What have I done?'

'I'm slightly concerned that you may have unnecessarily scared Dr Moloney by linking these cases together.'

'Are you being serious?' Maggie's eyes widened.

'Yes. I am. Look, I'm not only speaking to you as your boss here. There have been a few discussions about how you sometimes come across as a bit arrogant.'

'What the hell, Nathan? You're the one who told me to speak to Kate. No one else was going to do it. I just wanted to be upfront with her. She's a friend as well as a colleague – and she may be at risk.'

'Hang on. Let me finish. People don't know you the way I and some of the team do, Maggie. We know how your brain works, and how you have this uncanny ability to connect the dots sometimes well in advance of when the rest of us do. But you need to tone things down. Be confident in your thoughts, of course, but let others share their theories and support them the same way you'd expect to be supported.'

Maggie's shoulders drooped. 'Do I really come across that way? It's not how I'd like people to see me.'

'I know. And it's not all the time. What I'm saying is, just be mindful in future.'

'I hear what you're saying, but it's not something I do consciously. I'll try my best. If you feel I'm overstepping the mark, just tell me. I'd rather that than have people talking about me behind my back.' Maggie's shoulders tensed.

'For the record, no one was talking behind your back, and you did also receive some high praise, especially from DI Rutherford who is impressed with your ability to spot things while focusing on all lines of enquiry.'

Maggie blushed. She'd never expected that DI Rutherford

would speak of her so highly. She was still pissed off with Nathan though. 'OK. Thanks for letting me know.' She huffed.

'Don't be like that, Maggie. I wouldn't be much of a boss – or a friend – if I didn't tell you.'

'Of course.' Maggie pursed her lips. 'I'm sure I'd do the same if I were in your position.'

Nathan shook his head. 'I'm sure you would.'

Maggie turned to go. She hoped this was just a blip and they could go back to how things should be. Nathan knew she'd always been self-conscious about how she appeared to others, and hearing it, especially from him, really knocked her back.

'Before you go, Bethany has been out to speak with the family of the missing woman, Tracy Holloway. I spoke to Dr Blake earlier and the forensic report should be with us at some point today. Contact any friends you can and I'll see you in the incident room shortly.'

'Yes, boss.' She stood.

Nathan had a funny look on his face but Maggie didn't want to push him. If he'd wanted her to know, he would have shared it there and then. She'd wait until the briefing.

Her shoulders tightened once again and her gut felt like someone had grabbed her insides and was having a tug of war. She didn't have a good feeling about any of this.

Chapter 15

DI Rutherford called the team together to discuss victimology. 'Good to see you all still smiling, though that soon may change once the details of Dr Blake's report have been read.'

Maggie's stomach tightened again. She looked to Nathan for some indication of what to expect, but he wouldn't look her way.

'Tracy Holloway was reported missing by her parents five weeks ago. She was last seen on her way towards Stafford town centre, where it is believed she was planning on catching a bus to her parents' home. CCTV places her at Victoria Park entering from the east side. Last sighted by the bowling grounds, but there's no other CCTV after this. The cameras lost her. It seems her abductor must have followed her or observed her in the park and made their move. It's likely they are familiar with the CCTV locations, so as to have avoided being caught.'

'That suggests the person is organised ... methodical even,' Maggie offered.

'I'd agree with that assessment. Her family have said that Tracy was a slave to her routines and that would've made it a lot easier for the killer, if we assume they had been watching her before making their move.' Rutherford tapped the evidence board. 'They also confirmed they had been waiting for her to arrive, and the route she took would further support that she was heading for their address. A boyfriend or ex was mentioned. They'd had an argument; she called her mother to say that she would be a little late but that was the last they heard from her.' The DI shuffled some papers on the table before her.

'Has anyone spoken to the boyfriend or contacted the DAHU?' Maggie didn't believe that this was a domestic, but it would be worth pursuing, if only to rule out that angle.

'It's proving a little difficult to locate him as all we have is a first name, Joshua, even though they'd apparently been off and on for at least a year. The database has been checked, and we're trying to locate anyone with that name, but there are more than we expected.' The DI raised a brow.

'What? You mean no one, not even her parents, knows his full name? I know there's a backlog in the DAHU, but surely they would be able to give us some idea?' Maggie's eyes widened.

'Afraid not on both counts. The Family Liaison Officer with the parents noted that the boyfriend wasn't popular with them. Apparently, they thought he was a waste of space and it seems Tracy generally didn't share much with them as it always ended badly. In fact, they weren't even aware that they were still a couple – albeit off and on – until one of Tracy's friends mentioned it.'

'Sounds more like wishful thinking on their part if they didn't really like him. What did her friends or colleagues know about him?' Nathan sat back, crossing his leg.

'Just first-name basis according to the field team. Though one of her friends believes his last name begins with either an A or H.' DI Rutherford checked her notes.

Maggie sighed. 'Well that should be easy to decipher, shouldn't it.'

'Sarcasm duly noted.' The DI paused. 'I've requested that the field team and our partner agencies keep their ears to the ground. It seems odd that this boyfriend hasn't come forward despite the news reports. But there could be an innocent explanation.'

DI Rutherford didn't sound convinced to Maggie.

Bethany spoke up. 'When I spoke to some of Tracy's friends they described her as trusting and always looking for the good in people. That may explain why she stayed with a boyfriend who most of her friends and family didn't seem to like. A dangerous trait in this day and age, don't you think?'

'Hmm. She could have been easily lured by the killer. Maybe he pulled a Ted Bundy, pretended to have a broken limb so needed help loading something into the boot of his car – that sort of thing?' Maggie suggested.

'Good spot. You might be onto something. It might be a useful theory to raise at the press conference.' Nathan looked at DI Rutherford.

'Hold fire. That might give the public the false belief that we have a lead, or it may heighten the mood of any vigilantes out there to take action by misrepresenting the situation.' After the Raven case, DI Rutherford was treading carefully with the press. Maggie understood her reasoning even if she wasn't sure she agreed.

'I see your point, ma'am, but doesn't public protection need to come first? Maybe if we put our heads together and carefully word the release we can get the message out without causing panic?' Maggie caught the glare from her boss and instantly regretted opening her mouth.

'Her colleagues did point out that in the last few weeks prior to her abduction she'd been behaving oddly.' The DI scratched her chin.

'In what way?' Maggie wouldn't do herself any favours by

pissing off the DI. After the conversation with Nathan, she'd try to think more before blurting out her own theories.

'She was constantly checking her drawers at work. Looking over her shoulder. A bit jumpy – that sort of thing. When her colleagues asked her about it, they said she brushed it off and her excuse was that she'd been watching one too many horror films lately. According to her friends, after that, it looked like she was making an effort to appear normal, but she wasn't fooling any of them.'

'Was she an overly private person?' Nathan stared at the evidence board.

'Only in relation to her boyfriend, it seems. Otherwise, she was described as outgoing, fun and quite talkative. Why? What are you thinking, Nathan?' Maggie had to squint to read Rutherford's notes as she scribbled on the whiteboard.

'Hmmm ... it just seems at odds with the behaviour described today. Did any of them give a hint that they may have known something more? Maybe they pushed her on it, she had a go, so they're not sharing anything as they don't want to be involved or break her confidence?'

'Interesting you should say that as two of her work mates said they challenged Tracy and she did get very defensive, so they backed off. They didn't really think much of it after the fact as they said they assumed she was having a domestic situation. One said they couldn't remember the conversation and the other just went blank when questioned.' The DI paused and waited for some feedback from the team.

'Might be worth having another word. Maybe they were in shock after learning of Ms Holloway's murder,' Nathan offered.

'Yes. Bethany's going to interrogate Tracy's social media accounts. Maggie, you can speak to the work colleague and

Nathan, you're with me. Let's chat before the press conference this afternoon. We need to put something together that raises awareness so that people, particularly women, are more vigilant but without causing a bloody panic.'

Chapter 16

Nathan was coming out of his office with his coat on when Maggie grabbed his attention. 'Can I have a word before you shoot off?'

'I've only a few minutes. I've been summoned to a meeting with DCI Hastings after I speak with the DI.'

'Oh. Hope it's nothing serious. I just spoke to one of Tracy's friends and she mentioned that Tracy had been sent some random notes from someone but had hidden them from her boyfriend.'

'And what? She was seeing someone else?' Nathan appeared distracted.

'Well, that's what the boyfriend thought. According to the friend, the couple got into an argument; he was charged with criminal damage and was given bail conditions to keep away. Possibly the reason he hasn't come forward, so we should have his details on record. But why didn't those notes turn up when her house was searched?'

'You're losing me, Maggie. What's the significance of the notes?'

'Could they be from the killer? What if Tracy was being stalked too, like Kate?'

'Interesting theory but without the notes, it's hard to say – and

we can't just make up evidence to link this to Kate's situation.'
Nathan looked at his watch.

'I wouldn't do that. I just wanted you to know that I'm going
to go and talk to her friends and colleagues again. See if they
can shed further light on these notes. I'll update you if I find
anything of interest.'

'Sounds good, but tread carefully. I don't want you planting
any ideas in their heads – they need to be the ones who tell you
the details, not the other way around.'

Nathan left without waiting for a reply. Maggie went back to
her desk and made a list of the people she would speak to,
starting with Tracy Holloway's parents. They had already been
interviewed by the field officers and from what the records said,
it looked like Tracy had been close to them; she may have told
them about the letters or be able to direct Maggie to someone
who did know.

Chapter 17

'Hello. Is that Mr Holloway?'

'Yes, who's this?' His reply was abrupt.

'My name is DC Maggie Jamieson; I'm calling about your daughter's case. I know you've already spoken to the police, but some new information has come to light and I just wondered if you could help me?'

'New information? Have you arrested someone? I'll do anything to end this nightmare. My wife is beside herself. Not eating. Not sleeping. We just want this whole ordeal over so we can grieve properly.'

'I absolutely understand that and I'm sorry if I gave you the wrong idea. We haven't arrested anyone. I've spoken to a friend of Tracy's and she mentioned that Tracy had received some letters that may have caused friction with her boyfriend. I wondered if you knew anything about that?'

'Not this again. Her boyfriend would use any excuse to slander my daughter. We never heard of any such nonsense. For whatever reason, Tracy loved him; she'd never do anything to jeopardize that. Though we don't know why. He showed his true colours when they fought, didn't he!'

'Did she have any close friends or colleagues she may have spoken to about her ... erm ... relationship?'

'Well, yes. Of course, she did. I don't know what *he* told you, but despite his best efforts, Tracy had many friends. Rona has been her best friend since they were toddlers. I can get you her details, if you want.'

'We haven't located the boyfriend yet and that would be really helpful. Thank you so much.' Maggie wrote out the details and said goodbye. Mr Holloway was very defensive and clearly didn't like his daughter's boyfriend. She didn't want to upset him further and doubted that their daughter would have shared anything about her relationship or any problems she may have had with them, given the hostility. Maybe the best friend would be more helpful.

Maggie dialled the number she had been given and her shoulders slumped at each ring. Just as she was about to hang up, the phone was answered.

'Hello?'

The voice was barely audible.

'Hello. Is that Rona?'

'Yes.'

'My name is DC Maggie Jamieson and I'm calling to clarify a few points in relation to Tracy Holloway. Are you able to talk?'

'Sure. What can I do to help?'

'We've learned that Tracy had received some … erm … notes that suggested she may have been seeing someone else? Do you know anything about that?'

Maggie heard a sniff through the earpiece.

'She wasn't seeing anyone else. Did that arsehole Josh tell you that?'

Rona seethed.

'No, it was suggested that he believed that was the case and the couple argued. Had she hidden them from him and he found out?'

Josh is an idiot. Some weirdo had been sending her notes; it really creeped her out. She hid them because she knew how he would react. And she wasn't wrong, was she? She didn't tell anyone about them at first. But I noticed she was really jumpy and I had to beg her to tell me. She was going to go to the police, but then ... well ...'

The woman burst into tears.

'I'm sorry to have dragged this up but that's really helpful. Do you mind if I ask just one more question?'

'If you think it would help, ask anything you want.'

'Did you happen to see the notes?' Maggie tapped her pen on her desk while she waited for a reply.

'Yes. She showed them all to me.'

'Can you describe them to me?' Maggie didn't want to lead the woman.

'Yes. They were in black envelopes. On black paper. With gold writing. Why?'

'No reason. Just want to make sure I have all the details. Thank you so much for your time.' Maggie clicked the receiver to end the call and took a deep breath.

Without seeing the actual notes, she couldn't be sure, but it looked very much like Kate's stalker could also be their killer.

Chapter 18

Maggie wasn't one for reflecting on other people's opinions of her, not out of arrogance, but more because things like that tended to eat away at her. However, Nathan's words from earlier had stung. She rolled a pen between her fingers. She didn't want to put people's noses out of joint by making assumptions about the notes Tracy had received, but all sorts of sinister thoughts were going through her head. Someone called out her name.

'Are you coming to the briefing? Looks like Dr Blake's worked some magic.' Nathan popped his head into the open-plan office area.

'On my way, boss!' Dr Blake must have sent the full forensic report.

She gathered her notebook, turned her phone onto silent, tucked it in her pocket, and picked up a pen before making her way to the incident room.

Nathan stood at the front of the room, alongside DI Abigail Rutherford. A few members of the field team were asked to sit in, and this made Maggie a little bit anxious. What did that pathologist report say?

DI Rutherford spoke first. 'Thank you all for coming. DS Wright will be introducing the details of the pathology report today, but I wanted to first say that this is an unusual case and one that we will need to be sensitive about. I've just passed the more sensitive information on to the FLO, so Tracy's family will be aware of the details. I'll leave you in the capable hands of DS Wright while I go and speak to the COMMS Officer.'

Maggie and Bethany looked at each other.

'Christ. I've goose bumps after that delivery. What the hell is going on?' Bethany leaned forward.

Maggie shrugged. She had no idea what they were facing but she wasn't liking what she'd heard so far.

'Thanks, guv. OK, folks. This is a case unlike any most of us will have come across in our careers. Until we know the motivation, we have to be very careful how we handle things from here on in. I've read the pathologist's report and it is quite disturbing. Tracy Holloway is a twenty-eight-year-old white female. Her hair had been dyed black by the killer. Once the pathologist was able to remove the stitching from her eyes, she found that blue contact lenses had been inserted.' Nathan pulled a picture from the folder in front of him and pinned it on the board. 'This is what Ms Holloway looked like a few days before she was abducted.'

Maggie gasped. Although she had seen pictures of their victim before, they had been poor quality and from several years ago. Seeing the enlarged photo showed just how much Tracy had been totally transformed. Had they not had the details that confirmed their victim was the woman in the picture, she never would have said they were the same person.

Nathan continued. 'The post-mortem concluded that Tracy died from a brain haemorrhage caused by trauma. According to Dr Blake, it seems that our killer attempted a leucotomy – more commonly known as a lobotomy – on Ms Holloway and punctured blood vessels causing internal bleeding on the brain. Tracy may have suffered from headaches, seizures and various other symptoms before her death. Our killer then left her in the park, face down.' Nathan paused. 'The report also indicates that the victim had an infinity-shaped tattoo on her left shoulder blade. When her parents were first contacted, they advised that she had no distinguishing marks or tattoos, but we'll need to speak to her friends or others who knew her perhaps more intimately to confirm this. She may not have told her parents she'd had one done.'

'Oh my god, Nathan. For once, I am at a loss for words.' Maggie stared at the picture of Tracy on the board. 'What would possess someone to do this?'

'That's exactly what we need to find out.' Nathan then pointed to the side note on the board which had Kate's details following her report of harassment. 'It's still too early to link Dr Moloney's stalker – and I do believe we are also dealing with a stalker – at this time; however I think we need to look into this report further.'

'Can I ask why the sudden change of heart?' Maggie was both pleased and worried. If this murder was linked to the person who was stalking Kate, her friend may be in more danger than they all had thought. Maggie was reluctant to share the information from Rona about the letters at this time, as they had not been found. If she disclosed this now, and it turned out to be wrong, Nathan and the rest of the team would not be impressed.

'I think we have to accept that the resemblance to Dr Moloney is not easily dismissed. The fact that Ms Holloway's appearance was changed, and that Dr Moloney has recently been the victim of unwanted gifts and letters with a sinister undertone, makes it more than likely that the same person who has been sending Kate these items is our killer.'

'If that's true, he's escalating. Do you think we should let Kate know about this?' In normal circumstances, Maggie would have been straight on the phone to Kate, but without any concrete evidence, as Nathan had warned, she knew this could cause more harm than good.

Nathan shook his head. 'No. I'm talking to DI Rutherford about how best to approach this. But until we can make a definite connection, we don't want to upset Dr Moloney.'

Maggie took a deep breath before responding, but she couldn't help herself. 'I totally understand that, but if we wait too long we could actually be placing Kate in jeopardy.'

'I can assure you no one wants that, Maggie. We are aware of the risks, but we have to be careful here.' Nathan glowered at her.

Maggie let the words seep into her mind. She didn't like this one bit – her instincts to protect Kate were screaming, but Nathan was right, they needed more to connect the cases. 'Fair enough. Where do we go from here then?'

'I'd like the field officers to find out more about Ms Holloway's habits. Did she have a tattoo that she may have hidden from her family? Had she had any unwanted attention recently and the like? Bethany, I'd like you to dig further into her social media accounts. Any new friend requests? Anything that seems unusual. Also, let's try to piece together her last movements based on CCTV and information from those we speak to. Maggie, I'd like you to speak to Probation to see if they have anyone on their books who's raised some eyebrows recently and then go to Ms Holloway's home. There are some forensic officers still there. See if anything stands out to you. That's it for now. Keep me updated on anything that may be of importance.'

Maggie waited behind as her colleagues shuffled out of the room. 'Can I have a word, Nathan?'

He nodded.

She waited until everyone was gone, stood up, and closed the door. 'Between you and me, how concerned about Kate should we be? And please,' she touched his arm, 'don't sugar-coat it or feed me the standard line.'

'In my honest opinion?'

'Yes. I need to know the truth.'

'OK. I think we should be very concerned about her but I was instructed not to share this with the team yet as everything we have is only circumstantial. However, I'm using my own judgement now and I'm going to Markston Police Station shortly. I've already spoken to DI Calleja and shared my concerns. We've agreed to speak to Kate together and let her know.'

Maggie's head pounded and she rubbed her temples.

'I need you to stay focused, Maggie. It's hard when one of our own is targeted. But we can't let our feelings – no matter what those feelings are – cloud our judgement. Am I being clear?' His brow rose.

Maggie nodded. 'Right, of course. I'm going to contact Probation and see if there's anyone acting out of the ordinary. And thank you for being honest, I appreciate that.'

Nathan squeezed her shoulder and left the room.

Maggie looked up at the board. They needed to find this killer before Kate was the next one on the mortuary slab.

Chapter 19

Back at her desk, Maggie couldn't sit still. Her curiosity was getting the better of her. She wanted to know what information DI Rutherford and Nathan would be sharing with the press and whether they would allude to the connection with another stalking case.

She snuck in the back of the room and stood against the wall, her hands behind her, to stop her from reacting to anything that might lead to further frustrations. Looking at the attendees, she noticed that gobby journalist who had been out to get her during the Raven case. At the time, she had been investigating the dismembered remains of Bill Raven's alleged victims while he had been appealing his conviction. The reporter had made a point of sensationalizing the case and making Maggie look like she was incompetent. She'd also thrown around accusations that Maggie had coerced an innocent man into confessing and was trying to sabotage his release. She shuddered as the memories raced through her mind.

Maggie listened as her DI advised the press on the current situation with the discovery and formal ID of Tracy Holloway's body.

'Our victim was discovered in the early hours and declared dead on the scene. After speaking with our colleagues in the

Misper Unit, we can now confirm the victim has been identified as Tracy Holloway, who had been reported missing some five weeks ago. On discovery of her body, we've learned that her hair had been dyed black and clothing that she did not own was placed on her, presumably by her abductor and killer.'

'Can you tell us if she had been sexually assaulted in any way?' One journalist shouted out.

'No, I can't confirm that at the moment. As soon as more forensic details have been passed on to us, we'll be sharing what we can with you. Our message today really is to ask you all to respect the family's wishes and allow them time to grieve.'

'What about the eyes being sewn shut?' The mouthy journalist called out.

Maggie's eyes widened. *How the hell did she know that?* She needed to find out the journalist's name.

'I'm sorry? I'm not sure where you got that information from, but I am not at liberty to discuss any aspects of the ongoing investigation.' DI Rutherford's face had reddened, and Maggie knew the reporter would not give up so easily.

'But you're not denying it then, are you? And the mouth too. I heard she had an almost doll-like appearance.'

Maggie clenched her fists behind her; she could feel her knuckles graze the wall. She noted the smirk on the journalist's face.

'As I said, I'm not at liberty to discuss anything more with you at this time. I'd like to thank you all for attending today. If you have any further questions, you can direct them to our COMMS Officer via the usual channels.' DI Rutherford straightened her suit jacket and made her way out of the room, with Maggie quickly in tow.

'What the hell was that?' Maggie whispered to her boss.

'Fucked if I know. How did that journalist get those details? I specifically told you all in the briefing that we wouldn't be giving out those details to the press. Our whole case could be compromised now with all the nutters who are going to call in saying it was them.'

'Do you think we have a leak in the team, ma'am?' Maggie had to quicken her pace to keep up with the DI.

'We'd better not or heads will roll! And what was that crap about looking like a doll?'

Maggie grabbed DI Rutherford's arm. 'Wait. Dr Blake said something like that at the crime scene. I don't think it was recorded anywhere, so the leak could be anyone who was within earshot.'

'Are you serious? Right, I want you to speak to Nathan and check the records, statements, and any notes available. I'll be calling everyone together in an hour. If we have a leak, we need to know. I'd also like to find out more about that journalist. We need to shut this down as soon as possible before she prints something that's going to cause a panic in the community.' DI Rutherford carried on to her office, and Maggie went to Nathan's.

'Did you hear what happened?' Maggie blurted out.

'Where? When? Sorry, I'm not psychic so I have no clue what you're talking about. Care to enlighten me further?'

'Sorry.' She took a breath. 'At the press conference. Remember that journalist from the Raven case – the one who clearly had it in for me? She knew about the eyes and mouth being sewn shut in this case and—'

'What? Did she say where she found out that information?' Nathan interrupted.

'Well, if you'd let me finish ...' Maggie smiled. 'She also knew about Dr Blake referring to the victim as looking like a doll, but she wouldn't say where the information came from and Rutherford basically ended things there.'

'The guv must be fuming. But the doll thing – was that said in any of the briefings?'

'I can't recall. I know Dr Blake said it at the crime scene, but I can't for the life of me remember if it was something that was mentioned with everyone at any of the discussions or even casually in the office. That's what worries me more. Only someone at the scene would have heard that.' Maggie sat. Her legs felt like jelly.

'Well, let's find out the facts first. We should be able to narrow down where the information originated and then how the journalist got hold of it.'

Maggie knew Nathan was right. 'DI Rutherford wants me to go over the statements to see what information was recorded. That may give us a lead. She's also asked me to get Bethany to do some digging on that journalist. We'll have to stop her from sensationalizing this whole thing – imagine what Tracy Holloway's family are going to think if they read about that in the papers.'

Nathan's computer pinged. 'Go and make a start on those tasks; we're meeting in an hour. Can you ask Bethany to come in here? I'll work with her on the journalist side of things and see if we can get at least those aspects suppressed. Though I'm sure we're going to have to give her something to stop her.' Nathan scratched his head and picked up his phone. That was her cue to leave.

She walked over to Bethany. 'Nathan needs you in his office.'

'Erm. OK. Any clue what it's about?' Bethany frowned.

'Just the case. Sorry, I need to do something before the briefing.

Don't look so worried.' As the words came out of her mouth, she knew she sounded harsher than she'd intended but Bethany was already out of her chair and heading to Nathan's office before she could explain further.

Maggie opened the statements on her system. She trawled through the details but could find no mention of Dr Blake's comments from the crime scene. She looked through the notes she'd jotted down from the briefing but then realized that even if the doll-like reference of the victim had been mentioned, she wouldn't necessarily have noted that herself. Her next port of call would be DI Rutherford's PA, but with her only working part-time, she may well have gone for the day. She picked up her phone and dialled the extension. The answerphone kicked in. *Damn.* And then a thought crept into her head and the hair on her arms stood on end.

What if the killer was in contact with the journalist?

Chapter 20

The television blared from the front room as he made the coffee. 'I hope it's not too loud for you. It's just that I enjoy this reporter. She doesn't pull any punches.' He wondered if she'd heard him, but just in case she hadn't he popped his head through the doorway and called through, 'It is pretty loud, isn't it? I'll turn it down a notch. I don't want to give you a headache.' She seemed more responsive today.

Her head lolled to the side. 'Oh no. Hang on a minute. I'll just pour the coffee and then I'll help you out. Two secs, my princess.' He whistled as he poured their drinks and then shuffled back into the front room, placing the cups on the coasters. 'OK then. Here we go.' He tilted her head back and repositioned her in the chair. 'Are you thirsty?' He pointed to the coffee mug. 'It's a little hot at the moment, but when it cools, I can help you if you want.'

No answer.

'Come on now. How am I supposed to know what you want if you don't answer me?' He nudged her shoulder and her head fell backwards, hanging over the back of the chair.

'Oops. Sorry.' He straightened her again. 'Why won't you talk to me? I need you to say something.' He brushed the hair off her face. 'You feel hot. I hope you don't have a fever.' He went up to the first floor via the stairs and looked in the cupboard under the sink in the spare bathroom. He pulled out the small bag and inside he found the thermometer.

He returned to the living room. 'Open wide.'

Nothing.

He placed two of his fingers on her lips and used his thumb to prise her mouth open. 'Good. Now don't let this fall out.' He placed the thermometer underneath her tongue and gently closed her mouth. He sat opposite her, and while he waited he picked up his mug and focused on the television.

'Do you see why I like her? So feisty! I suspect the police aren't always thrilled with her reporting of the crimes in the community.' He chuckled to himself. His interest was piqued when the reporter mentioned Tracy Holloway. 'Oh. This should be good.' He turned the television up again.

'In other news, the police still don't have any leads in the case of Tracy Holloway. Ms. Holloway was found face down in Granger Park by two teenaged boys. When I spoke to the family, they expressed concerns about how little information was being shared with them by the police. My questions to the police have remained unanswered.'

'I think I need to speak to this reporter. Maybe I can give her some of the answers she's looking for. What do you think?' *She could be my voice.*

No response.

He placed his mug back on the table and shook his head. *What am I going to do with her?* He stood, walked over, and pulled the thermometer from her mouth. 'One hundred and three. Shit.' He wiped his sweaty palms on his trousers. 'You definitely have a fever. I'm sure I have some antibiotics around here somewhere. I'll get you a cool cloth for your forehead too.

You need to rest.' He removed the rope from around her chest. He had stopped tying up her wrists and feet when he realized she wouldn't be struggling. 'Let's get you back to bed.' He lifted her in his arms and hummed a soothing lullaby, one his mother used to sing to him when he was poorly, as he struggled to carry her upstairs.

He pushed the door to her room open with his foot, walked over to the bed and placed her on top of the covers. 'I'll get a light blanket to cover your legs.' He left her and went into his own room.

'Now, where did I leave those meds?' He rummaged in the top drawer of his dresser until he found the bottle he was looking for. He checked the date. Not expired yet. These will do. He went over to his closet and pulled out the throw he had washed the other day. He sniffed it. 'Perfect'.

He went back to her room and dropped the blanket and tablets on the floor.

What the hell?

Her hand was clenching the bedsheets. She had moved! A smile formed across his face. He picked up the items he had dropped and, placing them down on the nightstand, he opened the small cupboard by her bed where he had stored the ropes and a leg chain. The reality was, she had probably spasmed because of the treatment and her infection. He didn't care though. Better safe than sorry. He didn't want to hurt her because he knew she was unwell, so he loosely tied her hands and feet to the bedposts. 'I'll be back.'

He returned to the room a few minutes later with a cool, damp washcloth and wiped her face. He folded the cloth and placed it on her forehead. He popped two antibiotics from the bottle, raised her head and held the glass of water from this morning to her mouth as he popped a pill into her mouth and let her head go back to swallow. The gag reflex took hold and he was pleased that she did not have dysphagia, which suggested to him there wasn't brain damage. Maybe it was just an infection and once it was gone, she would be back. His living doll ...

He massaged her throat and when he felt her body shake his heart sank. *Shit.* She was choking. He sat her up and thumped her back. After three hefty thwacks, something shot out of her mouth. He lay her back down and sat on the edge of the bed as he dissolved the contents of the medicine in her water. It may not work, but he would try it until he could get his hands on something else.

It took almost fifteen minutes to get the liquid inside her. He watched her for a further fifteen minutes to make sure she didn't convulse again, gently caressing her hair. She stared at the ceiling and he wondered what was going through her mind. Was she thinking of him? Did she want to speak but her body refused to do what her mind was screaming? He hoped so. He needed her to stay alive as he wasn't ready to lose her just yet.

'Sleep well, princess. I have something special planned for you soon. Something that will bind us together for all eternity. You'd like that, wouldn't you?' He traced a symbol on her arm with his finger. 'I'll leave the light on for you, just for tonight mind.' He stood and stretched his legs. He wished he could share his plans with her, but that would ruin the surprise.

He needed a nap but he still had one task he wanted to do. He rubbed his eyes and gently closed the door as he left her room. He went back downstairs to his desk. He was feeling excited as he sat down and took out a black envelope, a black sheet of writing paper, and his gold pen, and began to write.

Chapter 21

Maggie looked at her list of priority tasks. After updating Nathan on her plans, she finished off her coffee before she picked up the phone and contacted Markston Probation. Location wise, it seemed the best place to start, given the address of Tracy Holloway and where she was found.

After a few rings, the phone was answered and Maggie asked to be put through to Sarah Hardy.

'Markston Probation. Sarah speaking. How can I help you?'

'Hi Sarah. It's Maggie – I'm actually hoping to pick your brains a bit, if I can.'

'Oh hey! Great to hear from you. What can I do for you?'

'We have a case that's left us all a bit baffled. I can't go into too much detail, but I wondered if you or any of your colleagues have anyone on your caseload who's raised a red flag recently.'

'Can you give me a little more than that?'

Maggie had to be careful with what information she shared, so she tried to give as much as she could without compromising the case. 'Let me think. Anyone who has a previous history of violence, harassment, stalking, kidnapping even. Targets females. Perhaps they've recently stopped reporting. Or even the opposite

– previous poor compliance but they're now attending every appointment.'

'Wow. That's quite a bit to digest. Let me have a chat with my colleagues and we can put a list together. I can't think of anyone off the top of my head, but I do have close to one hundred cases at the moment, so it may take a bit of time. I can email a list over to you as soon as possible.'

'That would be great. I'm kind of relieved that no one screams out at you at the moment, but if you could go away and discuss it with your colleagues, I'd really appreciate that. And if your manager needs to speak to anyone regarding the sharing of information, they're more than welcome to ring DI Rutherford.'

'Great. Speak to you soon.'

Maggie ended the call. She tried to log the information on her computer, but the screen was playing up again. Probably a loose connection. She dialled the HR department and asked if they could send someone from maintenance out to fix it. There was always a free desk in the office, so she used one of the other computers to record the information and then gathered her things together. Her next task would be to visit Tracy Holloway's home. Bethany was still looking at the social media accounts – Maggie informed her where she could be found if anyone needed her and she went down to the enquiry desk to grab the keys and sign out one of the pool vehicles.

At this time of day, the drive to Woodend didn't take long. The area was decent enough, if not a little run-down, and Maggie surmised that the rent was probably affordable for a young person trying to live away from home. She used the code that had been given to the police by Tracy's parents to get into the building and walked up the two flights of stairs, as there was a massive puddle in front of the lift and Maggie didn't want to have to guess what it was.

She stopped on the landing to catch her breath before entering the second-floor hallway. She knew she was out of shape and if she didn't do something about that, she'd fail the next fitness test and be stuck on desk duties. She made a mental note to start exercising again.

The victim lived in flat 212, and it was easily recognizable as there was a police officer standing just outside the door. Maggie showed her ID and signed the form he shoved in her direction. Inside, Maggie was instantly hit with the smell of vanilla. The flat was tidy and decorated minimally, and there were candles everywhere. She suited up and snapped on the latex gloves so she could begin looking around. There were a few people still dusting for prints.

'You all OK if I just have a look in the bedroom?'

'If you're suited up, knock yourself out,' one of the forensic officers responded.

The first door led to the bathroom and Maggie's heart nearly stopped when she opened the door and came face-to-face with a masked man.

He jumped back. 'Whoa! You gave me a fright.'

Maggie laughed holding her hand over her heart. 'Snap! Sorry, I didn't realize anyone was in there.'

'Yeah, just collecting prints. All yours if you need it.'

'No. I was looking for the bedroom. I'm guessing it's that other door.' She pointed.

'Yeah. I was headed there next. Do you mind if I follow?'

'That's fine. I'll just have a look around and then leave you to it.'

Maggie walked ahead and entered the bedroom. There was a double bed which had been made up. *So Tracy was meticulous and tidy.* One bedside table with a small lamp and a notebook. A chest of drawers and a small closet.

She opened the closet. Everything was hung neatly and looked to be in order of type: dresses, blouses, jackets, and trousers of various colours. *The clothes she was found in did not match her usual style.* The floor of the closet had shoe boxes full of trainers and pumps. No boots. A few scarves hung on a hook on the inside of the door. She closed it and went over to the chest of drawers next.

Socks, underwear, T-shirts and pjs were folded neatly. Maggie lifted a few things to see if perhaps Tracy hid any valuables underneath her clothing. Nothing there. Maggie looked under the mattress – nothing. And nothing under the bed either.

Finally, Maggie went to the bedside table. There was a smaller drawer with a cupboard compartment underneath. Inside the cupboard she found make-up, a hair dryer, curlers, and a make-up mirror. Then she opened the drawer and her heart stopped. She pulled out her mobile and with shaking hands scrolled until she found Nathan's number, and hit connect.

Nathan answered almost immediately.

'Hey, Maggie. What's up?'

'Sir, we have a problem. Have you spoken to Kate yet?'

'I'm with DI Calleja. We're just waiting for Kate to finish a call before she joins us. What is it, Maggie?'

'I'm at Ms Holloway's flat and have just found a bundle of letters. They're in black envelopes with gold writing.'

'OK. You've lost me now. Is that significant?' Maggie was surprised Nathan hadn't connected the dots. He had obviously not taken Kate's stalker seriously.

'Very. Kate received the letters in black envelopes with gold writing from her stalker.'

'Oh shit! I've got to go. Kate's just arrived. Make sure they're bagged up and hand them over to the forensic team then head back to the station. I'll see you there.'

Chapter 22

Maggie raced back to the station – she hoped she didn't end up with a speeding ticket. DI Rutherford wouldn't be too happy, even though it would be Maggie who had to pay. She ran up the stairs, two by two, to the office.

'Bethany, have Markston sent over the items relating to Kate's complaint yet?' Maggie bent over, resting her hands on her knees. She needed to catch her breath.

'Hang on. I'll check. By the way, Luke from HQ came by and replaced your monitor while you were out. He said it was easier to replace than to try to fix the whole thing.'

'Wow, that was fast. It usually takes ages to get someone to come out. They seem to be getting better at responding to call-outs.' Maggie was pleased as she hated not having everything to hand. Getting used to another workstation would have been a pain.

'He said he had a few call-outs here so brought a new monitor to save having to come back. Nice guy. Right, I'd better make that call.' As Bethany called downstairs, Maggie headed over to her desk and turned on her computer. Signing in, she scanned over her emails to see if anything further had come in from forensics. Just then, Nathan returned and was looking a little stressed out.

'Everything OK? You don't look so well.' Maggie stopped what she was doing.

'Yeah. Though Kate didn't take the news about your discovery too well. Can you come into my office and tell me everything about the victim's address?'

Maggie did as instructed, and relayed what she'd found. 'The envelopes were exactly the same, Nathan. Black with gold writing. I had a brief glance at the contents and that was similar too. Little messages as if written by someone known to her ... or watching her. I'm really worried about Kate. Where is she now?'

'Probably still arguing with DI Calleja. She was definitely spooked, especially now we can say there's a clear connection between the murder of Tracy Holloway and Kate's stalker. Shit.' He shook his head. 'We need to get a handle on this. Has anything else come in?'

'Not yet. I've asked Bethany if she can find out whether the items Kate brought in to Markston have been sent up here yet. If not, I'm half tempted to go and collect them myself and have a word with Kate if she is still there.'

'Sorry, but you can't do that. Let's keep the chain of evidence as clean as possible. Kate mentioned you invited her to stay with you while she was having a security system installed. Do you really think that's a good idea?'

'I offered as a friend. And that offer still stands. It may put off whoever is following her. They've clearly been watching her movements and will no doubt know from the news that I'm a police officer—' Before Maggie could finish, there was a knock on the door.

'Come in.' Nathan waved.

'Sorry to disturb you both, but we've had a call from the enquiry desk. Tracy Holloway's boyfriend is downstairs and demanding to speak with someone.'

'Thanks, Bethany. Can you check his details on our system and let the enquiry desk know that Maggie will be down in five minutes?'

'Will do, sir.' The door closed.

'Go and see what the boyfriend wants.'

'Sure. It'd be great to find out where he's been all this time.'

'Get any risk details from Bethany and report back to me when you're done.'

'OK. But just to be clear, I'm still offering Kate my spare room.'

'I figured that was the case. We'll pick up this conversation later. Go see what this guy wants.'

Maggie walked over to Bethany's desk. 'Any background on the boyfriend before I go down and see him?'

'Joshua Hinks but goes by Josh. Thirty years old. The police were called out to Tracy Holloway's address when neighbours heard shouting. When police arrived, there was a hole in the wall. He was charged with criminal damage and due back in court for sentencing next week.'

Maggie scratched her head. 'Well that's interesting, but why didn't anything come up under her name when we searched?'

'Looks like all the details were recorded under his name and address, and only with her first name. Someone could end up bollocked for that one.'

'I'd hope so. Can you do me a favour and contact the DAHU? See if this guy has been flagged up on their books at all.'

'On it.' Bethany picked up the phone while Maggie jotted down the details on Josh and made her way downstairs.

She opened the door into the reception area using her ID. The boyfriend looked nervous. He was pacing around the small area. 'Mr Hinks. Would you like to come through?'

He stomped his way to the door and followed Maggie. She could almost feel the anger burning. 'It's just through here.' She opened another door and led him into an interview room. 'Take a seat.' She waited until he sat down across from her.

'My name is DC Maggie Jamieson. I understand you wanted to talk to someone about Tracy Holloway.'

'Of course, I do! How come I had to hear about this on the fucking news?' His lip trembled.

'I'm sorry about that, but we couldn't locate you. We spoke to her family ...'

'Oh, well that explains it. They bloody hate me. Hated that Tracy and I were together and tried everything to keep us apart.' His face reddened.

'Why did they hate you?'

'Not good enough for her, was I? We got into an argument and I punched a hole in her wall. Her parents convinced her I was no good and she ended the relationship. I got angry, and I shouldn't have. That's the last time I saw her.' His shoulders shook and Maggie waited for him to gain his composure before continuing.

'What were you arguing about?'

'Isn't this in the police statement? Have you even bothered to check?'

'I came down to speak to you at your request. I don't know the details of the outstanding matters.' Maggie didn't like this guy's attitude one bit and was even more furious now about the incorrect logging of details. It was things like that which made her job more difficult.

'She'd hidden some love letters from me; obviously, she was having an affair. She denied it though. I lost my rag. I mean, you tell me. Why would she hide the letters if some random sent them and they meant nothing?' His hand thumped on the table repeatedly.

Maggie's interest was piqued. *He believed they were love letters.* She didn't want to agitate him further so steered the conversation in another direction to calm him down. 'How long had you and Tracy been in a relationship?'

'Nearly a year.' He rubbed his eyes.

'Why didn't any of her friends and family know your full name?'

'Yeah, they fucking knew! But they obviously didn't know she was playing around on me!' He slammed his hands on the table again.

'Mr Hinks, you need to calm down. I'll be asking you questions that might upset you, but we need to find out who did this and I'd appreciate your cooperation.'

'Hang on a fucking minute. Are you saying I'm a suspect? Do I need a solicitor? I came here to speak to you and now you're accusing me of hurting Tracy?'

'No one has accused you of anything. I'm just trying to paint a picture of what was happening in the time leading up to Ms Holloway's disappearance. Can you help me with that?'

'Uh, yeah. Sorry.' He leaned back in the chair.

'Can you tell me about these letters you found?'

'Letters might be stretching it. They were just notes. Things that said "Missing you" or "You looked beautiful today", shit like that. I found them when I was looking for my gloves. They were tucked in a bag in the back of the drawer by her bed. She denied it of course. Said some weirdo was sending her things and she was advised by her friends to keep hold of them just in case she needed to report it.'

'Were there gifts included with the notes? How do you know that it wasn't some random?'

'Who knows if there were gifts? I only saw the notes, but it wasn't some random – I mean, why hide them? Why not tell me about them? I'll tell you why, because she was cheating on me ... and now she's gone.' His emotions were all over the place. One minute angry, the next crying. Maggie knew he wouldn't stick out an interview much longer.

'Can you account for your whereabouts for the last few weeks and, more specifically, where were you for the 24 hours leading up to discovering Tracy's body?'

'I've just come back from staying with family in London. I've been there for the last three weeks and got back last night. That's why I came here this morning as soon as I heard.'

'And your family can verify that? Why have you been away for three weeks and what about the initial two weeks before that?'

'Yes, none of them left me alone for a minute while I was down there. After Tracy and I argued and I was arrested, I just couldn't cope. Bail conditions stopped me from calling her, but she didn't even try and call me. You know, to see how I was. I was warned not to contact her at all, so I had no idea any of this was happening. Why didn't anyone contact me and ask me if I'd seen her? Who am I kidding? It's not like her parents were going to tell me, is it? My parents told me to come down and stay with them for a while. Until things calmed down up here. So I did.'

'What about your bail?' Maggie wondered if Josh had been given conditions to sign in at the police station that they could easily verify.

'This is the first time I've been in trouble. We had an argument and I overreacted. I pleaded guilty as soon as I could because I knew I was in the wrong. Fuck, this is just too much.' He put his head in his hands. 'Why won't you tell me if she suffered? I can't cope with all this ... I can't ...' His voice choked.

'I can't give out the details just yet as it's an ongoing investigation. Can you give me the details of where you're currently staying, as well as your parents' details, so we can verify your alibi? Someone will be in touch to explain to you what's happened and offer you some support. I know it's a lot to take in.' Although he'd still be considered a person of interest until his whereabouts could be checked, Maggie's gut told her that Josh didn't have anything to do with the murder. It was no coincidence that she'd been receiving the same notes that Kate had.

'Yes.' He began writing his information down and, once done, Maggie escorted him back to the reception area.

'We'll be in touch soon, Mr Hinks.' She watched him leave before heading back up to her desk.

'Any luck then?' Bethany looked over as Maggie sat down.

'I don't think this is our guy. He messed up and took full responsibility for the argument, which landed him the court appearance. He was angry, but that's understandable – I would be too if I found out by watching the news my partner had been murdered. I'm updating the system with the information he provided.' She reached across and handed Bethany his parents' details. 'Can you see if his whereabouts checks out and I'll go and let Nathan know.'

'Sure. I contacted Probation and the DAHU. He has a pre-sentence interview with Lucy at Stafford Probation Office but he's not known to them.'

'Thanks. I'll try and speak to Lucy after she meets with him. See what her thoughts are.' Maggie uploaded the information onto her computer and then grabbed a coffee before going into the briefing room. Although caffeine was probably the last thing she needed, she had to make sure she had something in her system or she risked collapsing.

One question stuck in her mind though: how were Kate and Tracy Holloway connected?

Chapter 23

The large file was slammed on the desk and Maggie nearly fell out of her chair with fright. She had never seen DI Rutherford this angry – at least not in front of a group of people.

'We have a situation here, folks, and as you may have guessed I'm absolutely livid!' There was a pause and Maggie took the moment to look at the faces around the room. She hoped she could identify the guilty party from their expression, but no one stood out.

'Which one of you shared information with the press?' Rutherford paced the floor as she glared at the team. 'I've asked you a question. Which. One. Of. You. Leaked. Details. Of. This. Case. To. The. Press?' Officers' feet shuffled and there was a lot of movement in chairs as everyone looked around the room at each other, waiting for someone to come forward.

'No one's going to hold their hands up?' She sighed. 'OK then, Maggie, what have you found out?'

All eyes shifted to her and she wanted to shrink into the chair. She felt like her colleagues were accusing her of being a grass, when she was only doing what she was asked. 'I'm still waiting for your PA to come back to me, guv, but so far it doesn't look like any mention of ... well, you know, was said in the briefings, although the eyes and mouth being sewn shut was.' Maggie waited for Rutherford to respond and when nothing was said, she continued. 'There's always the possibility that someone who was present at the crime scene spoke to the press. I'm waiting for the parents of the witnesses to come back to me.'

'Thanks. Well, I don't want to believe any member of my team would break protocol and go behind my back by speaking to the press. However, I'd like to make something crystal clear and put it on the record. If I find out that any of you have done so, I will have you suspended so fast you won't know what's hit you. Do you understand?'

There were mumbles around the room.

'I said, DO YOU UNDERSTAND?' DI Rutherford raged.

A flurry of 'Yes, ma'ams,' came from the room.

'All right then. Let's get back to work and hope I don't have to revisit this again. Maggie and Nathan, I'd like you to stay behind for a moment, please.'

Maggie's eyes widened. *Fuck.* She could just imagine the whispers among her colleagues. *Teacher's Pet. Grass.* Would they trust her again after this?

When everyone had left the room, DI Rutherford sat down. 'I bloody hate when I have to do that. It drains my energy. But I will not tolerate disobedience of any kind – especially in what may prove to be a very high-profile case.'

'We understand, ma'am. What do you need?' Nathan spoke up first.

'I was speaking to DCI Hastings and he had an idea that I wanted to run by both of you first. Just between us, I'm not convinced it's the best plan, but if you both think it's worth a try, I'll do it.' She wrung her hands together. 'He suggested that we give out a small detail of false information. Something significant enough that the press might be interested in, but it can't have huge implications or impact the investigation.'

The three looked at each other. Maggie herself had wondered whether this would be a good idea, but worried that people might think she was being arrogant had she suggested it. 'If I may, guv. I like this idea and think we should definitely explore it. The problem is, we still wouldn't know who the leak was if we shared the same information with everyone. I think we need to perhaps identify a few people we may have concerns about and feed each one a different bit of information. That way we'll know for sure.'

A smile formed on the DI's face. 'I like it. A staggered effect. We can tick people off the list with some assurance that they aren't involved. That's clever.' DI Rutherford looked at the ceiling. 'OK, do we have any thoughts of who it might be?'

'I don't think it's anyone from our team directly, so that rules out us three and Bethany. There are a few new PCSOs and a couple of people on the field team who I've had some concerns about. They may be our first port of call,' Nathan offered.

'Write their names down, will you, then we can discuss what detail we want to feed to whom. What's the matter, Maggie?'

'Two things really. Although I agree that Bethany is not involved, if people find out what we're doing and that we left our own team out, what are they going to think? Secondly, what about Dr Blake's team? I think we need to speak to her as well. She mentioned that she has a lot of new people – temp agency staff – many of whom were at the crime scene. If I call her and discuss what we're doing here, she can replicate with her own team and feed back to us.'

'Yes. You're right. We can't start accusing only the police when it could have come from another agency. Did Bethany manage to find out any details about that reporter before the briefing? We'll need to speak to her as well.' DI Rutherford sat back in her chair and crossed her arms.

Maggie looked through her notes. 'No, there's no intelligence on her, unless you class being a pain in the arse as an offence. I know that journalist won't share any information with me, and I'd rather not be the one to talk to her, if possible.' Maggie could just imagine how that conversation would go.

'Why's that?' DI Rutherford queried.

Before Maggie could respond, Nathan interjected. 'That specific journalist was pretty hard on Maggie during Bill Raven's case, you might recall. Nasty headlines, accusing Maggie of all sorts. Even though she was wrong, she slammed Maggie every chance she could get. No rhyme or reason to it, guv. I concur with Maggie's assessment – it needs to be someone else who speaks to her.'

'Thanks for volunteering, then. While Maggie is coordinating with Dr Blake, I want you to track down and speak to that journalist. Use your charm if you have to. You do know how to do that, don't you?'

Maggie laughed as Nathan's face turned beet red. 'I'm sure he can dig deep and pull something out of the bag, guv.'

'Get started then. The sooner we find the leak, the sooner we plug the hole.'

Maggie didn't envy Nathan in his task. The journalist in question took no prisoners and if Nathan said the wrong thing, he could be next in the firing line.

Chapter 24

Maggie rubbed her eyes. She'd been trawling through records in the hopes of finding a solid lead when Nathan dropped a photocopied piece of paper on her desk. He pulled up a chair without saying a word. Things still weren't right between them after he'd called her out about her often solitary working methods, but neither of them would let any of those feelings get in the way of solving this case. Maggie looked at him, waiting for an answer and when one was not forthcoming, she picked up the copy and looked closely at the words on the picture. A popular meme about fixing broken dolls.

'What the hell is this?' It sounded familiar but Maggie couldn't place it.

'That's from our journalist friend. She claims it came anonymously in the post along with a note telling her the details from the crime scene and signed with the infinity symbol. She penned the name "Living Doll Killer" in her article.'

'Is she claiming that no one told her of the living doll reference made by Dr Blake at the scene then?'

'She denied any knowledge. Not sure I believed her though. Then she just showed me this,' he pointed to the meme, 'and the other letters, which I've handed over to evidence. She claims the killer is reaching out to her and she's only trying to help the police and make sure women remain vigilant.'

'Hang on. You said "letters". What else did they say?'

'Mainly nonsensical – poetry, references to family, finding a perfect match. That sort of thing. Once they've been processed, we'll have the opportunity to examine them further and see how they fit in with what we know. But there was something interesting about them.'

'What's that then?' Maggie sat up in her chair.

'They were all written with a gold pen on black paper. Like the notes Kate received.'

'I was hoping you weren't going to say that. They are legit then and there can be no doubt about Kate, Tracy, and now the journalist having had the same contact. I think Kate is the main target, but why is he taking these other women? What's the plan?'

'That's what we need to figure out. Our journalist friend wants to meet with you. She thinks she can set a trap for the killer in her articles and wants to work with you and only you on arranging this.'

Maggie stood. 'No fucking way, Nathan. That is NOT going to happen. The fact you've even mentioned it leads me to believe you told her it might be possible, so I suggest you get on the phone with her and tell her no bloody way.'

'Sit down and listen to me.' He waited while she sat back down in her chair. 'I know she's not on your list of favourite people at the moment, but I think she may be on to something and I'd like you to just have a conversation with her ... over the phone if that would make it easier for you to swallow. See what her ideas are and then we can talk about it further.'

Maggie crossed her arms. 'What about the shit she put me

through on the Raven case? If this all goes pear-shaped, she will crucify me in the press ... again. Absolutely not, Nathan. I can't believe you're even asking me to consider this. What is she playing at? Hasn't she done enough damage already?'

'I'm not asking. I'm telling.' He looked over his shoulder in the direction of DI Rutherford's office. The DI was standing in her doorway and nodded at Nathan. 'I've spoken to the guv and we both feel this is something we need to pursue. This is a direct order. I need you to call her and hear her out. Once you do that, you, me, and DI Rutherford will meet and come up with a strategy.'

Maggie's jaw dropped. 'I see. I have no choice or say in the matter. Right then, you'd best leave me to it.' She turned her back on Nathan. 'Just leave her details on my desk and I'll get to it once I've finished what I was doing.'

'Maggie, don't be like that. Put your pride aside and remember we're doing what's best for the case.'

'Of course, *sir*.' Maggie stared at her computer screen, hiding the tears that threatened to fall. She'd never thought Nathan would place her in this kind of position. Although she knew he was right, it irked her that he didn't seem to take her feelings into consideration at all.

That bloody reporter won't get the best of me this time.

He stood and dropped the journalist's card on her desk. He mumbled 'fucksake' as he took the few steps back to his office and closed the door.

'Wanker.' She picked up the card and looked at the details. She now had a name to put to the face: Julie Noble. Flicking the card between her fingers she took a deep breath before she picked up her phone and dialled.

'*Stafford Gazette, Julie Noble speaking.*'

Maggie froze. Just the sound of this woman's voice made her want to scream.

'Hello? Is there anyone there?'

'This is DC Maggie Jamieson from the Major and Organised Crime Department at Stafford Police Station. I understand you're expecting a call from me.'

'Well, well, well. DC Jamieson. I didn't think your boss could convince you. Even though he assured me it wouldn't be a problem.'

'Did he now?' Maggie slung daggers at Nathan's door. She hoped he could feel each one of them tear through him. 'My only concern is catching this killer, so why wouldn't I want to be involved?'

'Considering the looks you've thrown my way whenever I've seen you – and I'm guessing they're the same ones you're throwing at your boss as we speak – I figured you might be a little reluctant.'

Maggie had to bite her tongue. 'Mrs Noble. Can we just start discussing what your idea is, please? I'm kind of busy and don't have time to waste.'

'It's Ms. And yes, of course. However, I'd rather not do this over the phone. So, when can we meet?'

'As I said, I'm rather busy and can't really drop what I'm doing to meet you for what may turn out to be a no-go.'

'It's face-to-face or nothing at all. Unless you'd rather I just do things my own way, DC Jamieson. The choice is yours.'

Maggie cursed under her breath. She knew Nathan would order her to go if she didn't so she may as well get it over and done with. 'Fine. I'm tied up at the moment, but I'll meet you in town at the café on the corner just down from the police station at 3pm. Do you know the one I mean?'

'*There's only one, so yeah, I do. I'll see you then.*'

Maggie threw her phone onto her desk. This had better be worth it.

First things first. She needed to see the letters.

Chapter 25

After retrieving the evidence and making copies, Maggie walked into the incident room and examined each piece carefully. One of her first thoughts was whether Julie Noble had at least had the sense not to handle the items too much before handing them over to the police. *Doubtful.*

She was immediately drawn to the quote about fixing broken dolls. Did their killer think the women were broken in some way? Maybe they were looking at the case all wrong. Was there something in Tracy Holloway's background that the police didn't know yet? And how did that fit in with Kate? She jotted down some points and put the meme aside.

At first glance, the notes appeared to be an exact match to those Kate and Tracy Holloway had received. No stamps on the envelopes, so they had been hand-delivered to the newsroom. *Maybe he had been picked up on CCTV.* Another avenue for Bethany to explore. Maggie didn't envy her. Fortunately, she enjoyed what she did, and was incredibly knowledgeable on just where to look and what to look out for.

There was a tap on the door. 'What are you doing in here?' Maggie assumed Nathan was checking to see if she had followed through on contacting the journalist.

'Just looking at everything before I meet up with Ms Noble.'

Maggie tried not to be frosty in her response, but she wasn't sure she had succeeded.

'I get that you aren't happy about this, but just think, she owes you an apology. Who knows, you may even end up as friends.'

'The damage is already done though, isn't it? My name splashed in all the papers virtually screaming incompetence. Even if I do get an apology, it won't change the public's perception. As for ending up friends ... When hell freezes over.'

He held up his hand. 'OK. Message received, but let's be realistic here. With so many other news stories dominating, it's unlikely your name is going to stick in people's minds. As for Ms Noble, you may be able to find out if there's anything she's keeping from us. You have good instincts and I certainly got that impression. It would be good to have your opinion on the matter.'

'Fine. I'll get over this eventually, it's just still very raw. I'm just pissed off that she took so long to even let us know about this. It's a bloody murder investigation and she was withholding vital information. What does she gain from that?'

'Who knows. Perhaps she was hoping to maintain a connection with the killer? Maybe lure him out somehow? But that's a dangerous game – we've seen what he does to people. Once we have everything, we can come up with a stronger strategy instead of grasping at things and having no clear direction. It feels like we're just chasing our tails. This also means we won't have to waste our time planting false information with our colleagues. Can you imagine the uproar if we did that and they figured it out? I could kiss goodbye to being a DS permanently.'

'Exactly! Do you want to look over these with me for a few minutes? I just want to thrash out some thoughts before I meet with Julie.'

'I have about twenty minutes before I have to meet with DI Rutherford, so let's make a start.'

'Well, the similarities are evident – they were all hand-delivered so our guy either knows he won't be captured on CCTV or else he has someone else dropping them off, either not knowing the significance of the letters or actively working with him. I think it's the former.'

'I'd agree. He's managed to keep out of view this long, so why would he change? The abduction and what followed was personal – a solitary task. He doesn't have someone else working with him. Didn't someone deliver one of the boxes to Kate – one of those motorcycle delivery services? Did Markston ever trace that guy?'

'Yes. It was all through Acer Deliveries. A cash payment. When the owner and staff were questioned, neither the woman who received the package at the depot nor the delivery guy could remember anything significant. Everything is done out of a tiny room. No CCTV.' Maggie tapped her pen on the table.

'The notes don't say much either. A few weird poems and quotes. The latest one to Julie was interesting.' Nathan held up a page. 'Says he sewed their eyes so they wouldn't have to see the evil in the world and their mouths so they wouldn't speak of any evil. Bloody bizarre. The post-mortem confirms that the sewing took place after death, so could there be a ritual element to it?'

'I'd actually say it was more a part of his signature, like the tattoo he left.' Maggie noticed Nathan frown and knew she would need to expand on her thought process. 'Our experience tells us that some serial killers sometimes perform unusual, bizarre acts and routines that aren't considered a part of their MO; for instance, it's believed that the original Night Stalker in the US, before he became a serial killer, raped women. The women told the police that during some of the rapes, he would sit down and cry, called them by their first names, and made personal statements about himself in front of them. This would be considered ritualistic behaviour because it just can't be explained in any way. What did he get out of that? Do you see what I mean?'

'Hmmm. OK, I see what you mean. The infinity tattoo – he's showing his connection to the victim forever, maybe? What did Kate think about the eyes and mouth being sewn shut?'

'I don't think she verbalized anything at the time. She was in a bit of shock and wanted time to process things. It'd be a good idea to call her. You've been a big help. I've had so many things ticking through my mind – it's good to bounce the ideas off someone else. Like the old days. I'll catch you later.'

Maggie placed the copies of the evidence on the incident board before heading out to meet Julie Noble.

Chapter 26

It only took Maggie fifteen minutes to get to the café. She stared into shop windows as she passed, trying to think of questions that wouldn't give the reporter any additional information to use. The sun glared off the glass and Maggie had to shield her eyes. Before stepping through the café door, Maggie ran her fingers through her hair. *Best get it over with.*

'You showed up, and on time. I'm impressed, DC Jamieson.' Julie Noble smiled.

Maggie cringed. Everything Julie Noble said had an edge of sarcasm to it. Or at least it sounded that way to her. 'Can we just get on with this? I don't have time for any games.' Maggie sat.

'Do you want anything? My treat.' Julie pushed her chair out.

'Stay where you are; this won't be a long meeting. What I do need is some answers though. Why didn't you come forward when the killer contacted you?'

'I didn't actually know if the letters were a hoax until I saw your boss's face at the press conference when I asked about the living doll reference.'

'On that, I looked at everything you were sent, and nowhere does it reference living doll. Where did that come from?'

'The way she was dressed up. Plus sewing the eyes and mouth

shut, like a doll. I thought "Living Doll Killer" had a nice ring to it.'

'I still don't see how you drew that reference. Did someone from the police or crime scene contact you? Please don't bullshit me either. If we have a leak on our team, we need to know. You're jeopardizing our investigation by holding back information.'

'Oh please. It sounds like you're fishing and that I'm on the right track.' Julie sat back in her chair and crossed her arms.

Maggie needed to play her cards right and keep Julie onside. She could just hear Nathan chirping in her ear, reminding her that she could come across as an abrasive know-it-all at times – perhaps not the exact words he used, but it was what had been implied. 'You haven't denied what I asked. Look,' Maggie leaned forward, 'I am intrigued about your name for this killer. Are you sure you're telling us everything?'

'Why wouldn't I share what I know?' She paused, and Maggie gritted her teeth. 'OK, OK. You got me. He sent me a CD with that song, "Living Doll" on it. I figured it must be significant so I stuck it in. Happy now?' Julie looked directly in her eyes. 'You're a fascinating woman, DC Jamieson. Tell me what you know. Tell me who's on your persons-of-interest list.' She leaned forward.

Maggie's face reddened.

'Wait. You do have a list, don't you? There must be someone you can tie to this case.'

'I can't talk about the details of an ongoing investigation.' Maggie was sick of saying that phrase.

'You don't need to. It's written all over your face. Don't ever take up poker; your face would give you away.' She clapped her hands together. 'So it looks like you need me, DC Jamieson. How does that feel?' A coy smile formed on the reporter's face.

Maggie clenched her fists under the table. 'That's why I'm

here. You offered your assistance. Or is this just another way for you to embarrass me?'

'Embarrass you? What do you mean?' Julie's eyes widened.

Maggie lost it then. 'Are you bloody serious? The Raven case. You and your newspaper accused me of putting an innocent man behind bars. You still owe me an apology for that, you know.'

'An apology? Is that what's got your knickers in a twist? I reported the facts at the time, and they were correct. What happened afterwards was another matter, if you recall.'

'Forget it. Sorry, I can't do this.' Maggie stood. 'When you have something to add to this case, perhaps we can talk then.' She dropped her card on the table, turned, and walked out of the café.

Fuck. Fuck. Fuck. Nathan was going to have her head on a platter, but that woman knew how to push her buttons. She walked back towards the office and then heard her name being called. A hand touched her arm and she turned, placing her free hand on her baton in case it was needed.

'Whoa.' Julie removed her hand. 'I think we got off on the wrong foot. If it's an apology you're after, then I'm sorry. I don't know why the killer reached out to me. Maybe he was playing off the fact that we know each other professionally and that I haven't always been complimentary towards you? A message to the police that he's in control? Do you think you might know this person?'

Maggie didn't want to reveal the connection to Kate just yet. 'I don't know. I'm heading back to the station to look over everything.'

'Great. Two heads are better than one.' Julie started to walk alongside her.

'Sorry, I should have made myself clear. I appreciate your help and I'll be in contact if I have any further questions, but I'll be going back to the office on my own.'

'Oh. Right. Of course. Well, you know my number if you need anything.' Julie waved as she walked off.

Don't sit by your phone waiting for my call, Ms Noble.

Chapter 27

As she walked into the office, trying to forget the way Julie Noble made her feel, her desk phone rang and disrupted her flow of thoughts. She'd been trying to piece together when the killer had made his initial contact with the reporter and why he'd chosen her. She ran across the room and picked up the receiver.

'DC Maggie Jamieson speaking.'

'Hi. It's Julie Noble here. Do you have a moment to talk?'

'I'm still on the line, aren't I? What do you want?' She'd just left the woman; she could have her done for harassment. Maggie smiled to herself at the thought.

'When I got back to my office, I found another note waiting for me. Thought you might be interested, but if you're going to be arsy about it ...'

'Hang on. Sorry, OK, I'm sure you'll appreciate the pressure we're under and why you may not be my favourite person. Please tell me you haven't opened it yet.'

'I could tell you that, but I'd be lying.'

'Fucksake. I thought you wanted to help us. What did it say?'

'He makes references to Jeffrey Dahmer. That serial killer in the US? Didn't he kill boys and men?'

Maggie tapped her pen on the table. 'Dahmer, eh? Anything else?'

'*Just some sketch of a little girl and signed with something that resembles a figure eight, I think. It slants slightly to the left.*'

The line went silent.

Julie Noble didn't seem to recognize the significance of the infinity symbol, which meant the killer hadn't spelled things out for her. At least they had that to hold back from the public. 'What are you planning on doing with the information?'

'*Well, I was hoping we could come to some sort of an arrangement. We work together on this and you give me an exclusive when this is all over.*'

'I can't agree to those terms. I'd have to speak to my boss. But let me make one thing clear: you're not a police officer, so leave the investigating to us.'

'*Do you always take things so literally? All I meant was, I'd share anything that I receive and agree not to report on the case until the killer is caught. But in exchange, I want to be the one to break the story. Go and speak to whoever you have to and call me back.*'

Maggie heard a click and the line went dead.

Who the fuck did she think she was? As much as it pained Maggie, it would be better to have Julie onside than constantly fighting against her. She needed to speak to Nathan, and she turned in her chair to see if he was in.

No time like the present. Maggie took a deep breath and walked into Nathan's office, tapping on the door as she said, 'Hey boss, do you have a moment?'

'Sure. Take a seat. What is it?'

'I just got off the phone with Julie Noble. She's received *and opened* another note from our suspected killer and she wants an exclusive in order to keep this latest off the news.'

'I thought I already gave the go-ahead for that? Why didn't you sort it when you met up with her?'

'We didn't exactly get around to that. She pissed me off and I left.'

'Well, call her back and tell her that as long as she continues to share everything with us, she'll get the story first. But any pissing about, and that offer is withdrawn. What did the note say?'

'References to Jeffrey Dahmer and the figure eight as well as some drawing. But what she did fail to mention to you before was that he sent her a CD. With Cliff Richard's "Living Doll" track highlighted. When I call her back, I'll make arrangements to have everything picked up and I'll make it clear that if she receives anything else, she's to leave it until we can pick it up.'

'Dahmer? Cliff Richard? What's the significance?'

'Don't know, boss. Could he be hinting at something? I'm sure I read somewhere that Dahmer used to lobotomise his victims. Maybe he's just confirming what the pathologist found? Could he be using Julie Noble as his way of explaining things to us? Or he could be leading us down the wrong path, knowing Julie would come to us. But I do know that she has no idea about the infinity symbol, so at least that's something.'

'True. Go make your call. If anything else comes up, let me know.'

Maggie returned to her desk and called the reporter, relaying Nathan's instructions. 'So where are you now?'

'Markston Police Station.'

'What the hell? Why are you there?'

'I thought I'd speak to Dr Moloney and get her take on things while I waited for you to come back to me. Speaking of which, here she is now. See you soon, DC Jamieson.'

'Wait! Leave Dr Moloney out of this for the time being.'

'Why? What do I get in return?'

Maggie kicked her desk. This woman was infuriating.

'I can't offer you more than the exclusive you already have.'

'How about you tell me how Dr Moloney is involved in all of this … when the time is right. That seems fair.'

Maggie bit her nail. If she promised Julie the information she wanted, she may be putting Kate in jeopardy. Julie wasn't known for her tact. But if she didn't, Julie would do it anyway.

'Fine! But I'm serious. Keep away from Dr Moloney. Do you hear me?'

'Great. I look forward to your update.'

She paused and Maggie could hear her breath in her ear.

'I probably should tell you before you jump into a car, I'm not really at Markston. I had a hunch and you confirmed my suspicions. How would I have got to Markston so quickly after leaving you? C'mon, detective. Use that brain of yours. Don't you think we'd make a great team?'

The journalist laughed down the phone.

'You bitch! I should charge you with obstruction.'

'Mind yourself now, DC Jamieson. I could be recording you.'

Maggie screamed as she flung the phone down onto her desk. She wouldn't let Julie Noble get the best of her. At least she knew Kate hadn't been contacted.

Kate wasn't aware that the killer had been in contact with the news, though given the recent stories, it wouldn't take her long to put two and two together. It irked her that she had to keep things from her friend due to a conflict of interest, but Maggie knew Kate was already stressed enough knowing the killer and her stalker were one and the same. She didn't want Julie Noble to push her friend over the edge.

Chapter 28

In the conference room at Markston Police Station, Kate stared blankly at Lucy as she told the team about her plans for the refuge for which she had just received the seal of approval from the Ministry of Justice. She was finding it hard to concentrate on work at the moment. If this was someone else, she would be telling them to deal with the situation, but she didn't want to appear weak and she didn't want her colleagues to question her judgement on the job. So she buried it. But it was crawling to the surface and she was torn.

'Ideally, I'd like referrals from yourselves, for both men and women, and these can be discussed at the Domestic Abuse Forums. Sharon Bairden has agreed to do some group and one-to-one sessions. Claire Knight has also agreed to work with those who have children known to Social Care. It's all coming together – though there is still a lot to be done.' Lucy's pride was obvious.

'Well, we work with the perpetrators, so how would the DAHU fit into your plans?' PC Kat Everett rubbed her chin.

'I'd like to ensure a strong relationship with you guys for risk purposes. Everyone who has been referred and is either staying on the premises or attending the voluntary assistance groups will be informed that the haven will be working closely with the police and other agencies. They'll be asked to sign their consent so that if any of my staff learns of a situation that may put themselves, us, members of the public or children at risk, we'll be sharing that information with the police.' Lucy looked around the room.

Kate rubbed her neck. Everything Lucy was telling them sounded promising, but something niggled at her. 'I thought Probation didn't need consent to share that information. If risk is involved, that's surely a given? And wouldn't that lead to the residents hiding things for fear of reprisal?'

'I'm glad you brought that up. Remember, this is not a Probation hostel. It's mainly self-funded with accreditation by the Ministry of Justice. I do have to adhere to certain guidelines set out or I wouldn't be allowed to work directly with you or other agencies. The haven will also receive some government and charity funding, so I have to be able to meet targets that are set – I won't bore you with them all, but most agencies have to jump through hoops these days. My own experience has been that even though people may initially be reluctant, my staff and myself will be working to build up trust with the residents. So, we have to be upfront with them. If they choose not to sign, or if they break the rules, they'll have to leave. Though saying that, the door will always be open. I wouldn't want them to feel they were stuck for help – it just might be they were not ready at that time.' Lucy's brows creased and Kate saw a flash of pain on her face, but it went as quickly as it came.

'Well, I'm sure I speak for everyone here when I say you have our support and we'll be more than happy to work *with* you.' PC Mark Fielding smiled.

'Thanks, Mark. But let's be honest, there will be frustrations on both sides as you'll want information from me that I can't share and vice versa. I'd like to work with Kate on finalizing the referral form, if possible. I'm not ready to be fully up and running just yet; there are some maintenance and security issues being ironed out. But I do have news I'd like to share with you all.' Kate smiled as Lucy seemed to take delight in holding them all in suspense. 'Do you remember Vicki Wilkinson?'

Vicki had been attacked and left for dead by one of the domestic abusers who the DAHU had previously monitored. The offender had been murdered before he could be convicted of the crime, but Kate recalled the details as if it was only yesterday. It had been her first experience of using her profiling skills to work a murder case. Last she heard, Vicki had been undertaking various therapies to re-learn basic skills after suffering some brain damage.

'I don't think any of us will forget Vicki. Why?' Kate hoped Lucy had some good news.

'She'll be volunteering once a week at the haven when she is ready and able. Vicki is still in therapy but has done remarkably well considering what she's been through. She'll be one of the Drug and Alcohol mentors and running a workshop with anyone who comes to the haven with past or present substance misuse issues.'

'Fucking hell. That's just brilliant!' Kat blurted out what most of the team were thinking.

A sense of relief came over Kate; she had enough bad news to occupy her mind. Lucy wrapped up the session and agreed with Kate a date to work on the referral form. Something else to keep her focused.

Chapter 29

He prepared their meal with care. He knew exactly what she liked, and he wanted to be sure he made no mistakes. While the roast chicken cooked in the oven, he chopped up the potatoes – he'd have to partially boil them before he stuck them in the oven to roast, otherwise they'd take ages to cook. While he waited, he dug out the special napkins from the bottom drawer. The ones he had been saving for this very moment. He never really had the opportunity to open this drawer, the special drawer that was filled with candles, real napkins, and silver napkin rings his mother had given him.

He set the table and was pleased with how it looked. He stood back and scanned the room. There was something missing. He looked out of the window and admired his neighbour's roses. *Surely, they wouldn't notice if I cut a few for the table? Now, where did I leave my secateurs?*

He went back into the kitchen and kneeled down to dig around in the cupboard where he kept his basic gardening tools and weed killer. It was a mess. He'd have to tidy it one of these days.

Ah. There you are. A sharp pain shot through him as he pulled himself up. A few deep breaths and all would be fine.

'I won't be long, princess. I've a surprise for you,' he called up the stairs.

He walked across his lawn and looked around. He hoped no one was snooping. The neighbour's car wasn't on the drive, so he bent over and snipped off four fresh roses. He quickly returned to his house. He didn't want to have to explain to anyone who the roses were for if he was caught.

His heart was racing when he closed the door behind him. He would need to find something to put the roses in. He'd never had a need for a vase before; the only steady woman in his life was his mother and she didn't deserve anything nice. He returned to the kitchen and found an old jar. He gave it a good rinse and trimmed the bottom of the rose stems so they would fit. Perfect. Filling the jar halfway with water, he placed the four roses in and then set it on the middle of his dining table. He hoped she appreciated the effort. Checking the dinner once more before he collected her, he turned down the heat and walked upstairs.

'Knock. Knock. Are you decent?'

He pushed open the door slightly and peeked into the room. She sat staring straight ahead. Her chin was wet with drool.

'Oh, darling. You'll ruin your make-up.' He entered the room and picked up the handkerchief that rested on the table beside her. 'Are you not up to doing this yourself yet?'

No reply.

'Would you like me to help you downstairs?'

No reply.

'OK. I'll try not to ruin your dress.' He bent down and picked her up, carrying her in his arms down the stairs and into the dining room. Lifting her was becoming more of a struggle lately. He pulled the seat out with his foot and his arms shook as he gently placed her in the chair. He wiped the sweat off his brow with his sleeve as he propped her up and used the rope to secure her.

'There you go. Look at the beautiful flowers I picked for you. I'm going to go and plate up the dinner and then we can chat about your day.'

But he knew the conversation would be one-sided.

She couldn't speak.

She couldn't function.

She couldn't be his princess. He had failed again.

Time to make other plans ...

Chapter 30

Maggie tapped on Nathan's door and he waved her in, but before she could get any words out, his desk phone rang. She noticed the colour drain from his face as the call ended.

'Grab your stuff – another woman has been found. Goth-like appearance.'

'You're shitting me, right? Our killer could be escalating.' Maggie stood.

'Looks like it. Can you ask Bethany to call Markston and make sure Kate doesn't leave the office until we can get over there.'

'I definitely think there can be no doubt now.' Maggie relayed her earlier discussion with Julie Noble, who had already concluded the same, after realizing that Dr Moloney bore a resemblance to the dressed-up version of Tracy Holloway. She rushed over to Bethany. 'There's been another body found. Same MO as the first. Nathan wants you to contact Markston and make sure Kate doesn't leave until we get there.'

'Bloody hell. OK, on it. Do you want me to call you when that's confirmed?' Bethany was trying to hide her concern, but Maggie could see through her.

'Erm ... send me a text. Unless she's already gone, then give me a bell. I'll see you later.'

Nathan and Maggie drove out to the latest crime scene. Another park, though this one was a little more secluded – and it didn't take long for Maggie to realize the village was again in close proximity to where Kate lived. Maggie wondered if they could use the geographical profiling that Kate had trained them in to see if they could pinpoint the possible anchor point where the killer worked or resided. It seemed too coincidental that both victims were dumped in locations surrounding the area where Kate lived.

Nathan pulled up behind the ambulance that was present at the scene. A crowd was gathering behind the police cordon that had been put up. 'I'm going to see if the SIO is nearby and find out more. I'll meet you at the Forensic Investigation van.' Nathan turned off the car and got out.

Maggie checked her mobile. One message from Bethany to confirm Kate was still at Markston. She tucked her phone back in her jacket pocket and got out of the car, headed over to the forensics van and put on the crime-scene suit, trying to see past the crowd of people who were clearly fascinated by whatever lay beyond the police cordon.

Nathan made her jump as he approached from behind. 'Sorry. I really need to stop doing that, don't I?'

'Yeah, you do. Jesus.' Maggie's heart was thumping so loudly in her chest, she thought everyone could hear it. 'What did the SIO say?'

'Female. Approximately twenty-five to thirty years old. Black hair. Sounds like she was dressed almost exactly the same as Tracy Holloway. Dr Blake is there now. They're sending the ambulance away. No need for it – she's definitely dead.'

Maggie followed Nathan as they made their way through the crowd and under the police cordon. They signed in with the crime-scene manager and followed the path laid out by the forensics team to the body in the crime-scene tent. The victim was positioned in almost the exact same way as Ms Holloway – similar clothing, face down, no personal items like a handbag nearby. Maggie shuddered.

'Ah, Maggie, Nathan, how are you both? I was just about to head back to the lab while my team finish up here. Glad I caught you though.'

'Hi, Fiona. I'd say we're good, but two bodies within such a short amount of time is never a good sign. What can you tell us?'

'My initial observations are that this victim has not been dead long due to the presence of rigor mortis. We are looking at similar circumstances to the first murder – so same killer.' Fiona beckoned for them to come forward as she pulled down the top the victim was wearing and revealed an infinity symbol tattoo on the right shoulder. 'First thing I looked for. I don't think it's coincidental that both victims have this, do you?'

'Damn. Damn. Damn.' Maggie slapped her hand against her leg.

'My feelings too, Maggie. No full black eyes this time – slight bruising on the one, but they are sewn shut, as is the mouth. Also, no other discernible lacerations or injuries to her body that I can see. She has marks on her wrists and I suspect her ankles – once I get those boots off, I can check. Though they seem to be fading.' Dr Blake shook her head. 'I don't think her death was as quick as the other one. Right. I'm heading back. As per usual, I'll send you over my findings as soon as they're available.'

'Thanks.' Nathan left the tent and was looking around the area. Maggie followed him and they saw a PCSO talking to a lone male. 'That must be the witness. Go over and see what you can find out. I'll meet you back at the car. I'm just going to call Dr Moloney and let her know we'll be there within the next hour.'

Maggie nodded and headed towards the PSCO and witness, who seemed more interested in the body than in answering whatever questions were being asked of him.

Chapter 31

Maggie introduced herself to the PCSO and witness and stood directly in front of him to block his view of the body, but he still tried to see past her. *That's curious.*

'I know my colleague here is taking your statement, but could you just give me a quick run-down of how you came across the victim?' She took out her notebook and pen.

'Yes. Yes of course. Anything to help. I was on my way to work and decided to cut through the park as I was running a bit late. You see, I never normally go through the park, but the bus comes at ...'

'Sorry, I don't mean to rush you along, but I just need the basics. I'll get the details from your full statement.' Wondering if she was being too abrupt, she added, 'If that's OK with you. I wouldn't want to delay you any further.' She smiled.

'Oh, right. OK. So I was walking through the park and I noticed what I thought were filled bin bags – you know, all black, and from a distance ...' He peered over Maggie's shoulder. 'As I came closer, I realized it was a person. You can imagine my shock. I may even have screamed.' A nervous laugh escaped his lips. 'At first, I thought she may have fallen and injured herself, so I rolled her over ...'

'Wait. You touched the body?' Maggie frowned.

'Well, yes. How else was I supposed to check if she was breathing? I placed her back exactly as I found her, officer.' He held his hands up and smiled.

'Did you tell this to the police when they arrived?'

'Hmmm. I'm not sure. I must have done. I'm afraid you'd have to ask them.'

'Can I just get your name, please? You'll need to go down to the station and provide your fingerprints and DNA – to exclude you from any evidence that's found. Did you happen to notice any personal items nearby? A handbag or mobile phone?'

The man fiddled in his pocket. 'It's Oliver and no. It was just her ... um ... body lying on the ground.'

'OK, Oliver. Thanks for your time.' Maggie turned to leave when the man grabbed her arm.

'That's it? Don't you need me for anything else?'

Maggie looked at his hand and then into his eyes. 'Kindly remove your hand from my arm, please. No, I have what I need for the time being. Once your statement is taken at the police station, I'll be in touch if I have any further questions.'

Maggie didn't like the fact that his lips curled slightly when he responded.

'Oh, OK. Good. Good. I look forward to that DC Jamieson.'

In fact, Maggie didn't like anything about this guy at all.

Chapter 32

Kate paced her office like a caged lion, looking at the clock on her wall as she waited for Maggie and Nathan to arrive. Her brain was in overdrive trying to figure out who would be doing this to her and these women and what their motivation was. She rarely socialized, so couldn't for the life of her figure out who she could have angered so much to do this.

'You OK?' A voice snapped her out of her thoughts.

Kate jumped back.

'Jaysus! You frightened the life out of me. I'm fine. I just hate waiting.' Kate hoped Mark believed her; she wasn't in the mood to get into any deep discussions.

'Well you don't look OK. This must be freaking you out a bit, but we won't let anything happen to you.' He puffed his chest out and laughed. 'That light still flickering?' He pointed to the random bulb that didn't seem to know whether it was off or on. It had been driving Kate mad.

'Yeah, I logged it with HR again. Hopefully, someone will be out soon and ... thanks.' She gave him a nervous smile. 'I'm just waiting for Maggie and Nathan. There's been another murder and they're coming by to collect me once they're finished at the scene.'

'You're not going home, are you?' There was a look of concern on Mark's face and for a moment, Kate felt emotional.

'To be honest, I'm not sure what I'm going to do. I've got a security system being installed at some point, but Maggie has offered me her spare room until all that's sorted.'

'I think you should take her up on that. If you need any help or a lift, just holler. Don't let your pride stand in the way of your safety.'

'I wouldn't ...'

Mark raised his brow. 'You would. But don't. We're here for you and you don't have to go through this alone. In fact, if the shoe were on the other foot, you'd make sure the help was taken.'

She smiled and raised her hands in defeat. 'OK, I promise. I just wish they'd get here as the waiting is worse than the not knowing.'

Mark left her office and Kate sat down at her desk. She could hardly concentrate on her work with that bloody light flickering but she needed to focus on anything other than what was happening. She opened her emails and browsed through the endless queries, answering those that were simple enough and flagging those that needed a more thoughtful response. And then she saw it. She didn't recognize the sender but her gut told her this wasn't a spam email that had slipped through. With shaking hands, she clicked the mouse to open the email.

See you soon xx

She pushed herself away from the desk, nearly knocking over the cup of coffee that had now gone cold. She shook all over. *Why the hell is this happening to me?*

Chapter 33

Maggie walked back to the car and rolled her eyes as Nathan watched her go around to the passenger door.

She opened the door, sat down and buckled up. 'That guy was weird.'

'Why? What did he say?' Nathan started the car, indicated, and pulled out onto the road, heading towards Markston.

'It wasn't so much what he said. It was his behaviour. He kept trying to look over my shoulder at the body. He seemed to get excited when telling me he touched the victim.' Maggie looked out of the window at the scene as they headed back to the station.

'What the hell? He touched the body?' Nathan turned his head towards her.

'Yes, he said it was the only way he could see if she was alive. What I also found strange was, instead of leaving her face up and explaining what he'd done, he placed her back in the exact position he found her.' She rubbed her chin.

'I take it he'll be going to the station to provide prints and DNA.'

'Most definitely. I'll be looking into him a bit more, that's for sure. Does Kate know we're on our way?' Maggie looked at her watch.

'Yes. DI Calleja will have told her, so she's expecting us, and then I think we'll have to formulate a plan of action to make sure the risk to Kate is minimized and figure out how the public should be kept informed. If this person can't have Kate, they're likely to abduct another female until they can get to her.' Nathan looked in the mirror and changed lanes.

'What has the press been told? This guy is escalating and I'm not sure how we can explain who may be a target without revealing something about Kate, or at least her appearance.' Maggie scratched her neck.

'I disagree. Tracy Holloway bore no resemblance to Kate until our killer made her look that way, and I'd bet the same applies to this current victim. Physically, their features are similar – small build, tiny but pointed nose, full lips and high cheekbones. But that could describe thousands of people. We have to be careful what information is shared with the press.'

'Yeah, I know. Christ, this is just so frustrating.' Maggie saw the sign for Markston Police Station, and before Nathan had even stopped the car fully, she had grabbed her bag and was ready to get out of the car.

'Hang on, Maggie. I don't want you barging in there and raising anxiety levels through the roof, OK?'

For a moment, Maggie felt angry. Was Nathan implying that she would let her emotions cloud her judgement? She'd never done that before. Then again, she'd never been in similar circumstances before. After a few deep breaths, she calmed down. He was right. This case was different, and she needed to look at it from a totally different perspective. Each of the women were important and deserved the same treatment.

'I promise. And Nathan ...'

He turned and faced her. 'Yeah.'

'Thanks. I needed to hear that.' Things had been tense between them since he'd told her some home truths that she was finding difficult to process. She hoped he could see she was trying.

Nathan smiled. 'I know. Now let's get this part over with.'

Maggie exited the car and jogged up the stairs. When inside, she went to the enquiry desk and signed in. Nathan did the same. Because Maggie had previously worked at Markston, her pass still allowed her access to the station. She swiped her card and walked through the doors to the stairway.

When they reached the floor occupied by the DAHU, Maggie stopped and stepped out of the way to let Nathan pass. She needed a moment to collect her thoughts, and Nathan realized this as he pointed in the direction of DI Calleja's office and raised his hand. 'Five minutes ...'

Maggie had dealt with a lot of death and sadness in her time with the police. But she'd never had an investigation hit so close to home. Beyond the friendship, Maggie had stronger feelings towards Kate and she needed to compose herself. She'd make sure she did nothing that would compromise her friend or the case. Maggie plastered on a smile and walked through the door, heading to DI Calleja's office.

You can do this. If she told herself enough times, maybe she would believe it.

Chapter 34

He wore his anger like a coat, pacing up and down the hall, furious with himself.

With her.

With everyone.

I should have kept her longer. Now I'm alone again.

He smacked his head with an open palm.

Stupid! Stupid! Stupid! Each hit brought a sense of calm.

He wanted to scream, but the neighbours might hear him and he didn't need any attention drawn to him or his home. After leaving the last one to rest in the park, he hadn't been able to go into work. He rang them and said his mother was ill – she wasn't, but how would they ever find out?

This one hit him hard. He'd thought she was his princess. That she'd wanted to live. To be with him. To be a special one. But he'd been able to tell she was dying and leaving him, like they all did. He'd had to take matters into his own hands.

There was only one thing left to do. This time, it wouldn't fail. *I need her. I need Kate.* In his mind he believed that Dr Kate Moloney would accept him. That she would understand why. He saw it in her eyes when they spoke. She knew. She knew why.

He was foolish to think he could recreate her. She was so

unique. She may not have been the first, but she would be the last.

He'd watched the police arriving at the park from a distance. He'd seen DC Maggie Jamieson – the worry on her face had made him smile. He'd had to leave as soon as the police had started doing their door-to-door enquiries though, as they would surely have stopped at his car and asked what he was doing at a crime scene. It was too early for questions. He wasn't ready.

He needed a plan. He stopped at a café and grabbed a bacon sandwich. He was famished. He took out the burner phone he'd used to send Kate the email. He wondered if she had read it yet. He'd need to dispose of the phone. Even though it wasn't traceable, he didn't want to take any chances. He couldn't wait to see Kate.

A smile replaced the frown on his face.

Chapter 35

DI Calleja's office was not made to fit the number of bodies that were filling it at the moment. Maggie squeezed her way to the front and listened as Nathan shared the details of the latest victim.

'Another one that resembles me?' Kate paled.

'I'm afraid so, Kate. After we found the letters in Tracy Holloway's flat, we have no doubt that whoever is doing this feels some connection to you. This must be your stalker – and he's spiralling out of control now. You can see why we're all concerned.' Maggie listened as Nathan relayed the information in a soothing manner. He clearly didn't want to upset Kate any further.

Kate turned to Maggie. 'Did they tell you I got another email?'

Maggie looked at Nathan and DI Calleja before turning back to Kate. 'No. What did it say and when did you get it?'

'It just said "see you soon" with two kisses. It arrived while I was waiting for you both. I sent it over to Bethany and she said they'd run a trace on it, but like the other one, he's probably covered his tracks.' She ran her fingers through her hair. 'What's the plan then?' Kate looked around the room.

Nathan was the first to speak. 'We can provide you with a personal alarm and have one installed in your flat. Your address is already red-flagged, so any calls from you are classed as an emergency. I understand that Maggie has invited you to stay with her until your security system is installed. I think that's a good idea. Otherwise, I'll have to issue you with an Osman warning.'

An Osman warning, currently known as a Threat to Life Warning notice but often referred to under its old name, was issued if police had intelligence of a real and immediate threat to the life of an individual. Maggie hoped Kate would realize the seriousness of the situation if Nathan was suggesting one at this stage.

'It would make me feel much better, but I don't want to place Maggie or her brother at risk from this person.' Kate sat down, her shoulders tensed.

'Hey. Nathan assured me that the same flag and alarm system would be placed on my house. Plus, how much safer can you get? Having your own police officer on call.' Maggie smiled, hoping it would ease Kate's mind.

'You can't babysit me twenty-four-seven. That wouldn't be fair on you and I wouldn't feel comfortable myself.'

Nathan interjected. 'How about we leave you two to discuss the details while DI Calleja and I go and speak to the field team and make sure that a risk assessment plan is in place? We'll see you both shortly.' DI Calleja followed Nathan into the main office.

Maggie sat across from Kate and tried to reassure her. 'Andy works nights mainly, so it would be nice to have some company in the evening. But I know how much you like your privacy, so there's enough space in my house that you can go off and be on your own, knowing that there's someone around for company. We can travel together into work and meet up to come back home. The less you're alone, the better *I* will feel.'

'Are you sure? Have you told your brother? He may not like the intrusion.'

'Leave Andy to me. I know he lives there, but it's my house. And I honestly don't think he'll mind at all. Like I said, we'll be gone during the day when he sleeps and sleeping when he gets home, so no toes will be stepped on.' Maggie reached over and squeezed Kate's hand. 'Please consider it. Plus, I may need your help – if you have any idea of who might be doing this, tell me. I know you can't actually work the case, but if I had any questions it would be handy to be able to talk to you ...' Maggie winked. She could be disciplined if she did discuss the case with Kate and anyone found out. She'd be as careful as possible.

'OK. I'll stay, but only until my flat is secured. After that, I'm going home. What am I going to do about Salem?'

'Oh shit. I forgot about him. I'm not sure how Scrappy would take to having another cat in the house. Plus, I have a cat flap. What if Salem got out and wandered?'

'Yeah, that's my worry too. I have a neighbour who's quite friendly. I'll see if he minds looking after him for a few days. Right, I guess I'd better get home and sort all this out.'

'You do know I'm coming with you, right?'

'I'd be surprised if you didn't.'

Maggie thought she saw a smile forming.

'I'll just let Nathan know what we're doing. Don't leave the building without us.'

'Yes, ma'am!' Kate laughed.

Chapter 36

He parked his car a few houses away so he wouldn't be seen. He knew from which direction Kate usually arrived home. He'd been following her for a while.

He frowned.

She was in a car and she wasn't alone.

He smacked his steering wheel with the palm of his hands. *Why were the police with her?* He gripped the steering wheel so tightly his knuckles turned white.

Maybe the DC is just stopping by to pick something up. He smiled. It won't be long now – he would finally have his princess. She would be his and his alone. Kate wouldn't need anyone else once they were reunited.

He watched her building for what seemed like hours, though it wasn't that long in reality, before Kate and the others came out again.

She had bags with her. He shook with fury. *No! No! No!* This wouldn't do. He couldn't go another night without her.

He waited before starting up his engine and watched as the pair stood on the path chatting before getting into the car. Kate got into the back, while Maggie rode in the front alongside her boss. He ducked down as the car came towards him. Once he was sure there was enough distance, he started his car, turned around, and followed. He wasn't about to lose Kate now, not when he was so close to having everything he'd ever wanted. He hoped Mr Policeman was more focused on the road ahead than the rear-view mirror.

Wherever you go, my sweet, I will find you. I told you, we'll be together soon. Very soon.

Chapter 37

Kate thanked Nathan as she got out of the car and waited by the front door as Maggie talked with him. Ten minutes passed by the time Maggie finished her conversation and Kate guessed it had something to do with her from the sideways glances she caught now and again.

Maggie ran up the path towards her. 'Sorry, I should have just given you the keys.' She unlocked the door.

'That's OK. I would have probably just stood in the hallway if you had. Everything OK?' Kate got the impression Maggie was keeping something from her.

'Huh? Yeah, sorry. Everything's great. Follow me, I'll show you where you're staying.' She went up the stairs. 'Make yourself at home – I'll just leave you to it and when you're ready, come downstairs and I'll make us something to eat.' Maggie pointed at a door at the end of the hall and left Kate to her own devices.

Opening the door, Kate reached around and felt for the light switch. The blinds were closed, so the room was a little dark, but that soon changed once the light was on. She held her hands up to her eyes. *Christ, that's bright!* She noticed a small lamp on the bedside table and switched it on before returning and switching off the main light. Bright lights often triggered head-aches. Kate's mother was always telling her that she probably needed glasses, but Kate refused to believe her sight wasn't fine.

She dropped her bag on the floor, took out her mobile phone, and called her neighbour. She wanted to see if her cat, Salem, was settling in and sighed in relief when her neighbour assured her that he was curled up in a corner, purring away.

She sat on the bed and, lifting one leg at a time, she removed her boots. Placing her feet on the floor, she curled her toes on the carpet.

She closed her eyes.

Her chest tightened and the blackness descended.

Deep breaths, Kate. She could feel a panic attack coming on. Counting backwards from ten slowly, she managed to calm herself down enough that the tightening in her chest subsided.

She stood and started unpacking her things. She'd only taken enough clothes for a few days as she was adamant she wasn't going to let someone keep her from her home. Truth be told though, she was glad to have some company.

Maggie shouted up the stairs, 'Would you like me to bring you up a cup of coffee or something stronger?'

Kate smiled to herself. She'd never pictured Maggie as a hostess. 'Uh ... I'm just going to give my parents a call and then I'll be down. Hope that's OK?'

'Of course! Take your time.'

Kate wouldn't tell her parents what was happening. It would only worry them. She found their number on her phone and hit the connect button.

'Hello?'

'Hi pops! How are you?'

'Ah, Kate! So lovely to hear from you. Your mam isn't here. Do you want me to get her to call you back?'

Her father wasn't one for talking, and she was almost glad

her mother wasn't home as she would probably have kept pestering Kate for answers.

'No, it's fine, Da. I just wanted to let you know I'm staying at a friend's as I have ... erm ... painters coming around to redecorate. Figured it was best not to stay with all those fumes.'

'Good idea. You'd end up with headaches. OK. I'll let your mam know.'

The line went silent.

'Thanks, Da. Love and miss you both and I'll call again soon.'

'Right, love. Speak soon.'

She heard the click as he ended the call.

Kate changed from her work clothes into leggings and a sweatshirt. She plugged her mobile phone charger into a socket on the wall and charged her phone. Maggie would be bugging her if she didn't; she hoped she would remember to put it in her bag in the morning. Kate left the bedroom and walked the few steps to the bathroom where she splashed her face with cold water. Looking in the mirror she could see dark circles forming under her eyes. She needed sleep because she couldn't risk not being on the ball at all times. Her life might depend on it.

She headed downstairs and found Maggie curled up on the couch in the living room.

'Mind if I join you?'

Maggie moved over on the couch. 'Of course not. If you want to watch anything on TV just change the channel. I usually just flick through it anyway.'

'I don't want you to change your routine for me. Do whatever it is you normally do, and I will happily just work around that. OK?' Kate sat down.

'OK. So, first thing is, what do you want to drink? Secondly, what do you want to eat? I'll be honest with you, I've never been much of a cook and haven't done a proper shop in a while, so I can't promise anything exciting.'

'How about we order something in? My treat. I'll grab some things after work tomorrow and cook as well. It's only fair. And as for a drink ... if you have any wine, I could murder a glass right now. Otherwise, coffee would be grand.'

'Wine it is!' Maggie reached across Kate and pulled some takeaway menus off the side table that had been buried underneath a pile of magazines. 'Choose what you want, and we'll take it from there.' She handed the pile to Kate.

While Maggie went into the kitchen to get them wine, Kate leafed through the menus and settled on Chinese. Maggie seemed pleased with the choice and put the order in. Kate nearly jumped out of her seat when she heard the knock on the door.

'That can't be the takeaway already?'

Maggie walked to the window and peaked out from behind the curtain.

'Nope. Just some guy. You see if there's anything interesting on TV and I'll see who it is.'

Kate made herself comfortable and started flicking through the channels. But then she was interrupted by Maggie talking to the man outside. She knew that voice ...

Chapter 38

When Maggie opened the door, the man in front of her shoved a piece of paper her way.

'Have you seen my dog?' The man's head was down and he held his arm out, waving the missing dog poster about.

Maggie took the piece of paper from his hand and looked at the little shih-tzu staring at her with its bulging eyes. 'Uh, no. Do you live around here?'

'Why does that matter?' He peered over her shoulder, but Maggie blocked his way.

She frowned. 'Well, it doesn't really, but if you don't, what makes you think your dog has come to this neighbourhood?'

'Oh, I see what you mean. It's not my dog. I'm just helping a friend ...' He looked down and shuffled from foot to foot.

'Well, I haven't seen your dog.' Maggie caught Kate looking through the curtains and, just as the man turned to go, Kate retreated. *Weird.*

'If I see your friend's dog, is there a number I should call?'

The man ignored her, turned, and walked back down the path, briefly glancing back at the house. Maggie closed the door and returned to the living room.

'Did you know that man? Why was he here?' Kate rubbed her arms.

Maggie shrugged. 'No idea. Said he was looking for his dog. Are you OK? You seem a bit on edge.'

'I thought I recognized his voice but when I peeked out of the window, I didn't recognize him. I think my mind is just working overtime.'

Maggie squeezed Kate's hand. 'Hey, it's OK. He's gone now. He was definitely a bit of an oddball.'

Maggie and Kate waited for the food they'd ordered. Maggie brought some plates and cutlery from the kitchen and was just placing them down when another knock on the door made them both jump. Looking at each other, they laughed.

'What are we like? That'll be our dinner and, I don't know about you, but I'm starving.' Maggie stood and walked to the door to collect their meal.

Kate rubbed her stomach. 'Me too.'

They filled their plates – Maggie wanted to talk about the stalker-turned-killer, but she wasn't sure whether Kate would be up for a serious discussion.

Should I just wait for her to raise the subject? Her stomach grumbled. She'd wait until after they had eaten.

Chapter 39

Kate watched as Maggie collected the dinner plates and took them to the kitchen. She wanted to talk to Maggie about her own thoughts on the stalker-turned-killer but didn't know if she would be overstepping the mark.

When Maggie returned to the room, Kate couldn't keep her thoughts in any longer. 'I know DI Rutherford won't let me be involved in the case, but would you mind if we talk a few things through?'

Maggie's eyes brightened. 'I was hoping you'd say that. You're right that it's a conflict of interest, but I know you must have put together some thoughts and I think they would be helpful for the team. I can give them to Nathan, and he'll decide how to take it forward.'

'OK. Great. I'll just go and grab my notebook from upstairs.' She raced up the stairs and rifled through her bag. *Shit. I must have left them at my flat.*

She returned to the living room and slumped in the chair across from Maggie. 'I think I left them at home, probably in the rush of things. I can go by and collect them tomorrow.'

Maggie frowned. 'Not without someone accompanying you. We agreed and you promised.'

'OK. I'll make sure someone from work comes with me. How about we talk through what I can remember?'

Maggie nodded as Kate began to speak.

'Stalkers are categorized in a few groups – I think the type of person we're dealing with is someone seeking intimacy. I think this person is lonely. Given the way he tried to make the women into ... how can I explain it? Childlike, almost. What did that reporter say? A living doll. A compliant, personal plaything. Victims are usually strangers or acquaintances who become the target of the stalker's desire for a relationship – I don't think I know this person, but that's not to say I haven't come across them.' Kate looked off into the distance recalling an incident from her past, but immediately dismissed it and carried on her conversation with Maggie. 'This type of stalker may have delusional beliefs about their victim, such as the idea that they're already in a relationship, even though none exists. The notes, the gifts to me ... as creepy as they were, he probably thought he was making a connection rather than trying to scare or threaten me or the other women. The initial motivation is to establish an emotional connection and an intimate relationship. The stalking is maintained by the satisfaction that comes from the hope that they are closely linked to another person. Not all will escalate to killing, but this one clearly has. I definitely think my stalker is our killer.' Kate stared directly ahead.

'That's a lot of information to take in, but hearing you say it out loud, it makes sense. And I'm assuming it's escalated because you went to the police, or at least that's contributed to it.'

'I'm afraid that's probably true. The first victim was abducted around the time I reported the incidents, right?' This was part of the reason she was reluctant to share things with the police. Every time she did, something bad happened.

'Off the top of my head, I can't say for sure – but that's easily checked. Saying that though, I hope you're not blaming yourself for this.' Maggie looked reassuringly at Kate.

'It's hard not to feel responsible in some way, but I've studied this type of individual long enough to know that regardless of my actions, it could have ended up this way. Right now, I have to consider that I'm the one at most risk. Rejection can be taken hard and even though he may not see it as rejection at the moment, he was clearly angry that I went to the police. I still can't get my head around how this person knew my work email.'

'Bethany said he's covered his tracks. The email is untraceable. These types of accounts are easy to set up. The reality is, we all know how sometimes people just give out details without checking someone's credentials. He could've called the office pretending to be someone, and when you're busy at work, you sometimes just forget protocol. I've probably done it myself and we may never find out. You said you may have come across this person before. Do you think you know who it might be?'

'No. Ignore me.' Kate hoped her nervous laugh wasn't noticeable. 'No one comes to mind, though I've met quite a few new people recently with all the training I've been on. Maybe I met them that way?'

'You mean a colleague?' Maggie's head cocked to the right.

Kate laughed. 'Not necessarily. It could've been someone who takes the same train or bus as me. It could be someone who saw me in town. I guess I really don't know as I don't think this person has approached me directly yet.' Her mind was leading her down all kinds of paths and none of them seemed to lead anywhere.

'Would you know if you did? Our minds can be our best

friend or our worst enemy. You'll be jumpy anyway with all that's happening. Are you really OK?' Maggie leaned forward.

'I suppose you're right.' Kate stared at the wall. 'It's just so unnerving. I hate that someone has this much control over me. I'll have to change my routines, or I'll end up making myself a prisoner in my own home … or your home.'

'I can't imagine what you must be going through. Have you considered talking to someone about it?' Maggie rubbed her knees.

'That's what I'm doing right now.' Kate smiled.

'Yes, but I meant someone professional. Someone who can help you deal with all the feelings you'll be going through.'

'I'm OK. Just a bit pissed off. But I do know professionals if I ever do need to go down that route. Right now, I want to help catch this guy … even if it is from the sidelines.'

Chapter 40

Kate felt exhausted. Thoughts of a time in London kept creeping into her head – an unknown stranger pestering her with calls. Nothing had been done about him and Kate had felt like a fool for going to the police at the time. They'd made her feel that way. She was grateful that Maggie had a knack for cheering her up and the meal and conversation had worked a treat. They were just about to choose a movie when Maggie's brother arrived home from work and popped his head into the living room.

'Well, hello. You must be Dr Moloney. I'm Andy. Pleasure to finally meet you. I'd shake your hand, but I'm rather grimy I'm afraid.'

Kate smiled. 'Nice to finally meet you too! And please, call me Kate. Are you going to join us?' He was better looking than Kate had imagined. Nice smile.

'I'm sure Andy will want to get a shower, right?' Maggie glared at her brother and Kate was surprised at the frosty tone in Maggie's voice.

'Er, yeah. Best get cleaned up.'

She watched as he made his way up the stairs and turned to Maggie. 'He seems nice.'

'I guess so. What do you want to watch?' Maggie flicked through the films.

The mood in the room seemed to have changed and Kate couldn't figure out why. Maybe she was overthinking things. With everything going on, that would be understandable.

'Do you like horror? I don't really watch any fluffy stuff ... Oh, that sounded bad, but you know what I mean, right?' Kate wasn't interested in a happily-ever-after film.

Maggie laughed. 'Yes. I'm sure we can find something – a thriller maybe?'

While Maggie searched the menu on Netflix, Kate moved over to the couch and stared out of the window. The man with the missing dog poster popped back into her head. His voice. This would play on her mind until she remembered.

Andy returned to the room a short while later. 'Can I get you ladies a drink? Or something to munch on while you watch your film?'

'We're OK here.' Maggie carried on flicking through the options.

'Actually, I wouldn't mind a tea if you're making one. Thanks.' Kate flashed him a smile.

'No problem. Maggie? You sure you don't want anything?'

'Well if you're making one, I'll have a coffee.'

When Andy had left the room, Kate whispered, 'Is everything OK between you two? I haven't said anything out of order to upset you, have I?'

Maggie shook her head. 'Sorry, no. Everything's fine. I'm just feeling a bit on edge.'

'Shouldn't it be me that feels that way?' Kate nudged her leg, trying to lighten the mood.

'You're right. The case is just getting on top of me. We don't have any good leads and the longer the killer is loose, the riskier it is for—' Maggie stopped short.

'For me. The riskier it is for me, Maggie. Please don't walk on eggshells around me. I want to know what's happening. Well, as much as you're allowed to share. It'll help me get a solid profile and that', she tapped her friend on the knee, 'will help you catch this guy sooner. OK?'

'OK. Can I ask you something?' Maggie turned to Kate.

'Of course.'

'This guy has escalated; I think we agree that it's the same perpetrator in both the cases. How long do you think the stalking of each victim has been going on? And why has he moved from the letters and gifts to abduction and murder?'

'Hmmm. All great questions and something I've been running through my own head too. Based on what we know, I'd say I've been on his radar for a least a few months; when I was initially receiving items, it was some time ago, just before the Raven case came to light. I just hadn't realized the significance. I'd say that with the other two women, he could have been stalking them for a similar time frame, perhaps even at the same time – and without sounding crass, these women were his backup plan.'

'Why do you think that?'

'Because he dresses them to look like me. They both looked very different before he dyed their hair, changed their outfits and, at least in the first case, he even put in the blue contacts. I know it's not a popular belief, but I definitely think this person has some medical knowledge. Maybe they went to med school and failed, but I'd say there's a certain skill used that demonstrates a limited knowledge of procedures. Though ...'

'What?'

'Maybe they have a fascination with serial killers who have done this before. Like Jeffrey Dahmer. He crudely attempted lobotomies in the hope that his victims would stay with him forever.'

'He mentioned Dahmer in the notes he sent to that reporter, Julie Noble. I wasn't aware that Dahmer had any medical skills.'

'Interesting! And you're right – he didn't. Dahmer failed to keep his victims alive for a significant time ... well, a significant enough time. I know in this case, the first victim died fairly soon after she was taken, but I'm betting that your latest victim lasted much longer.'

'Christ, Kate. What kind of monster are we dealing with?'

Kate shook her head. 'I don't know, Maggie. But we need to find him fast – he could be hunting his next victim as we speak.' The significance of that last sentence was not lost on the two women.

Chapter 41

The following morning saw both Kate and Maggie up early. A cryptic message from Lucy had intrigued Maggie. It was an address just outside of Markston and the sentence:

Come as soon as you can.

As DI Rutherford had cancelled all annual leave, given the murders and concerns about Kate's safety, an idea popped into her head.

'Do you want to have some time out before going into work? I don't start for a few hours and you must be sick of being stuck here with a chaperone,' Maggie interrupted Kate's reading.

'Now that sounds interesting! Where are you thinking of going?' Kate placed her book on the table.

'I've just had a strange message from Lucy inviting me to an address. If my detecting skills are any good, I am assuming this is the S.A.F.E refuge address. I know Lucy said it was just about ready to open, so perhaps we're getting an early viewing.' Lucy Sherwood had set up the refuge, aptly named S.A.F.E, where men and women who were in abusive relationships could escape to find strength, acceptance, freedom and empowerment.

'Do you think she would mind if I tag along?'

'I doubt it.' Maggie was sure Lucy would be pleased that Kate was interested.

Kate's phone bleeped indicating a message had come in. Looking at the screen, she smiled. 'Message from Lucy. Guess we're going out then.'

'Excellent. A change of scenery will do us both some good.'

Maggie waited outside while Kate got her things together. They walked to the train station in silence.

Forty minutes later, including a short bus journey, they arrived at their destination. Maggie observed that it was far enough outside of the town not to put locals' backs up as well as remote enough to keep the residents safe. They walked up the gravel drive to the front door. There was a security buzzer installed and Maggie pushed it, waiting for someone to answer.

'Smile for the camera, ladies …'

Lucy's voice came through the speaker. Maggie looked around and noticed a small camera on the right-hand side above the door. Looked like Lucy was on the ball with the security measures. If Kate's installation fell through, Lucy might be able to recommend someone more reliable. They heard some clicks as the locks were undone and smiled back at the face that greeted them.

'So great to see you, Lucy! This looks fabulous from the outside!' Kate and Maggie hugged their friend.

'I'm delighted you both could make it. Mark, Sharon, and a special guest are just in the room through there.' Lucy pointed down the hall and followed behind them once she locked the doors again.

Maggie greeted her colleagues and squealed when she saw Vicki Wilkinson hiding in a chair behind Mark. 'Oh my God!

Vicki! How wonderful to see you.' Reaching for her crutches, Vicki struggled to stand up, and Maggie rushed over, giving her a hug.

'Hi guys. Bet you never thought you'd see the day. In fact, there were times I didn't think I would either.' A crooked smiled formed on Vicki's face.

Vicki had been attacked last year by her ex-boyfriend and left for dead. She had suffered extensive injuries and had been in a coma for months. But everyone was willing her on and knew she was a fighter. Today proved that.

'This is Dr Kate Moloney. She's a criminal psychologist and worked on your case.' Kate walked over and shook Vicki's hand.

'It's really great to see you all. Lucy has done an amazing job putting this all together.' There was a sense of pride in Vicki's voice. Her face beamed and it was obvious she was grateful for the opportunity to be a part of working in the haven after her own experiences.

'Hope you don't mind me asking, but how has everything been?' Maggie knew Vicki had been a long-standing drinker and had dabbled in drugs.

'I've not touched a drop since this all happened. I attend my AA meetings and I'm also a mentor at the drug and alcohol services. I've had enough of that shit. I've been given the opportunity to stay clean and turn my life around and there's no bloody way I'm going to fuck that up. I don't want to let anyone down, least of all myself.'

'She really has beaten the odds and I'm more than happy to support her. Vicki will be a resident keyworker here when she's ready and able. I've a room set up so she has somewhere to stay until she feels ready to get her own place. But there will be no pressure from me; as long as she delivers her workshops, stays clean, and can lend a hand when needed, she'll be welcome to stay.' Lucy winked.

'I'm really impressed with you both. Any chance of a tour?' Kate looked around the room.

'Absolutely. Follow me, folks. Will you be OK, Vicki?' Lucy tilted her head.

'I'll be fine. I've got my phone and can catch up on things while you show them about. Don't forget to show them the therapy room!' Vicki's face contorted slightly as she eased her way back into the chair, resting her crutches against the wall. She obviously had not fully recovered but Maggie was so impressed with how far she'd come.

Lucy showed them around each room and then pointed out back to what looked like three large sheds.

'What are those then?' Maggie moved closer to the window to get a better look.

'Old sheds that have been turned into studio flats, a recreation room and a group room. It's where the men will reside. Having both male and female survivors on the premises means we have to take all things – feelings especially – into consideration. We'll be piloting a mixed group in the future though, focusing on shared experiences in domestic abuse, but for the time being they'll be done separately.'

Maggie thought she saw movement behind one of the sheds. 'Is someone out there?' Maggie made a move to the door.

'There shouldn't be, why?' Lucy peered through the window.

'I'm pretty sure I just saw someone behind that building.' Maggie opened the door and called out. 'Hey! Can you step out, please?' Her body tensed.

No response.

Maggie turned to her colleagues. 'Stay here. I'm just going to check it out.' She could see the look of concern etched across their faces. Lucy's hand reached out for Kate.

Maggie ran to the back of the first flat. 'Hey, I said come—' No one was there. *What the fuck?* She could've sworn she caught a glimpse of a person. She waved back to the house. 'Never mind. Seems I have an overactive imagination.' But she wasn't sure she was wrong.

They finished the tour and Maggie congratulated Lucy on how far she'd come. She pulled Lucy off to the side while the others chatted. 'Can you check any CCTV you have out back and surrounding the building? If you do see anything, send it over.'

'Of course. I'll do that as soon as I can, but not all the cameras are up and running just yet.'

'It could all be in my head, but I'd rather be safe than sorry.' Maggie looked at her watch and then at Kate who nodded. 'We have to go now, but fantastic work on the haven, Lucy. I'll be in touch soon.'

Chapter 42

Maggie had said goodbye to Kate at the train station as they boarded trains in opposite directions. Kate had assured her that she had her personal alarm and mobile phone, and had been clear that she didn't want to feel scared about being on her own, though her eyes told a different story.

When Maggie arrived at her desk, DI Rutherford called her into her office. They had an ID on the latest victim, who had a previous caution for shoplifting from her younger years – Kelsey Gilbey. Maggie watched the DI as she gazed out of her window in thought. She knew that below the calm exterior, DI Rutherford was probably as anxious as they all were. They needed to find the killer and keep Kate safe in the process. Turning to Maggie, DI Rutherford smiled.

'I'd like you to go with Nathan to Kelsey Gilbey's house and speak to her parents. See if you can look around her room. Find out if anyone has been around there or if she'd mentioned anyone following her. The field officers tried to get answers last night, but the parents were too distraught. Forensics may well be searching the property when you arrive, so keep focused and get what you can as quickly as possible. OK?'

'Absolutely. Do you know where Nathan is? I didn't see him when I got in.'

'He's just speaking with the COMMS Officer, giving them an update so the vultures are fed. He won't be much longer. It might also be a good idea to follow up with our Probation colleagues at some point.' She waved her hand, dismissing Maggie.

Normally this would infuriate Maggie, but she knew DI Rutherford didn't mean any harm by it. When her head was away on a case, she acted without thinking. Much like Maggie.

Maggie grabbed her jacket when she saw Nathan coming down the corridor.

'You ready to go?' He jangled the keys in his hand.

'Wow. You're organised this morning. I thought I'd be waiting ages for you to get yourself together.'

'Ah, you underestimate me. I've had to sort my head out with this new role. Too many things happening at once; if I didn't pull my finger out, I'd be drowning by now.'

'Better you than me.' She smiled and followed him out to the pool car. Maggie was glad now that, although she had passed the sergeant's exam at the same time as Nathan, she hadn't applied for the Acting DS role. At first, she'd been a bit shocked that Nathan had pursued it, but with a wife who wanted to start a family, it made sense that he wanted to settle into a more managerial role. Maggie still loved the operational side of things and wasn't ready to give that up yet. Though it seemed Nathan wasn't either – and not by choice. The team were short-staffed and the higher-ups, when they were around, didn't want to employ anyone new just yet.

While driving to Kelsey Gilbey's parents' house, Maggie noticed how close to the last victim the addresses were. Only two villages away, less than twenty miles.

'Remind me to speak to Bethany when we get back to the office.'

Nathan quickly glanced at her. 'OK. What for?'

'Well I've been thinking about all that geographical profiling stuff Kate talked about a while ago. I don't know if you've noticed how close in proximity this address is to the Holloway case, and how close they are to where Kate lives? Also, the disposal sites. I just think it would be something worth looking at.'

Nathan's forehead creased. 'Yeah ... you're right. Good job.'

Maggie smiled. They were approaching the address. Although she'd been nearly twenty-nine years old, Kelsey had still lived at home with her parents. The notes Bethany had emailed over indicated that she'd been studying part-time and had worked part-time at a bar in Markston town centre – The Smith's Forge. She'd been at work on the night she disappeared. Initially, her parents hadn't reported her missing as sometimes she'd go for a drink with her friends, crash at their house, and then dash home in the morning to change. When Kelsey hadn't returned the following evening, they contacted her friends and learned that she hadn't been in college and no one could get hold of her. That's when they contacted the police and reported her missing. It was two weeks later that her body had been found.

Maggie knocked gently on the door. The FLO answered and pointed towards a room down the hallway. It was a grand living room, furnished with antiques. Maggie noticed there were a lot of pictures of Kelsey around the room at various ages but none of the couple together. The tension in the room was thick as Maggie looked at each of the parents in turn; there didn't seem to be any intimacy between the two. Mrs Gilbey sat with her body turned away from him, while Mr Gilbey crossed his arms and just stared ahead. Maggie whispered to Nathan, 'Do you think there's something else we should know here?' She flicked her head in the direction of the couple.

'We're not deaf, you know. Was there something you wanted to ask us?' Mr Gilbey huffed.

'Sorry. That was rude of me. I'm DC Jamieson and this is DS Wright. We just wondered if anything else has happened because you both look angry ...'

'Not that it's any of your business, but as well as our daughter being murdered, we are also in the middle of a separation.' He shot a glance at his wife. 'Which will probably end up in a divorce.'

The woman beside him gasped and burst into tears. 'How can you do this to me at a time like this and then tell complete strangers our business!' She stood and ran out of the room, nearly knocking Maggie over as she pushed through the door.

'You'll have to forgive me. That was out of order. I'm just finding this whole situation difficult to cope with. Why are you here? Has there been a new development?' He crossed his arms again.

Maggie walked over to the man. 'Do you mind if I sit down?'

'Of course not.' He pointed at the chair in front of him. Nathan sat beside him, in the seat his wife had left vacant.

'We've no new leads at the moment to share with you, I'm afraid. Just more questions. Did Kelsey mention to you any odd things happening in her life? Was she afraid of anything?'

'I went over all of this with the other officers – don't you share details with each other? Kelsey and I were never very close. I couldn't even tell you what her favourite colour was, let alone name her friends. Her mother might know more, but as you just saw, she's in no fit state to talk at the moment.'

'Can you tell me anything about where she worked? Maybe her colleagues know more.' Maggie opened her notebook and pulled out a pen.

'All I know is she was registered with a temp agency. She got temp jobs through them, secretarial work, some seasonal work, and some bar work. I wasn't too happy about the bar work though. A young girl like her, around all those drunk men ... recipe for a disaster if you ask me.'

Maggie raised her brow at Nathan. 'Do you happen to know the name of the agency she was registered with?'

He stood and walked over to a desk by the window and scrambled through the drawers. 'Here you go.' He passed the card to Maggie and she looked at the name before tucking the card in her notebook.

'Thank you. Would you mind if we had a look around Kelsey's room?'

'Not at all. Your crime people were here earlier. They left it in a mess. You may as well look at it now too.'

'Sorry for that and thank you. We won't be long.' Maggie followed the grieving father upstairs. He showed them his daughter's room, before leaving them to their search.

'Do you think we're going to find anything that the forensics team missed?'

'No, probably not. I just want to get a feel for her.' Maggie looked around the room. The father was right. The forensics team had left the place in a mess. She stepped over items on the floor. Placing protective gloves on, she shuffled things around in drawers.

'Where would someone hide something if they wanted to keep it a secret?' Maggie eyed the room.

'This is a grown woman, Maggie. Why would she feel the need to hide anything?'

'I got the impression that this is a family of secrets. She wasn't close with her father. Her mother is very emotional – regardless of the circumstances. Perhaps she displayed one personality for her parents and another in her life away from home?'

'Hmmm. I'm not sure I agree. Look around her room. All those pictures. It looks to me like Kelsey was friendly, fun, and sometimes a bit feisty but I don't think she hid anything from anyone.'

'Maybe you're right. But I think I'll still leave that bit open to interpretation. Something feels off. Has anyone spoken to the agency where she was registered?'

'Not that I am aware of.' He looked at his watch. 'It will have to wait for tomorrow though; we'll head out first thing. Let's wrap up here and we can check it out in the morning.'

'Makes sense. I'll just let her father know we're going.'

Maggie thanked the parents and couldn't help but feel sorry for Kelsey's mother. The woman was in a fragile state, and Maggie hoped she would have news to share soon so the family could find some closure.

Chapter 43

Maggie looked at the address details Bethany had left on her desk that morning. ArrowRoot agency was within walking distance of Markston Police Station. After clocking in at work, Maggie and Nathan grabbed a pool car and headed to the agency to see what they could find out. On the drive, she wanted to pick his brain while she had him to herself. Her thinking was that without the walls listening, he may be more forthcoming.

'Do you have any idea who we'll be getting to replace you? Will it be a PC or another DC?' Maggie wasn't holding her breath for a reply. Since taking on the DS post, Nathan had become very much a closed book and she was struggling to deal with that at times. When they'd been equal partners, they'd told each other everything. It was one of the reasons why he knew how important it was for Maggie to keep Kate safe. Nathan knew exactly what her feelings for the doctor were.

'Even if I did know, the guv made it clear that she'll keep us informed.'

'OK. OK.' She held her hands up. 'I just wondered if Kat was being considered ... that's all.'

'Kat Everett? I thought she was still with the Domestic Abuse and Homicide Unit.'

'Well, technically she is but she's been fast-tracked down the DC route, and rumour has it the DAHU will be disbanded and absorbed into the Integrated Offender Management Unit, the IOM.' Maggie tapped her nose. 'I hear things, you know.'

Nathan laughed. 'OK, Sherlock. Even if that were true, they may already have a placement for Kat. Let's just trust the guv to get us the best person for the job, eh? We'll park at Markston station and walk from there. I don't want to be there all day.'

They arrived at the agency and Maggie scanned the open-plan area. The men and women were all very young and some reminded her of those dodgy salespeople in pinstriped suits you would avoid if you were just looking around. A woman greeted them.

'Welcome to ArrowRoot – if you could take one of these each, sit down over there and fill in as much detail as possible, someone will be with you shortly.' She handed them both a clipboard with a form to complete.

Maggie took Nathan's and handed them back to the woman. 'Sorry, we should have introduced ourselves first. My name is DC Maggie Jamieson, and this is DS Nathan Wright.' They each held up their ID. 'We're actually here to talk to the manager. We need some information.'

The woman's cheeks went red. 'Oh, I'm so sorry. I just assumed you were here to register with the agency. Follow me, please. I'll see if my manager is free.'

All eyes were on them as they passed rows of desks and were led to the back of the building. Two offices were hidden behind large room dividers. Maggie guessed this was to provide some level of privacy. There was an office with a very large window just beyond that. It looked like that was the room they were heading to.

The woman tapped on the door and asked Maggie and Nathan to wait while she talked to her manager. Maggie noticed the man frown when he looked at them but then he smiled – one of those smiles that doesn't reach the eyes.

'Officers. Please come in. How can I help you today?'

'Thank you for seeing us. We'll get right to the point as we know you're busy. Were you aware that two people who were registered with your agency have recently been murdered?' Nathan didn't sugar-coat the situation.

The man sputtered the coffee he had just taken a sip of. Droplets of brown liquid ended up on his shirt, but he didn't seem too bothered. 'Erm … I'd heard about the murders on the news, and that explains all the whispers around the water cooler, but I'm sure you'll appreciate that I don't personally know everyone who's registered here.' He must have realized how he came across as he then added, 'Terrible news. The poor families of those women. But what does this have to do with my agency?'

'Well, it could be nothing at all, which is why we're hoping you'll cooperate. We'd like to eliminate any links to the agency as soon as possible from our line of enquiry. Could you provide us with a list of people who registered here six months before the victims, Ms Holloway and Ms Gilbey, registered, and anyone new who registered up until five weeks ago?' Maggie waited for a reply.

'Don't you need a warrant for that? We take GDPR very seriously here and can't just give out people's private details.'

'Yes. We understand and we'll have a warrant shortly. In fact, DC Jamieson – can you just call in and see how far we are with obtaining it?'

'Yes, sir.' Maggie left the room and called Bethany. Bethany confirmed that the warrant had been granted and she would scan a copy over to them. Returning to the room, she opened the handheld computer device issued to police officers. 'It's right here ...' She showed the manager the warrant. 'A paper copy will be provided to you shortly, but in the meantime, can you provide us with that list, please?'

'Well, that could take a bit of time. I'm busy here.'

'We appreciate that, but the sooner we have the list, the sooner we can leave.' Maggie didn't like this guy's tone.

'Fine.' He tutted and went over to his computer. Within ten minutes he had the list and printed them a copy.

'Your cooperation is appreciated.' Taking the list, the pair left the agency and collected Nathan's car from Markston Police Station. Maggie couldn't figure out why the manager had been so difficult.

Maybe he had his own secrets to hide.

Chapter 44

'Look alive, peeps. Tell me what you know so far.' DI Rutherford tapped the evidence board beside her.

'Well, guv,' Maggie spoke first, 'after speaking to the manager at ArrowRoot agency who finally gave us access to the records, we now have confirmation that both victims were registered there. I don't think it's coincidental. Either our killer works at the agency or he's registered there. I'll be interviewing the manager to see if there's anything else he can add. I got a funny feeling when I spoke to him.'

'OK. Follow that instinct and Bethany can start on the list when we're done. We'll be able to weed out most of the people though, I suspect, if we look at the profile and compare.'

Bethany nodded.

'OK, what else?'

Nathan stood and went to the evidence board. 'I was chatting with Dr Blake and she's confirmed, albeit unofficially, that both victims were put through some form of rough lobotomy. It was like the killer was trying to make these women into his own personal plaything, as crude as that sounds. Both had the infinity symbol tattooed onto their backs and neither had any tattoos before.'

'Hmm. Why do we think the killer is fascinated with Kate?

Is it someone she's met?' DI Rutherford looked directly at Maggie.

'Kate can't recall anyone specific – she has come across a few ... erm ... weirdos in her line of work, but we all could say that. I've asked her to make a list of anyone she has come into contact with who could be a person of interest, but I'm not holding my breath.'

'Why's that then?' DI Rutherford's head tilted.

'Whether Kate will admit it or not, this is really affecting her. I think she may be blocking out some things that could be significant as well as seeing things that may not be there.'

'Can you explain that further?' DI Rutherford pushed.

'The other night someone knocked on my door. A guy was helping his friend look for a lost dog. Kate became really agitated afterwards. Said she thought she recognized the guy's voice. But then calmed down and everything went back to normal.'

'Did you check this guy out?'

'Well, I didn't ask for his personal details, guv. He was looking for a lost dog, so I had no reason to be concerned. But I did find the missing dog poster, contacted the owners and they confirmed they had a few people canvassing the area, so it seemed legit to me.'

'OK. I'm just going to add the information anyway – in case we need to refer back to it at any time. I do think that while Kate is staying with you, you should keep an extra eye out – any suspicious vehicles in the neighbourhood, people coming to the door, that sort of thing. I'm assuming you have decent security and that the panic alarm has been set up? Your house has also been red-flagged, but let's just be that one bit more cautious.'

'Yes, ma'am. Sorry, I should have taken down his details to be on the safe side. I won't make that mistake again.'

DI Rutherford looked at Maggie and smiled. 'Great. OK, Bethany I'd like you to check CCTV in Maggie's area; see if we can find this guy just so he remains on our radar. If Kate felt she recognized his voice, I think we need to investigate that further. To put your mind at ease, I'm looking to add another member to the team. With Nathan Acting Up, we have a gap and I think I'm close to having that filled. I don't want any of you burning out.' She looked in Maggie's direction and held up her hand. 'Before you jump in and ask, no I won't be sharing details just yet. Nathan will take over from here. Keep me posted.'

DI Rutherford left the briefing, and Nathan stood to take the floor. He had an odd look on his face, and Maggie was keen to hear what he wanted to share with the team.

Chapter 45

The creases on Nathan's forehead spoke volumes.

'I know you're probably all a little tired, so I promise not to keep you much longer. I'd like to look at location. Maggie noted something significant the other day when we found Kelsey Gilbey and I think it's something we need to take into consideration. Bethany, you may be able to help with this line of enquiry.'

'OK, guv. I'm all ears.' Bethany sat forward.

Nathan walked to the board and started noting down the locations of Tracy Holloway's house and where the team suspected she'd been abducted from, taking into account all the information they had. He then drew a line connecting this to where her body had been found. Next, he wrote down the details of their second victim, Kelsey Gilbey. Her address and potential abduction location, followed by where her body was discovered. He turned back to the team. 'You'll notice that the distance between where Tracy and Kelsey were taken is approximately eighteen miles. Each park where they were found is about ten miles from where they lived. The parks are around fifteen miles each in distance from where Dr Moloney lives – on either side.' Nathan removed the clear sheet and placed it over the map of Staffordshire he had blown up for the meeting. In a bright red marker, he circled an area that was in the middle of everything else. 'If we follow the same logic that we did in the Raven case, here's where our killer will live or work.' He tapped the circle on the board. The room was quiet as everyone concentrated on the location: Forrester Grove, and the surrounding area was highlighted on the map.

'Bethany, if you cross-reference any persons of interest who may crop up from the agency, chances are the majority *will* live in the area, but I think we can rule out the females. We can then pull out any specific persons of interest.'

'Would it be worth pushing Probation now? I asked Sarah to speak to her colleagues about any cases that have raised an alarm recently. Also, what about having Kate look over the list when we have it whittled down? See if she recognizes any names?'

'Good call, Maggie. Though we'll have to tread carefully on both fronts, as if something does come up, we don't want it to be thrown out at a later date because we involved Kate.' Nathan looked at his watch. 'I've kept you all longer than I promised, I know. Just a few more things to go over but it looks like I may have something to share with you all today.' Nathan pointed to the doorway and, for once, Maggie was speechless.

Chapter 46

Maggie's jaw dropped as the newly appointed DC Kat Everett walked into the room. 'Oh, sorry. DI Rutherford told me to pop in and catch up with things. I've been seconded to help with the investigation.'

Maggie couldn't help the smile that danced on her lips. 'Good to have you on board, *DC* Everett. We're just about to go over what we know about the killer. I can catch you up on everything else if Nathan wants, after we've finished here.'

'Welcome, Kat. I think you know everyone on the team. Good to have you on board. Where were we?' Nathan directed his question to Maggie.

She turned to her colleagues. 'The profile on the killer so far is that we think he falls into the category of what is termed an Intimacy Seeker. This type of stalker seeks an intimate or romantic relationship with the victim – who in this case we think is Kate. When rejected by the victim, they will continually phone, write letters, and can become jealous and violent if the victim enters into a relationship with someone else. I think we can presume that Tracy and Kelsey must have rejected him in some way, and this led to their abduction and subsequent killings. No phone contact has been made in Kate's case and we're not sure what specifically has triggered the killer – Kate's not in any romantic relationships, as far as we are aware.' Maggie's lip twitched.

'But she did contact the police when this fucker overstepped the mark with notes that were of a more threatening nature. I'm sure I read that somewhere,' Kat interjected.

'You're right. She did and that's around the time that the first victim was abducted – so maybe he felt betrayed? Wanted to punish Kate somehow?' Maggie looked around the room and then stood and walked to the board. 'We know he must watch his victims; he alluded to as much in some of his correspondence, in that he knew things. The murders are of particular concern. Kate mentioned a serial killer who attempted to lobotomise his victims – keeping them alive but rendering them helpless. He wasn't successful. Based on what Nathan shared earlier from Dr Blake, it seems our killer is trying to do the same. Also of interest, a reporter has been contacted and there were references to Jeffrey Dahmer. The newspapers have now called him "The Living Doll Killer"... There have been some hints that our killer has a medical background. So I think we need to bear this in mind when looking at the background of any persons of interest.' Maggie noted all her findings in point form on the whiteboard.

Maggie had seen #TheLivingDoll trend across various social media platforms and it made her blood boil. Sensationalist reports only fuelled the flames and she worried that extreme members of the public would try and take matters into their own hands. 'Let's just hope there's no vigilante action because the press couldn't keep it under their hats.'

'Bethany will be keeping an eye on social media and alert us if anything of concern comes up.' Nathan would take no nonsense from the press. He'd made it clear to Julie Noble that if she took one step out of line, he'd make sure she regretted it.

'Given what we know from the pathologist's report, I think we do need to focus on the medical-background angle.' Maggie loved that Kat just got stuck in.

'We're definitely looking into that but, according to Dr Blake, having knowledge of medical procedures isn't a given.' Nathan shrugged.

'I like Kat's way of thinking. Maybe they don't have medical expertise, but could they be a failed medical student, or even someone who may have wanted to be a doctor or surgeon? YouTube videos and reference manuals would probably give detailed reports on how to perform these types of procedures,' Maggie offered. She wasn't ready to strike that line of enquiry just yet.

Nathan seemed to take that on board and Maggie was pleased. After their discussion about how negatively she was sometimes coming across, she felt like she was walking on eggshells at times.

'I read that there were tattoos found on the victims. An infinity symbol? Does Kate have this tattoo?' Kat flipped through the notes in front of her.

'No. We believe this is part of his signature. He's marking these women and letting them know he's a part of them forever.' Maggie waited to see if Kat had anything further to add before continuing. 'His actions suggest that he is obsessed but also organised. He's methodical in his approach to abducting the women, in not being seen, and in the way he attempts to immobilize them – he doesn't cut them. It seems that once he's performed the lobotomy, the restraints are removed as the women are incapable of doing anything to escape.'

Bethany shuddered. 'Christ. It doesn't even bear thinking

about what those women must have gone through when you put it like that.'

Maggie sat and jotted down some thoughts while Nathan took the floor again.

'Now that we have an extra pair of hands, I'm going to be working with DI Rutherford in the background, but I'll be available to chip in if need be. Kat and Maggie, I'd like you two to work together on the information that Bethany pulls together from the agency staff – interview people again if it's necessary. Our persons of interests so far include: the witness from the park, Oliver; the lost-dog man if we can find out who he is; the mystery man Maggie thinks she saw at the refuge, once we can confirm from the CCTV; our creepy agency manager and anyone else who raises a red flag. Leave no stone unturned. Even if you're not sure – get the details on the board and follow it up.'

'Sounds good, boss.' She winked at Nathan. 'I'll just give Kat a run-down on everything she's missed.'

'Thanks everyone. If anything comes up, I *want* to be disturbed, OK?'

They nodded and Maggie waited for everyone to leave the room. 'Well, this is a fantastic surprise!' She reached across and gave Kat a hug.

'I know. I was gobsmacked that I got the transfer. I know it's only temporary, but I hope if Nathan gets the DS role permanently, I might be able to stay.' Kat's eyes gleamed with excitement.

'Fingers crossed! Have you read anything about the case or has DI Rutherford given you a summary of where we're at so far?'

'I know a few things. Kate is considered the main target now. I saw her before I came over and she's definitely looking stressed. Is she staying with you?'

'Yes. Her flat is being done up with extra security, though they're taking their bloody time. She wants to go back home after that, but I'm going to try and convince her to stay a bit longer or to at least have someone stay with her.'

'By someone, do you mean you?' Kat smiled.

'Why do you say that?' Maggie rubbed her neck.

'I didn't mean anything by it, other than you know the case, you and Kate are friends, and you're trained in self-defence. Might be safer if someone she knows from the police stayed with her, don't you think?' Kat raised a brow.

'I definitely agree. But you know how stubborn Kate can be. Hopefully, we'll catch a break in this case soon, and I guess we have to respect her wishes. Right, I need to speak with Dr Blake. Why don't you get settled.'

Maggie showed Kat her desk, then grabbed her things and shouted out to the team, 'I won't be long,' before heading out to the pathologist's office.

Chapter 47

Maggie's footsteps echoed down the cold, clinical halls. She pressed the buzzer once she reached the doors leading to the pathology department at Stafford Police Headquarters. Unique to Staffordshire, the lab was purpose-built, and Dr Blake based herself there as often as she could.

'A visit without an appointment. To what do I owe this honour?' Dr Blake removed her glasses and held the door open for Maggie.

'Sorry to just show up, but I did try and call and it just rang out. Where are all your admin staff and assistants?'

'Don't get me started. Agency staff at the moment, need I say more?' She rolled her eyes.

'I just wanted to speak to you in person because I'm at a loss. I plan on going to both the crime scenes, to look at things from a different perspective I guess, and I'm hoping you can give me something from your findings to narrow my focus.'

'Everything you need to solve these crimes and find your killer is here.' Dr Blake spread the crime-scene photos across the table. 'Let me help you see what I see, see it through the killer's eyes, and you'll find exactly what you need.'

'You make it sound so simple. I don't think like a killer ...'

'OK. Think of it this way. When you arrive at a crime scene

and see my guys and gals standing around, looking, talking to each other ... what do you think they are doing?'

'Deciding where to start?'

'In a way, yes. They're initially looking around to establish what may have happened before deciding what tests they need to do and which items they need to take back for testing.'

Maggie put her finger up to her lips. 'Right. When I get there, I need to look around and see the likely entry point. Which direction the killer came from and I might be able to establish why. It also might point me towards the likely area where he resides.' Maggie knew all this but had really been feeling off her game so far and she hoped that saying it out loud and talking it through with someone not so close to the actual investigation would help her focus. Her ability to process the simplest information was skewed by the fact that her friend was in danger.

'You're definitely on the right track. So now you've had my help with that, I'd like some help from you.'

'Do you mind if I sit down?' Maggie had forgotten to eat again and was starting to feel light-headed.

'Please do. I was speaking to one of our document analysts about those letters that were sent over. No fingerprints or saliva found, but I think we all knew that would be the case. However, they also advised that handwriting is unique and personal to each individual. The writing habits we pick up in school tend to stick with us over the years, even if we vary or adapt the style as we get older.'

'I'm sure I've read about handwriting analysis in the academy – or maybe it was uni. But don't we need a sample to compare it to?'

'Yes, they've compared the notes sent to Kate and to Tracy Holloway and confirmed that they were written by the same person. We can conclusively say that Kate's stalker has turned into a killer, if we assume that the person who sent Tracy the notes is the person who abducted her. I think that's a safe assumption. Once you have a suspect or persons of interest, let us know and the analysts can do a complete comparison. However, we don't want to give them the opportunity to disguise their handwriting, so chances are you'll have to gather the samples when their home is searched, or you can get them to write something when they're being interviewed. Don't suspects write out their statements? If not, I'm sure you can use your imagination and come up with a creative reason to get them to write something. It will take a little longer to analyse, but it would definitely be more conclusive.'

'Right. I'll bear that in mind. I'm sure the team and I can come up with something.'

Dr Blake's phone rang, and she checked the screen. 'I'd better take this. See you later.'

Maggie let herself out. She hadn't planned on spending that long at the lab but Dr Blake had left her with a lot to think about. She texted Nathan to let him know her plans. The pool car wasn't due back at the station for another two hours, which would give her just about enough time.

In the car, she set the GPS and left Police HQ. It was time she channelled her inner killer.

Chapter 48

It took her about half an hour to arrive at Granger Park in Hartley, the first crime scene, where Tracy Holloway had been discovered. It was overcast today and made the park setting seem eerie and menacing. No one was around, but people were likely to be in work and all the kids in school. Just as well because it would make her task easier if she wasn't disturbed.

The first thing she wanted to do was establish the likely entry point since the park had three different routes. One entrance, to her left, was via a long path, covered in brambles. Although it was accessible and led out to a road, it was unlikely that the killer would have chosen this path while carrying a body. She ruled it out.

The next entrance was slightly to the right of her and had limited parking but did come from the direction of town. It would have been a straight enough route to come in this way, until the killer reached the pond. He would have had to walk around and potentially leave a lot more footprints because the ground was softer in that area. There was also the rock garden to contend with.

That left where she was standing. The road she herself had come down led straight to a dual carriageway. She looked up and noticed very few streetlamps – those that were present were far apart and therefore this was the more secluded entrance compared to the one to her right. She began to walk towards the tree where the body was found. She estimated about one hundred steps. She turned around and looked back the way she'd come, took out her mobile phone, and snapped a picture.

She believed she'd found the killer's point of entry. Maggie jogged back to the car and entered the GPS coordinates for the next crime scene forty minutes away.

A thought entered her head; she'd check it out after the next scene, and if she was correct, she may be able to pinpoint the killer's location and stop him before he chose his next victim.

With traffic being so light, she arrived at the second crime scene earlier than she'd expected. Looking at her watch, she realized that schools would be letting out soon so, in order to avoid attracting unnecessary attention, she'd need to get on with things quickly.

Rose Park in Kirby was like an island dropped into the middle of the village and this would make things trickier to deduce. The killer could have entered at any point; however with only two viable ways to drive into the area, Maggie had a fifty-fifty chance of guessing which it would be. She walked over to where the victim had been found. Flowers adorned the ground, with cards and candles placed as a memorial. A lump formed in her throat. She always tried to remain objective in her cases, but when they struck close to home, it was hard not to feel something.

Recalling the crime-scene photos in her mind, she saw Kelsey Gilbey on the ground before her. Given the position in which she had been arranged, it was more than likely that the killer would have come from the right, as he would otherwise have needed to turn around, and logically that didn't make sense. Armed with the information, she returned to the pool vehicle and headed back to Stafford Police Station.

Time to make the murder map.

Chapter 49

'Where have you been all this time?' Bethany huffed as she brushed past the maintenance man who was fixing yet another flickering light to pass Maggie a message. 'This building is falling apart.'

Maggie looked up and nodded at Luke.

'I was with Dr Blake for a bit and then drove out to the crime scenes. Nathan knew all about it. Why? Have I missed something?'

'Was your phone switched off or something? That bloody reporter has been hassling us all afternoon looking for you.'

Maggie took her phone out of her pocket. 'Shit. Sorry. I must have switched it to silent. I needed to concentrate and, looking at the number of missed calls I have from Ms Noble, I'm glad I did. You could have just radioed me. I wonder what could be so important. I'll ring her back.'

Bethany's desk phone rang. 'Bet this is her again. Stand by.' Bethany put on her professional voice and answered the call from the enquiry desk. She nodded in Maggie's direction. 'Yes. She's here now. You can put it through to her extension.' She hung up the phone and returned to the task on her computer.

Maggie answered after the first ring and waited as the call was patched through.

'Is that you, DC Jamieson?'

'It is. What in the hell is so important that you had to harass my colleagues? If you'd left me a message, I would have got back to you. This had better not be a waste of my time.'

'I can assure you, it isn't, and I did leave messages, but hours have passed and you've still not returned my calls.'

Julie Noble sounded exasperated.

'Fair enough. I was out on police business. I can't drop everything just to take a call from you. If you had informed my colleagues about the nature of your call, one of them would have been able to get in touch if it was urgent.'

'Point taken. Now, do you want to know why I called or shall we continue to be passive aggressive for a few more minutes?'

Maggie was tempted to hang up on Julie Noble then and there. *Who the hell did this woman think she was?* 'What is it then? Spit it out.'

'I received another note. This one was hand-delivered to my home, and before you get all high and mighty, I called the local police station and informed them. They told me to hang onto it and someone would be around to collect it, but hours passed, so … I opened it.'

'You what?' Maggie wanted to reach down the phone line and smack some sense into the journalist. 'I hope you at least wore gloves to avoid cross contamination.'

'We both know that none of the other envelopes had any prints on them, so why would he slip up now? But yes, I used my Marigolds. Only gloves I have in my house.'

Maggie couldn't picture Julie Noble doing any cleaning, let alone washing the dishes. They were probably there for whatever poor soul she hired to tidy her home.

'What did it say?'

'*He wants to meet.*'

Julie paused.

'*Hello? Did you hear me? The killer wants to meet with me.*'

'I heard you. I'm just processing. Give me a second to think.'

Nathan walked into the office and Maggie waved him over. 'Julie, I'm going to put you on speakerphone. DS Nathan Wright is with me, and I'd like you to repeat what you've just said.' Maggie hit the speakerphone and lay the receiver down on her desk. 'OK, whenever you're ready.'

'*I received another note from the killer. Same paper and what looks like the same writing, in gold pen. It had a few doodles on it, that figure eight again, an eye, and something else I can't make out. It reads: "I think it's about time we meet. I'll share my story if you'll share yours. Thanks for the name, by the way." And he signed it #LDK.*'

'What the hell does that mean? What's your story, Julie?' Nathan looked at Maggie and raised his brow. When the line went quiet, he nudged Maggie.

'Did you hear what DS Wright asked? What does he mean by "sharing your story"?'

They heard her clear her throat before she responded.

'*I've no idea. Honestly. Maybe he's got me confused with someone else?*'

'He seems to know his details; he's meticulous. I can't see him getting something like that wrong, so either he thinks he knows something about you that no one else does, or you're lying. Which is it?'

'*Honestly, I have no clue. The only thing I can surmise is that he knows I've been talking to the police. What now?*'

'As far as you're concerned ... nothing. We'll get some uniforms around to collect the note as soon as, so stay put. Don't be doing anything foolish, OK?'

'I'm never foolish, DC Jamieson. I'll wait for the officer, but I won't make any promises.'

The line went dead.

'For fuck's sake. This woman is getting on my last nerve.' Maggie slammed the phone down. She hated that the journalist always got the last word in. But she had to put Julie Noble aside for the time being and return her concentration to the case. Maggie emailed Sarah Hardy to see if she would be free for a chat in the morning. Within minutes she had a response. Looked like she'd be paying a visit to Probation in the morning.

Chapter 50

Maggie arrived at the Probation office in Markston just before 10am. Sarah Hardy reported that after discussing some cases with her manager, a few had stuck out in relation to recent risky behaviour that were causing staff concerns. One case had even been referred to MAPPA, the multi-agency public protection arrangements. MAPPA cases were the riskiest and involved various agencies, each taking a certain responsibility to manage the risk of the individual when they were released back into the community on licence.

'Great to see you. My manager, Andrew Bourne, will be attending and the Probation Officers who manage the specific cases will also be available to speak to you if we need them. Come with me, it's just through here.' Sarah led the way to a meeting room with Maggie in tow.

Maggie greeted the Senior Probation Officer, Andrew Bourne. She remembered him from her time within the DAHU and how helpful he'd been in allowing the police to liaise directly with staff when they were hunting for the killer of the domestic abusers.

'I think it's fair to say that we all want this killer caught. The news seems to be all over it like a rash and the last thing Probation wants is to find that someone we're supervising is involved in this in any way. After the government decided to split us into public and private sectors and now they're trying to put us all back together like Humpty frigging Dumpty – well, we just don't need that kind of negative press.' Andrew rubbed his chin. Maggie could hear the unease in his voice.

The public never seemed interested in the police or criminal justice agencies until something went wrong. Then it was all the failings that were pointed at – and all the positive work went down the drain, so Maggie could sympathize with his views.

'What are we looking at then?' Maggie scanned the pile of paperwork in front of Sarah and was eager to leaf through the pages. She could see highlighted at the top were the words: HIGH RISK OF SERIOUS HARM TO FEMALES. She felt a cold shiver down her spine. Could the break the police needed be somewhere in these files?

'Within the folders are four men who Probation have identified as being at high risk of serious harm to the public, but particularly to females.' Sarah pushed the papers towards Maggie.

'What's significant about these ones in comparison to other cases with the same risk flags?' Maggie needed to be sure that Probation had highlighted the most relevant cases.

'When you called and asked me to find out if anyone was causing concern to their officers, these were the cases that were brought to my attention,' Sarah confirmed.

'Can you talk me through them one by one and we'll look at whether or not they can be removed from the list or added as persons of interest.'

'Makes sense.' Sarah looked at her boss and he nodded his approval. 'OK, Harry is on a Suspended Sentence Order for harassment. The reason his officer flagged him was because he's stalked quite a few females of various ages, for a number of years. He recently fell into breach of his order after kicking off in a group programme and then going AWOL.'

'When did he last attend and can you tell me a bit more about his stalking? Is it following women? Does he approach them?' Maggie thought this guy sounded like a good one to follow up, especially since he'd recently stopped attending appointments.

'According to his breach report, he last attended eight weeks ago. He's not responded to any telephone calls or letters, so breach action was instigated and a warrant is outstanding. His pre-sentence report states that he made numerous telephone calls and followed women. In one case, he did approach the female and offered her flowers. He became very aggressive when she refused them and she called the police.'

Maggie highlighted the points as Sarah spoke. 'And the address on this report is his current one?'

'As far as we are aware, yes. When officers attended to enforce the warrant, there was no answer – maybe you'll have better luck finding him.'

'Great. Who's next?' Maggie would definitely be following up on that one.

'Oscar Reed.' Sarah pulled out the paperwork. 'I'm not too sure he meets what you're looking for. He seems to fall under the domestic abuse category as all his offending, including the harassment charges, relate to ex-partners. In fact, I think he probably needs to be on the DAHU's radar.'

'I'd say you're right on both counts. Our killer appears to be targeting strangers – at least as far as we are aware – but tell me a bit more about why his officer flagged his case.'

'He's also in breach, this time for the restraining order, but he was flagged because his latest threat to his partner included her ending up "like the girl in the park". His ex-partner also has long black hair and dresses like a Goth.'

'Definitely one to check out further. Was he living with the ex, prior to his conviction?' A tinge of excitement coursed through Maggie's veins. This one sounded promising.

'According the report, they separated soon after he was arrested, and yes, he had been living with her. Do you think that rules him out?'

'Not necessarily. I'll definitely look into him a bit more.' Maggie couldn't mention the notes on black paper as that detail had not been released to the public, but he could be targeting females in an effort to scare his ex … although how Kate fit into the picture was not yet clear. But if there was a link, she would find it. 'I see the next guy has a history of serious sexual assaults and rapes against females.'

'Yes. Richard is on licence and currently residing in one of our Approved Premise hostels. Looks like he's taken an unnatural interest in the murders you're investigating, which is why his officer flagged him.'

Andrew Bourne interrupted then. 'The papers never mentioned whether the women were sexually assaulted. Is that because you're holding back information to weed out any prank calls?'

'Between us, it hasn't been mentioned because there doesn't seem to be a sexual element in the murders. The women were not sexually assaulted. However, I'd appreciate it if you kept that under wraps – not because we're withholding it, but it could definitely be used to weed out any callers who are trying it on.'

'I'm guessing that this one probably wouldn't fit your profile. His offending is definitely sexually motivated. He's on the register indefinitely.' Sarah shrugged.

'I'll make note of his name and check him out on the ViSOR

database, but I think you're right, he probably isn't one to focus on. OK, so who's the last one then?'

ViSOR is a database used as a management tool by a wide range of agencies, to manage risky individuals as part of MAPPA. It allows each agency to share information with relevant partner agencies and contribute to the risk management of offenders at the click of a button. Maggie knew it could help weed out some of these cases so that they didn't waste any time.

'The final one, Ian McNally, is on licence and the officer managing the case has referred it to MAPPA because he suspects Ian has formed a relationship with a female but is refusing to disclose, despite licence conditions specifying that he must.'

'Can I stop you there for a second? If licence conditions say he needs to disclose, and he hasn't, why hasn't his officer recalled him back to custody?' This seemed like a no-brainer to Maggie, but she knew that there were other factors to take into consideration.

Andrew took the lead. 'If only it were that simple. In order to recall, we need evidence and when a home visit was arranged, there was nothing to substantiate the concerns. It's all based on hearsay, which is why we're involving MAPPA now. It will allow us to keep a closer eye on him until we have enough information to return him back to custody. We just have to hope that nothing happens between now and then ...' Andrew's voice trailed off.

'How do you know he's in a relationship then?' Maggie didn't always like protocol but she understood when agencies' hands were tied.

'We've highlighted a few areas in the case notes where he's hinted at a love interest but then retracted the statements or denied saying them at all. His officer was so concerned at one

point that he asked a colleague to sit in the interview room as
a witness to the claims.' Sarah pulled out the copy of the case
notes and handed them to Maggie.

Maggie read the notes carefully. Ian McNally definitely alluded
to having a relationship but the words were what raised the red
flags with her. Everything he said seemed to be one-sided. He
had informed his officer that 'she doesn't know it yet, but we
were destined to be together' but also that he, 'often watched
out for her when she left work'.

'I'm guessing we don't have a name of who he was talking
about?' Maggie searched the document to see if she had just
missed the information.

'No, we don't. As you can see, he's very evasive. But what did
stick out with me after speaking to his officer was his current
address.' Sarah pointed to the bottom of the sheet. 'Isn't that a
few miles away from each of the victims' addresses? It is also
within easy transport of Stafford and Markston. We know he
drives as he found himself a job as a delivery man.'

'A delivery man? With his record, how was that employment
approved?' Maggie was in shock. Surely Probation had a say in
what type of employment one of their cases took on.

'Our hands were tied with this one. Arrangements were made
via an employment agency that works directly with prisoners
prior to their release. They undertook an assessment and because
he wouldn't be alone at any given time, it was felt that it would
be a suitable employment opportunity for him on release.' Sarah
sighed. 'This is the problem – one agency assesses risk one way
and sometimes ignores Probation's concerns.'

'I thought you raised these things in parole reports?' Maggie
was growing more agitated by the minute.

'We do. But in this case, our concerns were noted as we

initially refused to back parole, but he played ball at the oral hearing and the panel agreed to release him. We then had to manage the risk as best we could.'

'Oral what?' Maggie's brow furrowed.

'Sorry, I forget we don't speak the same language at times. When Probation don't support parole, the prisoner has the right to appeal and an oral hearing is held at the prison. The panel will consult a wide range of reports and hear evidence from professionals who are working with the prisoner. They're looking for evidence of change in behaviour and attitude since their offence was committed and they ask what it was about their situation that led to offending behaviour, and whether they've addressed those issues,' Sarah explained.

'OK, but from what you've said, it sounds like his Probation Officer did address those concerns, yet the man was still released? What the actual fuck?' Maggie shook her head.

'This can often happen, which is now why, after the disclosures in supervision sessions, we're referring the case to instigate MAPPA Level 2 provisions. We don't have enough to recall him yet.'

An idea popped into Maggie's head. 'Would you happen to have any samples of his handwriting?'

'Yes, we would have his signature on his licence and any worksheets he's had to complete as part of his supervision. Why?'

'We've some handwriting samples but nothing to compare them to in terms of identified persons of interest. If we had copies, we could easily eliminate or possibly identify our killer. Can I see them?'

'Hang on, DC Jamieson. We have a protocol to follow, as I'm sure you're well aware. I'd have to check that out with our Public

Protection Team before I can give Sarah the go-ahead on that front,' Andrew interrupted.

Maggie had known it was too good to be true but noticed a smirk on Sarah's face. 'What do you know that I don't?' Maggie was curious now.

'We might have to wait for sign off to get the worksheets, but the police should have a copy of his licence already.'

'And that helps us how?'

'It would have their signatures on it ...'

Chapter 51

Maggie left the Probation office with a newfound vigour. On her way back to the train station she called Bethany. 'Hiya. I wondered if you could do me a favour?'

'Fire away.'

'Can you pull up the licence copies for the following people?' She rattled off the names provided by Probation in a hushed tone. 'I'll explain everything when I get back to the office.'

'You're coming back here? Wouldn't it be easier to finish work out of Markston station? I can email you the documents.'

'As great as that sounds, I may need to speak to Nathan, so it's probably easier if I just come back. Everything I need is to hand and it will save me from hassling you every five minutes.'

'Then do come back! I'm busy enough as it is. By the way, Kat and I spoke to that witness, Oliver. He has a solid alibi for the murder but he was, erm ... very enthusiastic about being interviewed, so I can see why you had some concerns.'

Maggie could hear the smile in Bethany's voice.

'Great. At least that's one off the list, though I'd rather have a solid person of interest. Anyway, I'll see you soon. One final thing – can you ask Nathan to look up Ian McNally on ViSOR. Tell him I'll explain when I get in as I don't want to say too much over the phone.' She looked around the station.

Only certain individuals could access and update ViSOR. Maggie had undertaken the relevant training, but she wanted the information to hand when she arrived and figured Nathan wouldn't mind. He seemed to enjoy the geeky side of policing and now that he was a DS and spent a lot of time at meetings or strategizing, any time he could dip his toe in an investigation, he did.

She grabbed a coffee while she waited for the train and gave PC Mark Fielding at the DAHU a call. 'Hey, it's Maggie. How are you?'

'Hey stranger. All good here. Busy but probably not as crazy as it is with you. Kate was filling us in on some things, and don't worry, she was vague as hell so all I really grasped was that you lot are up against it. What can I do for you?'

'One day I'll fill you in properly but as a side note, just keep your eye on Kate for me, OK? I just get worried she's internalizing everything and she needs to be sharp, not distracted.'

'Well that's a bit cryptic, but OK. What was the reason you called then?'

'Yeah, sorry. I was just at Markston Probation and they highlighted a case which sounded pretty concerning. I think they're going to refer him to the DAHU, but I wondered if he was on your radar already? His name is', she looked around to make sure no one was in earshot, 'Oscar Reed and I wondered if there was any intelligence on him that you could share?'

'Stand by.'

Maggie waited while Mark looked up the information on the database.

'We have him on our monitoring list but we're not officially managing his case. Is there something we need to know?'

'That's good to know. I'll fill you in a bit more when I can, but keep your eye on him. I'm going to ask Probation to get that referral over to you ASAP. In the meantime, can you email me whatever you have on him? If I can share more, I will.'

'*On its way.*'

'Thanks. My train is just about to arrive. Say hi to everyone and we'll catch up soon, I promise.' Maggie ended the call and ran to the platform. She just caught the train before the doors closed. There were plenty of vacant seats and Maggie took the opportunity to close her eyes for a few minutes. All the information she learned today whirled around in her head.

Could one of the Probation cases be their killer?

Chapter 52

Back at the station, Maggie greeted her colleagues. 'Did you manage to find out anything more, Bethany?'

'Everything's on your desk or inbox. I had to leave a message for Nathan about ViSOR because he hasn't been at his desk for ages. Have you tried contacting the MOSOVO unit?'

The MOSOVO unit managed sexual and violent offenders and fell under the public protection umbrella; they used the ViSOR database to record and flag the relevant MAPPA cases.

'Next on my list. I can access the database myself now, so can you retract the message to Nathan? Sounds like he's busy enough without me adding to his tasks.'

Bethany nodded. Maggie knew Bethany had other priorities and she didn't want to keep her any longer than necessary. Everyone was working so hard on these cases.

Maggie logged in to ViSOR. She rarely had the opportunity to use the system and had to reset her password. She typed in the first name on her list. As she suspected, the information from Probation had been passed on and recorded in the system. The MOSOVO unit didn't seem overly concerned with his behaviour, but Maggie copied down his current and previous address details. She'd see if Nathan would accompany her on a home visit, but she'd need to let the MOSOVO unit know what she was doing and why; if they had enough manpower, one of the officers might want to accompany her to tick off a few boxes. Her concern about this was that they'd become territorial and she didn't want to jeopardize the investigation. She input the next name on the list and it drew a blank. She would have been surprised if he'd appeared since his offences didn't meet MAPPA criteria ... yet. The final name was the one that caused knots in her stomach. The little information that she'd gathered from Probation sent shivers down her spine. She typed in his name and what she read caused all kinds of alarms in her head.

Ian McNally had a long history of stalking and harassing strangers dating back to his early teens. He spent much of his younger years behind bars and on different forms of probation supervision. His offences ranged from criminal damage, burglary, harassment to various public order offences. Just for good measure, there were also a few violent offences, including a manslaughter against a female for which he received ten years. The woman had been his partner at the time and he'd injected her with heroin. She'd overdosed and died beside him – he'd watched her die and then waited almost three hours before calling the police. His reason? He was too high himself to deal with the situation. Her friends and family swore blind she'd never used drugs before and she'd not been known to the drug services, so the question was whether he had forced her by injecting her with the drug. Given his history, it was likely to be the case that he had, but without evidence, he'd been convicted of manslaughter and not murder. Maggie rubbed her temples. Cases like that infuriated her, but her professional side understood that they could only convict on the evidence.

She felt a breeze on her back and when she turned, she realized that Nathan had snuck by her and gone straight into his office. She must have been too involved in what she was reading to hear him. She closed down ViSOR and went over, hoping he would have a minute to spare.

'Knock, knock ...' She tapped gently on his door. 'I wondered if you had a couple of minutes to go through something with me?'

He appeared distracted. It was only then that Maggie noticed the stubble on his face and his dishevelled hair and realized she had been neglecting her friend. 'Are you OK? You look a little ... ragged.'

'Gee, thanks. Just what I wanted to hear. I'm fine. Sit down and tell me what's on your mind.'

There was a terseness in his response and Maggie thought it best not to push him. If he had wanted to talk to her, he would have. 'It's about my visit to Probation earlier. It's thrown up a few avenues that I'd like to explore and possibly some persons of interest. I'd like to cross a few off before I bring them to the team. Would you be OK with that?' Maggie filled Nathan in on the details.

'Yeah, a few of them sound pretty promising. Have you contacted the MOSOVO unit? They can be a bit precious ... understandably, given the nature of the offenders they manage. Let me contact their DS and give him a heads-up. I don't want you going alone either, so pull someone from the field team with you – that Brian fellow you know; he seemed a big help in the Raven case.'

'I could do that, or I could see if someone from the DAHU was free, maybe Mark Fielding? I believe some of these offenders are or will shortly be on their radar. Certainly, the ones that have yet to be MAPPA'd. If MAPPA don't take them, the DAHU probably will.'

'I don't think that's a good idea. I know you trust him, but we should really keep this within the MOCD if at all possible. Tell you what, if Brian isn't free then take Kat with you. She can always liaise with the DAHU, but be clear, she's not to discuss the case with anyone else. With that reporter already knowing too much, we have to keep as much as we can to ourselves to weed out any of the false confessions.'

'Absolutely. Thanks. I'll go and speak to Brian and see what happens. Given the time, it will probably be first thing tomorrow that we get started and it will be more likely that we do catch these guys at home in the morning than now.'

'Agreed. Keep me posted. I'll just contact MOSOVO now.'

Maggie returned to her desk and dialled Brian's extension. A female voice answered, telling Maggie:

'Sorry, he's away all week. Holiday. Can you believe the nerve of some people?'

The woman snorted as she laughed.

'Can I take a message?'

'No. That's OK. Thanks a lot.' She smiled and ended the call. Kat wasn't at her desk, so she rang her mobile.

She answered, out of breath.

'Sorry, did I catch you at a bad time? It's Maggie.'

'Damn. If I had known it was you, I would've carried on leaving.'

She sensed the smile even if she didn't see it.

'I'm downstairs, on my way home. My mobile was stuck in my pocket.'

It was Maggie's turn to smile then. 'Sorry to disappoint you. I do have a favour though.'

'OK. Ask away.'

Maggie relayed the details. 'Would you be free tomorrow morning to do some home visits? If anything, we might even get a few arrests in for recall. Save the Enforcement Team from going out.'

'*Two secs. I'll just pull up my diary. I'll ring you back if we get cut off.*'

Maggie waited as Kat checked her plans for the next day and breathed a sigh of relief when she responded with:

'*Totally clear until 1pm. Do you want to make an early start? If we get started at 6am we should be able to grab some of them before they leave for work.*'

'Good thinking. I won't keep you any longer. Should I head here in the morning then?'

'*I can easily pick you up – saves all the fucking about.*'

'Great. I'll text you my address and see you in the morning.'

Maggie hung up her phone and shouted in to Nathan. 'Brian's on holiday so Kat has just confirmed she's available. We're going to head out early and I'll be in the office by 1 or 2pm, if not before.'

Nathan waved and Maggie gathered her things. She'd need an early night, and hoped they would get some answers tomorrow.

Chapter 53

On the one day that she didn't want to be late, Maggie had overslept. *Shit! Shit! Shit!* Poor Scrappy had no idea what was wrong, as Maggie unintentionally flung him off the bed when she threw the blankets off and raced into the shower. No time to waste with make-up or hair; Maggie grabbed something casual to wear and put her hair in a bun.

Perfect timing, she heard Kat's horn toot gently and ran down the stairs. Picking up her backpack which held her work things, and her handbag, she didn't bother worrying about whether she would wake Kate or Andy up as she slammed the door shut.

Opening the back door of the car, she threw her bag on the seat and then closed the door before getting in the passenger side.

'You'll wake up the whole neighbourhood. You OK?' Kat greeted her and pointed to a coffee in the holder beside her.

'You're an angel! Sorry. I overslept and thought I'd be late.' She took a deep breath. 'I hate being late for things. Do you mind if I just text Kate and Andy to explain? I probably woke them both up.' Maggie was embarrassed; she liked to be in control of things and when her timings were off, she felt off for most of the day.

'Knock yourself out. We have about twenty minutes before we arrive at the first stop. Hope he's in.'

Maggie sent the same text to Kate and Andy and asked them to feed Scrappy before they went anywhere. In all likelihood, she thought it would be her brother who read it first, but she was surprised to see that Kate answered and assured her that her cat would not starve for the day.

She put her mobile back in her front pocket. 'Did you have a chance to look at the email I sent you about these guys?'

'Yeah. Bloody hell. How were they not on the DAHU's radar? Especially that Oscar Reed. They'll probably be taking him on, but they'll need the thumbs up at the operational meeting next week. Do you think any of these guys are persons of interest in the investigation?'

'I'm a bit on the fence with all but one. Wait. That's not true. I don't think Richard is, as he's a persistent sexual offender and there's been no evidence of sexual assault in the murders. That Ian McNally really stands out to me, but then he doesn't fit some of the criteria we've highlighted. Interviewing him might change that though.'

'Right. First up – your man, Ian McNally. Let's see what he has to say for himself.' They both exited the car and made their way up the stone steps. Maggie was surprised at how nice the building was. She wondered how he could afford it. They headed directly to his apartment and knocked on the door, loudly enough to be heard but not so loudly as to wake up the whole floor.

Maggie put her ear to the door and listened. There was definitely someone inside and then she heard a deep voice: 'Can you move your face away so I can see who the fuck I'm letting in.'

Maggie reddened and stood back. They both took out their warrant cards and held them in front, so they would be visible through the peephole.

The door opened a crack. 'What do you want? I haven't done anything ...'

'Can we come inside, please, Mr McNally? Unless you're OK with the whole floor listening in on your business.'

'Suit yourselves.' He opened the door and let them inside. 'Don't expect any tea or coffee; I don't plan on chatting for long. I have to go to work.'

'We know. That's why we've come this early. We wanted to be sure to catch you before you went. My name is DC Maggie Jamieson and this is my colleague DC Kat Everett. We'd like to talk to you about some concerns raised by Probation.'

'Should have known those arseholes would be behind this. What are they saying I've done now?'

Maggie caught a familiar scent in the air. 'Are we alone here, Mr McNally?'

'Yes, not that it is any of your fucking business.'

She looked around. 'Well, let's have a seat then.' Maggie headed to the couch and made herself comfortable. She noticed the look of concern etched on his face as his eyes darted towards the bedroom.

'Are you deaf? No time for sitting around, I have to go to work.' He looked at his watch as if to prove a point.

Maggie motioned for Kat to sit down. She frowned as she sat, and Maggie leaned in and whispered in her ear. Kat nodded and sat back, crossing her arms.

'I think you should do as my colleague says and have a seat. The sooner we get through this the sooner you can go.' Kat glared at him.

Maggie had purposely sat so that Ian's back would be away from what she assumed was the bedroom door. It would throw him off as she asked her questions.

'Fine. But you're wasting your time. This is all a load of bullshit. Probation would do anything to see me back behind bars and it looks like you pigs are happy to help them.'

Maggie pulled up the copy of his licence that she had emailed to herself and read out the section which referred to disclosure about partners. 'You signed this, so you understand that condition.'

'I'm not an idiot. Course I understood it.'

'So, you're saying that you're not currently in a relationship, Ian?'

'Yeah. That's exactly what I am saying. Don't they train you people? Are you thick?'

'Who's in the bedroom?' Maggie leaned forward, ready to jump up if he tried to make an escape.

But he didn't.

'Don't know what you're talking about. I'm alone.'

'If I go over to that door, I'm not going to find a woman in your bed?' Maggie looked over his shoulder and pointed.

He stood. 'You've no right to search my house. Where's your warrant?'

'Actually, I have every right. Your licence is very clear.' Maggie walked around the couch and stood in front of the door. She noticed the sweat forming on his forehead.

'This is police harassment.' He made a move towards Maggie and Kat intervened, her hand perched on her baton, ready to take it out and use if necessary.

'I wouldn't do that if I were you, Ian. You'll only make things more difficult for yourself.' Kat put her hand on his arm and he shrugged it away.

'Get off me, pig.' He growled. 'Go on then, open the door. See what you find.'

Maggie tapped gently on the bedroom door. 'Hello? Stafford police here. I'm just advising that I will be entering the room.' She cracked the door open slowly and her jaw fell to the floor. In the bed was a man. Naked from the waist up. Long, polished nails. A dress had been discarded on the floor. Make-up from the night before, crusted on his face.

'Well, hello, officer. What can I do for you?' The stranger smiled and gave a flirty wave.

'Apologies. Sorry for disturbing you.' Maggie backed out of the room and closed the door.

Ian McNally began to laugh. A loud, raucous laugh that filled the room. 'You happy now? I told you there wasn't a woman in here. Shove that licence up your arse – no breach. Sam is all man, though he likes to dress up now and again. Go and tell my fucking Probation Officer what you found.' He pointed at the door. 'Don't trip on your jaw as you go.'

Maggie didn't like his arrogance. Although the licence did stipulate females, given his history, disclosure of any intimate relationship was covered. 'Wind your neck in. Your licence clearly states intimate relationships with the addition of, specifically, females. I'll be informing your officer and whatever action they take is up to them. In the meantime, we'd still like you to come down to the station to help us with our enquiries. Maggie took out one of her cards and wrote on the back. 'Tomorrow. Late afternoon so as not to disrupt your job any further. But I suggest you attend and tell my colleagues whatever they need to know.' She held the card out to him, but he just looked at her with steely eyes.

'I'll just leave this here then.' She dropped the card on the table.

Chapter 54

Maggie tugged the handle of Kat's car when it stuck as she tried to open it. Once in, she sat and turned towards Kat. 'Shit. That totally caught me off-guard.' Maggie buckled her seatbelt.

'Your face did give that impression. To be fair, I wasn't expecting it either. Probation will make the call on whether recall or a warning is appropriate. I think they'd have a strong case.'

'He's definitely someone I'd like to see questioned further, though I didn't see anything inside his flat that set my alarm bells off ... well ... other than his companion, that is, and that's only because of McNally's history of violence.'

'OK. Next on the list is Harry. Let's have a chat with him and see what comes up.' Kat indicated and pulled away from the kerb.

Maggie stared out of the window as Kat drove them to their next destination. She wasn't feeling very positive about the home visits. Her mobile rang, shaking her out of her thoughts.

It was the station. She answered and listened to the information that was relayed. 'OK, thanks for letting me know.' Maggie ended the call and placed her phone back in her pocket. 'That was Bethany. Seems Harry was found dead in his flat. Overdose it looks like, so that's one off our list. Who else do we have?'

'The next two live fairly close to each other so it's your call. Oscar Reed and Richard Patterson, but Mark advised that the DAHU were going out to speak with Oscar and if they feel anything relevant to our case comes up, he'll let us know. I suspect they'll add him to their list of nominals, so really there's no need for us to waste our time. If I'm honest with you, I don't think either is your man. If there was a list of what you're *not* looking for, these guys would tick all the boxes.'

'I agree with you and anyway, the MOSOVO team are going to be involved with Richard, but I think we should speak to the hostel staff and check his whereabouts on the relevant dates. Even if he had managed to sneak out, where was he holding the women?' Maggie was talking more to herself than to Kat and she guessed by the silence that Kat understood.

Kat pulled into the small parking lot just behind the Approved Premises building. 'Wow. Nice place. Are all APs in old, listed buildings?'

'No, but it's surprising how many are.' Maggie reached into the back seat and pulled the notebook out of her backpack.

They walked up to the door and pressed the buzzer, looking directly into the camera to identify themselves and then waited for the buzz and click that would signal they were free to push the door.

Once inside, they walked to the reception window and showed their ID. The receptionist buzzed them in and directed them to the main office. The woman at the desk smiled at them. 'Hello. You must be DC Jamieson and DC Everett. I'm Amie Humphrey, the Senior Probation Officer and manager of this AP. I had a call from Sarah Hardy yesterday to let me know you'd be coming. Though I wasn't expecting you here this early.'

'Yes, sorry about that. We wanted to make sure we caught

Mr Patterson, in case he had something planned for the day.'
Maggie shook Amie's hand.

'So how can I help you? I understand you have some concerns
about Richie. I came in early and checked his records. He has
a bit of an attitude problem, but generally engages with the work
here and is looking to move on from AP in the next few months.'

Maggie wondered if they were talking about the same person
as that was not the picture painted by Sarah Hardy. She'd leave
it though for the moment. Police and Probation didn't always
see eye to eye, and she'd feed her concerns back to Sarah and
see what the officer said. 'What kind of attitude problem are
you referring to then?'

'Like most people who are referred here on release, he didn't
want to come. A lot of offenders feel that it's just as bad as prison
with all the rules and some think they are better off staying
inside until the end of their sentence.'

'Really? Are the rules that strict? I would've thought that
they'd prefer to be in the community.' Kat's eyes widened.

'Strict enough. It all depends on risk level – but most APs
only take the high-risk-of-harm cases. We have Probation staff
on site, the hostel is manned twenty-four-seven and they have
to attend various groups, get drug or alcohol tested – any breach
and they could be recalled back to custody.'

'I guess we didn't know as much about hostels as we thought.'
Maggie shrugged.

'Not many people do. But you didn't come here for that and
I'm sure that you've much more pressing matters to deal with.'
Amie pulled up Mr Patterson's records on her computer. 'What
dates are you interested in? I can tell you what he did that day
before you speak to him. It might help form a better picture of
whether or not he's going to be helpful.'

'We're keen to know his whereabouts over the last five weeks or so. Also, does he stay anywhere else or have access to the properties of friends or family?' Maggie was about to take out her notebook to jot the details down when she looked over and saw Kat was doing it.

'Well, I can answer the second part of your question easily. Richie's on a curfew from 7pm to 7am Monday to Sunday. He can't stay anywhere overnight without permission from his Probation Officer and the Home Detention Curfew team at the prison. The governor has to sign that off and there has to be good reason and evidence for that to happen, especially in cases where the person is deemed at high risk of serious harm.' She took a sip of water before continuing. 'In his notes, there's no mention of family or friends, only acquaintances he's met here or in prison. I assume that they probably stopped contacting him when he was arrested or convicted.' She scrolled down the notes on her computer. 'As I suspected, he's presented every night without fail at his curfew time and there's no information or evidence to suspect that he left the property afterwards. Not only would his tag go off and notify the tagging company, but we have cameras that are manned by night staff. No one flagged anything of concern relating to his whereabouts.'

'Hmmm. OK, thanks. Can you think of anything else we need to be aware of before speaking with him?'

'Yes, there's one thing. Richie has a massive scar on the left side of his face. He was napalmed in his last prison. He also prefers being called Richie to Richard.'

'Seriously? Is it bad?' Maggie cringed at the thought of the pain that must have been. Napalming in prison circles was when a combination of boiling water and sugar were mixed and then thrown on the skin. The mixture sticks to the skin and intensifies burns, one of the principal effects of jelly-like napalm bombs, hence the name.

'Yes, he suffered some major burn injuries and nearly lost an eye. He is partially sighted in the left eye now because of the injury. He's very self-conscious of it and may become aggressive if he feels you're staring. So, if you're ready, I'll take you through.' Amie glanced at her watch. 'He should be in the group room we set up for you to interview him.'

Chapter 55

Richie Patterson was facing them as they entered the group room. The chairs they were to be seated in were the closest to the door – as per health and safety regulations. He didn't look at them as they sat down, and Maggie noticed him fidgeting with the sleeve of his shirt.

'Hi, Mr Patterson. My name is DC Jamieson and this is my colleague, DC Kat Everett. Did Ms Humphrey or anyone explain why we're here?'

He grunted and mumbled something incoherently.

'Sorry, I didn't quite catch that.'

'I said, yes. But you're wasting your time. I haven't done anything.' He looked Maggie in the eye. 'Oh, you're not bad looking, what did you say your name was?'

Kat leaned forward and Maggie touched her hand before she spoke.

'DC Jamieson, and we're not here to talk about me. I'd like to know why you seem to have taken such an interest in the murders of two females, Richie.'

'Do you think I was involved? Hah! What a joke. Call yourself detectives! I haven't done fuck all. Have you seen the security in this shithole? The only privacy I get is when I go to the loo, and even then, I'm not sure those perverts aren't looking at me.'

'Interesting choice of words. Remind me again why you're here?'

'Do you think you're clever, DC Jamieson? I was stitched up, that's why I'm here. What's that got to do with you? I did my time. Now I am stuck in here until they find me another place or—' He stopped and licked his lips.

'Or what?'

'Or I do something that lands me back in prison.' He sat back and smirked.

'Enough of the bullshit. Have you ever met or did you know Tracy Holloway or Kelsey Gilbey?' Kat tapped on the table, her impatience obvious.

He looked past them. 'Never. Look, I haven't been with a woman since I was convicted. I'm getting tired of being blamed for shit I ain't done. Not worth the fucking hassle.'

'Are you working at the moment?' Maggie wanted to calm the situation so returned to basic questions, hoping to catch him off-guard.

'Nope. Who the fuck is going to hire me?'

He made a valid point, but Maggie knew it depended on how honest he was in applications. She'd seen many sex offenders and violent offenders land jobs that were not appropriate because some employers were lax in doing the proper background checks.

'I hear what you're saying but it doesn't mean we aren't going to check.'

'Knock yourself out. If you find someone who's hiring, pass on my details, will ya? Is there anything else? I have a session to attend and I'm not about to receive a warning because you lot wasted my time.'

'I think we're done here, unless my colleague has any further questions for you?' Maggie looked at Kat and she shook her head. 'Thanks for your time; we'll be in touch if we think of anything else.'

'Yeah. You do that.' Richie stood and headed for the door, mumbling expletives as he left Maggie and Kat in the room.

'I don't think he's our guy, and like he said, everything checks out in terms of the timeline. I'm still going to ask Amie to send the CCTV footage to Bethany. Better safe than sorry.'

'Despite his little outbursts, he was pretty calm throughout the interview. The details of the crimes, from what I know about them, don't seem to fit his MO. Even if he had escalated to murder, there's no sexual element to the offences.'

Amie Humphrey returned just then. 'Did you get everything you need?'

The pair stood. 'Yes, thanks so much for your time. I'm going to ask one of my team to contact you about the CCTV; we'd just like to cover all bases.'

'Sure. I'll let my manager know and we can take it from there.' Amie escorted Maggie and Kat out. As they were getting in the car, Maggie looked up and noticed Richie staring at her from the window. He was trying to intimidate her, but she dealt with people like this every day and she wouldn't give him the satisfaction. She waved and his smile turned into a scowl.

'What an arsehole.' She sat down in the car and looked at her watch. It was just coming up to noon. 'I feel like we're missing something. None of them really fit the profile, but that Ian McNally, there's definitely something about him that doesn't sit right.'

'Well, we can do a bit more digging and see if there's anything you can pull him on, or maybe keep an eye on his movements.'

Maggie nodded. Time was running out. They would need to trawl through the information to see if something stood out. The Raven case had knocked her confidence and Maggie feared the answer wouldn't be obvious, and the implications of that could be devastating.

Chapter 56

Maggie hadn't been back at the office for five minutes before Bethany handed her the list of individuals registered to the agency that she had put together. It took her almost an hour to scan the paper; her eyes immediately focused on one she hadn't expected. She recalled a conversation she'd had with Kate when she first started receiving the notes. Kate had mentioned a few incidents which, on their own, would appear to be coincidences but in light of the current situation there could be something more sinister at play.

'Anything of interest then?' Bethany popped her head around the desk.

'Actually, there are a few people, but definitely one in particular.' Maggie pointed to the name.

'Oh, shit. I knew that name looked familiar. Doesn't he ...?'

'Yes. Dr Blake will not be happy.'

'Have you already let Nathan know?' Bethany bit her lip.

'Not yet. He texted me earlier to say he'd be in a meeting when I got back, so I'll have to wait, but in the meantime, is there any way you can do a background check without raising suspicion?'

Bethany smiled. 'Of course. Leave it with me.'

Maggie tapped her pen on the desk. They would need to

approach it sensitively because if the press found out ... Maggie didn't even want to think of the repercussions this could have.

She picked up her phone and dialled Kate's extension at Markston Police Station.

'*Markston Police Station. Dr Moloney speaking, how can I help?*'

'Hey! I wondered if you could share with me again a bit of information. I'm just running through things, so I apologize if this is slightly repetitive. Remember when we were talking about strange people you may have come across or who've made you uncomfortable? Can you just remind me of them again and maybe what made you feel weird around them?'

'*Erm … All right. Is this one of those times I have to just give you what you ask and trust that you have your reasons?*'

'I'm afraid it is.' Maggie hoped Kate would understand.

'*I don't have names for everyone. Like I told you at the time, I've just been getting weird vibes off people. You know that guy who works in the forensic department?*'

Maggie could hear Kate snapping her fingers.

'*The forensic assistant. I see him everywhere. He has no idea about personal space or boundaries and sometimes he just seems overfamiliar. But maybe I'm reading too much into things. You know, seeing things that aren't there because this whole situation is just eating me up inside?*'

'Hey. It's natural to feel that way.' Maggie reassured her and checked a name on the list. 'Anyone else?'

'That guy who came knocking on your door. He said he lost his dog? He creeped me right out. His voice sounded familiar, but when I peeked out the window, I didn't recognize him.' Kate sighed. 'See, none of this makes sense and, in fact, it makes me sound like a paranoid lunatic. Sorry I can't be of much more help.'

'Actually, you've been a big help. I'll speak to you later, and I know this is easier said than done, but try not to worry. We're working really hard to crack this, OK?'

But even Maggie didn't believe what she said. Kate *should* be worried, as they were no closer to finding her stalker or the killer.

Chapter 57

Maggie prepared herself for what she was about to do. It was never easy interviewing people you worked with. They either knew what you'd be asking and had answers prepared, or they became defensive and personal. It never ended well. The internal line rang on her desk phone and she listened as the enquiry desk told her that he was here.

Maggie collected her pen and notebook and walked downstairs to the reception area. She buzzed him in and took him to the nearest interview room. 'Thanks for coming down to the station at such short notice. We've just a few questions to ask, to clear a few things up.' Maggie motioned for him to take a seat.

'Well I have to say, this is a bit of a surprise. Have I done something wrong?'

'Why do you ask that?'

'DC Jamieson, I'm a Forensics Officer. I know what happens in police interviews, and you wouldn't have me here if you didn't think I may be involved in something of a criminal nature.' He cocked his head to the left and the accusation in his voice was clear.

Maggie noticed how calm he was. His breathing was normal

and he was relaxed in the chair across from her. 'We're just checking some lines of enquiry and your name popped up. As I know you, I thought you might be more comfortable and assured if we spoke, rather than a stranger. I'd like to ask you some questions, if you're OK with that?'

'Fire away. I've nothing to hide.'

'Can you just confirm that you are currently registered with ArrowRoot agency, here in Stafford.'

Maggie noticed he shifted forward in the chair.

'Yes. I am. But I'm hoping it won't be for long.'

'And why's that?'

'Well I've had my final probationary period review. I'd like to think that Dr Blake will take me on permanently.'

'So no plans to move on elsewhere in the near future?'

'You're asking some odd questions, DC Jamieson. What's this really about?' His eyes brightened and Maggie suspected he'd finally figured out the purpose behind the interview. 'You think I've something to do with the murders, don't you?'

'I haven't mentioned any murders. Do you have something you want to share with me?' Maggie looked him directly in the eye. She believed that a person could lie from their lips but their eyes would always deceive them.

'Why else would you have me here? Are you afraid I'm after Dr Moloney?'

Maggie stiffened. 'What has Dr Moloney got to do with the murders?'

A sly smile crept across his face. 'I'm not an idiot, DC Jamieson. Even in the forensic department, we hear things. I saw what was sent to her. She's being stalked, isn't she?'

Maggie sat in silence. Watched his mannerisms. The confident smile never left his lips, even as he spoke words of concern. 'I can assure you, I've nothing to do with these crimes or any interest in Dr Moloney. In fact, I thought we'd got on pretty well. I'm shocked I'm even here, but you must have some reason and I'd be interested in hearing what that is.' He sat back in his chair and waited for Maggie to respond.

He seemed composed and, for once, Maggie found she couldn't read him. Could they have got it wrong? Maybe she should just be direct.

'Did you know either Tracy Holloway or Kelsey Gilbey?'

He paused before answering. Maggie noticed he fidgeted with his tie. 'Not as far as I can recall.'

'Well, we have a witness who described someone who looks just like you and can place you with Kelsey Gilbey. How do you explain that?' When Bethany had done some further checks, a description of someone who fit Charlie had been found in one of the witness statements, and Maggie hoped her instincts would pay off.

'Really?' His eyes widened. 'I'd be very interested in knowing more about that. Where was this alleged sighting of me?'

'The Smith's Forge. You were seen talking to Kelsey and our witness described you as', Maggie looked through the notes in front of her, 'creepy and unable to grasp the concept of personal space, when you tried to chat her up.'

Charlie's face reddened. 'I ... I don't kn-know what t-t-t-t-to say.' A noticeable stutter caught Maggie's ear. She waited.

He composed himself. Maggie watched as his chest rose and fell. 'I'm embarrassed now, DC Jamieson.' He waved his hands in front of himself. 'I'm not the best-looking guy out there and I admit that when it comes to chat-up lines, I'm ... well ... pretty shit. Pardon the language. I'm sorry I made the witness feel uncomfortable. If truth be told, after talking to a few women, and being shot down, I left the pub with my tail between my legs. I haven't been out socially since.'

This time, Maggie could tell he was being honest, and her shoulders dropped. Perhaps they had got it wrong and he wasn't their guy. 'Would you mind submitting a handwriting sample?'

'Seriously? What has my handwriting got to do with anything? Haven't you shamed me enough? I can just imagine you all gossiping about what a loser I am.' He covered his face and leaned on the table. His shoulders shook.

'There's no need to get upset.' She passed him a tissue from the box in the drawer. 'I can assure you that you will not be a topic of office gossip. I'm sure you can appreciate that we need to get to the bottom of this and having a sample of your writing could eliminate you immediately.'

'Fine. Just give me a piece of paper and let's get this over with.' He huffed.

Maggie removed a sheet of paper from her notebook and provided a phrase which would allow the analysts to compare easily. She watched him closely as he wrote. He was left-handed, but his hand shook as he wrote. According to Dr Blake, the killer may be left-handed based on the nature of the injuries but the notes were written by someone who was right-handed – this was confirmed by the handwriting analysists, but could they have got it wrong?

'There. Happy now?' He shoved the paper towards her.

Maggie looked at the paper and put it in her notebook. 'Thank you, Charlie. Can I ask one more question before we wrap this up?'

'I don't think I have much choice in the matter. What is it?'

'Have you noticed anyone behaving unusually lately? Perhaps late for work? More stressed than normal? Maybe those who are not on the permanent payroll?' Maggie worried she'd said too much by hinting at agency staff, but it didn't seem to register with Charlie.

'Not that I can think of. Everyone is stressed at the moment. We've been working around the clock on the murders. If I do think of anyone, I'll let you know.'

'Thank you. That would be helpful. I'd ask that you keep the nature of our conversation to yourself for the time being too.'

'Don't worry, DC Jamieson. I'm not about to brag that I was questioned by the police, am I? Shit. Does Dr Blake know about this?'

'Not to my knowledge. I think it's reasonable to assume we'll have to let her know, but it's up to you whether you want to disclose it first.'

'Are we done?' Charlie stood and waited for Maggie to confirm the interview had been concluded.

'Yes. I'll show you out.' Maggie led Charlie back to the enquiry desk.

Before he exited, she touched his arm. He stopped and turned towards her. 'I'm really sorry about all this. I hope when you have a moment to reflect on it all, you'll understand why we had to speak to you.'

He simply stared at her, the hatred burning in his eyes.

The damage was done.

Chapter 58

'Any chance you can have a quick look at this, Bethany?' Maggie waved the paper with Charlie's handwriting sample.

'Sure. What's it for?' Bethany took the paper from Maggie's hand.

'It'll need to be formally analysed, but if you could compare it to the notes we have on file from the killer we might be able to provisionally rule out Charlie. The sooner we can do this, the better. He was pretty pissed off.'

Bethany took the paper and began searching the records. 'I'm not surprised. I'd be pretty pissed off too. But surely he'll understand our reasoning?'

'I wouldn't count on it. If he wasn't a murderer before, he definitely wants to kill now.'

Nathan walked into the room. 'Who wants to kill and why?'

Maggie filled in the details and Nathan shook his head.

'He'll calm down eventually. How close does his handwriting match up? Anyway, we've nothing to apologize for – part of our job is questioning everyone who has come into contact with our victims just prior to their deaths. Unfortunately, Charlie was one of those people. If he can't see the logic, perhaps he's in the wrong field.'

Maggie smiled. Nathan made a good point and if Charlie did

lodge a complaint, at least she was confident that Nathan would back her up.

'OK. At a glance, I'd say that the person who wrote this note', Bethany held up Charlie's paper, 'was *not* the same person who wrote these notes. See the difference in the slant, spacing and the letters?' She held up the evidence. 'They are pretty distinct. Did he write this quickly or did it look like he was concentrating?'

'Pretty quickly, but his hands were shaking. Why?'

'My thinking is, if he'd taken his time, it's possible that he purposely changed his handwriting style. But let's let the professionals have a look and make the final decision. I'm no expert.' Bethany loaded the document information onto the system. 'I'll send the original over now if you like.'

'That'd be great. He's worried about his colleagues finding out. The more we can contain this, the better.'

Nathan interrupted. 'I think we'll need to inform Dr Blake. He's agency staff and she'll want to know what's going on. She'll be furious to learn that we questioned one of her team without giving her a heads-up.'

'I was hoping you weren't going to say that. The question is, who is going to tell her? You or me?' Maggie batted her eyelashes hoping that Nathan would take pity on her.

'You're off the hook for this one. It needs to come from me. I'll reassure her that we didn't want to cast any doubt on her team until we had spoken to him first. But don't be surprised if you start getting the cold shoulder. She may be reasonable, but she doesn't take kindly to her assessment skills coming under scrutiny.'

'No one was questioning that though.' Maggie didn't want to jeopardize her personal or professional relationship with the pathologist.

'You pulled one of her team into the police station to question him about a possible link to the murders. How would you feel if the tables were turned?'

Maggie looked away. She could see how Dr Blake might take the news, but there was nothing they could do about it now. It had been a long day. The team were shattered. Maggie packed up her stuff and headed out the door.

Chapter 59

Maggie had a restless night. She stretched her arms and forced herself out of bed. She wrapped her housecoat around her and made her way to the kitchen where she smelled the delicious aroma of coffee.

Maggie was still half asleep and not quite firing on all cylinders due to the lack of sleep, so she wasn't quite sure she'd heard Kate correctly when she spoke. 'Can you just say that again?'

'I'd like to go and speak with Dr Blake about the latest autopsy and her findings if I can. Do you think you can arrange that?'

'I'm not sure that's going to be possible, given your involvement. Not only that, why would you want to find out more? Even if I get the OK from Nathan, I'm pretty sure DI Rutherford will raise serious objections, not to mention your own DI.'

'Leave DI Calleja to me – I'm a civilian so I'm not sure what kind of influence he'll have over the matter.' Kate looked away.

'He's still your boss, and you haven't answered my question. Why? Why would you want to put yourself through that?'

'I actually want to help tighten the profile. I think we're missing something and being on the sidelines is making an accurate picture impossible. From a personal point of view, I also want to know what I'm dealing with. Sometimes I feel like things are being blown way out of proportion and other times I'm a nervous wreck. For my own peace of mind, I just need to do this. Plus, I may be able to come up with some tips for the public, what to look out for, without causing a massive scare.'

Maggie eyed her suspiciously. 'That's a good argument. I guess we can run it by the higher-ups. I'll ring DI Rutherford now and, if she's OK with it, I'll contact Dr Blake and we can see if we can head over there today.'

Kate nodded and left the room, presumably to get ready and give Maggie some privacy. Taking a deep breath, Maggie picked up her phone and contacted DI Rutherford.

'What is it, Maggie?'

'Morning, ma'am. Sorry to bother you so early. Kate has a request and before you shoot me down, I'd like you to hear me out.' She wanted to warn her boss that it wasn't going to be something she'd appreciate, while also allowing her the time to flesh things out and present a reasonable argument.

'I'm listening …'

'Kate wants to meet with Dr Blake and discuss the post-mortem findings.' Maggie heard a slight noise coming from the other end of the phone, but Rutherford let her speak without interruption. 'She thinks if she knows more details she may get a better understanding of the person we need to focus on. At the same time, it may highlight ways she can keep herself safe. And perhaps she can assist in putting together a press release for the public?' Maggie waited with bated breath.

'I don't like it, but … I'm also going to go out on a limb and OK this. DCI Hastings will not be happy, and if he was here more, perhaps I'd care. Sorry, that remark was uncalled for. Right, if we can do the majority of it under the radar, then I'm happy to take any residual flak as, in all honesty, we have nothing and the longer this carries on the worse it's going to get. However …'

Maggie had known there would be conditions, but if it meant they could speak with Dr Blake, she would oblige.

'I want you to keep Nathan informed and if Kate becomes at all affected by any of this, you stop it immediately, whether she likes it or not. Do I make myself clear?'

'Yes, ma'am. I'll keep a close eye on her. We appreciate your backing.' Maggie suspected Kate would have found a way if the idea had been shot down, so it was better to have everyone onside.

'Speak soon.'

DI Rutherford ended the call.

'Kate. We have the all-clear. I'm going to ring Fiona now and see if she can fit us in.'

Kate popped her head in the room and smiled, giving Maggie a thumbs up.

The call with Dr Blake was brief. She had a few hours free but they would need to get to Stafford Police HQ as soon as possible. Maggie grabbed what she needed and left a note for Andy. He'd have to take a taxi to and from work today as she needed the car. Given the circumstances, Maggie figured he wouldn't argue.

They arrived at Police HQ within the hour and were greeted by Dr Blake's assistant. It seemed every time Maggie attended the mortuary, there was someone new. He led them into Dr Blake's office.

'Morning, ladies. I didn't have the chance to ask when you called, but to what do I owe the pleasure of this visit?' Maggie sensed a frostiness from Dr Blake.

'I'll save Maggie having to repeat herself again,' Kate started the ball rolling. 'I'm hoping you can talk me through some of your findings in relation to both of the victims. I've a general profile in my head of the type of person who may be committing these crimes, but there's something that just doesn't fit. I'm hoping you may be able to help fill in those blanks.'

Dr Blake's forehead creased. 'This is all a little unorthodox, isn't it, given the circumstances and your situation. Are all the powers that be on board with this? I'm not prepared to have any grief at my door if I do decide to assist you.'

'I've spoken to DI Rutherford and Nathan is aware. We all share your concerns.' Maggie looked at Kate. 'But we're no further ahead with a solid lead, strong suspects, or identifying any persons of interest … and that's where your expertise comes in.'

'Fine. Let's get started.'

Chapter 60

Kate stared at the pictures on the screen. The likeness was uncanny. Both of these women could be her twin. Her chest felt tight. Her eye twitched. *What the actual hell is happening?*

'Are you sure you want to do this, Kate?' Maggie reached out and Kate shook her hand away.

'Yes.' She cleared her throat. 'It'll help ... with the profile. We need to get a handle on this before I ... before someone else gets hurt.'

Dr Blake explained to them both her initial findings. 'If you look here', she pointed at each woman's face around the eye area, 'the killer used an ice-pick-like tool to go in behind the eye. As I pointed out in my report, I believe he's left-handed because of the angle used ... but there is still something odd about the injury that I just can't put my finger on ... anyway.' She shook her head as if clearing her thoughts. 'The problem is that in Ms Holloway's case, he hit blood vessels, which caused internal bleeding on the brain. She didn't die instantly, but she wouldn't have survived long.'

Kate looked away momentarily. The realization of what Tracy Holloway had gone through hit her hard. 'What do you think the purpose of that was? I have my own thoughts ...'

'In simplest terms, it's a crude lobotomy of sorts. If I had to guess, I would say he was trying to keep them alive but compliant.' Dr Blake pulled up the next photo.

'What's that on their backs?'

Maggie's face turned red as she'd clearly 'forgotten' to share this detail with Kate.

'It's an infinity tattoo,' Dr Blake offered.

'And they both had one? That's a coincidence, isn't it?' Kate watched as Maggie looked at Dr Blake; the doctor turned away.

'What? What am I missing?' Kate glared at Maggie.

'We think the killer put those tattoos on the women. Family and friends confirmed that neither had any tattoos. It may be his signature.'

'For Christ's sake, Maggie. Why didn't you tell me this before?' Kate looked closer at the tattoo. 'He's marking them. Staking his claim. They are his ... forever.'

'I'm sorry, I couldn't tell you.' Maggie at least had the decency to look embarrassed.

'So that's why you asked me if I had any tattoos, is it?'

Maggie looked down at the floor. 'Yes. But we had our reasons—'

'Can we carry on, Fiona?' Kate cut Maggie off before her anger grew. She wished Maggie had trusted her more to share that detail.

'Some sedatives were found in both women, so at least we can hope that they didn't feel anything at the time. Kelsey Gilbey survived longer. Your killer's skills were better. She died of an infection but was alive at least a week or two. He was giving her antibiotics.'

'There's been some debate as to whether he may have a medical background. Is that what you're thinking?' Kate was wavering herself now that she was hearing more.

'He could've learned how to do this from anywhere – online or from a medical book. He may have dropped out of med school. There are numerous possibilities. I wouldn't just focus on someone who has medical expertise though, if you want my opinion.'

'Noted. What else do you think is important?' Maggie listened intently.

'There are some old contusions on each victim. I think they were initially restrained with a plastic tie or perhaps a rope – the markings suggest a mixture of the two. There was also some old bruising and cuts on their backs, which I believe may have come from being confined in a tight space. Maybe the boot of a car? The injuries could have been sustained from hits on their back from something within the boot.'

'I wondered that myself. How did he get them back to wherever he held them? A car boot makes sense for travel. Was there anything under their nails? Did they fight back?' Kate was firing off the questions in quick succession and tugged at her ear.

'The nails were meticulously cleaned. And a fresh coat of black nail polish applied just after death or possibly after he undertook his surgical procedure. If the women did fight back, there's nothing to show it.' Dr Blake showed some close-up shots of the hands and feet. The nails were a glossy black. She turned to the next photos and Kate flinched.

'Their eyes ...'

'Yes, when I removed the stitching, I found he had put in blue contact lenses.'

'Like my eyes.'

'There is a similarity, yes. Are you OK, Kate?'

'No. I ... can't breathe. I ... need to ...' She slumped to the floor.

Maggie raced over. Kate could see her but couldn't hear what she was saying. Everything was a blur.

Kate wasn't sure how much time had passed, but she was now seated in a room – no more pictures. But as she blinked, she could still see their eyes. Glassy, blue ... crying for help.

'How are you feeling now? You scared me there for a minute.' Maggie squeezed her hand.

Her throat was dry. 'Sorry. It just all became a little too much, too real. Can I have a glass of water?'

Maggie left her alone. Alone with her thoughts. There was no denying it now. She *was* the target. It was her stalker and Kate had no idea what his plans for her were.

Maggie came back in with a large glass of water. 'Here. Drink this. Let's talk it through. I don't want you having this on your mind all day.'

Kate couldn't share her real thoughts. She needed to process everything in her own way. 'I'm fine, I think it was just a shock to see how much they looked like me. But I think I can come up with a profile that will help focus the case. I also think that Dr Blake was right about medical knowledge. The leucotomies were crudely done. You can actually google and watch videos on how to do them – but I do think he may have some basic medical knowledge. You said he mentioned Dahmer to that reporter. Maybe that's where he found inspiration.' She tugged her ear. 'Leave it with me, and I'll get something together for you in the next day or so.'

'OK. I'll let DI Rutherford know. Do you want to come back to Stafford station with me?'

'No. I'll grab the train to Markston.'

Maggie's brow creased.

'Don't look at me like that. I'll be on a train full of people and Markston station is a ten-minute walk away when I get off ... in a busy public area. I'll text you when I get there if it makes you feel better.'

'No. Sorry. I'll get someone to drive you over there. In fact, I'm just going to call DI Rutherford, then I'll drive you there myself.'

Kate breathed a sigh of relief. She didn't want to be on her own.

'I'll pick you up after work as well. You ready?'

Kate stood and grabbed her bag. 'Yeah. Let's go.'

Chapter 61

Kate waved to Maggie and watched her leave. She waited a few moments before running up the stairs and heading to the ladies' room. She looked at her reflection in the mirror but all she saw was their faces. Glassy blues eyes. Silky black hair. She touched the mirror – she was them. They were her.

She grabbed the sink to keep her balance. Her head was spinning. In hindsight she shouldn't have asked to see the pictures, to hear what had happened. Every little detail spun in her mind like a web and she was the fly. Stuck. Struggling to break free. But who was the spider?

She was shaken out of her thoughts when someone walked into the bathroom and greeted her. A few token words and Kate left, going upstairs to her office.

She walked straight past those in the DAHU, giving a brief wave to whoever had shouted out hello before hiding behind her computer screen.

Deep breaths.

Kate knew she needed to place her mind elsewhere. The images flashing in her head would stop then. She slammed her hands down on her desk. *Stop! Get the fuck out of my head.*

'Kate. Are you OK?' She hadn't heard Mark knock or come into the room.

'Yeah. Sorry. Just frustrated with a project I'm working on.' *Please don't push it, Mark. Go. Just leave.*

'You've gone really pale. Are you sure you haven't picked up that bug that's been going around?'

'Maybe. I don't know. Come to think of it, I'm not feeling very well. I might just go and work from home.'

'If you can wait half an hour, I'll take you. I need to swing by Police HQ so I can drop you on my way?'

'No. That's OK. It's only fifteen minutes or so on the train.' She looked at her watch. 'If I leave now, I can catch the next one.' She grabbed her belongings and pushed past him. 'I'll ring DI Calleja and let him know. If anyone needs me, they can ring me on my mobile.'

She didn't wait for his reply, just ran down the stairs, and out into the fresh air. The train station was quiet at this time of the day – the train itself was empty and Kate sat back in the seat, gazing out of the window.

When she arrived at her destination, she paused and called DI Calleja to inform him she would be at Maggie's and available if anyone needed her. She felt like someone was watching her, but when she looked over her shoulder and around her, there was no one there.

Inside the house, Kate went to her room and got changed. She lay across her bed and closed her eyes. She nearly fell off the bed when she felt something brush across her leg.

It was Scrappy.

'Jaysus, Scraps. You frightened the life out of me.' She lay back for a moment as her anger mixed with fear. The killer was winning, but she wasn't through fighting. She stood and went to the closet. She pulled out the white paper and her markers. Taping the paper to the wall, she began writing.

1. *Obsessive behaviour: watches his 'targets', learns their habits, makes plans for when it's best to strike.*

2. *Unpredictable and dangerous: educated and professional which gives him power. No one would suspect him. May have a career or work in various professional capacities but probably doesn't socialize much.*

3. *Few or no real friends: keeps people at arm's length; may have difficulties forming friendships.*

4. *Organised in his planning: precise execution of finding, stalking, and then abducting his victims.*

5. *Stalking is often triggered by a life event that's difficult to cope with, e.g. breakup, firing, arrest, significant anniversary, illness or rejection. What has happened in his life to trigger his behaviour?*

Kate stood back and looked at what she'd written. She was determined to find him before he found her.

Chapter 62

'So how did it go with Dr Blake?' Nathan queried when Maggie arrived back.

'Can we go into your office?' Maggie looked around at her colleagues. It wasn't that she wanted to keep them out of the frame, but she needed to get things clear in her mind.

'Sure.' Nathan let Maggie lead the way. She sat down and took a breath. 'I'm worried I did the wrong thing today. You should have seen Kate's face, looking at the pictures and hearing what happened to those women. She crumbled.'

'Hang on, it was Kate's idea. How could you possibly have known how she would react?'

'I know, but you didn't see her. It's like the penny dropped and she knew she'd be next. I felt so helpless.' Maggie rubbed her knees. 'I shouldn't have made her go. I was being selfish. I thought if she saw the pictures, saw what he did to them, she would ... I don't know. Fuck, Nathan. I messed up big time.'

'Hey. Calm down. I played a part in this too, OK. I allowed it. I thought it would help her form a profile. No one forced her to go; it was her suggestion in the first place. Where is she now?'

'I dropped her at Markston.' Maggie then remembered that Kate said she would text her when she got up to the office. 'Hang on. Let me check my phone.' No text. 'Shit. I need to call

Kate. Two secs.' Maggie called her mobile, but it went straight to answerphone. 'Shit. Shit. Shit.' She called Markston Police Station; this was feeling a bit like déjà vu. Mark Fielding answered the phone.

'Mark. It's Maggie. Is Kate there? I can't reach her on her mobile.'

Actually, you just missed her. She left about twenty minutes ago. I think she has a bug. She was heading back to yours.'

'Did anyone take her, do you know?'

'I offered as I'm just on my way out to Police HQ, but she just left.'

'Fuck. Thanks, Mark.' It frustrated her that Kate wasn't taking her own personal safety seriously or even considering how her blasé attitude was affecting others ... well, affecting Maggie, to be exact. Maggie ended the call and dialled her landline.

Just when she was about to panic, a familiar voice answered the phone.

'Shit, Kate. Why didn't you let me know you were leaving work?'

'Sorry. Look, I feel like I'm a prisoner with all these check ins. First someone is stalking me and now I have to call you every time I leave a room. I can't do it.'

Her voice cracked.

'No, I'm the one who's sorry. I shouldn't have yelled. I'm just really concerned. You're right. I need to back off.' Maggie recalled the conversation she'd previously had with Nathan. She could be full-on and it wasn't helping the situation. 'I just panicked when you didn't answer your mobile. Your safety is more than just a job to me – you're my friend. Anyway, do you need anything brought back? My treat.'

Kate laughed and Maggie relaxed.

*'I know you mean well. All good here. In fact, I've been working
on a profile, something that might help when you have some
persons of interest in your sights. I'll show it to you when you're
back. Oh ...'*

Maggie heard some mumbling in the background. 'Is someone
there?'

*'Yes. Your brother just got in. We're all good now. I'm going to
go, OK?'*

Maggie steadied her voice. There was something there between
Andy and Kate. It unnerved her. 'Yeah. See you soon.'

The call ended and Maggie looked at Nathan. 'Do you mind
if I head off soon?'

'Actually, I do. Why? Is everything OK?' Nathan sat back in
his chair.

'Yeah, sorry. Of course I need to stay. I don't know what I was
thinking. Ignore me. Kate's fine and my brother is with her now,
so at least I know someone's around.'

Nathan eyed Maggie suspiciously. 'And there's nothing else
you want to tell me?'

'No. If we're through here, I'm going to go and speak with
Bethany to see if she's found anything on the social media
accounts she's been looking at.' Maggie saw Kat out of the corner
of her eye. 'Ah, there's Kat. She was interviewing the agency
manager. I'll check what he had to say too.'

'Sounds good. Keep me posted.'

'Kat! Do you have a few minutes to catch me up on your interview?'

'Yep. Not much to tell, really. The guy admits to perving on
Kelsey Gilbey and was worried if we kept asking questions his
wife would find out.'

274 *Noelle Holten*

'I knew there was something off with him. Can we add him to our persons of interest list?' Maggie held her hands out, waiting for Kat's response.

''Fraid not. He was at an anniversary dinner in London with his wife and then a show. Even had the ticket stubs in his wallet. He was at a conference in Sheffield when Tracy disappeared. Can you imagine all the slimy suited bastards there? I just confirmed it with the hotel. It was a week-long, team-building conference. Who does those things?' She shrugged.

'Damn. Thanks, Kat. Back to the drawing board then. Maybe Bethany had more luck with the social media profiles.' Maggie's excitement had quickly deflated, and if they didn't find something soon, Maggie feared she'd lose more than just her pride.

Chapter 63

Maggie went over to Bethany's desk and pulled out a chair to sit on. 'Have we found anything on the social media accounts?'

'Actually, something weird is going on with them. I can't find any new friends, as that's the first thing I would look for. But reading through some posts, it looks like someone has been liking and commenting on posts as if they were the profile owner.'

'Care to expand?' Maggie leaned in to have a look on the computer.

'Well, let's take Tracy Holloway's Facebook account first. When I scrolled back to around the time that we suspect the killer started stalking her, she has a few posts of places she regularly goes – which, by the way, is a big no-no, and more so with Tracy as she made her profile public. Absolutely no security whatsoever.'

Maggie shook her head. In this day and age, she would've thought people would be more careful about what they put on social media. This was why she hated it – her own Facebook account had often lain dormant for months and the posts she did put up generally revolved around cute pictures of Scrappy or news articles she found interesting.

Bethany continued. 'If we then look at a few posts from about a month before her abduction, you'll see there are some posts about not remembering posting or commenting on certain things. This could be our killer pretending to be her.'

'Whoa! A person can do that? I mean, I've heard of such things but mainly thought they were a myth.' Maggie's lack of understanding of social media showed just how little importance it played in her mind.

'Another thing of note, and a little out of the ordinary, is that there's no connection between our victims, either on social media or through what we know of them.'

'Why's that weird?' Maggie didn't understand the logic, but knew there would be a method to Bethany's work. Although Bethany was a PC, she took on a lot of the crime analyst's job. She seemed more at home behind the computer than in the field, so the team left her to it. However, now that they were short-staffed, she could be pulled at any time, so Maggie wanted to get as much work covered before this happened.

'I guess I would've expected some effort from the stalker to try and impose themselves in some way into the lives of the women he's taken an interest in. Perhaps they had some of the same friends or went to the same gym, but these women are definitely strangers to each other.'

'OK, but I'm still a little lost. We didn't expect them to be friends.'

'No. But you often find that fake profiles are made up, joint friends requested and, unfortunately, people aren't very savvy. They think they are and accept the friendship without question. That way, when the target receives a request, they find some common friends and that's it, the stalker is in.'

'That makes sense. Is there any other way they could do something like this but, let's say, less obviously?'

'Yeah, but they'd need access to the person's phone or computer. There's spyware technology that can be used to attain the real-time location of the target device and get a log for its past locations as well. Since the app runs in a stealth mode, it will let you track the device without being detected. It can also access the device's social media activity, key logs, call logs, contacts, photos, browser history, and more – all remotely.'

'Are you serious? I mean, I know there are ways that these things can be done because I've heard of parents putting apps on their kids' devices to GPS track them and stuff, but you could actually see texts, and everything? Holy shit! That's mental. So how would a person do this without the other person knowing?'

'Steal their phone, add the app, and then return the phone. It only takes minutes to set up for someone who's skilled in that kind of thing.'

'How would we know if this information was on our victims' devices?'

'We'd need the device to check. We've already checked both victims' laptops and tablets – there was nothing on there. These devices were located in their homes though, and our killer may know these people socially or through activities where they have close and regular contact with the person.'

An idea came to Maggie then. 'Has anyone checked Kate's phone for a spyware app?'

Bethany scrolled through the information log. 'No. It doesn't look like any checks have been done, and to be fair, we've been focusing on the murder victims, but I think you raise a valid point.'

'Leave it with me. I'm going to contact Kate and see if she'll be willing to have her phone scanned. Let's say there is an app on her phone. Would we be able to trace where it's being tracked from?'

'That will depend on a lot of variables, but it isn't impossible. Of course, that's way past my remit, so we'd have to pass that on to the forensic IT specialists, but I'm sure they would do a rush job given the circumstances.'

'Bethany, you've made my day.' Maggie slapped her on the back. 'We might be able to turn this around on our killer if my instincts are right.'

'How so?'

'I'm still working through some details in my head, but once I have, I'll let you know.'

Maggie returned to her desk and started to write down everything that was churning in her head. Could Kate's phone be the key? It may be the only thing they had to identify the killer's location.

Chapter 64

He threw his glass against the wall.

How can I make this work? I need her in my life.

The phone ringing pulled him out of his thoughts.

'Hello?'

'Oh, you're home. I was afraid you'd be at work and I'd have to leave one of those dreadful messages. Do you even get them? You never call back.'

'Yes, Mother. I get them. I'm just really busy. Is everything OK?' He rolled his eyes.

'Since you asked, no, everything is not OK. I need help. Why can't you come round and help me with the shopping? My arthritis has flared up and I can't do things by myself you know.'

He cringed at her moaning. 'You have a carer to help you with all that. I'm really busy, Mother. Anyway, I don't feel up to it.'

'Pffft. Too busy for your mother. After all I've done for you … It's not like you have any other family to look after, and you seem to be well enough to help everyone else. I gave birth to—'

'Enough!' He hadn't meant to raise his voice but sometimes he had no choice. 'I'll pop round this weekend, OK? Now, I really must go.'

He hung up before his mother could say anything further.

She demanded so much time. But that would change when Kate was here. She'd get all his attention and his mother would just have to accept that. His mother would love Kate. She was perfect.

He needed a plan. Now that Kate was staying at that police officer's house, he'd have to change his whole direction of getting her. He'd show his mother; he'd do things differently. Someone did love him.

He took his notebook from his drawer and scanned over the pages. Everything he knew about Kate was written in this book – her clothing size, the make-up she wore, her favourite food, even details about her cat. He couldn't always trust his memory lately.

Wait. He thought back to when Kate had moved into that police officer's house. He hadn't seen Kate take Salem with her in the car. That either meant she wasn't planning on staying for long or she'd left the feral fiend with a neighbour.

He'd find out. This could be exactly what he was looking for.

Chapter 65

Nathan stood at the front of the room and his stress could be felt in the atmosphere. 'Thank you all for coming at such short notice. I know it's getting late, but I think it's important with everything that's happened that we look at where we're at – we've been looking at things on an individual basis, but we need a joined-up approach. Bethany, can you talk us through the social media interrogation?'

Bethany stood and faced the room. 'I'm not going to bore you with all the specific details, but when I was going through Tracy's and Kelsey's social media profiles I noticed a few odd things. There were comments that noted unusual reactions to certain photos and, in each case, either Tracy or Kelsey denied any knowledge of making the offending remarks linked to their profile. When their laptops were searched, there was nothing of note; however, we now suspect that a spy app was downloaded onto the victims' phones which would effectively allow our killer to monitor and read everything that the phone owner did. In fact, the killer could have posed as the owner on various social media sites or via text message.'

'Bethany and I wondered if Kate's phone has also been compromised in this way. I've left Kate a message so we can check her phone ASAP. What we don't know is how Kate and these two women are connected – or even if they are connected at all. And we don't know how or when the killer got close enough to grab the phones, install the app, and return them without the women knowing. Bethany said it could take anywhere from ten to twenty minutes to download the app onto the phone.' Maggie nodded at Bethany to continue.

'That's right. Maybe they were all somewhere and they left their bags unattended?' She paused. 'Though, most people have their phones glued to their hands. I'm at a bit of a loss on that one.'

Nathan interjected. 'I'm not sure a connection is important, if I'm honest. Kate was his initial target months ago, but he never took any action with her. In fact, I think the two women were chosen almost as if they were test subjects. He tried his hand at making them compliant, then they died, which means he may well just go for Kate instead of another woman. We need her phone and I'm actually not very comfortable leaving her so vulnerable. I think he'll escalate and make his move sooner rather than later. We've seen it before. We may need to think about moving her somewhere safer.'

As much as Maggie enjoyed having Kate at her house, she knew her boss was right. 'Where do you suggest?'

'Leave the details to me. I'll have to speak with DI Rutherford, and the less the team know the better. Not that we don't trust you all, but we need to make sure that only the top brass know what's happening. Maggie, finish up the briefing and I'll let you all know what's happening when I can. I can't stress this enough – do not share any information outside of this room. Am I clear?'

There were a few grumbles from her colleagues – no one likes to be thought of as a leak – but they all nodded their understanding. Maggie waited for Nathan to leave.

'OK. Let's focus on those we've interviewed so far. Tracy's boyfriend, Joshua Hinks. We know they had an argument at the time she disappeared. Although his family confirmed his alibi, he also knew Kelsey Gilbey as he was a regular patron at the pub where she worked. We can't find any connection to Kate, but that doesn't mean one doesn't exist. For now, he remains a person of interest. Then we have Richard Patterson. Now, he made some strange references to the murders and has taken an unhealthy interest in the cases, according to his Probation Officer; however, there's no evidence that he left the hostel or has another property where he could hold these women. The bodies were disposed of in the middle of the night, so I personally think we can remove him from the list. His offences also have a sexual element to them and there is no evidence that the victims were sexually assaulted. What does everyone else think?'

'Hmmm. Just because no semen was found at the scene, doesn't mean he didn't masturbate and then get rid of that. I think we're jumping the gun if we remove him so soon. How do we know that he didn't figure out a way to get out of the hostel unseen – or remove his tag? I remember a case where the tag hadn't been fitted properly and the offender just pulled it off and on and went on their merry way committing burglaries. He was only caught when a fault in the ankle bracelet set off the box and when the tagging company came out, they found him climbing back in through the window,' one of the field officers offered.

'OK, maybe we leave him on the list and get someone to go back to check his tag as well as any blind spots in the building.

Good call. Right. Let's all go away and start piecing this puzzle together. I think we're probably closer than we realize.' Maggie clapped her hands together. She was trying to keep up staff morale and hoped her face didn't tell a different story.

Chapter 66

Maggie went over the unknown suspect's notes again and thought about the victims. She was struggling to make the connections, which was unusual. The personal aspect of the cases was obviously having more of an impact than she cared to admit. The killer always seemed to be one step ahead of them, almost as if he knew what they'd be looking for and then making sure no trace of his presence was found.

Think, Maggie! Think!

Bethany was waving a piece of paper. 'Just had a call come in. A female who thinks she may have some information. Do you want me to follow up on this?'

'Excellent. Is she coming in?' Maggie didn't want to get her hopes up but any new information could be the missing link they needed.

'Yeah. She'll be here during her lunch.'

'Great. I'll sit in with you, if you don't mind. I like hearing things first-hand.' Maggie was the first to admit she was a bit of a control freak. She knew her colleagues understood her need and way of working and she tried not to let that overpower her ability.

'I think it would be useful given what you know about the case.' Bethany smiled.

Maggie clocked the time she heard Bethany's phone ring, and once she got the thumbs up, she gathered her notebook. She'd leave Bethany to take the lead in the interview and only jump in if she felt her questions hadn't been addressed.

They made their way to the enquiry desk, and Maggie headed to the designated interview room while Bethany collected the witness. A few minutes later both walked into the room and Maggie smiled at the woman as she sat down across from them.

Bethany did the introductions and explained the purpose of the interview to the woman. 'Thanks for coming today. You mentioned on the phone that you might have some information for us?'

The woman tugged on the sleeve of her sweater. 'Uh ... yes. My friends think I'm overreacting and tried to discourage me from coming, but I just couldn't get it out of my head, so I thought I'd best leave it up to the experts to decide.'

'Couldn't get what out of your head?' Bethany softened her voice to put the witness at ease.

'Well, a few months ago I was in this pub. Not a fancy one or anything, but you know, like a Wetherspoons ... though I don't think it was one ...'

'Can I just stop you there for one moment? I can tell you're nervous. We don't have to rush through this, although I know you are on your lunch break. Let's just focus on the specifics and if we need further details about the location we can come back to that if there's time.'

The woman took a deep breath and appeared grateful for Bethany's words. 'Yes. Sorry. I ramble when I'm nervous. I met someone at the pub. This random guy just approached me and then offered to buy me a drink. I've read so much about that date rape drug that I prefer to buy my own now, so I turned him down.' She took a sip of water. 'So anyway. He didn't pay any attention to that and bought me one anyway; he was weird though. Despite being overconfident in some respects, he seemed totally out of place in others.'

This interested Maggie, although it was beginning to sound like the story told by the witness who'd come forward about Charlie and he'd been cleared from their enquiry.

'I mean, he sat waaaaay too close. No sense of personal space at all. Then he started asking me these strange questions. Like, did I believe in fate. And did I think it was possible for people to be together forever. I mean, what the hell kind of pick-up line is that?'

Both Bethany and Maggie nodded at the woman. The questions were a little too much for a first-time meeting.

'How would you describe this guy? Did you notice any distinguishing features?'

'Hmm. I think he was average height though I can't be sure. His hair could have been dark blond, or maybe light brown. Sorry.' She shrugged. 'He was an older guy – maybe late forties. That's not much help to you, is it? I have to be honest, I tried to avoid eye contact in case he thought I was encouraging him, so I spent a lot of the time looking at my watch or out of the window, hoping my friends would arrive and he'd leave me alone.'

'No problem. We appreciate it was a few months ago, but any detail you can remember would be worth recalling.'

'He did have a tattoo on his left wrist. Some squiggly mark. Looked like the "and" symbol, I think. I remember it because I thought it was pretty strange.'

Maggie scribbled something on a piece of paper and passed it to the woman. 'Could it have been this do you think?'

'Um ... maybe. But I'm not too sure. I only saw it briefly. What does that even mean?' Her eyebrows furrowed.

Maggie looked at Bethany and then turned back to the witness, they didn't want to give too much away. 'It could be nothing. Is there anything else you can think of?'

'When my friends arrived, he still hovered about but I think he got the message when I ignored him. I did notice him staring at me throughout the night. And before he left my table, he reached out and tried to touch my hair.'

'What did you do?' Maggie noted the woman's long black hair.

'I just leaned back and shifted over in my seat. He really was pretty bad at reading signals!' She rolled her eyes.

'Sounds like it. So why did he stay in your mind after all this time?' Bethany shifted in her seat.

'Oh! That's the weirdest part of it all. I'd been back to the place a few times after that and saw him there, but thankfully he didn't notice me. Probably because he spent most of his time at the bar, chatting up the barmaid – then I saw that she was murdered.'

Chapter 67

'Can you repeat that, please?' Bethany looked how Maggie felt – in shock. Both their jaws were open.

'Yeah. The barmaid who's been on the news recently. She worked at the pub I was talking about. I mean, I don't go all the time, but she was there fairly regularly. That's why I called you guys.'

'You probably should have started with that part.' Bethany smiled.

'I guess you're right. I just wanted to make sure I got everything in.'

Maggie interrupted. 'Can you tell us the name of the pub and its location? You said you've seen the guy there a few times? How often do you go to that particular pub?'

'It's The Smith's Forge in Markston, not far from the train station. My friends and I go on a Saturday mainly, but sometimes I'll stop off there with my colleagues during the week. Maybe three or four times a month. I definitely saw this guy chatting to the barmaid. She didn't look too bothered by him, but then again, she'd want a tip so she wouldn't be nasty, would she?'

'Thanks, you've been a big help. Can you think of anything else that might be important?'

'Um.' The woman bit her lip. 'No. I don't think so.'

Maggie pulled out a card and handed it to the woman. 'Here's my card. If you do think of something, anything, no matter how big or small, give me a call.'

Bethany ended the interview and escorted the woman out. She returned to the room a few minutes later and couldn't hide her disbelief.

'Holy shit. We need to see if that pub has CCTV. Was that checked at the time when we found out where she worked?' Bethany sat down.

'I don't think that's the pub we checked out. Remember, she was agency so could have worked at a few different pubs. Given this was a few months ago, the agency she's signed up to probably only provided us with the last and most recent place she worked. I could kick myself for not asking how long she'd been there. At least it confirms one thing ...'

'What's that?'

'He spends a long time choosing and then stalking his victims. We should go further back into Tracy Holloway's history too ... and Kate's.'

Chapter 68

While Bethany went out to interview the pub owner at The Smith's Forge and speak to the agency about the other places where Kelsey Gilbey had worked, Maggie did some digging of her own. After speaking with DI Rutherford, she waited for Human Resources to send over details about Kate's previous work history. It felt wrong; she'd wanted to go directly to Kate and ask the questions, but DI Rutherford and Nathan made it clear that it was not an option.

Her emailed pinged and she opened the message. Kate's work history was limited. She'd had a few jobs in Galway in her youth, which she had noted but hadn't gone into details on – the basics, various retail and fast-food restaurants. She then went to university in Dublin and ended up in London to start her career in criminal psychology. But there appeared to be a gap in Kate's history of a few months.

'Nathan! Can I get your opinion on something?' Maggie called across to him.

Nathan strolled over to her desk. 'Sure. What's up?'

'I've got hold of Kate's CV. I'm hoping to see if we can find anything in her work background where she may have come across her stalker, and our possible killer.'

'OK. Have you found something?' He leaned forward.

'I'm not sure. Look here.' Maggie pointed to her screen. 'There seems to be a gap in her history. Between this job at the university and the freelance consulting she takes a break and it notes that she left her previous employment due to personal reasons and nothing else. Knowing what we do about Kate, does that seem a bit … unusual?'

'Hmmm. I see your point. Maybe there was a family issue? Has Kate ever mentioned anything like that to you?'

'No, that's the thing. But I guess a lot of the time when we talk it's about work stuff. Maybe I don't know her as well as I thought I did. How would we find out more about that? Do you think there may be more information in her personnel file?'

'Even if there were, I don't think Human Resources would share that information with you. It's one thing to share a CV but you know we can't look up personnel records for other reasons, despite the current situation.'

'Damn. Do you think I should just come out and ask her? If I explain that it has to do with the case and looking at her background for possible links?'

'Won't she know that you've looked at her personnel file? And I thought the DI didn't want to push Kate on anything without due cause.'

'Perhaps I can slip it into casual conversation? It could be important to the case, don't you think? I'm at a loss here and, if I'm honest, I feel a bit like a shit officer and an even worse friend.'

'I'm not saying you're wrong, but if it turns out to be nothing you could ruin any trust that Kate has in you. Is that something you're prepared to risk?'

'If it means saving her life from a messed-up killer … then yes, I'll take that risk.'

Nathan shrugged and started to walk back to his office. He looked over his shoulder to make a final point. 'Before you do any of that, have you contacted the police in London to see if Kate made any previous complaints? That one call could save your friendship as well as a lot of wasted time dancing around the situation.'

'And this is why you're the boss! I'm sure I would've eventually thought of that, you know.' Maggie was missing things she should have picked up earlier, because once again her personal feelings were affecting her judgement.

'I'm sure you would. Now, why are you wasting time still talking to me?' A crooked smile on his face was directed her way. Maggie knew he would be taking pleasure in this and she wouldn't give him the satisfaction.

'Dialling now ... sir.' She saluted as he closed the door to his office.

Chapter 69

A half an hour later, Maggie hung up the phone with more questions than answers. She had spoken to a detective in London and learned that Kate had indeed made some complaints about nuisance calls, but as she'd had no real information and hadn't felt threatened by them, the matter had not been pursued. A frustrating and familiar response when the police had no other option.

Why didn't she mention this to us, or me? Especially given the situation.

When Maggie compared the dates that had been given, they tallied up with the gaps in Kate's work history but the police in London didn't have anything further to offer on that front. The only way she'd get to the bottom of things would be to speak with Kate herself. Maggie didn't want to pressure her friend. If anything came up from the conversation, she could always try and delve a bit deeper by dropping the case into conversation. It was sneaky, but Maggie knew it might be her only way to get Kate to open up.

What she was beginning to realize was the strong possibility that the stalker had connected with his victims in some way prior to escalating to abduction and murder. Although they still didn't know what the trigger was, she suspected it was something recent – and if he was masking his behaviour in friendship, Kate may remember someone who fit that profile. Kate could be the key to unlocking the mystery and if the memories were buried deep, she may need someone to help bring them to the surface.

Maggie dialled Kate's direct extension at Markston Police Station and scrolled through her emails as she waited.

'Dr Maloney speaking. How can I help?'

'Hi. It's Maggie. I just wondered if you had any plans after work? I thought it might be nice to take a bit of a breather away from everything and grab some dinner out this evening. What do you think?'

'Oh, OK. Sounds wonderful. Should I catch the train to Stafford when I'm done? I may be here until about 6pm or so. I've got a few things I'd like to finish before heading out.'

'Actually, why don't I meet you at Markston? I've heard of a new restaurant there that I'd like to try out. This is the perfect excuse.'

'That's grand. I'll see you later.'

Maggie wasn't sure how Kate would take the conversation and hoped it didn't make things awkward. She'd soon find out.

Chapter 70

Maggie got off the train at Markston and headed for the police station. On arrival, she said hello to a few of her colleagues before making her way up to the DAHU offices on the second floor. She was out of breath again by the time she reached the top and promised herself she'd start doing more exercise at the gym in the police station.

The DAHU office was quiet as everyone seemed to have their heads down working. 'Hey guys. How are you?' She waved. PC Pete Reynolds gave a wave back before returning to his telephone call.

PC Mark Fielding stood and walked towards her. He gave her a hug. 'Nice to see you! You just missed Lucy.'

'Ah bugger. That's too bad, I'd like to catch up with her at some point. I take it Kate's in her office?'

'Yeah. She's just working on a profile of one of our domestic abuse nominals. I won't bore you with the details but he's a nasty piece of work.' Mark shook his head.

'I'd better not disturb her then. Is DI Calleja in by any chance?'

'I think so. Do you want me to get you a drink? I'll ring through and see if he's free.'

'No thanks. If he's not free, I'll just grab one of the empty desks and catch up on some emails.'

Mark returned to his desk and called through to DI Calleja. Giving Maggie the thumbs up, she whispered, 'thank you' and left him to it. Maggie passed Kate's office as she wandered down the hall, and when she peered through the window, she saw that Kate was in the zone. She didn't even look up from her computer.

Maggie tapped on DI Calleja's door.

'Come in'

'Hi, sir. How are you?'

'Great to see you again. You've been a bit of a stranger since you left here.' He smiled and Maggie knew he was teasing.

'Unfortunately, we have some nasty murders at the moment. Keeps us all busy.' Maggie winked.

'Yes. I've kept my eye on those … for obvious reasons.' Maggie knew the meaning behind his words. 'Have there been any further developments?'

'I'm afraid not, sir. Do you mind if I have a seat and ask you a few questions?' He gestured for Maggie to sit. 'I'm not sure if you can help me, but I just wondered if you knew about any issues Kate may have had in London before she moved here – either personally or at a previous employment?'

He scratched his head. 'I can't recall anything. Have you contacted HR?'

'Yes, but they haven't been able to share. I'll be asking Kate, obviously, but I need to be discreet to avoid causing any undue stress when it could be nothing at all.'

'Why *are* you asking? I'm assuming this has something to do with that stalker?' DI Calleja looked at Maggie intently.

'We think that the killer has been stalking his victims for some time, including Kate. He may even know them on some level and since he's escalated to murder, we suspect there has been a recent event that may have triggered his behaviour. As we can't speak to Tracy Holloway or Kelsey Gilbey, Kate may know something and not even realize it.'

'Interesting theory. Let me make some calls and see if I can find out anything. I'll be in touch.' Maggie got the impression that she was being dismissed and thanked the DI for his assistance and discretion, closing his door behind her.

She noticed Kate's door was open and headed towards her office. Tapping on the door frame, she looked in. The office was empty. She looked around but Kate wasn't in view. She walked into her office and over to the desk. She glanced at the papers but nothing caught her eye.

'DC Jamieson, you won't find anything of interest there.' Maggie nearly jumped out of her skin as she turned and saw Kate in the doorway, smiling.

'Christ almighty! My heart is racing.' Maggie grabbed her chest.

'Well you shouldn't be snooping.' Her lips curled and her shoulders shook.

'I wasn't. I swear ...' She stopped herself once Kate burst out laughing. 'OK, you got me. Are you nearly ready to go?'

'I'll just pack up and then we can make a move.' Maggie sat as Kate went back to her desk, put her notes away and logged off her computer.

They walked through the main office and said goodbye to the remaining staff. Maggie tried to keep the conversation as casual as possible, hoping Kate wouldn't see through her. Time would tell.

Chapter 71

'If the food isn't to your liking, we can always go somewhere else. I just thought it would make a nice change.'

'Looks lovely to me. I know I'm a creature of habit, but it's nice to experiment every once in a while,' Kate answered.

They were pleasantly surprised by the interior as they entered the eatery and followed an overly friendly waitress to their seats. 'So far, so good. Should we get some drinks before we order?' Maggie sat.

'Oh yes. A white wine would go down nicely just now. Let's order a bottle.' Kate opened the menu.

Maggie ordered a bottle of a reasonably priced pinot as well as a jug of iced water. She had hardly eaten today and didn't want the wine to go straight to her head. They looked over the menu in silence, and once the waitress returned with their drinks, they both ordered a pasta dish and a salad to start.

'We're two peas in a pod, aren't we?' Kate smiled as she sipped her wine.

'Ha! Both as stubborn as each other, that's for sure.' Maggie wanted to start the conversation on a light note. 'I realized that we've been working together for nearly a year now and I hardly know anything about the time before you came to Staffordshire.'

Kate's left eyebrow rose. 'Well, there's not much to tell. You know I have my PhD in criminal psychology. I was born and raised in Galway, and I moved to London so I could finish my degree and secure a job in the field. I love the colour black, my cat, and candles. That's me in a nutshell.'

'What exactly did you do in London ... work-wise, I mean.'

'Once I finished university, I did some lecturing. I also registered with a consulting firm down there in the hope of securing some temporary work. A few jobs came through that, but ...' Kate coughed and took a sip of her water, 'I realized the various jobs weren't my thing and just continued with the lectures until I saw the job in Markston come up. I'd had my fill of London by that time and needed a change.'

As soon as Maggie had heard that Kate was registered with an agency, she wanted to know more. It might be that the killer had connected with Kate a lot earlier than they realized.

'I've only visited London a few times, but I've heard it can be quite a lonely place to live.'

'Really? That certainly wasn't my experience. I guess it depends on how much you immerse yourself in things and how comfortable you are being by yourself,' Kate offered.

Maggie could see that Kate wasn't going to give up anything. In fact, she wondered if Kate had realized that she was fishing. Maggie probably shouldn't have underestimated her or been so confident in her own abilities.

The meal arrived and Maggie thought it would be best to stick to small talk until they had finished.

Forty minutes later, their plates were cleared and Maggie poured them each another glass of wine.

'What has this evening really been about?' Kate leaned back as she placed her napkin on the table.

Maggie's eyes widened. 'Sorry? What do you mean?' *Shit*. She'd been caught out.

'Look, I hope you don't mind, but the other day your brother mentioned to me that you're bisexual. I really like you, Maggie, but we can only be friends.'

Maggie spat out the wine that she'd just gulped onto the table. Picking up her napkin and dabbing the puddle, she was at a loss for words. 'Oh crap. Sorry. I didn't mean to do that, but you caught me off-guard. Did you ... did you think this was a date?'

'Bugger. I was trying to be sensitive to your privacy. Have I got it wrong then? It's just with you asking me about my past and the nice meal ... well, I put two and two together and obviously got five.' Kate's face reddened.

Maggie was at a loss for words. She hadn't known that Andy had spoken to Kate about her private life, but she'd be asking him why and how that bit of conversation had come about. Now she felt she had to explain something so Kate wouldn't find out her real reason for bringing her here. At least now she knew where she stood and tried to rescue the situation with a bit of humour. 'Don't worry, you're not my type.' She was relieved when Kate smiled and her face returned to her normal colour. 'I didn't know you and my brother were so close.'

'Oh, I wouldn't say we are. We just happened to stumble on a conversation about relationships and I was curious whether you were in one because you seem to work so much – when I asked about boyfriends, thinking maybe you were in a relationship with another officer as that's often the case in professions like yours, that's when he told me that you were bisexual and as far as he was aware you weren't seeing anyone. The alcohol may have loosened his lips at the time.'

'Well, I would've been more than happy to chat to you and answer your questions, so don't feel bad. Now that you know about my background, why don't you tell me about yours ...' Little did Kate know, but she'd given Maggie the perfect way to delve a bit deeper. Andy may have done her a favour after all.

Chapter 72

Kate was embarrassed by her assumption. She hoped her face wasn't still as red as it felt and she brushed her hair forward to hide behind it. 'I really do know how to put my foot in it, don't I?'

'Seriously, don't worry about it. I'm not embarrassed by my sexuality; I just would rather not make it public knowledge. I'm not defined by who I'm attracted to and, if I'm honest, it still confuses *me* no end. But I'd rather have told you myself.' Maggie shrugged and Kate could understand her feelings.

'Well, if it's any consolation, I think any relationship is confusing as well as the emotions that go with them. I'm usually quite blind to those things.'

Maggie nodded and Kate wasn't sure whether that was because she felt the same or because Maggie had had a crush on her and she was oblivious to the signs. She had embarrassed herself enough this evening so she didn't ask for clarification.

'So now that you have the dirt on me,' Maggie swilled the wine in her glass. 'It's your turn to spill. Love of your life? Weirdos? Never-going-to-happens?'

'Ha! I guess it's only fair.' Kate shifted in her seat. She wasn't one to open up easily but then again, neither was Maggie. It'd be nice to have someone to chat to about things. 'I've never been married or come even close. I've had a few relationships, both back home and in London, but nothing since I moved to Staffordshire. I've also had my fair share of weirdos, but I think most people have.'

'Interesting. Tell me more about the weirdos. I'm always curious about those things. Unless it's too awkward to talk about.'

Maggie must have noticed her discomfort. 'Oh, you know how it is. Guys who won't take no for an answer or who are into things that you're not. I love my look, but I think it can give people an impression of me that just isn't true. Do you know what I mean?'

'Definitely. I've seen it happen before. Can't say that's ever happened to me, though I have had a few people misunderstand my intentions. It can make things messy. That could be why I keep things quiet about myself. It can work against you though. I knew this guy once who I liked as a friend but he just didn't get it. It wasn't because he was a bloke either, I just didn't fancy him. He kept calling me and in the end, I just had to block his number and threaten him with harassment if he carried on.'

'I've had that before. I don't even know who the guy was. He'd call from a number that couldn't be traced and play old music in the background. I reported it to the police, but they couldn't really do anything about it.'

'Wow. Sounds a bit scary. I guess the recent events have brought all that up again?'

'To be honest, I hadn't really thought about it much. At the time, it really affected me. I was working at various temporary jobs through the consultancy firm I mentioned earlier and I was a bit homesick, if I'm honest. I had to take a few months off; the university were great and let me use the time for research on a project I was involved in. I never went back to temporary work and of course I was lucky enough to get the job at the DAHU, so it was a new start.'

'Shit. Sounds like it really did a number on you. If you ever need to talk, you know I'm here for you, right?'

'I'd rather just leave that behind me now. Ironic right? Given that we have someone killing women and dressing them up like me. I guess I'm just trying to keep things together. I went into a really dark place; my anxiety was through the roof. I don't want to go back there ...' A thought occurred to her then and she looked Maggie in the eyes. 'You knew all this though, didn't you? That's why you brought me here. You think there's some connection between what happened in London and what's going on now.' Kate tugged on her earlobe.

'The thought did cross my mind. I had some idea that something had happened. I think there may be a connection with temp agencies, but I'm not one hundred per cent sure yet, so ...'

Kate pushed her chair back and the metal screeched on the floor. 'I wish you'd been honest with me. You could have just asked.' She stood and didn't know whether she was shaking from fear or anger.

'Hang on. I'm sorry. I didn't want to upset you if there was no lead to go on. And I actually enjoyed getting to know a bit more about you.' Maggie pointed to the chair and Kate softened and sat back down.

'I appreciate the apology but I've been hurt by so-called friends in the past. I don't like people, especially my friends, going behind my back. I get that you were doing it with the best intentions, but there's really no need to go behind my back again.' Kate had no time for drama; she'd had enough of it on her plate and, if she was honest with herself, she had hoped that her friendship with Maggie would progress to something more than talking about work every time they met. It would have been nice to have a female companion to confide in outside of work. Maybe she misjudged Maggie.

Maggie's shoulders slumped. 'Noted. Shall we finish these drinks and just go then? Or do you want to talk?'

'I've said all that I'm going to say on the matter. However, I think you might be on to something with the agency connection. Perhaps our guy works at or is registered with an agency. It can't be a coincidence that the two women were also temps, can it? But that wouldn't explain how he would know me.'

'I can think of two possibilities. Your nuisance caller from London is our killer and followed you once you left the consultancy firm. He may have then registered with an agency up here and happened upon his victims. Or …'

'Or what?' Kate felt the goose bumps rise up on her arms.

'Or he's agency staff and works with you.'

'What? A police officer? Someone at the DAHU?' Kate's breaths shortened.

'No. We don't have any agency police officers, but we do have some agency admin staff. I think we need to look more closely at who those people are.'

Chapter 73

Maggie didn't get much sleep after she and Kate returned home, and when she saw Kate the next morning, the black circles under her eyes weren't hidden by the make-up. Andy had a few days off work so didn't need the car, and Maggie was grateful as she felt more comfortable driving Kate to and from work, especially when she now had potential colleagues to look into with regard to the case. Maggie didn't want to think the worst of people she worked with, but if it was someone involved with the case, the implications would be astronomical.

Kate had been quiet on the way to Markston. Maggie would ask Nathan or DI Rutherford to speak with DI Calleja and keep an extra eye on her. It would be so easy to assume that Kate was handling the situation, but her mood and behaviour towards Maggie, as if they were strangers, told a different story. A revelation that Kate may work with a killer would no doubt be making her feel more vulnerable. Her job should be somewhere she felt safe and secure.

The first thing Maggie did when she got into the office was speak to Nathan and relay the conversation from the night before.

'I'm not sure what to say. That's serious shit if it's one of our own.' He ran his hands through his hair. Maggie could see the strain on his face.

'I know. But it also makes sense. In fact, I'm not sure why we didn't look at this angle before.' Truth was, Maggie was so wrapped up in her emotions and worrying about her friend, she'd failed to pick up on the simplest clues and that was messing with her head right now. 'The only problem is, we'd need to get the details from the firm Kate was registered with in London. How forthcoming do you think they're going to be?'

'Leave that to me. In the meantime, could you cross-reference new agency staff that started around the same time that Kate did? If we think he followed her from London, he will have started around the same time or shortly after. We could give two months leeway either side of her start date at the DAHU. Remove the women off the list and see what we're left with. Are you OK? I'd have thought you would have picked that up before any of us.'

'Of course, I should have and I will from now on.' She looked away, embarrassed that her superior saw her failings so quickly. 'I'll see if Bethany can get the ball rolling on that. Are we including other agencies? Ones we work closely with, as I don't think we should limit ourselves to police staff. My gut tells me that whoever we're looking for may know Kate in a professional capacity, but not so close that they'd get caught. Given the DAHU is a multi-agency team, it might be worth checking out Social Care, Probation, the drug and alcohol services ...' Maggie paused while an idea festered in her head.

'What is it? Your brows have gone all funny.' Nathan swirled his finger around her face.

'I don't know yet. I was just wondering about the nature of the victims' injuries. I know Dr Blake said that the killer wouldn't necessarily have or even need medical knowledge to undertake what they did to the bodies, but ...'

'Spit it out, will you!' Nathan's patience was growing thin, but Maggie didn't want to put an idea in his head that could be completely unfounded.

'I'm just recalling a few weeks ago when we found Tracy Holloway and I called Dr Blake's office. It took ages and she finally answered the call herself because she said she had a lot of inexperienced agency staff working in the forensics team.'

'Well we'll have to include them too as they worked closely with the DAHU when those domestic abusers were being murdered.' He looked at his watch. 'I've got to go now. I'll have DI Rutherford speak to DI Calleja and also reach out to one of my London contacts to help with the agency info down south.'

Maggie nodded and was just about to leave Nathan's office when he called out to her. 'Don't overstep the mark with anyone, OK? I know exactly what you can be like when you get an idea in your head, but right now, we still need everyone onside. We have to tread really carefully and keep this on a need-to-know basis. Dr Blake is still pissed off about what happened with Charlie.'

She was about to protest, but that would just prove her boss right, so instead she gave him a thumbs up and trudged back to her desk. She quickly wrote out all the departments that were linked to the DAHU and had agency staff on a regular basis. She tore off the paper, and walked over to Bethany's desk.

'This could prove to be a major task, so if you need to use the analyst or want to pass it on, let me know but it's crucial we get as much detail as possible while trying to keep things under the radar. Do you think you can do it?'

Bethany read the paperwork and nodded. 'Yeah, I can do this, but it could take a day or two to get it all together. It'd help if I had something more to narrow things down ... Wait, I can contact HR for some things. Leave it with me.' Bethany turned to her keyboard and made a start.

Maggie squeezed her shoulder. 'You're a star. I may be pushing it but is there any chance you can get it back to me by tomorrow?'

'You're joking, right? You do realize there could be hundreds of people given that Kate's been here well over a year. I was being more than generous with two days and now I think about it, it could be even longer.'

Maggie held her hands up in defeat. 'I was only asking. We need that information, but I get that it's a mammoth task, so as soon as possible will be great.' She didn't want to think about what could happen until then or she may lose her shit. Maggie smiled. She felt her confidence returning. She'd need that now more than ever if they were going to catch the killer before he chose his next living doll.

Chapter 74

'Maggie. Can I see you for a second?' Nathan called out from his office.

She'd been staring at her computer screen for what seemed like hours so the break would be welcome. There was a sound of urgency in his voice. She stood, gave her legs a quick stretch and headed to his office. Maggie tapped on the door and he gestured for her to enter.

'You might want to sit for this.' He pointed at the chair.

It must be serious.

Maggie waited for Nathan to continue. 'I called my contacts in London, like we spoke about. Turns out they have an unsolved murder dating back to 2016 of a young woman who was first reported missing in February of that year. About six months after her disappearance, her body was found in a park, dressed in a white top, black skirt and combat boots, all believed to be her own attire. The post-mortem found that her injuries were similar to someone who had undergone a severe head trauma. Does this sound familiar?'

Maggie gasped. 'We've been wrong in terms of escalation. He has killed before. By the sounds of it though, everyone else that follows has been modelled after her. She must have been the first.'

'Yes. Her name was Catharine but everyone called her Cate. She bears a strong resemblance to Dr Moloney and it may be why he initially started stalking her. We have to find out how he knew or came across her in London though, and we need to know more about Catharine's background.'

Maggie stood. 'I'll get onto that right now. Excellent intel, boss.' She raced out of the room and back to her desk. She had a feeling that today would be one she'd spend very much glued to her computer.

Maggie tapped her pen on the desk while she waited to be put through to Nathan's police contact in London. A man finally came on the line, identified himself and asked how he could help.

'Hi. This is DC Maggie Jamieson from the Major and Organised Crime Department in Staffordshire. I understand you spoke to DS Nathan Wright earlier and advised him of a missing woman who later turned up murdered in your area back in 2016.'

'Yes. I've heard a bit about your cases and, I have to say, it sounds way too coincidental for them not to be connected. What do you need from me?'

'Ideally, if you can send me anything related to any suspects, persons of interest, the pathologist's report and any background information on Catharine, that would be great.' Maggie gave him her email details, thanked him and hung up the phone.

When her emailed pinged she quickly opened the information and her heart jumped in her chest when she saw the picture of Catharine Hill. They say that every person has a doppelganger and Catharine was Kate's. Reading over the notes she clocked that Catharine had been a student at the University of London just before she was abducted and murdered. Next she looked over the suspect and persons-of-interest list, but, similar to her case, it looked like they had no viable leads, although two or three people had been identified as probable suspects – young men with whom Catharine had been in a relationship.

'Bethany, can I email you over a list to cross-reference with the ones you're going through?'

'Sure. Where did they come from?'

'There was a case in London, Catharine Hill. She was abducted and murdered in 2016. Come and have a look at her picture.' Maggie waved her over.

Bethany jogged across the room and looked at Maggie's computer screen. Maggie heard the intake of breath.

'Oh my god. If I didn't know better, I would say that was Kate.'

'I know, right? The resemblance is uncanny. I can't help but think there must be a connection. Do the murders here and stalking all start from this?'

'I'll split the list with our analyst so we can get through it quicker and I'll come back to you if we find any matches.'

'Thanks.' Maggie returned to her computer screen and before she realized it, she had started typing an email to Kate. She wanted to know if perhaps they'd been looking at things all wrong. They all believed that something recent had happened which had caused the stalker to turn killer, but what if Catharine was the key and an anniversary or special date was the trigger?

Maggie wanted Kate to recommend someone to discuss the profile. Although it might result in a few arguments and hurt feelings, she knew that Kate would understand eventually. With all the previous scrutiny Maggie's team had been under with the Bill Raven case, any stray from protocol would have DI Rutherford breathing down her neck and put Nathan in an awkward position.

The curt response from Kate confirmed her fears:

I've spoken to a colleague from London who advised she would be able to assist.

Send her the details and she'll put together something for you.

She hated that Kate felt left out of the investigation, but once they caught the killer, Maggie knew Kate would come back to her old self. Putting her personal feelings aside, she began collating the information for the profiler and hoped that the London case held the key they so desperately needed.

Chapter 75

Maggie arrived home; it had been a long and tiring day. The greeting from Kate had left her feeling even worse than she had earlier. She was still waiting for the profiler to get back to her, and every time her phone pinged, Maggie hoped it was an email.

'What time does your brother get home?' There was no smile on Kate's face. She just stared through Maggie.

'Why do you want to know that?' Maggie rubbed her hands. *Was I too sharp in my answer?* The last thing she wanted to do was make Kate feel even worse. She had enough on her plate to deal with.

'Oh, I didn't realize it was a sore spot. I just was planning on making dinner and wondered whether it should be for two or three. Sorry if I touched a nerve; it's not like I asked you to tell me about the case.' She turned her back on Maggie and headed back to the kitchen, but Maggie followed, gently grabbed her arm and spun her around to face her.

'Hang on. Look, you haven't touched a nerve. I shouldn't have snapped. I know you're angry with me and I totally understand that, so I guess I was responding to your anger. I have no idea what Andy's schedule is these days. I can text him if you want?'

Maggie combed her fingers through her hair. She needed to get a grip or she risked pushing Kate away.

'It's fine. I can see you're busy. Just give me his number and I'll drop him a text.'

Shit. 'Sure.' She picked up her mobile, found his number and read it out to Kate. Maggie went into the living room, and took out her notes to distract herself. When she heard giggles from the kitchen, her curiosity was piqued. She went to the kitchen on the guise of getting a drink.

Kate's back was to her.

Is Kate flirting with my brother?

'Ahem.' She made her presence known and pointed to the kettle mouthing 'do you want a cup?'

Kate nodded. 'OK. I'll save you some and leave it in the oven. See you later.' She smiled as she ended the call. 'Your brother is pretty funny.'

'Really? I hadn't noticed.' Maggie shrugged.

'Are you sure you're OK, Maggie? I feel like I've done something to piss you off and I'd rather we talk about it than let it fester.'

'Huh?' *Was Kate being serious?* As childish as it was, Maggie was only responding to Kate's cues and when her brow furrowed, Maggie decided it was time to call her out on it. 'You're the one who's been off with me, and before you get defensive, I totally understand you want to be involved in the case, but you need to see it from my perspective. My hands are tied; we risk compromising everything we've done so far if we get you involved. In fact I've probably already told you too much, but you've done nothing wrong, OK? I'm just feeling a bit pressured and I sometimes forget to deal with those feelings.'

'Projecting then?' Kate cocked her head and Maggie was surprised there was no apology forthcoming.

'Yeah. Sorry.' She smiled and handed Kate a mug of tea. Sometimes you had to choose your battles, and this wasn't one of those times.

'As long as you're OK ... *we're* OK. Let's leave it at that for now. Now shoo! I have a culinary masterpiece to prepare.' She motioned for Maggie to leave her to get on with making dinner.

'Sounds great! What are we having?'

'Macaroni and cheese.' They both burst out laughing, though Maggie noticed it seemed forced from Kate. At this point she'd take what she could get.

Chapter 76

The conversation between Maggie and Kate at dinner was stilted. Kate swirled her dinner around the plate while Maggie couldn't help fidgeting with her napkin. When Andy came home, they were finishing up and although Kate's mood had improved, Maggie couldn't help but feel that Kate was purposely not including her. Her brother was being overly friendly and Maggie began to wonder whether there was something more going on between the two of them. It was none of her business, but Andy knew how Maggie felt about Kate. When she saw him touch Kate's hand as he passed his plate for a second helping, she lost it.

Her chair screeched on the floor as she pushed it back and picked up her glass of wine, taking it into the living room. She turned on the TV and raised the volume up louder than she normally would. She knew she was behaving like a stroppy child, but Maggie didn't want to hear them talking. When they joined her twenty minutes later, she was outwardly polite though her anger simmered insider her. She'd thought her brother was better than that. Knowing her feelings for Kate yet openly flirting with her right in front of Maggie. Wasn't there some sort of sibling code, even if the feelings were not reciprocated?

When Kate had gone to bed, she took her brother outside

and let her feelings be known. He was lucky she hadn't punched him the way she had when they were kids and he'd pissed her off.

Andy had tried to calm things down. 'I'm sorry, Maggie. I don't know what the big deal is though. It's not like she was ever going to go out with you, you know that. Kate said she talked to you.'

'Fuck off, Andy. I see now why you told her about me. Trying to get in for yourself, were you?' She shoved him and he grabbed her wrists. Not tightly, just enough to stop her from hitting him again.

'Whoa! Where did that come from? Let's go back inside and talk about this like adults. OK?' Andy opened the door and looked over his shoulder.

Maggie followed him back into the living room and sat down. 'I'm not even angry at you ... well, I am a little bit and I know this is stupid and normally I don't care but ...'

'Maggie, I don't know what's going on in that head of yours.'

She turned and faced him. 'Normally I don't give two shits what people think of me, but I hate these feelings. I hate that people will judge me.'

'What people? Judge you about what?' Andy frowned.

'Everyone! People I work with, people like Dad ... Don't you understand? I feel like I'll never be accepted by him. What if I were to fall in love? Want to get married ... to a woman. A father is supposed to walk his daughter down the aisle and that will never happen. My whole life I've felt like I've had to hide the real me from him. My own father doesn't even know me.' The tears had started.

'Oh man. This has nothing to do with me and Kate, does it?

I hate to see you like this, but I don't understand. Kate is straight. You can't be mad at me because Kate doesn't fancy you.'

'That's just it.' Her eyes pleaded with him to understand so she didn't have to say it out loud.

'You've lost me now.' He shook his head.

'Kate is untouchable. For me anyway. I want what I *know* I can't have because it's ... safe. It means I don't have to explore my own feelings. Open up to someone. Risk rejection.' She wiped her eyes with her sleeve. 'I've been out with men. Plenty of men. I enjoyed every one of my relationships with them – they just fizzled out. I never found the one and always wondered if it was because maybe I was looking in the wrong places. I didn't pursue relationships with women, I *experimented*, as Dad would say, and any time I wanted to go further, it was like Dad was on my shoulder, shouting in my ear, "don't you dare go there". So, I didn't.' Maggie held a hand up. She didn't want to go on.

Andy raised a brow. 'C'mon, sis. You can tell me anything.'

'What's wrong with me, Andy? What the hell is wrong with me?' She punched the cushion beside her.

Andy handed her a tissue and rubbed her back. 'Nothing. Nothing is wrong with you. Your job and the current case you're involved in is high pressure. You're human. You have feelings. And guess what?' He lifted her chin and forced her to look at him. 'Not everyone is Dad.'

Chapter 77

Maggie woke with a headache. She was emotionally drained but glad that she and her brother had cleared the air. Now she had to clear the air with Kate. She couldn't have this hanging over her head.

After getting dressed, she went downstairs. The house was quiet. She saw that Scrappy had been fed and let out. His cat flap was creaking as the wind blew it in and out. There was a note on the counter from Andy letting her know that he'd taken Kate into work and was going to B&Q for some supplies. Looked like she wouldn't have the opportunity until after work to speak with Kate.

She grabbed two ibuprofen from the drawer and swallowed them down with a strong coffee before heading into work.

When she arrived at the office, she immediately logged in to check if the profiler had come back to her and nearly fist pumped the air when she saw that an email was waiting in her inbox. Her stomach was in knots as she began to read:

I read the details from the unsolved murder case of Catharine Hill first and came up with the following information. As I wanted to remain objective, I didn't read the information from your current cases until after I came up with my own profile of the killer for Catharine, or Cate as I understand she was known. I think you'll be very interested in my findings and I'd be happy to discuss them further once you've gone through the information. My contact details are at the end of the email. Please say hello to Dr Moloney when you next see her.

Maggie skimmed all the technical jargon the doctor used to explain her findings. Her main interest was who and everything else would fall into place.

Based on the information to hand, I believe that the killer of Ms Hill had spent a considerable amount of time following her movements first. This individual believes he was connected, whether romantically or on some other 'special' level with the victim. There was no evidence of sexual assault so this was not a crime related to power and control, in my opinion. It may be that the death was accidental. My feeling is that the killer is much older than Ms Hill – by at least 10 to 15 years, but more than likely more. He may have attended college or university but not received his degree, but feels he is skilled enough to perform tasks related to the subject – for instance, law, medicine, or a similar skilled profession. He may have come across Ms Hill in this sort of setting – university or work – and formed an unnatural attachment. The victim may have spoken to colleagues expressing her concern, so I'd advise that her close friends and colleagues are spoken to again – they may remember something significant now that they previously have dismissed.

The killer may have a personality disorder, but without being able to examine him it would be difficult to assess properly. He may experience delusions which allow him to firmly believe that his victim(s) have genuine affection for him, that they are happy to be with him and that it is external forces that are keeping them apart.

Maggie skimmed through some more jargon and then came across the doctor's assessment of The Living Doll killer. Her heart was racing as the report was similar to what Kate had surmised. What really stood out was the last paragraph:

It is my conclusion that the killer in Ms Catharine Hill's case is the same person in the South Staffordshire murders. I would suggest that the police focus their attention on a male, aged 35-55 years old, who works closely with Dr Moloney. We already know that this individual is capable of murder. I don't believe that he murdered anyone prior to 2016 – Catharine appears to be the main obsession on which everyone else is based, given that he's changing the victim's appearance to match her. However, he may have been fantasizing about murder for some time. As Dr Moloney already looks very similar to Ms Hill, it is my assessment that he feels closest to her. He is unlikely to cause Dr Moloney direct physical harm if she understands his reasoning and reciprocates his feelings; however if he feels rejected ... death may be inevitable and he will continue to stalk females until he finds another match.

Her stomach churned. Maggie was beginning to think that they should tighten up the security on Kate and on her own home – even if Kate fought her every step of the way. She'd need to speak to Nathan.

'Hey, boss. Have you read the report from the profiler in London?' Maggie hoped she wouldn't have to summarize the information for him as she was still processing it herself.

Nathan looked up from his screen. 'Yeah ... yeah, I have. I forwarded it to DI Calleja as he needs to be aware of what we're dealing with. The risk to Kate at this moment is very high, and she shouldn't be able to go out and interview without a colleague present. We don't want to give this arsehole any opportunity to make his move.'

'Yes, that's why I came in here. I wondered if it would be worth upping the security at my house? Or looking at putting Kate in a safe house?'

'Hmm. I think it's something we should be considering, but I'll have to clear any additional expense with DI Rutherford and, of course, Kate's own thoughts need to be taken into account.'

'I'm just grateful that Kate didn't read the report. Imagine knowing something like that.'

'How do you know she hasn't read it?'

She raised her brow. 'Well she'd have to have a copy of the report and I specifically asked that only you, me and DI Rutherford were informed.'

Nathan shifted in his seat and turned the computer screen to Maggie. 'Well the doctor didn't seem to take that on board. Did you not notice that Kate has been cc'd in?'

'Oh fuck.'

Chapter 78

A bead of sweat tickled her face as the enormity of what she'd just read hit her like a train. Her breaths became shorter and she knew she had to get a grip or risk being pushed to take enforced leave for her wellbeing. DI Calleja was aware of Kate's background and past issues with anxiety, but she hadn't shared any of this with her other colleagues.

Kate wouldn't let the killer get the best of her. She refused to allow the crippling feeling of anxiety to take hold. She hadn't had any new notes, gifts, or emails so it could be possible that he'd found a new target. Believing that might help her remain strong and focus. But she'd still have to be one step ahead of the killer while making sure her colleagues didn't put her in a glass bubble.

She re-read the line that sent chills down her spine: 'He is unlikely to cause Dr Moloney direct harm if she understands his reasoning; however if he feels rejected …'

The killer would already be feeling rejected as Kate involved the police and he was aware of this fact. The security firm that were supposed to be fortifying her property still hadn't responded to her emails. She'd paid extra money to make sure that the job was done more quickly than normal, but it felt like weeks had passed and nothing further had been actioned. Initially they had responded that another important job had taken priority and they would get back to her property as soon as possible. She dialled their number.

'Bullet Security Services, how may I help you?'

'Hi, my name is Dr Moloney. I'm just following up on when the work at my flat will resume. It's becoming a critical situation now. I've been waiting far too long and if I can't get any way forward with your company, I'll have no choice but to take my business elsewhere.'

'Critical, you say? I'll just be moment.'

Kate was put on hold and stared out of the window while she waited for someone to return to the phone.

'Dr Moloney. Apologies for the delay in coming back to you. We should be able to come back to the job by the end of the week. I've deducted some money off your bill and I promise that it will be completed in the shortest time possible.'

'Thank you. I don't want the job rushed though, and I know that sounds like I'm contradicting myself but I would appreciate it if I could move back into my home as soon as possible.'

'We'll do our best. Thanks so much for your patience. If I need anything, I'll be in touch; otherwise the next time you hear from me it will be to pick up your new keys.'

Kate felt more relaxed after hanging up the phone. She was desperate to speak to her colleague in London to discuss the profile, but knew that she risked having the information fed back to Maggie and the murder team. Should anyone then be arrested, the case could be compromised. That was one risk she wasn't willing to take.

Just then, her mobile rang and she wasn't surprised to see who it was.

'Hello, Maggie. What can I do for you?'

'*I'm actually calling to see if you're OK. I know you've probably read the profile that came through this morning. It wasn't an easy read.*'

'Save your concern. I'm fine, really. It's everything I had expected, so there's no need to worry. What I'm more interested in is whether another woman has gone missing. We know that the killer quickly replaces his victims, so I imagine your team is actively pursuing that line of enquiry with the Misper Unit?'

She heard a sigh down the line.

'*I can't discuss the particulars of the case with you. However, I can say that we've not heard anything about a missing person. We've asked to be kept informed of any calls that come in which may relate to our case.*'

'Hmm. Don't you find that curious?'

'*Please don't put me in an awkward position. I've already said too much …*'

'Forget I asked. Right then, I need to go and catch up on my work for Lucy and her risk assessment referrals. See you later.'

Kate didn't bother to wait for a reply. Although Maggie hadn't said much, she'd said enough. The killer had not abducted another female. That could mean only one thing: he was waiting to make his move on her and she wasn't going to make it easy for him.

Chapter 79

He clenched his fists. He needed to lure Kate away from that copper's house if he ever wanted to have a chance to bring her to her new home. Their home.

He'd found out that the security on Dr Moloney's flat was delayed – thanks to him ... It seemed an elderly person took priority over a young female ... At least his mother was good for something. That meant that Kate would be staying with DC Jamieson a little longer.

Wait! That might work!

He reached for his car keys and headed to his destination, a smile on his face. His song came on the radio. Again! The stars were aligning; he smiled as he hummed along to 'Living Doll'. He loved Cliff Richard. His mother had played that record over and over again whenever his father had put him in the basement with his *friends*.

When he arrived, he parked and went to the boot of his car. Rummaging through his bag, he took what he'd need – gaffer tape, plastic ties, his knife, a stun gun – and placed them all in his small holdall. He put the baseball cap on his head, pulling it down to hide his features as much as possible. He pulled the missing dog poster from his pocket and walked towards the building.

He used the key he'd made when he borrowed Kate's keys. She always left them on her desk. You'd think she would be more careful in her line of work. He'd have to talk to her about that.

The key worked. He breathed out with relief. He headed to the door and rang the bell, looking around to make sure no one would disturb him. A man answered and he held out the poster.

'Have you seen my dog?'

The man smiled and took the poster. 'Hang on a moment, I can't see without my glasses.' While the neighbour turned to retrieve his glasses, he removed the knife from his holdall, stepped inside the flat and closed the door.

'What the he—!' The man noticed the knife.

He could see the fear in his eyes. 'You're going to do what I say and I promise you won't get hurt. Turn around.'

The neighbour was shaking as he carefully placed the gaffer tape over his eyes. He directed him to a chair and pushed him down.

'Put your hands behind your back.'

The neighbour did as he was told and he used the plastic ties to incapacitate his victim. Using the gaffer tape once more, he bound the man's legs tightly.

'Where's your mobile phone?'

'It's on the table in the other room.'

'Do not make a sound. If you say or do anything, I will kill you. Do you understand?'

The man nodded. He kept his eye on him as he walked to the other room. Glancing in, he saw the phone on the table. He picked it up and returned to his captive. 'Do I need a code to unlock it?'

The man nodded. 'It's one-five-eight-oh.'

He saw a wet patch forming at the man's crotch.

'Oh dear. You've had an accident. You can sort that out when I go.'

The man scrolled through the contacts until he found the one he needed. He smiled. Pressing the 'Messages' button he began to write the text.

Hi Kate. Sorry to bother you, but I think there's something wrong with Salem. Could you come over?

He waited for the reply.

Oh no! I'll be over shortly. Kate.

He smiled and responded.

OK. See you soon.

And so, the wait began.

Chapter 80

Kate grabbed her keys from her desk, and her jacket and bag from the back of her office door and raced out into the open-plan office. DI Calleja was in a meeting and DS Hooper was nowhere to be found. She rang a taxi from one of the desk phones.

'Mark, could you let DS Hooper know that I've had to go out? I need to take my cat to the vet. Hopefully, I won't be long, but if I end up delayed, I'll call in.'

'Sure. I hope everything's OK. Do you need a lift? I can get someone to take you.'

'Thanks. I've sorted a taxi. I'm sure it's nothing, but he's pretty old. I'll see you later.' Kate headed down the stairs and waited out front.

When the taxi arrived, she gave him her destination and dug through her bag to find her mobile phone. It wasn't there. She checked the pockets on her coat.

No phone.

Shit. I must have left it in my office.

There wasn't time to turn around and go back for it. She hoped Maggie didn't try and call her – she'd be even more pissed off if she learned Kate had left it at work. But she was hoping that once she dropped Salem off at the vet, she could call from there and maybe get a lift back to work.

It took less than twenty minutes to arrive at her building. It felt strange being back even though she'd only been gone a short time. She gave the driver a £20 note and told him to keep the change. Running up the stairs, she pulled her keys from her pocket and unlocked the main door. Once inside, Kate ran to her neighbour's door and, as she reached out to knock, it swung open slightly beneath her hand.

He must have left it open so I could just come in. Not very safe, if you ask me.

She'd have a word with him once she got Salem safely to the vet. If Salem escaped, she would be devastated.

She called out as she entered her neighbour's flat. 'Hello. It's just me, Kate. Where are—?' She covered her mouth to stifle a scream as she took in the sight in front of her. Before she could turn and run, a hand came out from behind and covered her mouth.

He must have been waiting behind the door.

'You must forgive me, Kate. I was hoping the circumstances of our meeting would be different. Now, I don't want to hurt you so just relax; you'll feel a little prick and then everything will be OK.'

Kate flung her head back and heard the crack as the back of her skull met the man's forehead. He stumbled back and Kate looked around the room for a weapon. There was nothing.

'Oh Kate, why did you have to do that?' he snarled.

She looked at the masked man. There was something familiar about him, but she couldn't put her finger on it. 'Why are you doing this?'

He slowly approached with his hands out. 'Why? Why do you think? You're my princess. You've come back to me. You know that. Why are you playing these silly games?'

She had to be smart. Had to keep him talking while keeping her fear under control. 'Do I know you? Your voice ... it sounds familiar. Why won't you let me see your face?'

The man stopped. His eyes looked up at the ceiling like he was carefully thinking of his next words. Kate took that moment to make her move. She raced towards him with her hands out. If she could catch him off-guard, she may be able to push him aside and get through the door.

Her hands shoved his shoulder and he stumbled sideways. It worked. Just a few more steps and she would be out the door and able to raise the alarm. She was so focused on that task, she didn't see him twist his body and grab her leg. She fell forward and hit the floor full force. She was winded. Kate turned over onto her back and tried to sit up. He had got to his feet and stood above her. She watched as he reached into his pocket.

'We can talk more back at home. I didn't want to have to do this, but you've left me no choice.' It was then that Kate realized he was holding a stun gun. His movements were so fast as he bent down, she didn't have time to scream before she felt the volts course through her body.

The room went black.

Chapter 81

Maggie sat on the train and rubbed her growling stomach. She didn't feel like cooking when she got home, so she rang Kate to see if she wanted a takeaway. A new fish & chip shop had opened down the street from her house, and she thought she would pick something up on her way back. A peace offering.

There was no answer. Maggie left Kate a message, as she figured by the time she got to the takeaway, Kate should be back at the house. Markston was closer than Stafford. When she called again forty minutes later and there was no answer on Kate's mobile, Maggie called her own landline. If Kate had misplaced her own phone, she would answer – Maggie had told her to use the landline if she needed to.

No answer.

She shrugged and pocketed her mobile; Kate was probably in the bath. She had made Kate a promise not to panic so much and she wasn't going to break it, no matter how hard it was. At the takeaway, she ordered enough food for three in case Andy came home; she paid and walked towards her house. With everything that had been going on, Maggie was always extra vigilant when in her neighbourhood. The killer could be out there, watching. They'd know that Kate was now staying with her, so she looked at every car, licence plate, person, and house as she strolled home. She didn't want to take any chances.

Nothing unusual today.

Balancing the paper bag with one hand, she reached into her bag and pulled out her keys. Once inside she called out, 'Kate, are you in?'

No response.

Maggie and Kate had agreed that if one or the other had to work late, they would let the other know. She walked to the kitchen and put the bag on the counter. Pulling out her mobile phone, she double checked that Kate hadn't tried to call or message her, but her screen showed only the picture of Scrappy.

She dialled Kate's number again. 'Hey, it's just me. If you're working late, can you drop me a text? I just want to check that everything's OK.' She remained casual on the phone and ended the call before plating up her fish and chips. She placed the other two dinners in the oven. Kate and Andy could heat them up when they got in if they wanted to.

Maggie settled onto the couch and ate her dinner as she watched the news. The police hadn't released all the details about the murders in the hope that when an individual was caught, they'd be able to confirm that it was really their killer and not some nutjob looking for fame. What the police hadn't released to the press was the fact that both women had blue contact lenses inserted in their eyes. Although some had guessed about the sewing of the orifices, the police hadn't confirmed this. Maggie shuddered. Thick black thread had been used and it was macabre in nature. She struggled at times to get the images out of her head. She didn't even want to think about what the women had been through, but Dr Blake at least confirmed that both had been deceased when their eyelids and lips had been sewn shut.

She looked down at her plate of food and her stomach turned. Maggie took her plate to the kitchen and binned her dinner. She grabbed a bottle of water out of the fridge and went back to watch TV. Kate still hadn't returned her call, so Maggie texted Andy in the hope that maybe Kate had left a message with him. Within a few minutes, her brother texted back.

Sorry. I've heard nothing from Kate. Is everything OK? A x

She didn't want him to worry and sent a quick message back reassuring him that she was probably just overreacting. He knew what she was like when she was working a difficult case.

Maggie pulled the blanket that balanced on the couch arm over her and lay down. She hadn't realized she'd fallen asleep until she heard the front door close.

It was Andy. Kate must have come back and left her to sleep.

'What time is it?' She rubbed her eyes.

'Just gone two. Why are you up?'

'I must have fallen asleep watching TV. I'm going up now though. This couch is so uncomfortable. Night.'

'See you in the morning.'

Maggie tiptoed up the stairs. As she passed the spare bedroom, she couldn't help but peek in.

No Kate.

Fuck.

Chapter 82

'Andy!' Maggie's mind raced. 'Andy! Kate's not in her room. I need the car keys.'

Andy's thunderous footsteps would probably wake the neighbours if her shouting didn't but Maggie wasn't bothered. All she could think about was her friend.

'Calm down. You can't go out now. You need to sleep. You need a clear head. Maybe she's over at a mate's and forgot her phone. You know what she's like with that bloody mobile.'

'No. She wouldn't do that. She promised me. I need to call this in.' Maggie dialled 999 and explained the situation to the call handler. She needed to speak to Nathan. Her hands were shaking as she tried to find his number. Andy took the phone out of her hand.

'Sit down.' Maggie tried to fight him but felt exhausted with worry. 'I'll dial Nathan. Just sit there.' He pointed to Kate's bed and she walked across the room, hoping her legs were not going to give out on her.

'Nathan. It's Andy, Maggie Jamieson's brother. Kate's missing. I'm going to pass the phone over to Maggie now. OK. Yep. Thanks.' Andy handed the phone to his sister. 'I'll make you some tea,' he whispered and left Maggie to it.

She breathed deeply. 'Hi Nathan. So sorry to call you at this hour, but Kate hasn't come home, she's not answering her mobile, and frankly I'm bloody worried about her. I've called it in.'

'*You did the right thing, Maggie. Look, I'm going to ring the office and make sure that some officers are dispatched out to her flat, OK? Unless they find something, there's not much we can do until morning, so I suggest you try and get a few hours' sleep and come in with a fresh head, OK? You won't be of any use to anyone otherwise.*'

'But—'

'*I'm not going to argue with you. If I do hear anything, I'll let you know. Now, go.*'

She knew she wouldn't win this argument. Her brother came in and brought her a hot cup of tea with too much sugar. Their mother always made them super sweet tea when something was wrong and, as much as she appreciated the gesture, she wouldn't be able to drink it. She took a sip to satisfy her brother and then lay down. Andy squeezed her arm and closed the door when he left.

Maggie stared at the wall ahead of her. It was going to be a long night.

Chapter 83

Kate's heart thumped loudly in her chest as she realized where she was. Lying on her side with her eyes covered, every bump made her body ache. Something hard was pressing on her back and she winced. After her abductor had used the stun gun, he must have carried her through the back of the building and placed her in the boot of his car. She only hoped a neighbour had been looking out, witnessed the event, and called the police.

She didn't know how long she'd been in the back of the car, but it came to a stop. Minutes passed before she heard a car door open and gravel crunching beneath his feet. Kate felt fresh air on her face as the boot was popped open. She began to scream but then felt a gloved hand over her mouth.

'Oh Kate, ssshhhh ... Please don't do that. I don't want to hurt you, but I will if I have to.' She felt a prick in her arm and then she was woozy. 'Just a little something to calm you down. I'm afraid I won't remove my hand until I know you will be quiet.'

Her life depended on her playing his game. It wouldn't do her any good to fight at this moment in time. Her hands and feet were tied and her eyes were covered. She was at his mercy.

'Good. I'm just going to pick you up and take you inside. You're home now.' He grunted as he lifted her out of the boot.

An icy shiver went down her spine.

Kate woke up on a bed. Her hands and feet were once again bound, so she couldn't move. She felt a hand caress her face and tried to move away from his touch.

'I know this must all seem a bit unusual, but you can trust me, Kate. Don't you see, we're finally together. I only wish you hadn't made it so hard. I tried to keep away; I tried to use others. But I should have known they could never be the one. They left me. It was always you.' He gently prised the tape from her mouth.

She tried to speak but her throat was dry.

'Hang on. I'll get you some water.' He held her head up and a straw was placed between her lips. 'Here you go. Be careful you don't spill any on yourself.'

She coughed and turned her head away after taking a bit of the water. It was cold against the back of her throat. 'Where ... where am I?'

'Sshhh. Rest now. There'll be plenty of time for us to talk in the morning.' She could feel something hovering just above her face, but he didn't touch her this time. Instead, she felt cold lips on her forehead. 'You're home now. We have a lot to plan. Goodnight, princess.'

A tear trickled down the side of her face. The water must have been laced with something as she began to feel groggy again. The more she tried to fight sleep, the worse she felt. She gave in and knew that tomorrow she would have to try harder. She didn't know how long he would keep her alive, so every second counted.

Chapter 84

Her whole body ached and she felt sick to her stomach. The room was dark but not completely black. A dim lamp cast shadows above her. Kate had never come into contact with a stun gun before and she hoped it would never happen again. He had removed her blindfold at some point in the night.

'Oh good. You're awake. I was worried I had administered the wrong dosage and caused some damage. Would you like some water?' She recognized that voice – where had she heard it before? If he kept talking, she might remember.

Kate nodded. She had to stay in control even though every ounce of her being wanted to scream out. She tried to sit up but realized she was strapped across her head, chest and legs. Her wrists were cuffed to the metal bars on the bed. Was she on a hospital gurney?

He came back into the room. His face was hidden behind a mask. That was a good sign. If he didn't want to be identified, that might mean he wasn't planning on killing her. He held the glass beside her face and angled the straw towards her mouth.

'There you go, Kate. I'm so glad you're finally here. You were always the one.' He stroked her hair with his free hand.

She turned her head to get the straw out of her mouth, but

the strap made movement difficult. 'Where am I? Why am I here?'

And why the fuck did he keep saying she was the one!

'You're somewhere safe.' He turned his head but Kate couldn't see what he was looking at. She tried to look around the room, but all she could see through her peripheral vision were the white ceiling and blurry white walls.

'What is that? You don't need to do that. I won't fight you ...' Panic overwhelmed her.

'Ssshhh.' He caressed her cheek. 'It's just a little something to help you sleep. You do know I would never harm you, right?'

A tear rolled down the side of her face and tingled in her ear as it landed on her lobe and slipped inside. She tried to shake her head but to no avail.

'Please, if you let me go now, we can forget all about this. I don't know what you look like – you could let me go. I won't say anything to the police.'

A flash of anger blazed in his eyes. 'Don't do that, Kate. We both know you'd tell your friend, oh, what's her name ... Maggie. Yes, that's it. Then it would be game over and you would never know what happiness is. Don't you want to be happy?'

Kate realized that if she wanted to stay alive, she had to play along with this guy's fantasy or he would kill her. She had no choice.

'Of course. I'm sorry. I just panicked there for a minute. Can you remove the restraints? I'd like to sit up and talk to you.'

For a moment, Kate thought he was going to free her, but then he tightened the strap across her chest. She gasped.

'Please. That hurts. I ... can't ... breathe.'

'I know that's not true, Kate. But I forgive you. Let's not play games. I'm sure you're scared right now, but I know you'll soon grow to care about me. I'll protect you. I dreamed of this day from the moment I saw you.'

'I-I really can't breathe. P-p-please. Can you lo-loosen it a little b-bit?'

His head cocked to the left as if he was assessing her. Trying to figure out if her pleas were genuine. After a moment, he loosened the strap across her chest.

'Thank you.' She took a deep breath.

He didn't respond but continued to stare at her as he held her hand. It was unnerving. She wanted to turn her head, but feared he would take that as an act of defiance, so she looked him in the eye and smiled. Her mouth twitched.

He picked up the needle and let go of her hand. 'Now this might make you feel a bit dizzy at first, but you'll soon sleep. Ah, my sleeping beauty.' He stuck the needle into the muscle of her arm and the effects were almost immediate. She felt nauseous and then sleep quickly consumed her.

Chapter 85

Maggie stretched and picked Scrappy up when she felt him rub against her hand. Petting the cat usually calmed her, but not this morning. She put Scrappy on the bed and picked up her mobile from the nightstand. It was 4.30am. No messages or calls from Kate or Nathan. Although she'd barely slept, she knew she wouldn't get anymore sleep, so went and had a shower.

She returned to her own room to get dressed and heard her mobile phone ping. Nathan had texted her to say that she should get dressed and he'd be at her house in twenty minutes. Maggie threw on her black jeans and a burgundy blouse. She rushed around, picking up the things she would need for the day and slipped on her trainers. Grabbing her black leather coat from the hook by the door she had just enough time to put her hair in a bun before she heard two quick taps on a horn. Stepping outside she waved at Nathan and locked her door.

She ran down her steps and got into the car. 'What happened? Have you found her?'

'No. Field Officers went to her property and found her neighbour's door was open. When they entered, they found him tied to a chair with a gag in his mouth. It looked like he may have choked on his own vomit. Forensics are there now.'

'Nothing at Kate's flat? I mean, that could just be a coincidence, right?' Maggie was in denial. She didn't want to think that anything had happened to her friend.

'I wish I could say it was. The neighbour's mobile phone was checked and there were messages between him and Kate. Or more likely, the killer and Kate. Looks like Kate was lured to the property under the guise that something was wrong with her cat. It's more than likely the killer waited for her to arrive and then she was taken elsewhere. There was some blood in the flat, but until forensics test it, we can't say for definite who it belongs to. What they have told me is that it's not enough to assume someone was murdered. They think the neighbour was left in the hope that he would eventually be found and released.'

'That would suggest the killer either wore a disguise or a mask to hide his face.'

'Yep. But for whatever reason – panic, or perhaps he was injected with something – the neighbour ended up vomiting and, with the gag in his mouth, he choked.'

Maggie shook her head. 'How awful. But we still can't say that Kate made it to the property, can we?'

'I know you hope that's the case, but we have to be realistic here. I think it's safe to assume that Kate has been abducted. What we can hope for, though, is that her abductor was foolish enough to leave some evidence behind. Something that might lead us to finding Kate.'

'Fuck. I should have kept a closer eye on her. We shouldn't have argued. This is all my fault.'

'You argued? About what? And can I just say, none of this is your fault. We know this person is obsessed with Kate. If it wasn't today, it would have been another day that he attempted to take her.'

'No, you don't understand. We left things on bad terms. Andy and Kate really hit it off and I've just been a total bitch about things. I had no right to be. I was just thinking about myself because my ego was bruised. She didn't even talk to me before she left yesterday morning.' Maggie rubbed her temples. 'If she had texted me to let me know she was going to check on her cat, I could have made sure someone went with her.'

'Well that could have ended badly for another person. Take a deep breath, put those feelings on the back burner for now, and let's focus on finding Kate, OK?'

'You're right.' She opened the window and let the cool air hit her face. She took in three deep breaths.

'Are you OK now?' Nathan looked at her before turning his attention back to the road.

'Yeah. Much better.'

'Good. Can you close the bloody window now, I'm freezing.'

Maggie couldn't help but laugh as she hit the switch and closed the window.

They arrived at Kate's flat and headed directly to the neighbour's. They signed themselves in and put on the requisite gear for entering a crime scene. Just before going into the neighbour's flat, Maggie noted that a camera had been installed in the corner outside Kate's door.

'Look.' She tapped Nathan's arm. 'The security team Kate hired must have started their work. I'll leave a message for Bethany to contact them when she gets in. Maybe we can get some footage from this entryway at least.'

'Good spot. I'm just going to talk to the Duty SIO.' Nathan walked into the flat.

Maggie radioed into the call centre and left a message for Bethany asking her to ring her back as soon as she heard anything. Maggie didn't know how long they would be at the property.

Guilt flooded through her but she shook her head, took a deep breath, and walked into the flat. Fear gripped her as she took in the scene.

Chapter 86

'What the hell?' Maggie looked around the room, taking in the horror before her. Kate's neighbour was straddling a chair, legs and hands tied with plastic cuffs to make sure he was held securely. His head was tilted back, eyes bulging and vomit stuck to the side of his face. It was like an explosion had happened. Flecks of vomit were on the floor and nearby wall. Dr Blake tilted the man's head forward. She looked to be searching for something on the man's neck.

'What the hell, indeed. Not the most pleasant way to die, I'd say.' Dr Blake continued to examine the back of the victim's head and Maggie moved closer to hear the pathologist.

'What are you looking for?' She strained her eyes looking at the victim's neck.

'Puncture wounds. Before we bag him up and take him to the morgue, I was curious to see whether he was injected with something he may have had a bad reaction to. Nothing obvious at the moment, but I'll be able to tell you more after the PM. I'm going to head back now and I'll make this a priority.'

Maggie moved out of the way as Dr Blake walked past her and out of the door, calling out instructions to her team as she left.

She stared at the man. *What can you tell us?* There didn't seem to be any obvious answers. She joined Nathan. 'Do we have anything that can tell us where Kate may have been taken?'

'Looks like there was a bit of a struggle here and Kate may have been incapacitated somehow and fallen. They found some blood on the floor just over there.' Nathan pointed. 'And a broken nail – black polish, so I am assuming it's Kate's. Though we'll have to see what forensics say, and there's no way we can say for sure. However, Dr Blake advised that there were burn marks, consistent with a handheld stun gun, found on the neighbour's flesh.'

Maggie closed her eyes. 'So he could have been waiting behind the door and taken Kate by surprise? If knocked out by some sort of sedative, she may have fallen and when putting her arms out to break the fall, her nail may have been broken then?' She was trying to work out the logistics in her head.

'Are you OK, Maggie? If this is too much, I can meet you back at the station?'

'No. I'm fine. I need to be a part of this. Has anyone in the building been spoken to?'

'Kat and the field officers are doing that now, but from what I've heard so far, there's been nothing out of the ordinary reported. Not much else for us to do here. Whoever abducted Kate seems to have been meticulous enough not to have left any clues as to where they were taking her. What are we going to do about her cat?'

'Oh, shit. Salem. Where is he?'

'Through there, in the back room.'

'I'll take him back to mine and figure out what to do after. Can we do a quick stop by mine on the way back to the office?'

'Sure. I'll help you get the cat's things together.' Nathan

followed Maggie to the back room and they collected Salem and his belongings and loaded them into Nathan's boot.

'Has anyone searched Kate's flat?'

'Yes. No evidence it was broken into. Door was secure and nothing inside disturbed.'

'OK. Christ, Nathan, I really won't forgive myself if anything happens to her.'

'I told you. None of this is your fault. Let's get this cat dropped off before I have a sneezing fit. Did I mention I'm allergic?'

'Oh crap. Sorry. Do you want me to put him on the back seat?' Maggie went to move the carry case to the back.

'No, it's fine. It won't take long.'

Maggie dropped Salem off at her place, closing him into Kate's room with everything he would need. She left a note for her brother in case he came home, advising him not to panic if he heard sounds from Kate's room and to keep the door closed. She had no doubt Scrappy would be upstairs once he figured out there was another cat in the house. She couldn't worry about that now though. They had to find Kate.

Chapter 87

Kate couldn't move. Her head felt heavy but at least her eyes were no longer covered. She blinked to get some moisture and hoped that the blur before her would clear. She wanted to take in every detail for when she escaped. There was no way she would let him win.

She had recognized his voice. She was sure he was the one who had knocked on Maggie's door claiming to be looking for a lost dog. She would bet her life on it. Though he must have altered it slightly. He had been watching her enough to know she was staying with Maggie. The knock on the door startled her. She lay still. If he thought she was still asleep, he may leave her for a while. Allow her enough time to get her bearings. She felt so weak.

Tap. Tap. Tap. He knocked again. 'Kaaaaate. I know you're awake. Normally I wouldn't even bother knocking but I don't want to frighten you.' There was a calmness in his voice.

Really? So attacking and abducting me wasn't supposed to be scary?

She didn't respond and quickly scanned the room for cameras. He had to be watching her. That would make things more difficult. Was she in a child's room? There was a wooden chest in the corner that had dolls sitting on top of it.

'I have to go out. Rest up, princess, and I will see you soon.'

That voice. He *had* disguised it previously. He was still trying to disguise it. It wasn't just the lost dog incident. She had definitely heard his voice before. But where? Think Kate – Damnit! He was going out though. She'd need to try and take in her surroundings as quickly and as carefully as possible. If he figured out what she was doing, he would put a stop to it and who knows what else he may do. She wasn't going to be fooled by his friendly tone. He had already shown what he could do with … she wasn't going to focus on that though. She tried to lift her head but the pounding started. With her hands and feet tied to the bed, her movement was severely restricted.

Kate looked at the ceiling. Was that a hole in the ceiling? Could he be watching her from a room upstairs? Did that mean she was on the ground level or was there an attic? The questions made her head pound even more.

She didn't hear him approach the door and screamed when she heard him knock.

He opened the door a crack and whispered. 'Shhhhh. Nothing to be afraid of. I told you, I'm not going to hurt you. Don't you realize that?' There was an edge to his voice.

'Uh … ssss … sorry. I guess I'm just a bit jumpy being tied to the bed. I thought you were going out?' She wondered if reasoning with him would get her anywhere near her ultimate goal of escape. What did the email from her London colleague say? She needed to remember now because it could be the very thing that saved her life. She had to empathize with him.

'Well if you're good, we can fix that. But right now, I'm afraid you'll have to stay that way. I'm just leaving now. We'll talk more when I'm back.'

She wanted to keep him talking. 'Where are you going?'

'Out. Don't try to analyse me, Doctor. I was hoping you wouldn't, but I guess it's second nature.' He sighed. 'Don't be frightened but I am coming in.'

Kate felt every muscle in her body tense.

He opened the door and turned on the lights. The bright infusion in the room burned her eyes and she squinted until it felt more comfortable. The sight before her chilled her to the bones.

Chapter 88

Back at Stafford Police Station, Maggie saw that Bethany was still at work trying to get the information from the security team that had installed the camera outside of Kate's flat. Bethany rolled her eyes and pointed at the headset. Maggie left her to it but didn't hold out much hope.

'Any news from the crime scene?' DI Rutherford walked into the office.

Nathan recounted the information they had so far, and DI Rutherford's face was strained. Dark circles danced around her eyes and Maggie noticed she'd stopped trying to cover them with make-up lately. She made a note to check up on her once they had a solid lead – any sooner and Maggie knew that she would just be fobbed off. The focus would be on getting Kate back safely; anything else would take a back seat.

'Has anyone contacted the DAHU yet? I know they've been informed of Kate's situation, but it might help if we heard first-hand the last thing people remember before Kate left the office. Who did she talk to? Where did she say she was going? We know she received a text from her neighbour, but her colleagues may be able to tell us a bit more about her demeanour at the time.'

'I'll do that now, ma'am.' Maggie sat at her desk and dialled the direct number to the DAHU.

'*Domestic Abuse and Homicide Unit, PC Fielding speaking. How can I help?*'

'Hi Mark, it's Maggie here. I'm calling about Kate.'

'*Hey. What the hell is happening? Did you find her?*'

'No, we haven't. I'm afraid I don't have much time to talk, but I'd like to know if you or anyone spoke to Kate before she left work yesterday?'

'*Yeah. She asked me to pass on a message to DI Calleja. Said her neighbour called about her cat and she had to rush to the vet?*'

'Wait. She said she went to the vet or to her neighbour's to take her cat to the vet. This is important.'

'*Sorry. She was getting her cat to go to the vet. From her neighbour.*'

'OK. How did she appear? Was she nervous? Did she seem off in any way?'

'*Just upset. Like I would expect someone to be if they were worried. If I thought it was anything more, I would have contacted you.*'

'Shit. I know, Mark. Sorry. We're none the wiser then. Oh, one more thing. Did Kate have her mobile phone with her?'

'*Hang on. I'll check her office.*'

Maggie waited a few minutes before Mark returned to the phone.

'*It was on her desk. She's always forgetting it. Do you want me to drop it up to you guys on my way to HQ? I am heading up there shortly.*'

'That would be great. See you soon.'

Maggie ended the call with Mark placing the receiver back in its cradle.

'Any luck?' Nathan queried.

'No. Only that Kate doesn't have her mobile so we won't even be able to see if we can locate her through that. Dammit. I kept reminding her to keep that with her. Mark is dropping it up shortly. Maybe Bethany can find something useful on it – though I hate to breach her privacy this way.'

'I know what you mean, but right now, we need to focus on Kate's abduction and whatever we need to do, will get done.'

Maggie hoped they reached Kate in time. There was no telling what the killer would do to her or how long he would hold her before she ended up another one of his living dolls.

Chapter 89

'Did you expect to see my face? Did you hope I would reveal myself to you?' He walked towards the bed. 'All in good time, princess. We have trust to build, don't you think?'

She flinched as he touched her arm and for a moment he wondered if he had made a mistake in bringing her here so soon.

'What are you going to do to me?' Her voice shook.

'Do to you? Why would I do anything to you? I thought you knew how I felt about you. You're the one.'

'Yes, you keep saying.' She paused. 'Why ... why did you murder those other women?'

'Murder? Oh no, no, no.' He shook his head. 'They died. It wasn't intentional, just the circumstances. I'm a lover, a protector, not a ... killer.' Her brow furrowed and he was disappointed that she would believe the worst of him.

'Do we know each other?' Her head tilted and her eyes squinted as she tried to see beyond the mask.

He moved back. He wasn't ready to answer her, but wondered if she would figure things out before he revealed himself. 'I know you very well. I know everything about you. I know you like to use coconut shampoo. You prefer candles to lights. Your Irish accent is more prominent when you're angry or excited.' He smiled as he thought about all the habits and nuances Kate possessed.

She shifted in the bed, as if she was trying to sink into the mattress. A faint whimper escaped from her lips.

'You'll know everything about me in due course.' He coughed and winced as a pain shot through him. 'We have eternity to learn everything about each other. I think we have a lot in common ... Oh, look at the time. You've kept me longer than I planned.' He bent down and whispered in her ear. 'Don't worry, I'll be back soon. Get some sleep, sweetheart.'

He looked over his shoulder as he left the room and smiled. She was so fragile. So innocent. He'd look after her. As he closed the door, he removed the mask and left it on the table just outside the door. It was time to go to work.

Chapter 90

The briefing room was packed, and Maggie not only saw but could feel the strain on her colleagues' faces. Nathan was furiously writing on the whiteboards.

'What else do we know? We have a possible link to temp agencies – specifically ArrowRoot in Markston and FirstStop in London. The owner in Markston has been ruled out as a person of interest even though he seemed a good suspect at the start – he turned out to be a bit of a perv but mainly an arse. Our killer feels connected to these women and this stems from the unsolved murder in London. The killer must have had a relationship with the London victim. Was it unrequited? Is this what led him to kill again? But why is he here? What drew him to Stafford?'

'That's a lot of questions and not enough answers.' Maggie stated the obvious and Nathan glared back at her.

'Well, what do you have to add to the story? We're not here to criticize. We're here to find those answers.'

Maggie blushed. 'Sorry, boss. Um ... I still think that the connection is to one of the partnerships we work with. Think about it. This guy accessed Kate's work email – that's only known to people within the criminal justice system; everyone else is screened through HQ. He's also technically skilled. We're assuming he put spyware apps on the victims' phones. Which reminds me, any update on the camera outside Kate's flat and what did we find on her mobile, Bethany?' Maggie had been annoyed with Kate as she'd initially refused to hand over her phone to be checked. She'd wanted time to back up her photos and contacts.

'The security company hadn't connected the camera yet, so nothing from there. Uh ... there was definitely the same spyware app on Kate's mobile. Unfortunately, this person has been accessing the information through a sophisticated system and I couldn't tell how long ago it was added. He used something to cover his tracks and, like the emails, I can't pinpoint a location.'

'For fuck's sake.' Maggie fired Bethany a look and the PC shrank in her seat.

'Maggie!' Nathan glared.

Maggie's cheeks burned at Nathan's rebuke as she turned to Bethany. 'Sorry. It's just we don't know how long Kate has and the longer we piss about, the more I fear Kate will suffer.'

'No one has been pissing about. Let's look at what we *do* know about our killer: tech savvy; obsessive behaviour bordering on delusional – may have a history of concerning attachments to people; something has happened recently that triggered these new murders. We believe he killed Catharine Hill. Her friends and family say she was stalked for over a year before she was abducted. She was reported missing and held by the killer for three months before her body turned up in a park. All our victims have a Goth-like appearance – though we know that this was Ms Hill's actual appearance; the current victims were all made to look that way.' Nathan paused and Maggie took the opportunity to add to the briefing.

'The eyes and mouths of the victims were all sewn shut. We

thought this was because he was making some sort of statement or this was his signature – they won't speak or see – but what if it's simpler than that? What if our killer is a mortician? Dr Blake commented on the skill of the stitching in one of her reports.' Maggie leafed through the pages and held one up. 'Here, on page fifteen, Dr Blake states that the injuries and procedure imply someone who has medical knowledge. Surely a mortician would have this? Why haven't we spoken to any?' Maggie eyed her colleagues.

'Do you have any specifically in mind? Do you know how many morticians there are in Staffordshire? At a guess, I'd say just one hundred to one hundred and fifty. Without any evidence, we can't just go out and talk to them all. That's a waste of resources and time and you're just grasping at straws.' Nathan's tone was stern. He was losing patience with her, but she couldn't help feeling that there was an obvious answer and they were all too blind to see it. Maybe they were all too close to the case. It was clouding their perspective.

'Sir, there was one person who did raise some concerns but I couldn't find a London link ...' Bethany almost whispered. Maggie was embarrassed now that she'd made her colleague feel this way.

'Well, spit it out,' Nathan demanded.

'Charlie. But we spoke to him already and ruled him out.' Bethany looked as if she wished she'd never brought it up.

'You mean the forensics guy from Dr Blake's team? Why bring him up again?' Nathan tapped his foot.

'Well, everything Kate said about him, coupled with the fact that he's agency staff and, coincidentally, registered at the same agency as all of our victims. He's registered with a few other agencies too, but I wouldn't say that should have any bearing.

Charlie would have had access to Kate's phone – he's often based in Markston Police Station. He has medical and forensic knowledge. His background indicates that he dropped out of med school before turning his hand to forensics.'

'How long have you been sitting on this information? We need to go and interview him again, boss.' Maggie stood. 'Why are you all still sitting here?' She looked around the room.

Nathan walked to the door. 'Maggie, outside. Now. The rest of you, look at the evidence, find the connections. Get me some answers. I'll be back.'

Maggie followed Nathan outside the room.

'Go home and calm down. I don't want to have to take you off the case but your behaviour in there ... totally uncalled for.' Maggie went to interrupt and he held up his hand. 'Other than "OK, boss", I don't want to hear another word. Charlie has already been spoken to, and he has an airtight alibi for the timeframe that Dr Moloney went missing. We're not going to rake him over the coals. Get your stuff and go. I'll see you back here tomorrow morning.' He turned around and went back into the briefing.

Maggie just stood while her anger burned. She would speak to DI Rutherford before she left. Surely the guv would see sense.

Chapter 91

Maggie slammed the door behind her after she let herself into the house. She had initially tried to get the guv on side by asking if she was ok after pointing at the dark circles under her eyes. DI Rutherford hadn't taken too kindly to the comment and told Maggie to mind her own business. Now all she kept hearing was the voice of DI Rutherford drumming in her ears. *You're too close at the moment. Nathan was right. Go home, get some sleep, and come back tomorrow with a fresh head. Any mistakes now could result in us finding Kate's body and none of us wants that.* She was raging even though she knew her boss was probably right, but she had no idea how she would even be able to sleep.

She chucked her jacket over the bannister and stomped her way into the kitchen, nearly tripping over Scrappy as he let out a long and desperate meow for his dinner. Bending over, she petted him and whispered, 'All right, Scraps. No moaning, I heard you. The whole bloody neighbourhood probably heard you. Fish or chicken then?' She opened the cupboard and took out the tin closest to her. 'Fish it is. I'll save some for Salem too. You wouldn't want your roomie to get mad, would you?' She emptied the foul-smelling chunks into Scrappy's bowl, made a dish up for Salem and put it by the door. She flicked the kettle on. Kate had been making herbal teas the last few evenings and Maggie thought that if there was ever a time she needed to settle her nerves, it was now.

She sat at the breakfast bar and leafed through a magazine while she waited for the familiar click to let her know the water had boiled. Choosing a berry-flavoured tea, she poured the water into a large mug and let it steep. She went into the living room and sank into her couch, the tension in her muscles apparent as they ached. Scrappy sauntered into the room, licking his lips and rubbing against her leg. She caressed his head as he danced in and out of her legs, purring loudly.

Everything felt out of control at the moment and that scared Maggie. She liked order, thrived on knowing what her next step would be, only this time she had no clue. The team had spent countless hours interviewing the victims' families, friends, and numerous potential suspects and they were no further forward. Colleagues' backs were up when they were put in the frame, even though they understood the seriousness of the matter and why they may have been placed in the loop. And then there was Julie Noble. She frustrated the hell out of Maggie. She had hoped to spend some time with Julie when the killer had suggested a meeting, but something must have spooked him because Julie hadn't received any more notes or instructions that could help lure him out into the open. She jumped when her mobile phone ringtone snapped her out of her thoughts. Looking at the screen she didn't know whether to scream or smile when she saw who it was.

'Hello?'

'Hey. Are you busy?'

Julie Noble whispered into the earpiece.

'Why are you whispering?'

'I'm across the road from that forensic guy's house – in some bushes to be exact – and I don't want anyone to hear me.'

'What the hell? What do you think you're doing? He'll probably put in a complaint if he sees you pissing about outside his house. Get your stuff and go.'

'When we spoke about him, I could see the fire in your eyes. I don't think you believe he's not involved, do you? In fact, I bet you have your own separate list and are going through them in your own time.'

It frustrated Maggie that this woman knew so much about her without them even spending much time together, but she wouldn't give her the satisfaction of knowing that. 'You know nothing about me. Now stop playing detective and get your arse home. If my boss finds out you were anywhere near that house, she'll make me haul you in for obstruction.'

'We both know that's not true. Don't you even want to know why I'm here?'

'Frankly, I don't. If I get myself involved in this, it will be my arse on the line too. I have to think about Kate now. I've been sent home to recharge and that's exactly what I'm going to do.'

'Look, there's a coffee shop around the corner. Come and meet me. Let me tell you what I've found and if you still feel the same, I'll back off. Hang on … I see something.'

The line went quiet and Maggie could hear some rustling. What the fuck did Julie think she was doing? She'd have them both under fire if she carried on.

'Julie! Julie! For fuck's sake, will you answer me? What is going on? Are you OK?' Panic was beginning to set in the longer it took her to reply. 'Bloody answer me or I'm going to hang up the phone.' If she was messing about, that would surely get a response.

'*Sshhhh. I need to move closer. Don't hang up. I'll be with you in a min …*'

The line went silent again.

As each second ticked by, Maggie was more and more on edge. Her nails would be bitten to the quick at this rate. 'OK, I've seriously had enough. What the—?'

Before Maggie could finish, Julie came back on the line.

'*You need to get here quick. I'm not one hundred per cent sure but …*'

'What?'

'*I'm looking through the window and I could swear I see Kate in there.*'

Maggie had to catch her breath.

'*Hey. Are you still there? Did you hear what I said?*'

'You'd better not be messing me about. Text me the details and get over to the coffee shop you mentioned … NOW! I'm going to call this in and I'll be there as soon as I can.'

Maggie's hands shook as she ended the call with the reporter and searched for Nathan's mobile number. He answered after the third ring and sounded like he'd just woken up. Maggie was still angry with him, but also felt a little bad for disturbing him because she knew this was taking its toll on everyone.

'*I was just having a nap. Why do you sound so flustered? Has something happened?*'

Nathan yawned down the line.

'I've just had a call and I think I may know where Kate is. You're not going to like it …'

Chapter 92

'You can't be serious.' Maggie listened to Nathan rant about the implications this new information could have on the case.

'Well, it hasn't been verified, but that's what Julie told me. We have to check this out, don't you think? The last thing we'd want is for Julie friggin Noble to break the story on the news before we've even looked into it.'

'Fuck. I really don't want to do this, but ... OK, I think we need to confirm it's Kate before we go barging in. I'm going to call DI Rutherford; you grab Bethany and Kat and head to the address. See if you can get a sighting of Kate. Once confirmed, we can go in and worry about any warrants after – we'll think of something. Do not enter the property on your own or alert the suspect that we're there, do you hear me, Maggie? No bullshit superhero crap. We follow protocol, and sort out that reporter, will you? What the hell is she doing snooping around people's houses, and how did she know he was a person of interest or that Kate was even missing?' Nathan didn't wait for an answer, which was good as Maggie didn't know it, but she would do her damnedest to find out.

Maggie rang Bethany, who confirmed she'd pick her up in twenty minutes. She texted Kat the address and told her to meet them outside the coffee shop. She changed into her jeans and grabbed her trainers. If she needed to run after a suspect, she wanted to be prepared. She placed her phone in her back pocket and grabbed her coat just as she heard a beep outside. Locking the door behind her, she raced to Bethany's car and once inside relayed the information that she and Nathan had discussed.

'Do we know how Ms Noble knew that information?' Bethany stared ahead as she drove to the address Maggie had given her.

'No. Unless she's been snooping around and someone told her about him. I wouldn't put it past her to be paying someone for information. What I don't understand is why our killer had been contacting her before and feeding her information. He wouldn't identify himself and provide an address, so has he played her? Why did he stop all contact?'

'Nearly there, we'll soon find out.'

'There's the coffee shop. She said it's around the corner from the address. Drop me here and you go and park near the property but stay out of sight. If he leaves or anything looks unusual, call me, OK? Update Kat as well, if you can.'

Bethany nodded and pulled over, letting Maggie get out of the car. Julie saw her from the window and made her way outside.

'Good, you're here. What's the plan?'

Maggie waved Bethany off and turned back to Julie. 'You, get inside. We've a few things to clear up first.'

Julie followed her into the small café. Maggie ordered a coffee and sat down at the table where Julie had perched herself.

'When was the last time the killer made contact with you?'

Julie shifted in her seat. 'I told you all this. Aren't we wasting time here?' Julie tapped her foot. 'He hasn't for a while now. You know the last time – his little request for a meet up. Nothing since.'

'So how did you get this address and why were you hiding outside his house?'

'I overheard you and Kate talking about him, and then when I saw you'd interviewed him, I looked into his background. I thought he was curious. I had no idea that Kate would be there – I'd heard from a source that she was missing. You do realize I walk by the police station every day – I see and hear things.'

'Did you see Kate's face? Was she OK?'

'That's the weird thing. From what I saw, she looked ... comfortable. I didn't see her face but the mannerisms were the same. He was talking to her.'

That didn't sound right to Maggie. 'I need you to promise me you'll stay here and don't report about any of this.'

'What the hell? If it wasn't for me, you wouldn't even have this lead.' She leaned back and crossed her arms. 'I'm sorry, but I can't make those promises.'

'Julie, please,' Maggie pleaded. 'If this isn't Kate, you could be putting her at risk. We can discuss an exclusive once we know more. Is that fair?'

Uncrossing her arms, she smiled. 'OK. But only because it's you.' Julie winked at her.

'Erm ...' Maggie felt her stomach tighten. She was flustered and needed to focus. 'I'm going to go and meet my colleague around the corner. Let us do our job and then I'll be in contact.' Maggie stood. 'Please don't let me down. I'll have no hesitation in arresting you if I need to.'

'No need for threats, even if you have no grounds for an arrest. I'll keep my word as long as you keep yours. Oh, and Maggie ...'

Maggie turned and waited.

'I'm not averse to cuffs, just so you know.'

Maggie turned on her heels and left the café. There was no mistaking Julie Noble's meaning, and, uncharacteristically, Maggie was intrigued. She couldn't deny there was a spark between them, but she needed to focus on finding Kate. Maggie walked towards the address and saw Bethany's car parked two houses away. She slid into the passenger seat. 'Have you seen anything?'

'Lights on in the front room. All I could see from here were shadows. Two, possibly three people – but I can't be sure. Are we going to knock on the door?'

'No. Not yet. Nathan said we need to identify Kate before we barge in, given that it seems as if whoever is with him is there of her own accord. I'm going to try and get a closer look. Do you have any binoculars?'

Bethany shook her head.

'I guess I'll have to try and get as close to the property as possible. My phone is on silent but vibrate is on, so if you need to warn me about anything, call. Any sign of Kat yet?'

Bethany shook her head.

'Odd. OK, contact Nathan and let him know what we're up to. If it is Kate, I'll let you know so you can ring it in and come back me up.'

'Be careful.'

Maggie smiled as she left the vehicle and got as close to the bushes on the pathway as she could. As she neared the property, she crouched and slowly crept towards the front window. The curtains had been closed, but there was a sliver of light from the corner. She put her eye to the glass and strained to see in. Her heart caught in her breath. A woman with long, black hair and a slight figure sat with her back to the window. He was there, facing the woman, smiling and chatting casually. Maggie tried to get a closer look but as she stretched towards the window something snapped beneath her feet. She ducked down and, with her back to the wall, she hugged her body close hoping she wouldn't be seen. The light cast a shadow across the lawn and the sweat beaded across her forehead. Then darkness.

Fuck!

He had closed the drapes completely and now Maggie had to make a decision. Should they bust into the house and risk exposing their hand? She had to be sure. An idea formed in her mind – she just hoped Nathan would be up for it.

Maggie crept back along the route she had originally taken and made her way to the coffee shop. She ran her idea through her mind once more.

It could work. Then they would be sure.

She took a deep breath and walked into the café.

It's now or never.

Chapter 93

'Well? Is it her?' Nathan stood and looked as if he was ready to make a move.

'I don't know. Before I could get a good look, I made a noise and he closed the curtains.'

'Jesus, Maggie. I think we need to call it in and deal with what may come. We can't risk it; if it is Kate, any mistake on our part could have devastating consequences.' Nathan reached for his radio.

'Hang on, boss. I have an idea. Hear me out.' Maggie collected her thoughts and continued. 'What if we can get someone inside? Come up with an excuse, see how he reacts?'

'No. I don't like that. What if he panics? We could just be pushing him to take action.'

'Wait. Please. We can get Julie to knock on his door. Say she's doing a story on forensics and was given his name. Maybe along the lines of the work they are doing on the recent murders and how important his role is? That would feed into his ego; he may let his guard down.'

Nathan was pacing the coffee shop's floor. Maggie waited for his response and motioned for Julie to jump in and add something that would sway the argument.

'I'm totally up for that ...' Julie's enthusiasm was obvious.

'Stand by, Ms Noble. I've not agreed to anything yet. You do realize that you could be placing yourself at risk too.' He looked at his watch. 'It could take time to get a team here to wire you up. I don't like this at all.' Nathan's face creased. Maggie could tell he was having an argument with himself inside that head of his.

'We don't have time to wait. I'll leave my mobile phone linked to Maggie. You can listen in and record what he says. He may not even let me in, but if I could get a glimpse of the woman and confirm it's Kate – you could be close by. We could think of a word or something that will signal if it is Kate.' Julie looked from Nathan to Maggie.

Maggie pleaded with her boss. As much as she hated to beg, she knew this opportunity needed to be acted on fast.

'If the shit hits the fan, I'm holding you responsible. Do you understand?' He pointed his finger at Maggie.

'Absolutely. How about if Julie says something simple like asking him for a tissue if she sees Kate. If we hear that, we'll enter the property and make the arrest.'

'If it is Kate, do you really think he is going to invite a reporter inside?' Nathan was getting flustered.

'We can try, boss.'

Nathan nodded. 'OK. Julie, link your mobile with Maggie's now. I'll update the team and make my way to the property with Maggie about five minutes after you leave. That way, if he looks around, he won't see us. We'll find a spot close to the property and move in if you confirm it's Kate. But for the record, I don't like any of this one bit.'

Julie took out her phone and followed Nathan's instructions. She started walking to the door.

'Wait.' Maggie rushed over and grabbed Julie's arm. 'Are you sure you want to do this?' Maggie realized the enormity of the task at hand. She was placing Julie at risk and, as much as it bothered her to admit, she didn't want to put anyone else in harm's way.

'My. My. My, is that concern etched on your face, DC Jamieson? I'm touched. I'll be fine. This isn't the first time I've put myself in danger, you know. Remember, I survived your wrath.' Julie winked and Maggie couldn't help but smile.

'Are you two done? Let's get a move on, please,' Nathan interrupted, and Maggie cleared her throat.

'Right, boss. Julie, we'll be right behind you. Don't do or say anything that will put you in harm's way.'

Julie spoke into her pocket. 'I promise I won't. But I expect something in return, DC Jamieson. We'll chat when this is over.'

Maggie hoped no one else heard the comment, but her stomach did a flip. There was a definite flirtatious tone to Julie's words and Maggie wasn't sure how she felt about that.

Nathan motioned for Maggie to follow and the pair headed towards the identified property. Nathan crept along the left side of the property and Maggie the right. As soon as they were in place, he gave Julie a thumbs up and she rang the doorbell.

Maggie held her breath as she waited for the door to be opened. Although it was only seconds, it seemed like hours had passed, and then she heard the locks click and a voice she recognized.

'What the hell are *you* doing here?'

Chapter 94

Maggie listened intently as Julie introduced herself.

'Good evening. I don't know if you remember me but I'm a journalist with the *Stafford Gazette* and I'm doing a story on the role of forensics and crime scene investigations. I was told you might be interested in being a part of this feature. Do you mind if I come in?' Maggie watched as Julie stepped into the doorway, but Charlie stood firm blocking her from going any further.

'Isn't it a bit late to be dropping round someone's house? Speaking of which, how did you get my address?' Charlie popped his head out of the door and looked up and down the street. Maggie quickly retracted her head, hoping she hadn't been spotted. 'Who told you to contact me?'

Was that nerves or wariness Maggie heard in his voice? She wished they'd had enough time to set up video surveillance. Being able to hear but not see was unnerving – sometimes it was the little tells in a person's face that gave them away.

'The PR people at ArrowRoot actually suggested you. They did give me a few other names and details, but you looked to be the most experienced. If you're not interested, I can always approach them instead?' Julie was good at what she did.

Maggie was relieved that Julie had not said Dr Blake had

given the details, as Charlie would then know for sure that he was being watched. Dr Blake was a stickler for protocol. Maggie waited with bated breath as Julie turned on her heels and made a move to leave.

'Hey! Wait a minute. I didn't say I wasn't interested,' Charlie called after her.

She had him!

'It's just I am kinda busy at the moment.'

Maggie could just imagine the beads of sweat forming at his hairline. His voice shook slightly. Was he worried they would find out it was Kate he had in his living room? Had he gagged her to keep her quiet before answering the door? Tied her to the chair so she wouldn't move? Maggie needed to stop thinking about all the possible scenarios or she would blow their cover and burst into the house right now.

'Great! I won't take up much of your time, I just need a few bits of information and then we can pick a date to discuss it in more detail. My editor is a real witch when it comes to nailing something down. If I have something solid for her, I won't get a bollocking. I'm sure you understand.' Julie pushed past him.

Maggie couldn't see her anymore. She looked across for Nathan and saw a thumbs-up sign. He still had sight of Julie.

'Really, it's not a good time. How about you come back tomorrow or I can meet you at your offices? They're not too far from where I work.' Charlie's voice cracked. He was becoming more insistent and Maggie waited for what Julie would do next.

'Can you just tell me a bit about—?' Julie persisted.

'I said not now!'

Maggie jumped at the boom in his voice.

'Hey, what's going on out here? You only have another hour,

honey. Do you want to waste it chatting in the doorway or by doing something better with that mouth of yours?'

Who the hell was that?

'Oh! So sorry. I didn't realize you had ... erm ... company.' Maggie listened as Julie thanked him for his time. Two minutes later and she was out of the door. She didn't look at Nathan or Maggie but instead started walking quickly in the direction of the café.

Both Maggie and Nathan waited ten minutes before they left their positions and followed the reporter.

'Well, I'm guessing that it wasn't Kate in there given how quickly Julie left.' Maggie ignored Nathan as she ran the last few steps into the café.

'What the hell was that?' Maggie realized too late that she was being confrontational and raised her hands to acknowledge this to Julie.

'It wasn't Kate, that's for sure. Same build. Same hair. But jeez ... not the same face. My guess, he hired a prostitute for the evening. You should have seen how red his face was when she came into the hallway.' Julie laughed.

'If it wasn't Kate, it means we have even less time to find her now. I knew I shouldn't have listened to you. For fuck's sake.' Maggie bit her lip. Kelsey Gilbey had been found only two weeks after she was abducted. They knew he was escalating and the window between kidnapping his targets and their murder was getting smaller and smaller.

'Be careful, DC Jamieson. Burning bridges with me is not in your best interest.' Julie glared at Maggie.

Maggie squared up to her. 'Are you threatening me?'

'Ladies! We don't have time for this bullshit. Tear yourselves apart, shake hands, and let's move forward. Thank you for your help tonight, Ms Noble. I'll be in touch. Maggie, let's go. We'll have an early start tomorrow and I want you firing on all cylinders. Got it? Bethany is taking Kat home. I'm sure you can catch a lift too.'

Maggie scowled at Julie. This woman infuriated her but at the same time, intrigued her. 'This conversation isn't over,' she huffed. She wasn't going to give Julie the satisfaction of having the last word and stomped out of the café after Nathan.

Chapter 95

After last night's fiasco, Maggie was on edge. Tempers were frayed and everyone seemed to bite like rabid dogs at any comment or suggestion.

'Bethany, do we have any update from the digital forensics or handwriting analysis? We have to have missed something.' Maggie paced up and down the office.

'I'm just going over everything now. There's a strange anomaly here, but it doesn't fit with our line of enquiry,' Bethany offered.

'Well, what the hell is it?' Maggie ran her fingers through her hair. 'Sorry. I didn't mean to shout.'

Bethany kept her back turned and Maggie could just imagine the faces she was making at the screen.

'Well, we've been focusing on agency staff as that's where the evidence has taken us so far. But why haven't we widened the net? Looking at peripatetic staff – they go across all the stations and could have access to various pieces of information, including Kate's email, her phone, anything really.'

'Damn!' Maggie smacked her leg. This was something she should have picked up on herself. Her judgement had been clouded by the fact that someone she knew was in trouble and she felt completely helpless.

'I actually only just realized it now. When I thought about

the logistics of the case, I wondered how someone could know so much about everything we're doing and still have access to Dr Moloney. In fact, I'm a little surprised you didn't see it first. I had to be sure though, as I didn't want to send anyone on a wild goose chase.' There was a sarcastic edge to her words.

Maggie squeezed her hands into fists. 'OK. And you're right, I should have seen it. What have you come up with?'

'There are four permanent members of staff who have access to all buildings in South Staffordshire. Three of them have been to Markston Police Station numerous times in the last six months.'

'Let's have a look at them. If we call them in, and interview them, we might be able to rule them out and save some time.'

Maggie waited while Bethany pounded the keys on her computer. One by one a picture formed and Bethany used her IT skills to pull them together expertly and place them alongside one another – like a virtual line up.

'Hang on a minute.' Maggie's heart raced and she leaned in a little closer.

It can't be. He had hair ...

'That one.' Maggie pointed at the screen. 'Pull up his details.'

Nathan walked over to them. 'What's got you hopping about?' He looked over Maggie's shoulder. 'Who's that?'

Maggie turned and hugged Nathan. 'We've got him. *That* is our killer.' Realizing what she'd done, she quickly composed herself.

'How do you know? He hasn't been on our radar before this.' Nathan didn't sound convinced.

'Don't you recognize him? We've all met him ... including Kate! He was at my house too. Oh my god! I can't believe this bastard had the nerve to come to my house and I had no idea who he was.' Like a film, snapshots of the person on the computer screen were racing through Maggie's head as she pieced everything together.

'Whoa. He came to your house? When? And why wasn't I informed of this?' Nathan frowned.

'There was no reason to inform anyone at the time. Remember the guy who came knocking on the door? He had a picture of a missing dog with him and asked if I knew anything. I'm pretty sure that's him.' She pointed at the screen. 'He must have been wearing a wig and he was a little slimmer but ... there's no mistaking it. Kate said something was familiar about him ... his voice I think. Fuck! Fuck! Fuck!' Maggie kicked the leg of the desk in front of her and then hopped around after realizing she wasn't wearing her usual shoes with the reinforced toe. 'Dammit. He's been here plenty of times. We need to get him in here now. Can we pull up his work schedule? If someone interviews him here, I can take Kat and go to the house registered to his name.'

'You're jumping the gun. We'd need a warrant. All we have is the fact that you *think* you recognize him. That's just not enough at the minute.' Nathan put up his hand before Maggie could protest. 'Bethany, get his details. I'll speak to DI Rutherford. This has to be seamless.' He looked at Maggie. 'Find it.'

Tick tock.

Tick.

Tock.

Maggie placed her hands over her ears. All she could hear was the relentless ticking of the clock on the wall. She had spent almost an hour going through everything they had on the case so far, but couldn't link their suspect. There had to be something.

She stared at the picture again. And then an idea popped into her head. They knew that there was a possible connection to the case in London: the young woman with Goth-like features, who was strangled. The MO wasn't the same, but maybe they were trying to force a connection. What if it was something simple? Contacting HR, Maggie asked the admin to send her the CV. It had worked previously – maybe it was as simple as seeing whether this guy had any relations in London. She tapped her pen on her desk while she waited for the email to arrive.

PING!

'OK. This guy previously worked at the same university that Kate did, albeit with little overlap.' She didn't care if anyone noticed she was talking to herself. The picture formed in her mind as she spoke. 'I wonder if the pathologist in London has any samples left from the autopsy. Maybe the London killer left something behind since, we're assuming, this was his first kill.' She recalled that the officer had described the murder as one of a personal rather than a sexual nature. Catharine Hill had been strangled and, unlike the two women here, her face had been covered over when her body was disposed of in a park. That usually meant the killer had some sort of personal relationship with their victim.

Maggie called the London force and relayed her queries.

'That's an interesting theory, DC Jamieson. An ex-lover? A shunned boyfriend?'

'I'm not sure, but my gut is telling me that she's the key to all of this. If I can place her in some way with our suspect, I think everything else will fall into place.'

'Gut instinct shouldn't be ignored. If my memory serves me correctly, there was no trace evidence to link anyone. Do you have a picture of the guy? Details? Maybe I can run him through our system.'

'Sending it over now. You should get it shortly.'

'Have you looked at the picture of Ms Hill?'

'I've seen the post-mortem shots and the pictures in the newspaper – they weren't of much help as they were either grainy or she was quite young.'

'I'm sending you something now. If you can, pull them up side by side and tell me what you see. Look closely.'

Maggie's heart raced. What was he seeing? She didn't have to wait long before she spotted it. 'Holy shit. The nose. The eyes. Thanks for this. I'll speak to you later.' She hit print on her keyboard.

She threw the phone back down onto the receiver and shouted to Nathan. 'I have it. I bloody have the connection!' Maggie ran to the printer, picked up the piece of paper and dashed over to Nathan's office, waving the pictures in his face. She could have kicked herself for not seeing it sooner.

'What the heck?' He grabbed the pieces of paper from her hand. 'What am I supposed to be looking at?'

'Look past the make-up. Facial features. Build ...' She waited for the penny to drop.

'Damn! Although we still need to substantiate this, it's a start. Great work, Maggie. I'll speak to Rutherford and get Dr Blake to run some DNA tests to share with our London colleagues. Find out where he is and I'll get the warrant.'

Chapter 96

'Can I tell you a story? I missed out when you were young. I'd like to make up for that before it's too late again.'

Kate wasn't going to argue. She found that the more she complied, the more freedoms he gave her, and with the pain in her shoulder, she could do with sitting up. 'Can I sit up, please? My shoulder hurts.'

He cocked his head to the left and smiled. 'Of course, sweetheart. You're turning into a right daddy's girl, aren't you?' He attached the chain to her leg at the bottom of the bed.

The bed never moved and Kate guessed it must be somehow secured to the floor. He lowered the bars attached to the sides of the bed, and once he removed the restraints on her arms, she pushed herself into an upright position.

'Thank you. That's much better.' She rubbed the back of her shoulder and winced when a sharp pain shot down her arm.

'You're best to leave that to heal for a bit.' He sat at the end of the bed and rubbed her foot. 'How about that story now?'

Kate nodded and forced a smile.

'You may not remember, but I've met you before. The first time I saw you, my heart raced. I couldn't believe you had returned.'

Kate scrambled her brain. Although he still covered his face, every now and again there was a familiarity that caused her hair to stand on end. And his eyes. She was sure she'd seen them before; she just couldn't place where.

'I was still grieving. I thought I'd lost you. I didn't mean to hurt you, but your rejection ... it angered me. I just snapped. But then you came back. You were there, right in front of me.' He looked up to the ceiling. 'I had prayed for that moment but I was never one for religion. Inside I was torn apart.' He gripped his hands together. 'I really thought I had lost my chance to love you, to be a part of your life. I felt abandoned when you died. So many thoughts bombarded my brain. Now what would I do? Who did I have?' He coughed and moved a little closer. Kate had to force herself to sit still rather than jump out of his reach.

Who did he think she was?

'And there you were. My girl. Right in front of me.' He shook his head. 'It couldn't be true. I mean, I know what happened back at my flat in London. But you changed the spelling of your name. I can understand that. You didn't want anyone to know. You were protecting me.'

'I remember the bell above the door ringing and in you walked. Your raven black hair blowing in the wind and your piercing blue eyes – just like mine – looked my way and then you smiled. You had noticed me. I smiled back. Do you remember? I didn't want to cramp your style, though, as you walked past me to a group of people sitting behind. Playing it casual, like I was your secret. And you'd be mine. Our game.'

It came to her then. She recalled the moment he was talking about, but that had been years ago!

Kate had arrived at the coffee shop later than she expected. She was meeting some friends from the university.

When she walked through the door, a gust of wind had caught

her and blown her hair in her face. She brushed it back with her hand and immediately saw her group and waved. She smiled as she walked towards her friends. The coffee shop only had a few people in it – a lone man, two teenagers, and then her own group of friends. Kate noticed these things, took in her surroundings, but she hadn't taken much notice of him. She tried to recall the details of his face.

As if reading her thoughts, he reached up and pulled off the mask.

Kate gasped.

'You! B-but ...' She couldn't get the words out.

He moved closer. 'Sshhh. It's OK. I know it's a shock, but Daddy's here.'

Chapter 97

Maggie wasn't very religious, but she prayed they weren't too late. After the back and forth because of the name confusion, and then seeing the similarities in the facial features, all the pieces had started to weave together. Although there was a connection to the police, it had nothing to do with the agency, and now they had their killer and a warrant was issued so they could search his property. A call to Stafford Police HQ showed that he was not in work – Thursdays were apparently his regular day off. Another connection. Both victims were found on a Friday morning – the killer had used his day off to kill and then dispose of the bodies.

Today was Thursday.

A car had been placed outside the property to make sure that, if he was home, he wouldn't be able to leave without them knowing. Updates indicated that there was limited movement within the house. It was a fairly isolated property – an old, two-storey brick house with what looked like an added peak, making it three stories high – a loft room perhaps. Google Maps showed that it had some sort of balcony on the second floor. Further checks concluded that the property had been rented at the start of 2017, before Kate had moved to Staffordshire. They couldn't get hold of the landlord, but in one way, that was good, as they couldn't be sure if the landlord was involved too and it would be less likely for anything to be leaked to the press.

When Maggie and the team had arrived at the property, Nathan explained the strategy.

'This is a large building. We'll need all areas secured, so I want two of you in the back, two each at the sides of the building and two more to come in the front with Maggie, Kat and myself. Are we clear?' The team nodded and began to get into position.

Bang! Bang! Bang!

Three loud knocks on the front door.

'Police. Open the door, Luke. We have a warrant to search the property,' Nathan shouted.

No response. They waited a minute before repeating the process.

'It's in your best interest to cooperate. This is your last chance. If you don't open the door, we're coming in.' Nathan looked at Maggie and nodded. They stood aside as one of their colleagues knocked the door in with the battering ram. Once inside, Nathan and Maggie ran up the stairs – the two other officers searched below and would join them once it was clear.

There were a few rooms, none of which looked very lived in. Dust cloths covered furniture and Maggie hoped she didn't sneeze. She motioned to Nathan and Kat. 'Nothing here. But it looks like this floor is split over two levels.' She pointed to a small set of stairs. 'Do you want to wait for the other two to finish in the main area before going up?' As the words left her lips, the other two officers appeared and all five made their way to the next floor area. There were only two rooms here and Nathan directed the other two officers to go and check out the tower.

As they opened the doors and cleared the room, Maggie's

heart raced. Then she heard a scream coming from a door at the other end of the area. Maggie ran ahead, not caring whether Nathan or Kat were behind her. Sometimes protocol couldn't take precedence. She flung the door open and gasped.

Nathan burst into the room behind her. 'Where is he, Kate?'

Kate was shaking. Her mouth was moving but no words escaped. Her finger pointed at the open window. Maggie ran over to her, noticing her leg was chained to the bed. Kate was pacing but every time the chain reached its length, she jerked to a stop.

'I had to do it. He was going to kill me. I didn't mean for it to happen.' Kate kept repeating these words but they made no sense.

'It's OK now, Kate. You're safe. Nathan, where is he?' Maggie's eyes darted around the room and landed on the open window.

Nathan was looking out of the window, the one that had a balcony attached. 'I don't know, he's not here.' There was a shout from below and Nathan looked down. 'He must have fallen or jumped. He's on the ground. Officers are with him.' Nathan radioed in and Maggie consoled Kate – she knew the psychological scars would cause the most harm. Kate flinched when Maggie touched her shoulder. Maggie directed her to the bed and radioed for someone to bring the bolt cutters so they could remove the chain from Kate's ankle and take her out of this hell hole.

'Can you talk to me, Kate? We're going to get you to the hospital but has he hurt you?' Maggie looked her friend up and down. No visible injuries.

Kate just shook her head and that was when the tears flowed. Maggie wondered how long she'd had to keep it together. As Kate sobbed, Maggie held her friend.

DC Everett accompanied Kate to the hospital. Nathan wanted Maggie to stay and continue to search the property. When they looked in the little tower room at the top, a chill went down her spine. Images of Kate were everywhere, intermixed with photos of Catharine Hill. He had been following her for some time. Some of the pictures had been taken in Markston Police Station. Kate hadn't been safe anywhere. There was a picture of Maggie and Kate hugging and Maggie's face had been scratched out. A laptop, video camera, and two mobile phones were on a desk. The forensic IT team would probably find a lot of material on them. Maggie looked at the floor and shook her head. Something caught her eye. She moved her foot slightly to the left and noticed light. Bending down, she realized it was a hole which looked directly into the room where Kate had been held captive. The bastard had been spying on her. Maggie shuddered. The forensic team had arrived and it was becoming increasingly claustrophobic in the room.

Maggie needed to see this arsehole. 'I'm heading to the hospital.' She didn't wait to hear Nathan's response.

Chapter 98

He lay motionless in the hospital bed. Handcuffed to the side bar, Maggie listened to the steady beep of the machine that monitored his heart. His eyelids fluttered.

'Hello, Mr Bradford. Can you hear me?' Maggie pulled her chair closer to the bed and she heard the rasp in his breath.

He spluttered as he spoke. 'Where am I?'

'You're in the hospital. That was quite a fall you took. Your legs are broken and I believe the doctors are waiting for some further test results. All I care about, though, is that you're stable and can talk. Why did you do it?'

His eyes widened. Maggie held in her anger as she realized that he knew his secrets were out. 'D-do what?'

'Before we speak any further, I'm going to have to caution you. This is not a formal interview, but I'm not going to get caught up in the politics should you decide to change your story at a later time.' Maggie cautioned him. 'Do you understand what I've said?'

His demeanour changed. He wasn't the fragile maintenance man they'd all seen in the police stations. Eavesdropping on conversations. Watching Kate. Watching her. Maggie shuddered.

'I'm not an imbecile, DC Jamieson. I know what it means to be cautioned. How is Kate, by the way? She wasn't looking too well when I last saw her.' There was genuine concern in his eyes but Maggie still wanted to punch him in the face.

'Dr Moloney is fine. She's told us a lot. You'll be charged with her attempted murder, kidnapping and harassment. You're also quite a hoarder. We found the room in the loft. So you'll also be charged with the murders of Tracy Holloway and Kelsey Gilbey. We also have enough evidence to charge you with the murder of Catharine Hill. The City of London police are thrilled to be able to close that unsolved case. I'll ask again, why did you do it?'

'Sh-she was an accident. I didn't mean to kill her. I loved her. I just wanted her to be a part of my life. My children. Why have you taken away my children?' He sobbed.

Maggie did not feel any sympathy for him. 'Who was an accident?'

'Catharine. Her bitch of a mother never told me about her until she was older. The damage was done.' He spat the words out with venom in his voice. 'I tried to reach out to her, but it was too late.' He shook his head. 'She said such hurtful things to me. Imagine calling your own father a pervert? All I did was hug her. Isn't that what parents do? Catharine pushed me away. I got angry and grabbed her by the throat. I squeezed. Tighter ...' He sighed. 'Well, you know what happened to her. I had to leave London then, and nearly didn't when I first saw Kate. My mother's here in Staffordshire. I thought if I changed my name to hers, it would cleanse me, wipe away my sins. But it didn't make anything right.' The bars on the beds jangled as he tried to raise his hands to his face. He could only use one – the other was securely cuffed to the bed. 'Are these really necessary? I've two broken legs. I can't fly out of here, can I?'

'It's protocol. You're under arrest. A police officer will be stationed outside your door until you're well enough to be taken into the station and formally charged. You still haven't explained why you killed Tracey Holloway and Kelsey Gilbey. Why abduct Dr Moloney?' Maggie wanted answers and was determined not to let their killer get away with leaving the families and Kate asking questions.

'My daughter. I wanted to bring her back. To be the father I should have been. Don't you see, DC Jamieson? Kate *was* Catharine. She came back to me. How else do you explain all the coincidences?'

'What the hell are you talking about?' Maggie's hands gripped the arms of the chair. If she didn't keep them occupied, she was afraid of what she might end up doing.

'They're identical. Look in my wallet. I have a picture of Catharine. You'll see it then. It was her. She came back.' He kept repeating the same thing over and over again.

This guy was off his rocker but Maggie's curiosity got the better of her and she searched the hospital drawers for his wallet. Not there. Of course. It would be in police evidence along with anything else he had in his possession.

'Your wallet isn't here.' Maggie saw the panic in his eyes. 'It will be at the police station. You do realize that what you've said is not a defence, right? Dr Moloney is not your daughter. Are you trying to hide behind a defence of diminished capacity? I can tell you now, I will make sure that defence doesn't work. You'll spend your remaining days on this earth behind bars.'

A look of confusion came over him. 'You've got this all wrong, DC Jamieson. I never wanted to kill anyone. I wanted my girls to stay with me. Forever.'

Maggie thought back to the infinity tattoo. 'Is that why you branded the women with that symbol?'

He looked at her, confused. 'The infinity symbol? That was our thing.' He twisted his free hand and showed a similar tattoo on the inside of his wrist. 'Catharine had one on her back and now Kate does too.'

Maggie flinched. Since his arrest and hospitalization, she hadn't been able to speak to Kate properly. Maggie wondered if she was even aware of the tattoo that scarred her body. 'I'll be back to speak to you later. I suggest you start being honest with us. It will make things easier when it comes to your trial.'

'Tell me how my daughter is. Tell me!' His cry was pitiful.

Maggie stood and watched as Luke Bradford closed his eyes. She made her way to the door and as she was just about to leave, she heard him whisper,

'I need to be with my Kate ...'

Chapter 99

Maggie looked through the small window in the door and saw an older couple she assumed were Kate's parents sitting by the bed. The worried look on their faces was heart-breaking.

She tapped on the door and Kate gestured for her to come inside.

Maggie was startled by how frail Kate looked sitting in the bed. Sunken eyes, pale skin, and she was shaking, physically shaking. Kate introduced Maggie to her parents and it was obvious that they were angry with her. She didn't blame them.

'Stupid question but ... how are you?' Maggie half-smiled.

'I d-don't actually know how to answer that, if I'm honest. The nurses have been wonderful; they told me that *he* is in the hospital. I can't sleep. I know he has broken legs, but what if he tries to contact me or escapes?'

'Oh shit. We've all be so caught up in finally having him, we didn't think of the implications of you both being here. I'm so sorry. I'll see if we can have him transferred. I guess they brought you both to the nearest hospital. Leave it with me.'

Relief washed over Kate. 'Thank you. Did he tell you that he marked me? That infinity tattoo ...' Kate reached behind her to her shoulder and winced. 'It's still sore. The doctor said I can have it removed, but I'll never forget it was there. Has he told you anything?'

'Not much. Just that he thought you were his daughter because you apparently look just like her.'

'His daughter? Is that why he dressed the other women up? It wasn't me after all?'

Maggie could see the tears in Kate's eyes. She understood what her friend was thinking. She hadn't been the real target; she just happened to look like someone else.

'I don't want to upset you anymore. This will all be very confusing until we can figure out everything. We'll have plenty of time to discuss it when you're well enough and back at work.'

Kate's father interrupted then. 'She's not going back to work.'

Maggie looked from Kate to her father. 'What do you mean? Kate, what's going on?'

Before her father could say anymore, Kate touched his hand. 'I'm going back to Ireland.' She looked at her father and then back at Maggie. 'Just for a bit. I still need to talk to DI Calleja, but I have quite a bit of annual leave to take and while I'm away, I'm going to think about my plans for the future.'

Maggie couldn't hide her disappointment. 'Oh Kate, I get that you need time away to heal, but don't make any rash decisions.'

'DC Jamieson. My daughter knows exactly what she's saying. Don't you think you've done enough damage?'

The words stung.

'Da. None of this is Maggie's fault.' Kate attempted to smile but Maggie thought she saw something else in her eyes ... blame.

'I can understand you all being angry with me. I probably will always blame myself too – for not being more vigilant. For not putting stronger measures in place. But Kate,' she looked directly into her friend's eyes, 'you're a brilliant criminal psychol-ogist. Please don't throw all your hard work away ...' Maggie stopped as Kate held up her hand.

'Now really isn't the time for this. My head is all over the place, but I'll be back for the trial. Right now, I just need you to go, OK?' Kate reached out for Maggie's hand and held it tightly. 'I don't blame you for any of this. I know you don't believe me now; I can read you like a book.' A smile formed on Kate's face. 'But trust me. No one is at fault but him. We'll talk later.'

Maggie nodded and squeezed Kate's hand in return. 'I'll go and put in a request to have Luke transferred. Speak soon.'

She fought back tears as she left the room. Something told her that this might be the last time she ever saw Kate.

Chapter 100

After putting in a request to have Luke Bradford moved, Maggie returned to Stafford Police Station. Her head hung low as she walked into the office and all eyes turned to her for an update.

'I'm afraid I have some sad news.' The team waited eagerly for Maggie to continue. 'Kate is going back to Ireland with her parents once she's been discharged from hospital and her statement has been taken. She said she'll be back for the trial but ...' Maggie's emotions took over. She grabbed a tissue from her bag. 'I don't know if she'll be returning to her post at Markston.'

Bethany gasped. 'Oh Christ! Though I can understand her position, it can't be easy to deal with all this right now.'

Maggie knew they had no time to dwell on the situation and pulled herself together. 'Anyway. What do we have on Mr Bradford so far? He's been arrested at the hospital and there's an officer stationed outside his door. I've requested a transfer to a different hospital because Kate is not happy being in such close proximity; however, I was told that as Kate will probably be discharged shortly, it's unlikely he'll be transferred given the paperwork and cost of doing so.'

Nathan rolled his eyes. 'Well let's hope Kate doesn't find this out. She'll be furious. Bethany's done some digging. I can't believe he's been here, at HQ and at Markston Police Station. Christ! We've all chatted to him at some point. That being said, he seemed to be able to disguise his presence expertly.'

Maggie nodded. The police had found numerous wigs and body suits to alter his shape inside the loft room when it was searched. His position as a maintenance man allowed him access to all the police stations and explained how he could come into contact with Kate, and get her phone and her email details so easily. It also allowed him to find out information about the case, as he went about his day-to-day tasks, eavesdropping on conversations as he fixed lightbulbs, windows and any other task requiring his skills. No wonder he stopped contacting Julie Noble. He must have overheard the team discussing their plans. What angered Maggie most was that police checks hadn't identified his name change back in 2016 after his daughter had been in killed in London. In the scheme of things it didn't make much of a difference as he didn't share the same last name as Catharine Hill, but it may have alerted the police to dig a bit deeper when he had applied for the position. He led a fairly quiet life, lurking in the background as he stalked his prey. His many disguises explained why Kate felt she had known the killer but couldn't quite place him. Maggie slammed her hands on the desk in front of her.

'We really should have seen this. Focusing on the temp agency staff threw us off course.' She clenched her fists so tightly that her nails dug into the palms of her hands.

'We followed the evidence. There were too many coincidences not to go down that avenue. He hid his tracks well. Bethany, tell us what you've discovered so we have more to go on when we interview him.' Nathan sat down and instructed the team to listen closely. Maggie knew this guy was clever and would have answers for everything they threw at him. They needed to be prepared.

'I haven't had the chance to go through everything collected at the scene, but from what I can gather so far, Luke Bradford (aka Stockton) was born in Stafford but his family moved to London when he was a child. His father was a funeral director and the family lived above the funeral home he owned. He's an only child. When police spoke to his mother, she didn't appear shocked at all, describing her son as selfish and creepy. She rambled a lot about how he would 'play with the dead', so we can only assume that he spent a lot of time with his father.' Bethany scrolled down her computer screen and continued. 'His father died when Luke was in his early twenties. By this time, he was working in schools and universities, one of which was the University of London, and records show he was there when Dr Moloney was lecturing. That may be when he first came across her. His mother returned to Staffordshire not long after her husband died. It seems the pair were estranged for a period, but no information as to why. A possible area to explore in the interview. Our London colleagues advise that they spoke to Catharine Hill's mother and she admitted to having a one-night stand with Luke that landed her pregnant. She never disclosed to her daughter who the father was, but admits that he had pursued her relentlessly until she threatened police action. She only knew him as Luke, and she never told him she was pregnant. And she never even thought about him when her daughter was murdered because she assumed he had left the area. Everyone, even the police, believed that the murder was by an intimate partner—' Bethany sighed.

Maggie interrupted. 'I wouldn't put it past him not to have followed Catharine for years after finding out he was her father.'

Bethany continued. 'Whatever was the case, Catharine Hill was reported missing by her mother in 2016 and six months later, her body was discovered. We've all seen the pictures – she could be Kate's twin. But what I don't understand is, why did he abduct and kill the two other women before Kate? He's been working in the police stations for a few years now.'

'That's something we'll have to ask him. In fact, I was hoping we could do that soon in case they do decide to transfer him.' Maggie looked at Nathan.

'Yeah. I agree. Let me update DI Rutherford and we'll head over to the hospital now. Visiting hours will be over soon, so we're less likely to run into Kate's family and have to come up with an explanation.'

Maggie took a deep breath and gathered her thoughts. She headed to the pool car and, as she was opening the door to get in, her mobile pinged. A message from Bethany.

Mr Bradford has lawyered up. Apparently, he wants to 'cleanse his soul', whatever the hell that means. Nathan knows and is on his way down.

Bethany x

Chapter 101

When they arrived at the hospital, Maggie had no patience to wait for the lift and ran up to the second floor via the stairs. She had to catch her breath when she reached the top and that gave her enough time to compose herself and wait for Nathan as he exited the lift.

'Not sure what the rush is. It's not like he's going anywhere. You ready?'

'I am. Odd choice of words – cleansing his soul. What do you think that means?' Maggie walked alongside her boss.

'Is that what you've been thinking about on the way over here? I wondered why you were so quiet. I've no clue what it means.' They noticed a smartly dressed female enter their suspect's room with a jug of water. 'But it looks like we're about to find out.'

Maggie followed Nathan into the private hospital room. Luke Bradford was sitting upright in his bed, mumbling to himself. A small table and chairs had been set up at the end of the bed. Maggie pulled the digital recorder out of her bag and placed it on the table as she sat down. Nathan took the lead.

'Well, it looks like you have everything all set up, Mr Bradford. My colleague, DC Jamieson, will be recording this conversation and I'll formally caution you in the presence of your solicitor so this is all on the record.' Nathan continued with the introductions and formally cautioned Luke. 'Do you understand what I've said?'

He nodded.

'For the benefit of the tape, Mr Bradford nodded his understanding. Shall we start from the beginning then?'

'DS Wright, I have no intention of making any excuses. I have spoken to my solicitor and we've prepared a full and frank confession.' He gestured to his solicitor and she pulled out a wad of papers which Maggie took hold of. What did confuse her though was that according to his personnel files, Luke was left-handed and that was the hand that was cuffed to the bed. From memory, the writing looked similar, but Maggie was sure it wasn't a direct match.

'Did you write this?' Maggie looked at the solicitor while handing the paperwork to Nathan.

'No. My client wrote it.' She cocked her head to the right.

'I thought you were left-handed. How did you write this?' Maggie pointed to the cuffs secured to the bed.

A great roar of laughter, followed by a fit of coughing, came from the bed. 'I'm ambidextrous, DC Jamieson.'

That explained many of the inconsistencies that Dr Blake had noted in the evidence. They hadn't been able to figure out how the injuries sustained by the victims came from the left hand but the notes appeared to be written by someone who was right-handed.

'You didn't know, did you?' A sly smile formed on his face.

Maggie redirected the focus of the interview. She wouldn't play his games. 'Not that we're complaining, but why the full confession?'

He lifted up the side of his bedsheet and pointed to a small case which held some form of liquid medication. 'I'm dying. I almost wish when Kate pushed me she had done a better job of it. Could have saved me a lot of grief. The big C.'

'Dr Moloney didn't push you. You slipped.'

'Po-*tay*-to … po-*tah*-to. Whichever way, I fell. I only have months, maybe just weeks left. It was because of the cancer that I knew I had to get my affairs in order, get my plans rolling, be with Kate to make amends. A long, drawn-out trial is in nobody's interest. I already have a life sentence; I just won't be serving it behind bars.'

Maggie was furious. It felt like an easy way out. She wondered if there was any way that the CPS would expedite the trial so that at least Kate would see justice. It may make her change her mind about leaving the DAHU and Staffordshire.

'So why did you do it? I want to hear it from you. Why did you put those families through all that agony?'

'I just wanted my daughter back. Was that so much to ask? I could hear her every day. I wanted to explain that I didn't even know she existed until she found me.'

'But they weren't your daughter. You changed their appearance to look like her.'

'No. No. No! Kate was the one. The other two were merely a means to an end. I needed to see if I could make it happen.'

Maggie's forehead creased. 'Make what happen?'

'Make them stay with me.' He coughed and took a sip of water. 'Catharine didn't want to stay. She was angry. If I could make those women stay, make them care for me like a daughter should, I would have her back, don't you see?'

'But where did Dr Moloney fit into your plan? Were you going to do to her what you did to them?'

'Kate *is* Catharine. Don't you get it!' He grabbed the side of the hospital bed until his knuckles turned white. 'I just had to remind her. She ruined my plans. *You* ruined my plans.'

Nathan interrupted. 'We're going in circles here. I don't think we're going to get anything coherent out of him.' Nathan pointed to the side of the bed where the pump lay. 'The drugs must be kicking in because he's not making any sense. I think we should take everything back to the office and see what the CPS says.'

Mr Bradford's solicitor stood. 'Everything you need is in the papers I gave you. A detailed background history of my client. His signed confession. I think he needs his rest now.' She walked towards the bed and pushed a red button just above him. Shortly after, a nurse walked in and asked Maggie and Nathan to leave. Maggie tried to protest. She wanted to know more. She didn't want him to get a cushy sentence in a psychiatric ward when he deserved to rot in prison – cancer or no cancer.

'C'mon. We have what we need.'

As they walked out of the door, Luke Bradford whispered loudly enough for Maggie to hear. 'Goodbye.'

A shiver went down her spine.

Chapter 102

The following day there was an ominous presence in the office. Luke Bradford's statement made for grim reading. DI Rutherford had called everyone in for an early meeting. She seemed distracted. Maggie had heard that DCI Hastings had not shown up for work and no one could get hold of him. That left DI Rutherford to relay the news to the press, but she had a meeting with Julie Noble first, as Julie had been promised an exclusive.

'Can I have everyone's attention, please.' The room fell silent. 'I hope you've all had the chance to read the statement. The highlights are as follows: it looks like Luke Bradford may go down a diminished capacity route given he's adamant that Dr Moloney is his daughter. His claim that he had no intention of murdering the other women, that their deaths were "merely an accidental and unfortunate mistake" in his quest to ensure that he could spend his last time on earth with his daughter again ... Christ, I don't even want to go on, this is so sick.' DI Rutherford took a moment to compose herself. 'He seems to feel he has some connection with the dead. He mentions his father, a funeral director who has been deceased for some time now, locking him in the funeral home where the dead became his "friends". His words, not mine. He also refers to the American serial killer, Jeffrey Dahmer – for those of you not familiar with him, he attempted to lobotomise his victims to try and keep them alive ... unsuccessfully. The digital forensic team found videos of how to perform a lobotomy and many searches referencing the practice.'

'Have we heard anything back from the CPS yet? He's admitted the murders, so surely with his diagnosis we have a case to argue for an expedited trial?' Maggie shuddered. Kate had been so close to being the next victim.

DI Rutherford shook her head. 'Too early for that. They'll have to read the statements, have a psychologist assess his competence ... all that. Though they are in agreement that we can charge him formally at this stage.'

'Absolute bollocks.' Kat piped in. 'If this guy gets a cosy sentence ...'

'We all feel your anger, Kat.' DI Rutherford motioned across the room. 'But let's focus that anger on making sure we have all the evidence in place to ensure he gets his just desserts.'

'Has anyone spoken to Kate yet?' Maggie wanted to be the one to explain everything to her friend.

'Not yet. But there is a FLO with her and I understand she is being discharged from the hospital this morning. DI Calleja advised that Kate will be returning to Ireland and I've no idea when, or if ... she will be returning to the DAHU. Those plans we discussed will need to be put on hold now, Maggie.'

Maggie and DI Rutherford had been working on a proposal for the Police and Crime Commissioner to second Kate in the MOCD as a consultant. She'd work on profiles and assist on murder investigations.

'I thought that may be the case. Hopefully, time away will give Kate some closure and she may reconsider the offer in the future.'

'Get everything together to charge this bastard and take DC Everett with you. If Kate is still in hospital you can explain what's happening; otherwise head over to her home as soon as you're done – I don't want her finding out anything from the news. I'll update the FLO so he's aware of what's happening.' Maggie made a move to go, tapping Kat as she walked past, when she heard a mobile ring.

'Hang on a moment.' DI Rutherford held a hand up as she answered her phone. Her shoulders slumped, and Maggie returned to her seat. As DI Rutherford's face grew paler, Maggie's nerves were on edge.

'Guv, what is it?' Maggie frowned. DI Rutherford's hands shook and Maggie couldn't tell if it was from anger or nerves, until she spoke.

'That was the hospital. It seems Mr Bradford decided that his time on this earth was up and he self-administered a fatal dose of morphine about an hour ago, just after the doctor had made his rounds. He was pronounced dead half an hour ago.'

'That fucking coward!' Kat stood. 'He's lucky he's dead or I'd kill him myself.'

'That's enough, Kat. This changes things slightly. Nathan, can you inform the CPS of this development and also the victims' families. Take someone with you if you need to. I'll let the higher-ups know … if I can find any.' She rolled her eyes. 'And I'll also speak to that reporter, Julie Noble. We promised her an exclusive and even though it may not be the right outcome, it's something. Maggie, you and Kat can go and visit Dr Moloney. Make sure you update the FLO first in case the hospital staff leaks the information to the press – and try and be sensitive, OK? Emotions are likely to be running high and we need to contain things until we have the full details.'

Looking around the room, Maggie saw various degrees of disappointment, anger, and disgust among her colleagues. Kat was right when she called Luke Bradford a coward and now Kate would not get the closure she needed. Maggie could only hope that this would not sway Kate's decision and force her to leave her job permanently.

'Are you ready to go now? I've no idea what I'm going to say to Kate to make this situation any better. On the one hand, he's dead.' Maggie rubbed her hands. 'But now justice won't be served to either Kate or the victims' families, and I can just imagine what the press will make of all this. Somehow it will be our fault – especially since he was right under our noses all along.'

Chapter 103

When they arrived outside Kate's building, Maggie and Kat were surprised at the number of reporters. 'What the hell? We've only been out of the office for forty minutes. How did the news travel so fast?' Maggie received a text and when she saw who it was from, it all became clear.

Have you watched the news at noon? I got an exclusive feature. Thanks for making that happen. If you're free this weekend, the drinks are on me. X Jules

When had she become Jules? Maggie shook her head. 'Looks like the guv updated Ms Noble pretty sharp. There was a feature on telly about fifteen minutes ago according to the text I just read.' They'd have to be careful how they managed this with Kate. No doubt she would be well aware of the situation and she hoped that the FLO had at least had the opportunity to lessen the blow.

They exited the vehicle and pushed their way through the crowd of people, avoiding the flashes and questions as they walked up the stairs and into the building. Maggie glanced at the neighbour's door and shuddered. Memories of where it had started flashed through her mind; she could only imagine how Kate must be feeling.

DC Everett knocked gently on Kate's door. The FLO answered and ushered them in, closing the door behind them. 'They're just through there.' He pointed in the direction of the kitchen.

Icy stares from Kate's parents greeted them.

'Hi, Mr and Mrs Moloney, Kate. I'd ask how you're all feeling but I think I may know.'

'You think you may know? You haven't the slightest idea how any of us are feeling! Who do you think—?' Kate's hand rested on her father's arm.

'It's OK, Da. This isn't Maggie's or the police's fault.' Kate motioned for Maggie to follow. 'Let's talk in here.'

'I'm so sorry about all this. I guess you've heard the news.' Maggie didn't like how calm Kate appeared. 'It's OK to be pissed off, even if it's at me. I understand.'

Kate sat down. 'I've nothing to be mad about, do I? He was dying of cancer anyway, and it all makes sense now. His diagnosis must have been what triggered this whole series of unfortunate events. I have an answer now. It had nothing to do with me and who's to say he would have even made it to trial? I'm just glad it's over and I can begin to move forward. I do feel sorry for Tracy Holloway's and Kelsey Gilbey's families though. I think they'll find it a lot harder than I will to get closure.'

'Can I be frank?' Maggie needed to say what was on her mind.

Kate nodded.

'I'm a little concerned by how well you're taking all this.'

'For my own sanity, I just have to accept the outcome and move on. Making the decision to be away from everything and back home with my parents for a while will help with the healing. I know a few good counsellors I can speak to as well. I just need to be as far away from here as possible right now. In fact, I've handed in my notice to the landlord. I can't live here after all that's happened.'

'Does that mean you might be back?'

'I could be. Could I ask a favour?' Kate shifted in her seat.

'Of course.'

'Can I leave Salem with you while I sort all this out? I don't want to uproot him and cause him stress while I'm figuring out what's next. It might be for about a month. Would that be OK?'

Maggie reached across and squeezed Kate's hand. 'Of course. However long you need.' On a more selfish note, Maggie reasoned that while she had Salem, there was always the chance that Kate would be back.

'Thanks. That's one pressure off my mind. What happens with the case then?' Kate crossed her legs.

'We'll still need a statement from you. To close off everything. I know it's not the best timing, but could you do that?'

'I've already written out a statement.' Kate's lip curled. 'It's in the kitchen. I'll grab it for you before you leave.'

Maggie wasn't surprised by this. Kate, even under pressure, was always efficient.

There was an awkward silence. Maggie felt like this was the end of something and didn't want to be the first to speak. DC Everett walked in and helped move things forward.

'Fuck. What a mess, eh? I hope you're OK. Your parents just handed me this envelope. Said that you wrote up your statement in the hospital. Is it OK for us to take this? I got the impression your parents want us to get the hell out of your hair.' DC Everett looked at Maggie and Kate.

Kate laughed. 'Ahh yes. They're a little on edge and want me back in Ireland like yesterday. You should have everything you need there.' Kate changed the subject. 'So, what's on the cards for the team now?'

'Well Lucy wants us all to help out with the hostel. It's officially opening next week, so she's invited us all to pop round over the weekend.'

'That's grand! I'm sorry to be missing that – be sure to take some pictures and send them on. I'll drop her a line when I'm settled, but let her know I'll be thinking of her.' Kate tucked her hair behind her ear. 'Well, I guess you need to get back to work, and I have some packing to do.'

DC Everett hugged Kate and wished her well. Inside Maggie screamed – it was so unfair that Luke Bradford had won, even though his death might mean Kate wouldn't have to suffer through a long trial.

Kate approached Maggie. They looked at each other, sad smiles adorning their faces. 'Is this goodbye then?'

'I never say goodbye, DC Jamieson.' Kate winked. 'I hear you might have an opening on your team for a criminal psychologist in a month or so.'

'And I know just the person for that vacancy.' The pair hugged and Maggie's heart felt a little lighter.

Chapter 104

Lucy ran her hand along the couch that had been donated to the refuge. She smiled as she looked around the room. She knew exactly what her dead husband Patrick would be thinking and saying if he was here to witness her success.

Fucking slag. Who do you think you're kidding? YOU WILL FAIL at this, like you have failed at everything ...

She squeezed her hands so tightly her nails broke the skin on her palms. He would not ruin the day for her.

Her mobile phone pinged. She walked over to the table and picked it up. It was from Mark.

Do you still need help? I can be there in an hour. X Mark

Lucy smiled. She was so excited about opening the haven after getting the official accreditation from the Ministry of Justice and had roped all her friends and colleagues into helping her out.

She texted back.

It's OK. Sharon is coming by in a bit to go over the advocacy sessions. There may be wine. You're more than welcome to join us. X

She enjoyed Mark's company but knew she was keeping him at arm's length. Her healing was not yet over – it may never be – but she hoped one day she would be ready to trust again.

She stared out of the window at the dark clouds forming. Fitting. A storm was coming and her insides were in turmoil. She needed to shake this feeling out of her head.

Lucy walked over to the window and pulled it closed. She was startled by the thumping on her door. She looked at her watch.

Too early for Sharon.

Grabbing her cardigan off the couch, she wrapped it around her as she headed to the door. She thought she heard someone whimpering on the other side of the door. When she looked at the camera monitor, all she could see was a shadow.

Nothing would prepare her for the sight before her.

The young woman with the bloodied face reached out to Lucy. But before Lucy could catch her, she collapsed in the doorway.

THE END

Acknowledgements

I'd like to thank everyone who has cheered me on and supported me so far on my writing journey. You're all amazing! If I miss anyone out, it's not intentional!

I'd like to thank my family and friends both near and far, for the tremendous support they have given me – especially my dad, who was taken away from us so suddenly in Oct 2019. I didn't think I would finish this book on time, but he must have been pushing me from the heavens. I'd also like to thank my stepmom, Pauline Holten, for championing my books to everyone she meets in Ireland. My sister Julie and my mom – who fly the Canadian flag along with my brother Tony, Shane and my niece Josianne Boudreau. And to Paula, Christopher and Jimmie – you all mean the world to me.

A massive thanks to Charlotte Ledger and Bethan Morgan for their patience, understanding, guidance and belief in me as a writer and to the whole One More Chapter team who have been fantastic since this crazy journey began.

Special thanks to my beta readers and everyone who has allowed me to use their names! And for the most part, their characters are nothing like them in real life … ha ha!

A heart-felt thank you to all the authors and festival peeps who have been so incredibly supportive, you have no idea how much it means to me – particularly Angela Marsons, Martina Cole, Bob McDevitt, Jacky Collins, Kimberley Chambers, Mari Hannah, Heleen Kist, Christopher McDonald, Nic Parker, Graham Smith, Mel Comley, Emma Kennedy, Mel Sherratt, Ian Rankin, Robert Bryndza, MW Craven, Howard Linskey, Michael J Malone, Lisa Regan, Chris Merrit, KL Slater, Rona Halsall, Craig Robertson, Gordon Brown, Caroline Mitchell, Clare Chase, M.M. Chouinard, Karen King – a thousand #thankyous would never be enough. Apologies if I missed anyone out.

To the crime writing community – do you know how SUPERB you are? Seriously! I wish I could name each and every one of you – your kind words, encouragement, inspiration and over-whelming support continues to amaze me. Don't ever change.

To my amazing blogger friends, I want to name you all, but I can't – so if you are reading this and thinking "is she talking about me?" the answer is – Hell yeah, I am! Love you all. Special mention to #MyTribe and to Sarah Hardy for organising the most EPIC blog tours via Book on the Bright Side Publicity.

A massive thanks to the Bookouture team (both the authors and my colleagues) for all the amazing advice and cheers!

Of course, I will always mention Tamworth Probation/ Tamworth IOM; Stafford IOM; and all my remarkable ex-colleagues within the Police and Probation Service – both the public and private sectors. Your dedication and professionalism astound me – I may have been "paroled" after 18 years of service, but I think about your truly fantastic work all the time – and all the stories I now have to tell!

Finally, a massive thanks to all the readers. There are just no words to convey how much your support and reviews have meant to me. You make me believe I can keep on doing this and give me a reason to write.

A Note from Noelle

The series is set in Staffordshire; however, I have used some literary licence by making up names of towns/places to fit with the story.

Having been a Senior/Probation Officer for 18 years, I left in 2017. There are some references to the changes that were implemented in 2015, but I went all nostalgic and some of the work/terms refer to a time when Probation was all one service – though it seems I may have been psychic as the service is coming together under the public banner once again. Regardless, it made things a lot less complicated. Any errors to police procedure / probation or any other agency mentioned within the story are purely my own or intentional to move the story forward.